Before You Know Kindness

CHRIS BOHJALIAN

Before You

Know Kindness

A NOVEL

RANDOM HOUSE
LARGE PRINT

Grateful acknowledgment is made to Far Corner Books
for permission to reprint an excerpt from "Kindness" from
Words Under the Words: Selected Poems by Naomi Shihab Nye.
Copyright © 1995. Reprinted by permission of
Far Corner Books, Portland, Oregon.

Published in the United States of America by Random House
Large Print in association with Shaye Areheart Books, New York.
Distributed by Random House, Inc., New York.

Library of Congress Cataloging-in-Publication Data
Bohjalian, Christopher A.
Before you know kindness/by Chris Bohjalian.
p. cm.
ISBN 0-375-43418-6
1. Manhattan (New York, N.Y.)—Fiction. 2. Gunshot
wounds—Patients—Fiction. 3. Animal rights activists—Fiction.
4. Parent and child—Fiction. 5. Hunters—Fiction.
6. Vermont—Fiction. 7. Large type books. I. Title.

PS3552.O495B44 2004
813'.54—dc22
2004051572

www.randomlargeprint.com

FIRST LARGE PRINT EDITION

10 9 8 7 6 5 4 3 2 1

This Large Print edition published in accord with the
standards of the N.A.V.H.

FOR THE BLEWER WOMEN:

Sondra, Cecilia, Evelyn, Victoria, and Julia

Before you know what kindness really is
you must lose things,
feel the future dissolve in a moment
like salt in a weakened broth.

NAOMI SHIHAB NYE, "Kindness"

. . . she took a long breath and looked behind her up the long walk to see if any one was coming. No one was coming. No one ever did come, it seemed, and she took another long breath, because she could not help it, and she held back the swinging curtain of ivy and pushed back the door which opened slowly—slowly.

Then she slipped through it, and shut it behind her, and stood with her back against it, looking about her and breathing quite fast with excitement, and wonder, and delight.

She was standing inside the secret garden.

FRANCES HODGSON BURNETT,
The Secret Garden

PROLOGUE

Cavitation

The bullet—cylindriform as a rocket but tapering to a point almost sharp enough to prick skin with a casual touch—was two and a half inches long when it was in its cartridge in the rifle. The shank was made of copper, and the expansion chamber would cause it to double in diameter upon impact. The tip was designed to swell upon contact as well, ripping apart the flesh and muscle and bone as it made its way to the elk's or the bear's or (most likely) the deer's heart. It looked like a little missile.

The bullet did not hit Spencer McCullough in the chest that very last night in July, however, because that would have killed him pretty near instantly. Nor did it plunge into his abdomen, which—depending upon how much of his stomach, his liver, and his spleen were in harm's way—would have killed him over the course of minutes. A thirty-ought-six—a .30-caliber bullet atop the classic cartridge case developed by the U.S. Army in 1906—turns bowels into pudding.

Instead, it ripped into the man's body just above and to the side of his chest, slamming into him below his right shoulder. It shattered completely the scapula and his shoulder joint, demolished his rotator cuff (which would have been even more debilitating for his wife, Catherine, because she still gave a damn about her tennis serve), and mixed into a thick, sloppy soup the muscles that Spencer used to move his shoulder and lift his right arm. The bullet was traveling at two and a half times the speed of sound, and the tissue had to absorb the velocity: Consider the way a bullet does not appear to pierce a brick of Jell-O but, rather, causes it to explode.

What was of most importance to the two EMTs who arrived at the house at the very peak of Sugar Hill, New Hampshire, however, was that the bullet had also obliterated the first branch of the axillary artery—the superior thoracic artery—though as they were taking what remained of Spencer's vitals near what remained of his snow peas that summer night in the garden they tended not to use words like **axillary** and **thoracic**. They used words like **bleeder** and terms like **bleeding out,** and Evan Seaver—the male of the pair—allowed himself a small assortment of expletives and invectives. Evan was two decades younger than his partner, a fifty-one-year-old first-response veteran with hair the color of hoarfrost that fell over her ears and rounded her skull like a helmet. Her name was Melissa Fearon, but everyone called her Missy Fearless. She ignored Evan's occasional lapses in decorum that evening because he had never before seen a gunshot wound. He'd seen his share of grisly car and snowmobile accidents, and he had in fact been with her when they found the vacationing TV producer who'd been decapitated behind the wheel of the convertible he'd rented in Boston. But that gentleman was clearly dead—not dying—and so Evan hadn't had to get too close or spend any time with the corpse.

Both EMTs were volunteers who did other things for a living. Evan worked at an electrical wire factory in nearby Lisbon, and Missy taught math at the high school in Littleton. On at least a half-dozen occasions she had pulled her own students from their dads' toppled four-by-fours or their very own Geos, Escorts, and Corollas, the vehicles inevitably crinkled like the foil wrappers that folded themselves around sticks of chewing gum. She had dealt before with audible bleeding—hemorrhaging that seems absolutely torrential, the flow not in reality making the noise of a geyser but seeming to everyone present as if it is—and seen people (grown-ups and teenagers and, alas, children) impaled on the shards of twisted metal that once were parts of automobiles.

Spencer was well into the first symptoms of shock when they arrived: He was cold and clammy and pale, and he was having great trouble breathing. Consequently, he was what Missy Fearon and her more seasoned associates referred to as a scoop-and-run. She and Evan did little at the edge of the garden where they found Spencer (his body half in the lupine that bordered the vegetables and half in the ugly, knotted vines on which once had grown snow peas) other than apply a thick, gauzy trauma dressing to the wound—and then lots of hand pressure—slip a stiff plastic cervical collar around his neck to immobilize his head, and roll him onto a backboard. Then they were off to the hospital in Hanover. Somehow Missy managed to stick a saline IV into Spencer in the ambulance while continuing to keep weight on the wound. She thought of how the EMTs sat on patients or jumped on the rolling gurneys to maintain pressure in the TV dramas, but she couldn't imagine actually doing such a thing, especially with this poor guy. She'd be sitting on jam.

As for the emergency room physicians and the surgeon who, fortunately, lived within minutes of the hospital, once they had Spencer McCullough stabilized their greatest concern was the reality that before shattering all that bone in his shoulder and upper back, the bullet had done a pretty fair job of pulverizing the brachial plexus—the network of nerves that sends signals from the spine to the arm and the hand. Recall the Jell-O: Meaningful reconstruction was completely out of the question. Assuming they could even save Spencer's right arm (which was no guarantee), it was highly unlikely that it would ever do a whole lot more than flop at his side like a scarecrow's.

Inevitably, Spencer was right-handed. And so even though he wasn't the athlete his wife was (the rotator cuff was among the least of the surgeon's problems), this would be a severe disability. Even though he worked at a desk—Missy overheard enough as she worked to get Spencer into the ambulance to understand that he was a public relations guy for some animal rights organization in New York City, and this house he was at was his mother-in-law's—it was going to be a very long time before anything came easy to him again.

Once the physicians had started pumping the units and units (and still more units) of blood into him, done a chest X-ray, and gotten the only good news that Spencer McCullough's body was going to offer that evening—there was no hemorrhaging inside the thorax and a lung had not collapsed—they set to work trying to control the bleeding in his shoulder and washing out the wound. This meant, among other tasks, meticulously removing all those tiny fragments of bone, which were now little more than contaminants. It meant using a Gore-Tex sleeve that looked a bit like a miniature version of a radiator hose from a car engine to reconnect the severed arteries, and then—when they needed yet more tubing—stealing a part of a vein from his leg.

Weeks later, they might do whatever reconstructive surgery they could. They might perform a nerve-cable graft, taking nerves from the part of the man's leg where they had just taken a vein so that a portion of the pudding of sheared links in the nearly invisible wires in his right shoulder might begin to grow back. Or, if necessary, they might amputate the arm. In all likelihood, it was going to be completely useless. No, it would be worse than useless. It would be a hindrance, a limp and flaccid tentacle that hung by his side, caught on counters and tabletops, and banged against him when he tried to move his body in any manner that was even remotely athletic.

Still, Spencer McCullough was alive. And if someone had said to either Missy Fearon or Evan Seaver before they arrived at the house on Sugar Hill that a guy there had taken a bullet from a thirty-ought-six a couple of inches from his heart, they both would have assumed that they could have driven from the scene to the hospital at the speed limit with their siren and two-tone switched off, because all that was going to happen when they arrived was that the body was going to be declared dead and put on ice for the ME.

Only when they had deposited Spencer at the hospital and he had been rushed into the OR did either of them have the time to voice the questions that had crossed both their minds: Why the hell was there a loaded deer rifle on the property three and a half months before hunting season? And why in the name of heaven was a twelve-year-old kid—the guy's own daughter, for God's sake!—firing potshots into the garden on the last night in July?

Part I

THE DEER

One

The sun was up over Washington, Lafayette, and
the trio of nearby cannonball-shaped mountains
that were called the Three Graces, and Nan Seton—
elderly but far from frail—sat sipping her morning
coffee on a chaise lounge on the Victorian house's
wraparound porch. She noted how the sun was rising
much later now than it had even two or three weeks
ago: It was already the twenty-eighth or twenty-ninth
of July (it disturbed her that she couldn't grab the precise date right now from the air), and her children
would be arriving tomorrow. Friday.

A golden retriever—old like her but not nearly so
energetic—lolled near her feet on the outdoor rug.

She had been on the porch close to half an hour
and even the coffee in the stovetop percolator she had
brought outside with her was cold, when she heard her
granddaughters pound their way down the stairs. The
older girl, Charlotte, was twelve; the younger one,
Willow (a name that drove Grandmother crazy both
for its absolute lack of any family resonance and its
complete New Age inanity), was ten.

The girls collapsed into the two wicker chairs near
the outdoor table, opposite their grandmother and her
chaise. She saw they both had sleep in their eyes and

their hair wasn't brushed. They were still in their nightgowns, their feet were bare, and Charlotte was sitting in such a fashion—the sole of one foot wedged against her other leg's thigh—that her nightgown had bunched up near her waist and she was offering anyone who cared to see an altogether indelicate and (in Nan's opinion) appalling show of flesh.

"Good morning," she said to them, trying hard to resist the urge to put down her cup and saucer and pull Charlotte's nightgown back down over her knee. "How are my two little wildflowers?"

"Sleepy," Charlotte said, her voice already the uninterested drawl of an urban teenager.

"You girls are up early. Any special reason?"

"There's a bird on the roof," Charlotte said.

"A woodpecker," Willow added, and she reached down to pet the drowsing dog.

Nan nodded. She decided the bird must have been on the roof over the kitchen porch on the other side of the house, because otherwise she, too, would have heard him just now. "They don't normally drum this late in the season," she said to her granddaughters. "They—"

"Trust me, we are not making this up," Charlotte said. "It sounds like there's some guy up there and he's trying to open a tin of Altoids with a machine gun." The girl had two tiny hillocks starting to emerge on her chest. Not yet breasts and not visible in this particular nightgown. But they were evident in bathing suits and T-shirts. Her eyes were the shape of perfectly symmetrical almonds, her nose was small, and her mouth was a luscious pucker at once waiflike and impudent. She lacked her mother's paralyzingly sensual red hair, but her mane was thick and dark with natural hints of henna, and it fell on her shoulders like a cape. In a few years, Charlotte would be gorgeous, an absolute knockout. For the moment, however, she was in that murky world between childhood and serious adolescence. In one light she might pass for ten; in another she might be mistaken for fourteen.

"She didn't say we were making anything up," Willow murmured, and then she did exactly what her grandmother wanted most in the world that very moment: She reached over to her cousin from Manhattan and pulled the older girl's nightgown down over her knee so that taut and tanned twelve-year-old thigh once again was decently covered.

"If I had a gun, I would have shot it," Charlotte grumbled, widening her eyes as she spoke because she understood her remark was so gloriously inflammatory. But then—and here was that child—she still lacked the anarchic courage of a truly angry adolescent, and so she allowed herself a retraction of sorts. "Well, not **it,** of course. Dad would completely disown me if I ever did something like that. But maybe I would have shot near it. Scared it. Scared its beak off."

"Do you know why a woodpecker might drum in July?" Nan asked them.

"Because it's an idiot."

"Charlotte—" Willow began, but her cousin cut her off.

"It is! Why do you think we have the expression **birdbrain?** "

The woman watched Willow's round face carefully. The girl was two years younger than Charlotte, and she lived in northern Vermont—barely two hours from this house, actually. She had worried this whole month that Charlotte would (and the word had come to her the moment she had spoken to her own adult children that spring when they had begun planning the girls' annual summer stay in New Hampshire) **corrupt** young Willow. So far that hadn't happened, but she knew there was still plenty of time. She saw now that Willow was more hurt by Charlotte's tone than impressed by her attitude. The girl was gazing down at her toenails, and the salmon-colored polish that she had layered on them the night before. Her feet were elegant and small. The soles were smooth, the skin was soft.

"It's not likely the bird is stupid, Charlotte," Nan said. "He's either boasting of his responsibility for a second clutch of eggs or he's lonely and still trying to find a mate."

"I wish I spoke woodpecker, then. I'd tell him to go write a personal ad. It would be a lot quieter."

"Have you seen the crow?" Willow asked her grandmother.

"Yes, why?"

"It's so big. I never think of crows as big. But twice yesterday near the garden—by the apple trees—I saw it."

Charlotte rolled her eyes. "It's probably a raven then. Ravens are much huger. Right, Grandmother?"

"No, it is indeed a crow. There's a family with a nest at the top of one of the white pines near the strawberry patch. Try an experiment later today, if you feel like it. Before we leave for the club, place a dime in the driveway near the trees. Maybe even tilt it on its side so it catches the sun. When we return, there's a good chance the dime will be gone."

"Oh, good," Charlotte said, and she smiled. "A woodpecker so dim he thinks bashing on the roof will get him a girlfriend and a crow who's a petty thief. What nice birds you have, Grandmother."

"He wants the dime because it's shiny," Nan said simply, as she carefully placed the wicker tray that held her coffee on the table beside the chaise and stood up. "Now, what would you two like for breakfast? I actually have some pancake batter in the refrigerator from yesterday and, of course, sausages—"

"Dad would freak if he knew how much meat you were trying to feed us," Charlotte told her.

"Yes, your father probably would. You don't have to eat it. But Willow and I still eat—"

"Dead things."

"Yes, we do."

Willow's hair was the color of a sand dollar that has not yet been bleached by the sun. She looked up now, brushed her bangs away from her eyes, and said to her grandmother, "Maybe I'll just have pancakes this morning, too, please."

"What? No sausages?" Nan asked, unable to hide the surprise in her voice.

"No, thank you. Not today."

"Hallelujah," Charlotte said happily, and then she climbed off the chair and ran up the stairs to get dressed. The dog lifted his head, the vibrations from the human on the stairs causing his spot on the porch to shudder beneath his snout. Willow paused for a moment, and it seemed to her grandmother that there was something more she wanted to say. But then she stood, too, shrugged her shoulders and raced up the steps after her cousin.

AS SHE DROPPED the pancake batter—after nearly twenty-four hours in the refrigerator, it was thicker than pudding—onto the electric skillet, the phone rang. Nan Seton had never bothered to purchase a cordless phone, and so she made a mental note as she scooted in her slippers across the long kitchen to keep the call brief: She did not want the pancakes— which, because the batter was substantial and heavy, reminded her of small loofah sponges on the griddle— to wind up looking like charcoal briquettes.

"Hello?"

"Hi, Nan. It's Marguerite."

"I'm making the girls breakfast."

"Oh, I'll just be a minute. Do you remember how you noticed at the club yesterday that Walter Durnip's color wasn't very good?"

"Vaguely. He looked a little gray."

"He did, he did. Well, he died."

She sat on the wooden stool by the phone, and nodded to herself. "How?"

"In his sleep."

"That's how I want to go. What was it? A heart attack? A stroke?"

"I don't know. But when he went to bed, he didn't say anything to Elizabeth about how he felt. He just went to sleep, and when Elizabeth woke up this morning she knew right away he was dead."

"He was eighty-four, wasn't he?"

"Something like that."

"He wasn't even ill."

"At least not visibly."

"Oh, we would have known if Walter was ill. He wasn't particularly stoic."

Nan heard her friend laugh, but she hadn't meant this as a joke. It was, in her mind, a simple reiteration of an obvious fact: Walter Durnip was a man, and men were notoriously unwilling to keep pain to themselves—which was where, more times than not, it belonged. As a general rule, old people who talked about their ailments made Nan Seton uncomfortable. Too much . . . body.

"Elizabeth doesn't know for sure when she's going to have the funeral yet, but it will probably be the day after tomorrow. Saturday."

"Saturday? Too bad. Oh, well. At least by then I'll have a houseful, so the girls won't have to go. John and Catherine arrive tomorrow," she said, referring not to a husband and a wife but to her son and her daughter. Nan knew from years of conversations exactly like this one with her friend Marguerite that she did not need to explain that when she said Catherine she meant

Catherine and her husband, Spencer, and when she said John she meant John, his wife, Sara, and—now—their infant son, Patrick.

"How long are they staying?"

"Catherine and Spencer are both taking next week off. Isn't that nice? They'll be here for nine days—"

"And John and Sara are bringing the baby, right?"

"Of course."

"You **will** have a houseful."

"John and Sara will only be here for the weekend. Till Monday morning. Still, it will be good fun. I'm sure the girls miss their parents. The only hard part is going to be dinner because Spencer is just so difficult."

"Being a vegetarian is no big deal, Nan. Lots of people are!"

"There are degrees. And most people don't obsess about it the way he does or lecture their dinner companions the way he does. Soy milk. Soy hot dogs on the grill. Tofu. Yuck. It just makes things so complicated because I never know what to buy."

"Make him cook!"

"He does. Sometimes that's worse. Everything always seems to have lentils in it."

Upstairs in the bedroom above the dining room she heard a colossal thud and then she heard the girls laughing hysterically. Charlotte, she knew from experience, always woke up in a foul mood but tended to cheer up as the morning progressed. By lunchtime, she would be charming. Willow, on the other hand, seemed to grow tired as the day wore on and if she was going to be cranky (and it was generally rare for the younger cousin to grow irritable) it was likely to be at the very end of the day. Late afternoon, just before dinner. After they had returned from the club, where she had the children in a regimen of swimming, tennis, golf, and junior bridge lessons.

"How is Elizabeth doing?" Nan asked, referring back to her and Marguerite's mutual friend, a woman who—like her and Marguerite—was now a widow.

"Oh, I believe she's fine," Marguerite told her, her voice as light as a dandelion puffball in May.

"Good. Walter was a lot of work, wasn't he?"

"A **lot** of work," Marguerite agreed.

Across the kitchen, the deep black circles around the outer edges of the loofah sponge pancakes were spreading into the centers, and the acrid smell of badly burned batter was starting to waft through the house. Quickly Nan said good-bye and hung up. She flipped the pancakes, telling herself that if she scraped the creosote-like sludge off the bottom and served each one with the undercooked side up the girls would never know the difference. She didn't believe this for a second, but she wasn't about to waste all that good leftover batter.

WHILE THE GIRLS were picking apart their grandmother's pancakes with their forks—each curious in her own way as to exactly how the edges of the pancakes could appear charbroiled while the insides were the consistency of mayonnaise—Charlotte's father, Spencer, was standing before 150 executives and middle managers from the American Association of Meat Substitutes in the Ticonderoga Room in a conference center in Westchester County. The Ticonderoga Room was the largest of a series of meeting rooms in this wing of the building, all of which seemed to have been named after regional Revolutionary War landmarks (the Saratoga, the Delaware, the Yorktown Heights), though Spencer had yet to see anything anywhere in the conference center that in the slightest way reflected a colonial motif. Not so much as a bellhop in knickers and a tricornered hat, or a plugged-up wrought-iron cannon and hitching post along the exteriors.

Spencer was asked to speak here this morning both to provide the group with some light breakfast entertainment and to inspire them in their ongoing efforts to garner more (and more) refrigerator and freezer case space in the nation's mainstream supermarkets for their garden burgers and faux sausages, their Fakin Bacon and Foney Baloney, their ground round made from seaweed and soy protein.

In today's speech, before he got to his routine slides of the slaughterhouse in North Carolina that sent thirty-two thousand desperately frightened, squealing hogs to their death every single day (many of them dunked by mistake in vats of scalding water while still half-alive), he played a television commercial on the room's three large TV monitors. The ad was for a more individualized torture chamber called the Microwave Home Lobster Steamer. He chose this particular commercial to warm up the crowd—get them good and indignant before they had even finished their bagels and muffins and vegan granola—because this morning he was beginning his speech with his own restaurant experiences when he was nineteen, his very first summer in Sugar Hill. He guessed he was choosing this part of his life because he and Catherine would be flying to New Hampshire tomorrow for their annual summer vacation.

He had already told the crowd of the restaurant's snappish dying lobsters, those behemoth earwigs on steroids, and then of the busloads of senior citizens in their thin plastic bibs who came to the Steer by the Shore to devour them. They would come for dinner after gazing upon the craggy visage of the Old Man of the Mountain in nearby Franconia Notch—a curmudgeon who had since slid down the side of the cliff—someone inevitably observing that the natural granite bust indeed had a certain Daniel Webster–like resemblance from the side but from the front looked like nothing more than an outcropping of shale and rock.

"No one could cleaver a live lobster as quickly as I could," he said now, segueing from his well-practiced Alcoholics Anonymous Twelve-Step confessional tone into what he considered his Baptist preacher's crescendo. "That's not hyperbole, that's not immodesty. That's fact. I could kill two in a minute. One night I killed sixty-four in half an hour and change—enough for the whole bus! That evening every single man and woman on the tour ordered the restaurant's signature meal, the baked stuffed one-and-one-quarter-pound Maine lobster, and—honest to God, I am not exaggerating—I might have split even more if the restaurant's ovens had been larger, because there were three buddies from Texas on that sightseeing jaunt with their wives, and each of them volunteered his belief that the only thing better than twenty ounces of baked stuffed Maine lobster . . . was forty!"

The audience laughed with him, appalled, and he shook his head now, suggesting that in hindsight he couldn't believe what he had done. And, the truth was, he couldn't. He remembered those evenings well, especially the nights when there would be those sightseeing tours. As soon as the bus would coast into the dirt-and-gravel parking lot, he would retrieve the wooden coop with the torpid crustaceans from the walk-in refrigerator so that the creatures were right there beside him on the floor. Then, like an automaton, he would bend over and grab one from the container that reeked of low tide and pin the writhing, asphyxiating decapod (five pairs of appendages on the thorax, a word he'd found in the entry on lobsters in the dusty encyclopedia from the Coolidge administration he'd discovered in a spare bedroom in Catherine's mother's house) on its back. He would uncoil the springy ribbon of tail and hold down the bulbous crusher claw with his fingers for the split second it took him to line up the cleaver on the lobster's carapace (an unbuttoned sports jacket, he thought at the time) so that the animal's abdomen was exposed. Then he would press the metal blade straight down as it breathed.

But not, alas, breathed its last.

The point was to get the creature into the 450-degree oven while it was still alive.

And—whether he was cooking five or six lobsters on a given night or five or six dozen—after he had sliced the animal lengthwise down to the exoskeleton, he would pack the open cavity with rouxlike gobs of Ritz cracker crumbs and margarine, sprinkle paprika on the stuffing, and slide him off the cutting board and onto a baking sheet. Rarely did the animal have an aluminum leaf to itself, usually it would be one of three or four lobsters pressed together, the claws of one beside the tail of another, Y to Y to Y. Then he would deposit the creatures into the oven on whichever rack was not at that moment occupied by swirls of sole (wrapped around ice-cream-scoop dollops of the same Ritz cracker crumb and margarine paste), slabs of bluefish, or chicken breasts buried beneath bubbling puddles of tomato sauce.

"The animal would cook for ten to twelve minutes. I presumed it finished dying within the very first, but that probably wasn't the case," he said, his voice softening both for effect and because he knew this was true and it disturbed him.

First it's the whales, then it's the dolphins. Next it will be the tuna. It'll never stop, you know, until someone's protecting the bloody lobsters! The words of a whaler—an otherwise charismatic old bird with a furrowed, hard-bitten face—spoken to Spencer the year before last at a gathering of the International Whaling Commission he'd attended in Japan. He remembered their discussion now, as he did often when he talked about lobsters. **Well, yes,** he'd told the whaler. **That's exactly the point.**

In addition to being Lobster Boy—Spencer's title was actually second chef, but the grown men who were waiters all called him Lobster Boy—he also prepared the sole and the bluefish and the chicken Parmesan at the restaurant. The first chef, a burly guy who'd cooked on an aircraft carrier before enrolling in culinary school when he was done with the navy, worked behind a grill the length of a shuffleboard court in the dining room itself, searing the steaks and the chops before any customers who wanted to watch.

When Spencer would return to his girlfriend's mother's house, he knew he was sweaty from his hours beside the hot ovens and from his exertions—he moved quickly and he always pressed the cleaver down hard, convinced even then that it hurt the animal less if the evisceration was fast—but he knew he smelled mostly of fish. Consequently, in late June and July and early August, when the nights were still warm, he kept a bathing suit in the car and sometimes he would detour to Echo Lake before going home. There he would dive into the water and swim along the surface until he felt free of the smell of dead lobsters and sole, and the skin on his fingers no longer had an oily film from the bluefish.

He never went skinny-dipping, even though it was dark and he was alone, because he knew the lake was filled with crayfish, and he felt awfully vulnerable among them when he was naked. Most weren't even as

big as his thumb and he didn't believe they would try
to exact revenge for the way he slaughtered so many of
their saltwater genus kin, but the idea had crossed his
mind and so he always wore a suit—just in case.

He didn't tell his audience this part of his story. But
even at the podium he recalled those swims vividly.

"I must admit, at nineteen I took no small amount
of pride in my abilities as second chef, and I understood that Lobster Boy was a compliment of sorts," he
continued. "No one killed lobsters with my supernat-
ural speed, and speed mattered greatly to the waiters—and, yes, to the diners—at the Steer by the
Shore."

The fact was that Spencer took pride in most of
what he did, even then, whether it was cranking out a
five-page essay on Gogol at the last minute—usually
between 6 a.m. and the start of class at 9:10—playing
pickup basketball at the gym his first spring semester,
or butchering live lobsters in the summer that followed. He knew he was intolerant of ineptitude, and
he understood that as he grew further into adulthood
he would be the sort of person who was easily annoyed
by incompetence. He sensed this both because he was
impatient and because he viewed his impatience as a
virtue. Serene people annoyed him.

"At the end of the summer," he said, lowering his
voice once more as he prepared to build toward the
particular moment in his life that marked the turning
point for the sinner—the carnivore!—that he knew he
once was, "I took the bus from New Hampshire to the
Port Authority in Manhattan. I lugged my suitcase

across town to Grand Central in sweltering, Bombay-like late August heat. At nineteen, it never crossed my mind to take a cab, and the only subways I could find then were those that followed the island's avenues north and south. I met my father at the platform where the 5:57 to Scarsdale was waiting."

By design Spencer did not add that once he and his father had boarded the train, he asked to see pictures of the new house. While Spencer had been having sex with his girlfriend in northern New Hampshire and scuppering lobsters, his parents had decided to move. Again.

"That night at dinner"—in, alas, an unfamiliar dining room in an unfamiliar house—"I realized that something had changed. The lamb—an animal noth-ing at all like a lobster, I know—made me gag. There I was with my parents and my sister and a serving plate layered with skewers of shish kabob, and I thought I was going to be ill. Really and truly ill. And I knew—I knew!—at precisely that instant that never again was I going to yearn for meat or poultry or fish and that I would always find the slick, rubbery touch of bologna revolting. I might never have nightmares about lobsters, but nor would I ever again dream of meat."

With his thumb he flipped the small button on the remote in his right hand that dimmed the room's over-head lights and then the second one that controlled his PowerPoint presentation slides, and instantly the FERAL logo—an image of lions and tigers and bears and cows and chickens and dogs and goldfish and cats and (at Spencer's insistence) lobsters planted on a grid on a lentil-shaped oval that FERAL's critics insisted was a subliminal hand grenade—filled the screen.

THAT NIGHT IN NEW HAMPSHIRE, the last night when the house would still have in it only the dog, the cousins, and the girls' grandmother, the deer discovered the massive vegetable garden in the sprawling meadow beside Nan Seton's long and meandering gravel driveway. There were three animals, a pair of does and a yearling, and they smelled the radishes—which they wouldn't eat, but which they understood often seemed to coexist with so many of the plants that they would: the leafy oakleaf and Bibb lettuce that was just starting to go to seed, the lush, sprawling spinach rosettes, and the snow peas and the string beans and the purple vein-laden greens that towered above the golf ball–sized beets.

The animals had their summer fur, a rosy, almost reddish tan. They wandered silently through the broad, sweeping fields of lupine on which they would never dine, moving so quietly that the dog in the nearby house neither stirred nor lifted his aged snout. The next morning there would be tracks—twin mollusk shells pressed into the earth—at the edge of the garden and in some of the rows, but the girls and their grandmother would not notice them when they wandered out to weed and water the plants. This was the first time in a generation and a half that there had been a vegetable garden beside this house, and while

Willow's parents might have detected the deer prints and recognized them—John Seton, after all, had lived in Vermont most of his adult life, and his wife, Sara, had been there since birth—Willow herself did not. Nor did her cousin from Manhattan's Upper West Side or their grandmother, who lived across that city's vast ecosystem of a park from young Charlotte. After all, Nan only spent the summer and early autumn at this ancestral homestead surrounded by fields of lupine and—far enough down the hill that it didn't obstruct the house's views of the White Mountains to the east and the south—a small forest of sugar maples and pine.

Nor did anyone notice the way the whitetails had browsed the lower branches and twigs of the apple trees that separated the vegetable garden from the driveway or the scat that one of the creatures had left near the mounds from which had sprung the first tubular sprouts and broad leaves of the zucchini and squash.

They noticed instead the more obvious signs that the deer had visited: The leaves on many of the plants the girls' parents had placed into the ground with such care as seedlings or seeds over Memorial Day Weekend were gnawed or nibbled or gone, and a part of one of the rows of corn—finally knee high—had been knocked over. Stepped on. Crushed.

When the girls and their grandmother discovered the damage in the morning, it crossed all of their minds that when the middle generation arrived that afternoon—their idiosyncrasies and their hopes as clear on their faces as their receding hairlines and their adult-tired eyes—there would be discussion and there would be debate. There might even be action. Certainly Spencer, the catalyst behind the vegetable plot, would want to do something. But they all knew on some level that despite the exertions and proclamations of that energetic middle generation, there really was nothing they could do to prevent the deer from feasting on what was left of the garden.

Two

The morning after the deer found a veritable super-market waiting for them on Nan Seton's property, Willow was standing in a beam of phosphorescent sunlight in her grandmother's kitchen, adjusting the candy lilies and the yellow loosestrife she had picked in one vase and the snowcap daisies in a second, thinner one. She was using the counter between the antique dishwasher and the sink, working carefully because she wanted the arrangements to be perfect. When she was done, she threw the stems she had trimmed into the garbage and filled both vases with water. Then, taking baby steps so she didn't slop water onto the floor in the hallway, the stairs, or along the second floor corridor, she carried the flowers upstairs to the room in which her parents and Patrick would be staying when they arrived later that day—the room in which her parents always slept when they came here, since it had been her father's bedroom in this house when he was a boy.

Initially she placed both arrangements on the embroidered scarf on the dresser, but that looked too crowded and so she sidled around the crib that Grandmother had brought down from the attic and placed the daisies on the nightstand. Then she fluffed the pillows on her parents' bed one more time, made sure the welcome card she had created from colored paper and her grandmother's ancient Magic Markers was perfectly centered against the headboard, and adjusted the bedspread so that it was as flat as a tabletop. Her mom and dad would be arriving sometime that afternoon, and she wanted their room to be cozy and welcoming. She couldn't wait to see them.

When she turned around, she saw that her cousin was standing in the doorway in her string bikini.

"You should get in your suit," Charlotte said. "You know Grandmother will freak if you're not ready when she wants to leave for the club."

"She's still watering the vegetable garden, isn't she?"

"Actually, she's just standing there with the hose, staring at stuff. It's like she's had a stroke or something."

"Charlotte!"

The older girl rolled her eyes and started running her fingers over the red petals of one of the lilies in the arrangement on the dresser.

"Be gentle with them," Willow said to her, and then added quickly, "Please. I want them to look nice when Mom and Dad get here."

"The only reason we even have flowers this year is because my dad planted them."

"We all planted them."

"It was my dad's idea."

"So? You can pick some for your parents' room, too."

"Yeah, right."

"It would make them happy."

"It would take more than a couple of tired-looking lilies to do that."

"Don't say the lilies are tired. They're not," she answered. Willow knew enough not to either reassure her cousin that her aunt and uncle had seemed happy enough when they'd all been here over Memorial Day Weekend or to ask her what she had meant and thereby give her yet another chance to vent. She really didn't want to hear Charlotte's complaints right now about either her parents' marriage or how her father's job was constantly screwing up her life: how she was the only kid in all of New York City who had never been to the Bronx Zoo or seen the Big Apple Circus or (and **this**, Willow knew, was what really vexed her cousin these days) been allowed to own a leather skirt or a pair of leather dress shoes.

"No, you're right," Charlotte agreed, "they do look pretty. Your mom and dad will like them. And the card, too. You're sweet to do all this." Then she gave her that wide-eyed smile that Willow thought made her older cousin look like a beautiful young model in a face crème commercial and took her hand. "Now come on," she continued, pulling her from her parents' bedroom and down the hall to the one the two of them shared, "you need to get dressed for the club."

NAN SETON WAS SEVENTY, but she had more vigor than her forty-year-old son and her thirty-eight-year-old daughter. Sometimes, when John and Catherine would speak on the phone or visit with each other at one or the other's home or at this imposing Victorian with its top-heavy tower in northern New Hampshire, the siblings would try to convince themselves that Mother only **seemed** to have a vast storehouse of energy inside her because she didn't have young children the way they did. When she had been their age and they had been children themselves, she couldn't possibly have been so . . . vigorous.

Oh, but Nan Seton was, and in their hearts John and Catherine knew this. They remembered from their childhoods that between the Junior League and the Mayflower Society and the mornings she spent as a volunteer at the public schools in Harlem and Chinatown and the South Bronx, or the time she spent riding her bicycle in Central Park or attending lectures at the Fifth Avenue museums near their apartment, the woman never stopped moving. And that was just during the school year.

In the summer she was even more active: Then there were those train-schedule-precise, rigidly programmed days in New Hampshire in which she would play golf in the morning, swim in the afternoon at the lake or in the Contour Club's pool, take them on nature walks before dinner, and then insist—insist, as if it were homework—that they play badminton with her before the sun had set or they had cleared the dishes from the dining room table. Those days, John and Catherine lived very much the way their daughters did now for a month every summer, when the girls would attend what they called the Seton New England Boot Camp and spend the better part of their days hitting buckets of golf balls at the club, practicing the crawl or learning to dive at the pool, swatting tennis balls with the girl from Dartmouth who was serving this year as the club's informal teaching pro, or learning the nuances of bidding in the club's Young People's Summer Bridge League. Charlotte and Willow, too, had their nature walks with Grandmother and—a new addition this year—a vegetable garden the size of a truck farm to weed and fertilize and thin.

Granted, Nan Seton always had the luxury of help when her own children were young: There was an endless stream of au pairs, a cleaning woman twice a week in Manhattan and another once a week here in the country. And, until he died, there had been Richard Seton. Richard didn't do a whole lot around either the apartment or the house in New Hampshire, and by his own admission what went on in either world between, say, seven in the morning and seven at night was a complete mystery to him. But he was very, very good at running what had been his father's advertising agency, and then he was even better at managing the enterprise when the agency went public in the late 1970s. He never wrote a single line of copy or bought even fifteen seconds of airtime, but he created an estimable litany of frivolous but impressively glossy innovations, such as the "Button Club," a training program for young account executives that taught them such presentation morsels as the importance of buttoning their suit coats before speaking and of using their hands when they shared marketing and media plans with their junior clients. He made sure that his more senior clients received complimentary subscriptions to **Advertising Age** and the **Wall Street Journal**. And in an era well before e-mail and digital cameras and budgets that were lean to the point of malnourishment, he gave lavish holiday parties for the companies whose advertising dollars he spent. These parties, in his opinion, were about friendship—not pandering—because in his experience a person was far less likely to fire his friend than his ad agency. Granted there were always cases of Château Aile d'Argent and burgundies from La Vignée Bourgogne there, too, and Richard certainly was willing to look the other way in the late 1960s and 1970s when the younger account executives and copywriters were also offering their age-appropriate clients marijuana and controlled substances that Richard knew well were illegal.

But advertising for Richard was largely about relationships, and it was a testimony to the success of his formula that in the days after he died of a heart attack at his desk at fifty-one, Nan received dozens of sumptuous arrangements of flowers, all with accompanying cards expressing condolences and signed with appropriate gravity from "All of Us" at Warner-Lambert, Freeman-Duffy, Scott Paper, Coleman-McNeil, Lever Brothers, and Procter & Gamble.

He may not have been home all that often, but he enhanced an already sizable family estate and allowed Nan and John and Catherine to go about their lives without fear that the money might someday run short or Father might complicate their carefully managed end-of-the-day routines by showing up before dinner.

In all the years that Nan had been a widow, she had not, as far as either John or Catherine could tell, gone on a single date. The children presumed this was because there was no man her age who was willing to risk his health by trying to keep up with her. Of course, in the matriarchal worlds in which she moved—the Colony Club, the Contour Club, the garden clubs in New York and New Hampshire—a man would have been a needless encumbrance in any event.

Nan's eyes sat back a tad too far in their sockets, and without the inspired ministrations of a stylist her hair would fall flat against her skull. Her skin was deeply lined from her years in the sun, but because of the moisturizers she slathered on it at night it looked as oily as an adolescent's in the morning. But she had been a real beauty when she was young—that was clear even now—and her face was as adorably ellipsoidal as ever. She had grown into the term she had heard used to describe her own mother a quarter century earlier and become—and she accepted this most days with grace—a handsome woman.

She stood now at the edge of the vegetable garden, the end of the hose in her hands, while inside the house she presumed her granddaughters were climbing into their swimsuits and brushing their teeth. She had already packed the car with their towels and their tennis rackets and a couple of child-sized irons and drivers. Then she bent over with a lack of decorum that only would have been surprising had someone been present and stared closely at the decimated rows of peas and string beans and beets. For a moment she presumed this was the work of a rabbit or a raccoon, but then she saw the way that some of the corn plants had been toppled and overturned so that the roots extended into the air like wet dingy mop heads. This was the work of larger animals, she decided. Almost certainly deer.

She gazed down toward the trees at the edge of the sloping fields of lupine and then straightened up. Even from here she could see three of the large yellow signs that said **POSTED** in a bold, block sans serif type. The notices were nailed to the trees and informed possible trespassers that there was absolutely no hunting, fishing, or trapping allowed on this property and that violators indeed would be prosecuted. The prosecution was an idle threat, but the hardware store didn't stock any versions of the sign that didn't include it. She'd first had the warnings put up when Charlotte was four and Willow was a toddler, and the whole extended family decided to have an old-fashioned Thanksgiving in New Hampshire instead of Manhattan. It had been the last seventy-two hours of that year's rifle season, however, and there had been so much sniper fire in the nearby woods and fields that the grown-ups had joked grimly about living in Beirut and Charlotte had gotten scared.

The idea crossed her mind now to take the signs down before she went home in September. If she did not discourage people from hunting on her property this November, perhaps the deer would stay away next summer. Maybe the herd would figure out that predators skulked near the Victorian at the top of the hill.

Yes, if the family chose to spend Thanksgiving here again they might have to live with the snap and crack of rifle fire, and perhaps a deer might even be killed within sight of the house. But obviously Willow had seen dead deer in Vermont: Surely she'd noticed the newly killed animals when they were weighed on the big outdoor scales at general stores and town offices or when the disemboweled carcasses were hung out to dry on a house's front porch. Her own father had taken up the sport last year to vent whatever midlife steam had begun to accrue in his bones, and he'd actually spent four or five days tromping through the snow and the cold in the woods. Apparently he'd seen a doe and then a doe and a fawn but no bucks that either he could or would have shot.

His hobby was a family secret of which only she and Sara and Willow were aware. John Seton owned some kind of Adirondack brand rifle, a scope (and she'd held the little spyglass in her hands before he had attached it to the rifle barrel) that made things hundreds of yards distant look like they were a mere arm's length away, and camouflage clothing from some company with the frightening name of Predator that was crafted from a material with the equally disturbing moniker of Stealthtex. The fabric was wind and rain resistant, and when John was wearing it in the woods he was, supposedly, invisible if the conditions were right.

Well, not completely invisible. He also wore an orange cap with earflaps for safety, and the color was such an ill-advised shade—and **so** visible—that it looked at first as if he had wrapped his head in police tape when he modeled it for her.

She and her daughter-in-law both hoped this was a temporary fixation, triggered largely by Sara's amnio. When Sara and John had learned their little baby was going to be a boy, John had started babbling about how in years to come he and his son might do some real north country male bonding and bag themselves a buck. She'd presumed he was kidding, and Sara—who was on the phone with them when he called with the news—said that she wished that he were. No such luck. By the time hunting season rolled around the second Saturday in November, he had taken his Hunter Education and Safety course and gotten his hunting license for the sixteen-day rifle season.

Nan knew that her vegetarian daughter and son-in-law in Manhattan—oh, God, especially her son-in-law—could never be privy to the reality that John Seton owned a gun and hoped to use it someday to kill a deer. They would be appalled. Spencer would be particularly furious, and there was nothing more unendurable than Spencer McCullough's self-righteous indignation. At her sixty-fifth birthday party at the Colony Club, she had overheard David Linton, a retired bank economist and the husband of one of her bridge pals, Marisa Linton, admonishing Spencer very good-naturedly about some of FERAL's stunts, the realities of supply and demand in a free market, and how nowhere in the world was good meat more affordable than in the United States. And so when it was his turn to stand and raise his champagne flute,

Spencer had toasted her warmly but then gone on to rebuke everyone who was eating the Colony Club's beef Wellington—one of the two entrees she had chosen for the party, the other being a pasta primavera specifically for Catherine and Spencer and Charlotte—while insisting that FERAL did nothing ever but point out the obvious, and no one in the room would be eating that beef if they'd seen a cow emerge onto a slaughterhouse kill floor or been forced to witness a steel bolt being blasted into its forehead to stun it before it was butchered. She vaguely recalled him saying something next about the animal's tongue sticking out from between its teeth in shock and incredulity, but he was (once again) becoming such a spoilsport that by then she was trying hard to tune him out.

Which brought her back to posting. John and Sara wouldn't care if she chose to stop posting her land. If there was going to be any resistance to the idea, it was going to come from her daughter and her son-in-law. They were both not merely vegetarians, they were animal rights activists—Spencer professionally, Catherine as a reasonably enthusiastic amateur. Spencer, in fact, was something even worse than a vegetarian: He was a vegan, a word that sounded vaguely anatomic in Nan's mind and therefore caused her a slight, unpleasant shudder whenever she heard it. Spencer's peculiarity meant that she couldn't even serve something as comfortably plebian as macaroni and cheese when he was visiting, because one of its two signature ingredients was made with milk and milk came from cows. It was ridiculous, in her opinion, completely ridiculous. Thank God Catherine still allowed milk and yogurt and cheese to be part of her and Charlotte's diet.

Nevertheless, Spencer was the communications director for FERAL, a lobbying group that championed animal causes, and when he wasn't jetting to Washington to argue against things that seemed harmless to normal people—state dairy compacts and pet stores that sold tropical birds—he was meeting with magazine editors and appearing on TV shows defending positions that more times than not completely befuddled her. Why in heaven's name was it better for college students to drink beer than milk? Who really cared if wing tips or a wallet were made of leather: What were people supposed to do, wear plastic dress shoes? Keep their credit cards packed together in their pockets or purses with elastic bands?

And while Nan thought chimpanzees were cute and she understood that they were considerably smarter than, say, squirrels, she found her eyes glazing when Spencer would go on and on about the need to extend legal rights to chimps and gorillas and dolphins.

She knew that the **A** and the **L** in FERAL stood for animal liberation, and that **FER** stood for Federation. The group's official name was the Federation for Animal Liberation. This meant, in her opinion, that the acronym should more properly be FEDAL, since the first three letters of **federation** were **FED.** Or, perhaps, they could use the first five letters of **federa-**

tion and call themselves FEDERAL. She thought that had a nice historical ring to it. But FERAL? It made them sound like they were a bunch of wild animals, and what could possibly be the point of **that?** Still, she did like the way their letterhead and their magazine and even some of their T-shirts had a portion of some poem by Ovid—though she did wish they'd chosen one that wasn't quite so judgmental about "feasting on meat."

Spencer was not a particularly handsome man, even if, as Nan recalled, he had been a rather good-looking college boy. But he carried himself with the confidence of someone who was striking and tall and who knew it. You could see it (as she certainly had) when he was speaking before groups of people in libraries, local YMCAs, and even the larger, more urban Rotary and Kiwanis clubs. Moreover, he was so indefatigably self-assured about his positions on . . . well, on everything . . . and so facile with statistics and stories and seemingly relevant anecdotes that it was futile to argue with him. Nevertheless, Nan was often left wondering: Did anyone really care that Pythagoras was a vegetarian? Who, other than Spencer, even knew who the Manicheans were? The only reason the family even had this ridiculous vegetable garden was because it was easier to put the effort into the earth than into trying to talk Spencer out of it: Nan and her granddaughters were now weeding and watering more for his sake than for their own. Here in the country they accommodated his diet—his family's diet—even if it put desperate strains on Nan's admittedly limited creativity in the kitchen, they endured his monologues at dinner, and (yes) they gardened.

But then, of course, there was that other Spencer—the gentle and loving and almost farcically good-natured man whose sincere consideration of animals made him such an impassioned and (in small doses) charismatic champion of their rights. How he had loved Catherine when he was courting her here in the country at nineteen and twenty! It was so obvious and genuine and touchingly over the top. Breakfast in bed. Bouquets of lupine and wildflowers. Enduring hours of defeat at her hands on the Contour Club tennis courts. Nan had heard stories from Spencer's parents of the lengths to which he had gone to rescue raccoons as a child, to shelter birds with broken wings, to nurse ailing dogs and cats and (once) a neighbor's ugly ferret. Nan needed only to recall Julys past and how Spencer would read to Charlotte and Willow for hours before the children would go to bed to be reminded of her son-in-law's strengths. He would use voices so rambunctious and theatric that Nan would be left wondering why he hadn't wound up an actor. Moreover, as busy as he was—he seemed to be traveling all the time—when Willow and her family would visit New York, it was invariably Spencer who would take the girls to a Broadway musical or a children's ballet. He didn't always make time for the small things, Nan knew, such as teaching his daughter the names of the trees that grew in Central Park or showing her how to press a fallen leaf between wax paper in the fall, but then her husband, Richard, had rarely done those sorts of things with his children, either.

The difference—and this was what alarmed Nan periodically—was his utter unwillingness to listen to others, and the way he would dismiss those who disagreed with him when it came to matters of food and meat and animal rights. All too often he seemed more interested in animals than in humans. Than in his own family. Moreover, sometimes he seemed interested in animals in the abstract—as issues and causes—rather than as individual creatures with whom he might feel a special bond. It was as if he'd lost somewhere that little boy who would rescue a raccoon because it was furry and soft and he saw in its eyes the simple spark of life.

The irony in Nan's mind was that there had been a time when Spencer had not simply eaten like a regular person, he'd actually been a rather good cook. A chef, even! He was nineteen and he was dating her daughter, and the two of them spent the summer (the first of many) with her in New Hampshire between their freshman and sophomore years of college. It was only a year after Richard had died, and Nan was very glad to have a man around the country house so there would be someone to empty the kitchen garbage and change the lightbulbs in the ceiling fixtures—real man's work, in her opinion. Her daughter, Catherine, was a waitress at Gerta's Edelweiss Garden that summer, a restaurant with postcard-perfect vistas of the ski slopes at Cannon and the new condominiums at

Mittersill, while Spencer worked in the kitchen at the Steer by the Shore, a steak-and-seafood restaurant, which in lieu of a view had both a dining room big enough to accommodate bus tours and the area's first dessert bar—a novelty back then. Spencer started there over Memorial Day Weekend as a dishwasher but, through a combination of pluck and luck and the sudden arrest of the restaurant's second chef for cocaine possession, had ascended with meteoric efficiency. By the Fourth of July it was young Spencer McCullough who was slicing the chicken breasts and cooking the lobsters and making that delicious stuffing with the secret ingredient that tasted an awful lot like Ritz crackers and that Spencer protected like a spy. That summer she would not have been surprised if someday when he finished college Spencer had enrolled at the Culinary Institute of America or Johnson & Wales with the hope of becoming a serious chef or restaurateur.

Of course he hadn't. By late August, when he and her daughter were done with their jobs for the summer and the boy—and in so many ways then he really was still a boy—went home to see his family in Westchester before returning to college, it was clear that he would continue on the more predictable white-collar path taken by all of her children's friends.

And, in truth, why should she have expected him eventually to go on to cooking school? It wasn't as if Catherine ever again wanted to have anything to do with either a restaurant's kitchen or its dining room.

Spencer still enjoyed cooking—that was clear—and

he certainly enjoyed cooking here in New Hampshire. The problem was that he now cooked like a—and there was only one word for it—weirdo. She shuddered when she thought of the odd beans and curds and funguses that he considered legitimate sources of nutrition.

Behind her she heard the screen door clap shut and for a split second it had sounded to her like a gunshot, and she thought suddenly of the deer and her idea to remove the signs that forbid hunting on her property. She turned around and saw her two granddaughters racing toward her, Willow in a blue terry-cloth cover-up and her cousin in only that minuscule string thing that both Catherine and Charlotte insisted was a bathing suit. She sighed and then prepared herself for her daily battle with the older girl: The child might have only the merest hummocks for breasts, but she still could not arrive at the Contour Club dressed like a lap dancer. It was just that simple.

Three

John Seton was lying happily on the floor of his living room in Vermont, a wisp of black bang across his eyeglasses, watching enrapt as his son pedaled the pudgy water balloons that passed for his legs like an upside-down bicyclist. Patrick was not quite five months old, and any day now John was sure that his cherubic baby boy was going to dazzle him by overcoming his turtlelike inability to roll over and start spinning like a dervish on a ski slope. It could happen this very second, if only because the child might grow tired of feeling the Dijon mustard that in the last moment he had let loose into his diaper with the power and sound of a fire hose.

Upstairs he heard Sara in the boy's nursery, and he presumed she was getting the baby monitor off the nightstand and throwing a couple more onesies and doll-sized socks into the baby's suitcase. He and his wife—260 pounds of grown-ups—would share a single overnight bag, while their thirteen-pound eleven-ounce son would have to himself a piece of luggage the size of a steamer trunk. The clothes the boy wore might not be big, but he sure needed a lot of them. And then there were the pillows and the blankets and the menagerie of stuffed animals from his room here so his crib in New Hampshire would smell like his crib in Vermont.

The boy stared up at the ceiling and gurgled contentedly. He smiled at something John could neither see nor understand, and John smiled back. Then he sighed. Young Patrick was not going to roll over today—at least not this morning—and so he scooped his son up and carried him to the bathroom to change him.

As he passed through the kitchen with his boy in his arms the phone rang. He wanted to let the answering machine get it because in all likelihood it was either his office or Sara's answering service, and today was supposed to be a day off. They were driving to his mother's in New Hampshire, and they were hoping to leave by nine thirty—ten at the latest—so that they could stop by the club and surprise everyone while they were having lunch or whacking tennis balls or whatever it was that Mother had the girls doing at boot camp today. But he knew that if he didn't answer the phone Sara would. She'd only been back at work for two months, and so she was still in that professional's postpartum phase in which anything she did with one of her patients was more satisfying—and, in truth, easier—than hooking up a Hoover (either Patrick or the pump) to one of her breasts, or waking at one or five in the morning to feed the child, or trying (and failing) to quell the aneurysm-inducing stress that both of them felt when one or the other was trapped behind a hay wagon or dump truck and they were late for Patrick's 5:30 pickup at the day-care center in their village. The place was run by two women who were loving and gentle and kind during the day, but like werewolves were transformed into something unspeakably ugly at precisely 5:31. The family of any child remaining at the Mother's Love Nurture World at 5:45 would be charged an extra half day; three tardy pickups in a month and the child was subject to dismissal.

With his one free hand he picked the receiver from the wall like an apple and heard the secretary he shared with two other public defenders on the other end of the line.

"Hi, John. Sorry to bother you. I didn't know if you saw the newspaper yet."

"No," he murmured, shaking his head despite the reality that the woman couldn't see him. Patrick happily grabbed his nose with fingers that still resembled tiny pinchers and made a sound like a giggle.

"I hear Patrick," Sally said.

"Yes, you do."

"You sound like you have a cold."

"No. I have a baby who thinks my nose is a rattle."

"Oh, that's cute."

Actually, John thought, it was more painful than cute: The baby was trying to move his skull the way he himself had a moment earlier when he'd been shaking his head, and he was surprised at the amount of strength in that small hand and arm. The kid couldn't roll over yet, but his motor skills for exactly this maneuver had been perfected with weeks of practice on a stuffed animal the size of a butternut squash that he and Sara had christened Drool Monkey.

"What's in the paper?" he asked.

"Dickie Ames was busted last night. It was another DUI—"

"Oh, Jesus, he didn't hurt anyone, did he?"

"No. But he took out a fire hydrant. And because it was the zillionth time—"

"It was not the zillionth time," John corrected her. Sally was an excellent secretary, but she was twenty-three and her tendency to speak with adolescent hyperbole sometimes annoyed him. "It was, I believe, the third."

"Well, he blew a mighty impressive point-one. And, oh by the way, he was driving with a suspended license: He wasn't due to get it back until the week after next."

John wasn't defending Dickie Ames, but he needed the man to be a credible witness in a misdemeanor assault in a bar. Ames was a drinking and deer-hunting pal of Andre Nadeau and was supposed to explain to the judge at a bail review on Monday that Nadeau was acting in self-defense when he'd broken a heavy glass beer mug against the side of Cameron Gerrity's face in a fight—which, John believed, was exactly the truth. It **was** self-defense. Gerrity may have been the one to wind up with the thirty-four stitches in his cheek and a nose that would look forever like a boxer's, but John was quite confident that Nadeau had been provoked. Ames saw it all and he said so. Besides, there were extenuating circumstances John hoped the judge would consider. Nadeau was a single dad. John had seen him with his boys, and although Nadeau may have had a problem with drinking (yes, like his pal, Dickie Ames) he certainly didn't have one with aggression. He had no history of pummeling people in bars. He had no history of pummeling people anywhere.

If given the chance, Dickie Ames was also going to tell the judge what a fine father Nadeau was to those two boys and that whenever he had been together with the family at deer camp, the man was loving, gentle, and preternaturally responsible—especially when it came to teaching a couple of junior high school kids not to kill themselves with the family arsenal the grown men used to kill deer and moose and bears and any other mammals they happened to stumble across in the woods. John liked Nadeau—and not simply in the protective, fatherly way he liked all the pathetic drinkers and substance abusers and petty thieves who wound up at the office of the public defender. He liked Nadeau because the guy was raising his boys pretty much on his own since his wife had left him. The man had offered to take him deer hunting at his family's camp this November—help him track and kill a 250-pounder, perhaps—and John had readily agreed. Nadeau liked him, too, and respected what he did as a lawyer: He wouldn't mind that John was a complete moron in the woods and was still learning to hold a rifle and hunt. Nadeau had even told him about a friend of his in Essex Junction, a gunsmith, who would be able to remove the bullet—cartridge, to be precise—that seemed to be stuck in the chamber of John's rifle. It had been there since last November, since the last day of John's first hunting season.

Periodically he'd tried to extract it since then, retriev-
ing the gun from the locked cabinet in the guest bedroom and cycling the bolt over and over, but the bullet
had never popped out. His older friend, the justice
Howard Mansfield, had suggested he simply shove a
ramrod down the barrel and force the live round from
the chamber, but there was no way in the world John
was going to try that little maneuver. That was exactly
how newcomers to the sport—especially newcomer
flatlanders—blew off their fingers or hands. He'd considered simply driving to the edge of the forest and
discharging the weapon into the sky, but he feared that
perhaps whatever was causing the bullet to lodge in
the chamber would prevent it from leaving the barrel
as well. The thing just might explode in his face. He
understood he'd have to deal with the bullet before
hunting season, but since he only used the rifle during
those two weeks in November he hadn't seriously focused on the problem until Nadeau suggested his
buddy, the gunsmith.

He sighed now so loudly at the reality that Dickie
Ames had spent the night behind bars that Patrick
turned his little boy eyes on his father's face. At least,
John told himself, he wasn't Dickie Ames's lawyer, and
he took some comfort in this.

"Anything else I should know about?" he asked
Sally. "Sara and I were about to leave."

"I don't think so."

"Well, thank you."

"I guess you didn't need to know about Dickie
Ames. I guess it could have waited."

"No, you were right to call. I appreciate it."

"Tell you what: For the rest of today I'll only call you if I have good news."

"You have the number at my mother's house, right? The cell phone never works over there."

"I do."

He thanked her once again, pulled his nose from between Patrick's viselike fingers, and then continued on his way to the bathroom on the first floor of the house. After he had changed his son's diaper, he decided, he would toss the gun bag with his Adirondack rifle into the trunk of the car. On Monday they would be driving through Essex Junction on their way home from his mother's, and he could drop the weapon off with that gunsmith.

JOHN'S WIFE, SARA, hadn't spoken to Catherine and Spencer since Memorial Day Weekend, when they had all met at the Seton summer home to plant the vegetable garden, the cutting garden, and the beds and beds of berries: strawberries in a western field, blueberries along the house's southern foundation, and raspberries to the east. John and his sister, Catherine, seemed to speak weekly, however, and the two siblings spoke at least that often with their mother.

At first Sara had taken it as a compliment that she was allowed to call the family matriarch Nan while Spencer, Catherine's husband, had to call her Mrs. Seton. It was almost comic: Spencer had known the woman since he was eighteen, and still he was required to address her with Victorian courtesy and old-money solemnity. He and her husband each received Valentine's cards from Nan in February, and even after all these years the one to Spencer was signed "Sincerely, Mrs. Seton." It was only after she and John had been married for a couple of years that it dawned on Sara why she might be allowed to refer to her mother-in-law as Nan and Spencer was not: Perhaps it made Nan feel younger—as if the two of them were girlfriends—if they called each other by their first names.

As she and John and their baby drove now to New Hampshire, Sara decided that although she wasn't dreading the weekend before her, she wasn't looking forward to it, either. She was beginning to feel that her own house was getting back into some kind of order for the first time since before Patrick was born and she would have enjoyed a weekend at home. Moreover, the child was cutting a tooth—though he was sleeping right now in his infant car seat in the back—and poor John was exhausted. Could barely keep his eyes open at the dinner table last night and had spent most of the morning lying on the floor with the baby.

She was also troubled by the sheer amount she had felt compelled to pack. They'd be in New Hampshire a whopping sixty-eight to seventy hours, but between the excessive athleticism her mother-in-law cheerfully inflicted on the family (she had to remember tennis rackets and golf clubs and bathing suits, though she wanted to play neither golf nor tennis nor swim in that frigid alpine slush that Nan called a lake or that club pool that reeked of chlorine) and the accrual of health and beauty aids—sunscreens and powders and shampoos and lotions and teething gel and ointment and hair glitter and, alas, even lipstick for Willow because Nan had them all going to the club on Saturday night for a soiree of some sort and Willow had said on the phone that Charlotte would be wearing lipstick and so she wanted to wear some now, too—it felt to her as if she were packing for a monthlong expedition into a lost world without drugstores and shopping malls.

She thought she might be overthinking this because she was a therapist, but the problem with Nan—and with John and Catherine and, yes, Spencer when they were all together—was that they could never just . . . be. They didn't sit still well as a family. When she and John had been younger they'd smoked a little dope, and sometimes she longed to buy a bag of the most mellow stuff she could find and bring it with her to Sugar Hill. Sedate the whole bunch of them so they'd all sit on that wraparound porch and just stare at the beauty of the lupine. Maybe open the windows, point the speakers outside, and listen to music on that antique record player Nan kept in the living room. Play some of those old Sammy Davis Jr. and Mel Tormé albums that her daughter had presumed were oddly flat Frisbees when she'd been a first-grader.

Her daughter. Now, that was the part of the weekend that excited her. Though she spoke with Willow on the phone at least every other night, she hadn't seen her in just about two weeks now—twelve days to be precise—and she missed almost every aspect of having the girl in her life on a daily basis. She missed reading to the child in bed in the evenings or having the child read to her; she missed the way Willow moved slowly through the house with the grace of a ballet dancer, sometimes seeming to barely touch the stairs when she glided down them on her bare feet; she missed the way the girl managed somehow to eat cereal without making a sound—the spoon never touched the sides of the bowl, and Willow seemed to loathe the insectival sound of a slurp as much as any grown-up—and she missed the way Willow could calm Patrick with an almost paranormal gentleness. When the baby was in nuclear meltdown and neither breast milk nor rocking would silence the child's earsplitting siren of a shriek, somehow Willow knew precisely how to hold him or tickle him or rub him to bring both parents and newborn back from the brink. She also changed diapers, which certainly made things easier when Sara was trying to get something that resembled dinner on the table.

Willow was not a perfect child, of course, and Sara did not for a moment delude herself into believing that she was. She gave up quickly on math problems, it was easier to pull the witchgrass from the front garden than it was to convince her to clean her room or put her dirty clothes in the hamper, and she spent more time in front of a mirror than Sara thought any ten-year-old should. But she was sweet and sensitive and Sara loved her madly—so much more, she feared

on occasion, than she would ever learn to love her
baby boy with his tendency to pee straight into the air
like a geyser.

"Did we remember the nightlight?" John was asking her now.

"Darn it, we didn't," she said. She honestly didn't
know how much Patrick needed the nightlight, but
his parents sure did. It was bad enough to be awake at
one or two in the morning, but it was hell when you
slammed your shin into the crib, or nearly poked out
an eye on one of the airplane wings in the mobile that
dangled just beyond the lad's reach.

"Well, we can pick one up in Littleton."

"That means getting off the highway," she said, an
issue in her mind only because getting off the highway
would slow them down and thereby decrease their
chances of getting to the club in time for lunch.

"Maybe I can get one this afternoon, then," John
said. "I'll be happy to pick one up while Patrick's napping. I'll want to get a new can of tennis balls, anyway.
You know the ones Mother has are going to be so old
they'll bounce like rocks."

She nodded and glanced back at Patrick, resisting
the urge to squeeze his toes in his socks. Then she
closed her eyes, flexed her own toes once against the
straps of her sandals, and started to make an inventory
in her mind of everything she had packed and John
had wedged into the backseat and the trunk of the
Volvo. She was asleep before she had even finished
with the items in the diaper bag resting now beside the
baby behind her.

Four

Willow Seton curled her legs up against her chest, and wrapped her thin arms around her thin knees. She was sitting on the coralline cement that surrounded the club's swimming pool, and she could feel the pebbly stone surface through the blue Lycra of her Speedo tank suit. It was late morning, and with the exception of the two cousins, the lifeguard, and a pair of older women in pastel tennis skirts chatting near the diving board, the pool area was empty. Overhead there were a few dolloplike scoops of cumulus clouds, phosphorescent in the high summer sky, and when they passed between the sun and the earth Willow would pull her body into an even tighter ball.

She found herself scrutinizing Charlotte as her cousin draped her body languidly in the water atop three long, Styrofoam floating noodles: a hot pink one in the hollow behind her knees, a banana yellow one beneath the small of her back, and a red one that looked like a long piece of licorice behind her neck. She was wearing the black string bikini that drove their grandmother crazy. But their grandmother was taking a golf lesson right now and so Charlotte had raced directly into the ladies' cabana and changed from her tennis clothes into the bathing suit. Now she had the pool to herself, and she was acting as if she were completely unaware that her cousin and the lifeguard were watching her.

At least Willow presumed Charlotte thought the lifeguard was watching her: Charlotte seemed to believe that teenage boys always were watching her. In this case, however, Willow honestly didn't believe that Gary was aware of her cousin as anything more than a girl who swam well enough that it was unlikely she would find a way to drown herself on his watch. The fact was, Charlotte was twelve, a child like herself. Sure, she'd turn thirteen in the last week in August, a month before Willow would reach eleven, but Charlotte hadn't even started eighth grade yet. Gary, both cousins knew, had graduated from high school that June.

Still, Charlotte was a beautiful girl, and for the past two weeks she had managed to convince their grandmother that she was wearing sunblock when in reality she wasn't: Though this might mean she'd have to battle all kinds of skin cancers in that never-never land of adulthood, right now her skin was bronzed to the point of exoticism, and she was going to show off every single inch that she could.

By comparison, Willow felt like a jar of old craft paste: pale white because she had been wearing the requisite sunscreen, tired, and common. Even her bathing suit looked unattractive: The bottom had started to pill from all the hours she'd spent sitting on the cement around the pool. Until this week, it hadn't even crossed her mind that a Speedo could pill. She'd wanted to buy a new suit before her parents brought her here for the month, but because of baby Patrick there hadn't been time to go to the mall.

"I think I should pierce my belly button," Charlotte said abruptly, and though Willow was aware that the remark technically was directed at her, she knew her cousin had only broached the idea to get a reaction out of Gary. "I think I should get a silver ring. Don't you?"

"No."

"You don't think I'd look good with one?"

"I think your mom and dad would kill you."

"They wouldn't know. It's not like I walk around in a halter at home."

"Well, it's not like you do at school, either. So why do it?"

"It would be cool."

"You couldn't wear that bathing suit," Willow said, and for a moment it seemed that Charlotte was pondering this, but then the girl glanced out of the corners of her eyes at Gary—Gary with the peeling skin on his nose and the tawny young man's hair on his chest, Gary with the sunglasses and the whistle and the small stud of his own sparkling right now in his left ear—and she realized that Charlotte was thrilled that she had alluded to how scanty her bathing suit was in front of the lifeguard.

"That would be too bad, wouldn't it?" Charlotte said. "Maybe I'll wait till the end of the summer. When we go home. I'll bet this town doesn't even have a place that does body art."

"No," Gary said from the top of the chair, the sound of his voice—and the reality that he was actually listening to their conversation—catching them both by surprise. "There isn't a place in Franconia or Sugar Hill. But you could always try Yankee Art up in Littleton. The guy there also does tattoos."

"Yeah, Charlotte, why don't you get a tattoo? A belly-button ring and a tattoo. That'll make your mom and dad real happy."

"Of course," Gary continued, "you'll need to wait at least five or six years. I'm pretty sure it's against the law to tattoo a seventh-grader." He was smiling when he said it, and Willow wished she could see his eyes behind the mirrored lenses of his sunglasses.

"Eighth," Charlotte said, almost spitting the syllable up at him. "I'll be in eighth grade in September."

The lifeguard just nodded, and Willow could tell he was struggling not to laugh. Then she saw him look up at something behind her, and when she turned she saw her mom and dad and Patrick—the baby in a Snugli on her father's chest, his small pink hands the only visible flesh—wandering toward them across the grass between the main entrance and the clubhouse with its picture-window views of Mount Lafayette. They were early, she realized, because Grandmother had said they probably wouldn't arrive until midafternoon. Then her mom was opening the gate in the chain-link fence that surrounded the pool, and—forgetting completely for the moment that her cousin Charlotte was annoyed by enthusiasm in any form— Willow was on her feet and running across the cement deck toward them because the truth was that she missed her parents, even if they hadn't found the time to buy her a new bathing suit, and she was very glad they were here.

WILLOW BOUNCED her baby brother on her lap in a wrought-iron chair on the clubhouse deck by the dining room. His eyes reminded her of the pearly blue moonstones on the necklace Grandmother had given her for Christmas seven months ago, and his hair looked a bit like a baby chick's. She had already finished her grilled cheese, but everyone else was still eating—except for Charlotte, who had never gotten to join them because Grandmother had refused to allow her to leave the pool area until she put on a T-shirt and shorts, and so the girl had been left to pout in the ladies' cabana. Had been inside there at least half an hour now. It crossed Willow's mind that it was possible Charlotte had snuck out and was actually watching the older teenagers sunbathe on the grassy hill just behind the tennis courts—she was probably sunbathing **with** those older kids, in fact—but she certainly wasn't going to squeal on her cousin.

Her parents and her grandmother were talking about a funeral Grandmother was going to attend tomorrow for Walter Durnip. Willow knew Mr. Durnip largely as a heavyset man who seemed to walk in slow motion back and forth along the first hole of the golf course, but as far as Willow could tell he never played. He wore Bermuda shorts, and he had veins on his legs that looked like the topographic relief map in her classroom of the rivers in the Amazon rain forest. Her dad seemed a little sad that Mr. Durnip was dead. Apparently he had known the man his whole life, and the man's daughter had babysat him when he was a little boy.

"Maybe I'll join you, Mother," her father said, referring to the funeral. Both he and her mother were eating tomatoes filled with salmon, and Willow found herself wishing the sheer rosiness of the fish had been hidden better by the mayonnaise and the dill. What was it Charlotte was always saying? It's not meat, it's flesh.

"Oh, don't even think of coming," Grandmother began, shaking her head at her son and groaning. "You're on a weekend vacation. And I just know the funeral is going to be long, and there will be people there who will feel they have the right to talk."

"It's called a eulogy, Mother. Some people actually like to mourn."

"I don't mean the minister. I mean regular people. These days, it seems, anyone who happens to be in the church for a funeral is invited to speak. I was at a funeral last summer—that nice Mrs. Knebel—and easily a dozen people thought they had something worth sharing."

"I gather you thought they were mistaken."

"That church has very poor ventilation. And they had too many hymns. When I die, I want my funeral to last no more than fifteen minutes, and absolutely no one is allowed to speak but you or your sister, and the minister—whoever it is then. And no hymns. Are we clear?"

Her father took a long swallow of his iced tea and said, "We're clear, Mother. Show tunes, yes; hymns, no."

"I'm serious. I want a nice, short funeral—especially if there's sunshine. People should be outdoors."

Patrick burped and then smiled. His eyes were unblinking.

"If you die in the summer, we'll be sure to have the funeral here in New Hampshire and we'll be sure to have it outside," her mother said. "We could have it beside the new cutting garden." The cutting garden was a living room–sized block of perennials they had planted between the spindly apple trees and the garage. It actually had been among the easier tasks they had tackled over Memorial Day Weekend, because most of the flowers—the bridal veil astilbe, the red English daisies, the moss pink, the Canada and the Carolina phlox—were in shin-tall buckets and merely needed to be transplanted into the soil that had been tilled before they arrived.

"If you'd like—and you'll need to let us know ahead of time, Nan—we could even rent a little arch made with lattice from one of those rent-anything places," her mother continued, teasing. Sara was wearing sunglasses and holding her hair back in a tie-dyed scarf Willow had made for her at a summer day camp when she'd been seven. She looked a little bit like that First Lady from the early 1960s Willow had seen photographs of—the one who always seemed to be wearing sunglasses and scarves—except that her mother's hair wasn't quite as dark and her mother as a whole wasn't quite as glamorous.

Actually, Willow didn't think her mother was glamorous at all. But she was pretty and she was interesting: The girl did not know the details, but she had the sense from the occasional remarks her parents and her Vermont grandparents had made and from pictures she had seen in old photo albums that her mother had been rather wild as a teenager and when she'd been in college. She knew that her mother had once traveled to Cape Cod with a boyfriend on the back of his motorcycle, and that with two of her girlfriends she'd once taken her own father's car and disappeared for a night in Montreal. She had a thin tattoo of what looked to Willow like ivy wrapped around her left ankle, and a rose the size of a tablespoon in the crevice at the very small of her back—a spot no one ever saw these days but Willow, baby Patrick, and John.

"Oh, I have some bad news about the garden. The vegetable garden," her grandmother was saying.

"Yes?" Her father used what Willow recognized as his lawyer's tone when he said the word, drawing the single syllable out a long time and keeping his voice perfectly even.

"Deer. It was attacked by deer last night."

"Attacked by deer," her mother said, emphasizing **attacked**. Willow knew that her mother disapproved of language with needlessly violent imagery. "You make it sound like it was shelled."

"They might as well have shelled it. The peas and string beans and beet greens were eaten, and the corn—"

"We can't possibly have corn yet," her father said.

"And the corn **plants** were trampled. Not all of them. But some."

"But they didn't eat everything, did they? Not in one visit . . ."

"No, not everything. But they'll be back."

She watched her father wipe his lips with his napkin, the cotton cloth already discolored with grease from past swipes. "Spencer will try to stop them—humanely, of course. But he'll do something. That garden means an awful lot to him."

"I know it does, and for the life of me I don't understand why. He lives six hours away. If he liked gardening so much, he should have had a garden of his own when he lived in Connecticut. He and Catherine should never have moved back into the city if manure and fresh beets—"

"Endive," her father said. "Endive and kohlrabi . . . and manure."

"Whatever. If gardening was so important to him, he should have stayed in Long Ridge. Not bought that apartment on Eighty-fifth Street."

"He tried, Mother. Remember how he lost that garden to the deer, too?"

"If he couldn't stop them in Connecticut, how in the world will he stop them here?"

"Maybe he won't," her mother said. "But certainly he'll make the effort. It's not so much about the garden as it is about the house. The property. This place means an awful lot to him, Nan, you know that."

"Sara's right. I know my brother-in-law, and he will launch an absolute crusade to take back the peas."

"Trust me, it's too late for this year," Nan said. "All we can do now is stop posting the land and keep our fingers crossed that the hunters scare the deer away in the autumn."

"Oh, I wouldn't give up yet," her father said. "And you shouldn't, either. In the meantime, Mother, do you want to play some tennis? I have to get limbered up for Catherine."

Willow watched her brother try to wrap his hand under the strap of her bathing suit, but he couldn't quite wedge his fingers between the elastic and her shoulder. Still he struggled, and his small nails were starting to tickle her.

"I'd love to," Grandmother said. "I had a golf lesson this morning, but all we did was stand around with our putters. Boring."

"Honey, do you want to join us?" her father asked her mother. "Willow, you wouldn't mind watching Patrick, would you?"

She thought her parents were taking the news about the garden pretty well, and she felt another surge of that affection she'd experienced when she'd been preparing flower arrangements for their bedroom that morning and when she'd turned around at the pool and seen them approaching.

"Nope," she said, pulling Patrick away from the strap of her Speedo and kissing him once on his nose. The baby gurgled and sighed. She realized, much to her surprise, how happy she was to see him, too.

Five

Spencer McCullough had been watching the lakes with their impenetrable Native American names—Winnipesaukee, Sunapee, Squam—outside his plane window for almost ten minutes now, and so he knew they'd be on the ground any moment. Even in a fifteen-seat puddle jumper, the Friday afternoon flight from LaGuardia to West Lebanon was barely an hour. He glanced across the aisle at Catherine, saw she was focused on an article in her magazine, and turned back to the window. He thought of the garden. It wasn't its size that excited him: Anyone with enough time on his hands could plant a third of an acre of carrots or beets or squash. It was the garden's variety. Granted, he had appeased his mother-in-law and Sara and John—who, because they lived in Vermont, presumed they knew more than he did about growing vegetables in the faux tundra of northern New Hampshire—by planting rows and rows of the basics. But there were also yards of surprises interspersed in the dirt and clay, and he couldn't wait to see them. White icicle radishes. Kohlrabi. The arugula and the endive that he understood his daughter, his niece, and his mother-in-law already were eating and the blue Hubbard squash that by the fall would look like the pods from which aliens always seemed to spring in the camp horror films of the 1950s.

He could never, of course, have a vegetable garden on West Eighty-fifth Street. They lived on the ninth floor of a building full of co-op apartments.

Even when they had lived in Connecticut in the first years after Charlotte had been born, however—their postpartum foray into suburbia—he couldn't have had a garden like this. It wasn't that there hadn't been the time when he was home or that they hadn't had the space—though that was more limited in the suburbs than it was in northern New Hampshire. It was the deer. Those beautiful animals with their big dark eyes, their white plumelike tails, and their ridiculous Vulcan-like ears. He had tried three times in the four years they had lived in Long Ridge to have a vegetable garden, and each time the deer had devoured it. Eaten whatever they wanted, despite his attempts to deter them. Eaten the lettuce, despite the tobacco-tea—chewing tobacco in water, really—that he had sprinkled on the grass that bordered the garden. Eaten the flowers on the string beans, despite the garlic and Tabasco concoction he had doused on the plants themselves (a remedy that proved as bad as the ailment, since the smell had made the few plants the deer hadn't bothered to gobble completely inedible). Eaten the peas and the beet greens despite the old bathwater. The deer had ignored the mothballs he put in his yard (the nuclear option, in his mind, since mothballs contained naphthalene), and the myriad animal urines—bobcat, wolf, his own—that he showered along the perimeter. Alas, nothing could dissuade the deer that wandered contentedly in the night through those sub-urban backyards from eating whatever they wanted.

But, then, what did he expect? Sometimes he would ask himself if he honestly believed that he could outsmart an animal so perfect in terms of its evolution that its bone structure hadn't changed in four million years. A mammal that—unlike so many others—didn't become a mere fossil to study in the Ice Age but actually flourished in the midst of cataclysmic environmental transformation. Spencer understood that deer could eat virtually anything that grows up from the dirt—and, when pressed, had been known to stomp fish in shallow water to eat them—and were capable of living almost anywhere. Deep woods. Cleared farm-land. The suburbs. Cities. The whitetail existed in the coldest reaches of northern Alberta, in the scorching heat of New Mexico, along the Pacific coastline of Peru. Its cousins, the blacktail and the mule deer, filled in those western corners of North America where the whitetail was absent—the Nevada desert, the California seaboard—with the result that there were few crevices on the continent where there weren't deer of one kind or another.

Nevertheless, Spencer had convinced himself that New Hampshire would be different. In all the times that he had been to his mother-in-law's—the summers when he'd been a college student, weeks at a time ever since—never once had he seen a deer on her property. Two decades ago he'd seen them occasionally from the highway when he was returning home from Echo Lake, but he guessed those sightings were ten miles from Sugar Hill, and he knew from his work that deer tended to live most of their life in a world no bigger than a couple square miles. If there was enough food, some whitetails would spend a whole season in a few hundred acres.

Moreover, he presumed he saw deer off the interstate near Echo Lake because there was no hunting allowed in the state park. And hunting was the key. Neither wolves nor foxes nor drought nor mountains of snow could diminish a region's deer population for long. Only man could do that. All that hunting in the fall beyond the borders of the state park, Spencer guessed, kept the deer herd small and would prevent the creatures from sidling up to a Sugar Hill garden and eating the spinach. They knew the signs of a **real** predator when they saw one.

An irony, of course, was that Spencer himself would never kill a deer. Nor would he ever eat one. He hadn't touched meat since he was nineteen years old. He'd never hunted (and he knew he never would), and he positively did not approve of someone else taking a Savage 99 or a Browning A-Bolt or whatever it was that they used, and firing a bullet into a deer: Like the lobsters he'd slaughtered—like the hogs and the chickens in their minuscule cages in those deplorable factory farms, the air itself an unbreathable miasma of excrement, like the mink who were electrocuted or clubbed for a coat—they felt pain. They felt pleasure. They had parents.

But if two centuries of deer hunting in New Hampshire had diminished the herd to the point where he could plant the vegetable garden of his dreams—and have the satisfaction of knowing that his daughter, his mother-in-law, and his niece were savoring its bounty—so be it.

His family had never had vegetable gardens when he'd been growing up, not on any small (or large) square of land beside any of the houses in which they'd lived in a variety of suburban neighborhoods north of Manhattan. Not in Hastings or Rye, not in Stamford or Scarsdale. Not in either of the smaller houses in Hartsdale or the large Tudor one his mother had loved in New Canaan. They moved a lot, it seemed, for a family in which Dad never once relocated cities for work or even changed corporations. Bill McCullough worked, in fact, between the eleventh and the eighteenth floor of the same building on Madison and Twenty-third Street for forty years—working every single day for the very same insurance company—until his wife was diagnosed with lung cancer at sixty-two and he retired at sixty-three to help care for her. She died after a gloomy, febrile, excruciating seven-month battle—more with the chemotherapy and the radiation than with the disease itself—and he, well aware of the life expectancy for a now sixty-four-year-old widower, followed her quickly. A series of strokes at weekly intervals beginning nine months after her funeral. He spent a month in the hospital, unable to speak, then move, then breathe. Charlotte had been in kindergarten at the time. They returned from Long Ridge to Manhattan soon after that, though Spencer didn't really believe there was a connection.

As a child Spencer hadn't understood why his family moved so often and why he went to so many schools. Why he had to figure out so many unspoken dress codes—each one more subtle than the one that preceded it—between the seventh and twelfth grade. Obviously his father wasn't wanted by the law, and he traveled almost not at all for business. Still, Spencer didn't spend a whole lot of time with him growing up. And when he did, his memories were mostly about silence: His dad appearing once in a while—almost like a vision—in the small bleachers at the baseball field when his Little League team had a game. His dad tying a necktie in the mirror in the front hall of the house in . . . in either Rye or that first one in Hartsdale, Spencer couldn't be sure . . . before leaving unusually early for work one morning and whispering conspiratorially that they shouldn't wake his mother. His father falling asleep at nine thirty at night in front of the television set in the family room, alone, an unfinished scotch and water (mostly scotch, despite the ice cube that had melted) on the table beside him.

Sometimes Spencer and his sister, a girl only eighteen months younger than he, would water down the bottles of Cutty Sark and J&B Rare. They'd measure where on the schooner's sails the scotch was on the Cutty Sark label, pour out between half an inch and an inch, and then replace it with exactly as much water and—if they had noticeably diluted the color—a drop or two of their mother's dark apple cider vinegar.

He had few memories, he realized, of his father and his mother ever chatting with each other when he was a child. On some level, they loved each other: He saw just how much when his mother was dying. But other than he and his sister—and a shared tendency to drink way too much and then grow acrimonious—they really had very little in common. They never divorced, and it was only in college that he decided they probably should have. After all, he had an abundance of recollections of the two of them squabbling in six or seven different houses, and he wondered if everyone would have been happier if the two of them had separated.

Later, as a grown-up, he conjectured they might have moved so many times when he was a child because it gave his mother—a woman much smarter than his father—a way to fill her days. She could pack and unpack and redecorate, and perhaps she wanted something to do more than she wanted a divorce.

What Spencer lacked in close friends, he had tried to make up for in pets. He was never a brooding child or even a churlish one. But he did keep his emotional distance, because eventually that distance would become geographic and—to an eight- or a ten- or a twelve-year-old boy—prohibitive.

Thus there were, invariably, the dogs and the cats. He had both as a boy. In every neighborhood there was a golden lab that was pregnant or a stray cat with a litter of kittens in someone's garage. Only rarely did his parents deny him one. It actually became a part of the family lore, the stories his parents would tell their new acquaintances at cocktail parties in their new towns: The boy and his dogs. And cats. The boy who would rescue a raccoon. His mother regaled his mother-in-law with that tale the day they were introduced.

In New Canaan the menagerie peaked at three dogs and four cats. Then his father accidentally backed the Impala over the sleeping mutt that looked a lot like a springer spaniel. His parents fought and soon (once again) they had moved. In truth, Spencer knew, it had nothing to do with that dog.

It was odd, but he was convinced that one of the things that had led him to stay at Sugar Hill for entire summers in college after Catherine had first drawn him north was the reality that Catherine's father had passed away, which meant that her parents would never be squabbling there. Sometimes he thought this was an even more visceral part of the property's attraction than the fact that the house had been built by Catherine's great-grandfather and had been a stable part of the Setons' family life for four generations.

He gazed once more at Catherine, and once again she didn't look up. Her mouth was open just the tiniest bit and curled into a barely perceptible smile—as it was often when she daydreamed or read—an expression that always had held for him the power of an erotic summons: It seemed to suggest pleasures that were libidinous, secret, and wanton. Her hair, the russet red of an apple in fall, was hiding her eyes like drapes as she flipped through the pages in her lap, and he was torn between the desires to touch her and to leave her at peace. He wanted to murmur aloud that they were almost there, but the engines on these small planes were so noisy that he would have to shout, and somehow that would wreck the intimacy of the moment. Besides, so often this month with Charlotte away in the country, whenever either of them had opened their mouths to discuss anything that wasn't of the most prosaic nature (dinner, the location of the joint checkbook, whether he should bring an umbrella to work), for reasons he couldn't quite understand they wound up fighting.

Sometimes Spencer feared he was growing into a middle-aged bully—a verbose version of his occasionally sullen father—and he couldn't figure out why his simple desires for competence and order so often seemed to transmogrify into anger. Packing this morning had been a perfect example. Catherine had placed her empty suitcase on the bed beside his without noticing that his flat travel alarm had been there in a curl in the bedspread, and he had wound up spending twenty-five minutes searching for the clock before discovering it underneath her bag. Then, his mood fouled by the unplanned scavenger hunt, he heated up the last dregs of the coffee in a mug in the microwave, only to discover that Catherine had already dumped the dregs of his organic soy milk down the drain so the refrigerator wouldn't reek upon their return. And though he certainly appreciated her foresight, he wished she had asked him first because he absolutely loathed his coffee black. Finally, just when he had all of his clothing folded perfectly flat in his suitcase, Catherine asked him if he could squeeze into his bag bottles of their shampoo and conditioner and a few items Charlotte had asked them to bring north—including her riding helmet and boots because it sounded like the girls would have a chance to go on a trail ride in the next week or two.

"I can't fit her riding helmet in my suitcase," he'd said, and the iciness in his voice had surprised him. Where had that come from?

"The helmet's hollow. Stuff it with your socks and underwear. Then it'll fit."

"And the boots?"

"The boots are small."

"And covered with dirt and manure."

"They aren't."

"I took her last. Remember?"

"Of course I do. You do it so rarely."

Suddenly they sounded like his parents in one of their habitual, second-scotch skirmishes. Except it was the morning and he and Catherine hadn't been drinking. "My point is that I know exactly the condition of the stable in the park. It's filthy. And so the boots are filthy," he told her.

"Why didn't you clean them off then? Or ask her to?"

"I did clean them. I didn't disinfect them. It never crossed my mind they'd have to share close quarters with my clothes."

"Fine, I'll put them in a plastic bag in my suitcase. You take the helmet."

And so he had removed his shirts and his pants—khakis and shorts and even a pair of golf slacks—from his suitcase, stuffed the helmet with his underwear and socks, and then wedged everything back inside his very well-traveled American Tourister twenty-inch Cabin Carry-On. It wasn't nearly as neat as it had been, and so he'd spent the rest of the morning seething—more at himself than at her because he knew he had overreacted. But the end result was the same: a tense and wearisome silence. He retreated into the quiet of their two cats, pulling a dining room chair over to the living room couch on which they were dozing in the sun and noiselessly running his fingers over their fur. Then he reread for the third time the note they would be leaving for the teenage girl on their floor who was going to feed the animals and change their litter box. It was a complicated set of instructions, because it wasn't easy to keep a cat vegan.

There was no dog in their life and he wished that there were. Unfortunately, once in a mood of self-righteous obstinacy, he'd proclaimed their apartment was too small for one. He'd insisted it would be cruel to coop one up for a whole day there. He no longer believed that (had he ever?), but he was, he knew, disablingly—perhaps self-destructively—stubborn.

Now on the plane he resolved he would behave better. He reached across the aisle to feel (at once so like and unlike that of a cat) the soft down on Catherine's wrist and her arm, bare even in the chill of this claustrophobic passenger cabin. Lightly he stroked the skin just above her thumb and along the back of her hand. Though the house in New Hampshire belonged to Mrs. Seton, he had been coming here for two decades, and it was as close to a familial motherland as he had: a place with memories and roots that transcended the itinerant nature of his own suburban upbringing. He loved the house, he believed, more than did his wife and his brother-in-law, who had known it their entire lives and now took it for granted, and at least as much as his mother-in-law, who slipped into a life there each summer with the same blissful sigh she'd exhale when she'd plunge into the crisp waters of Echo Lake.

He gave Catherine's hand a small squeeze, but she continued to read. She was still angry with him. Once they were on the ground and he wouldn't have to shout, he would apologize to her for being a . . . a jerk. Yes, that was right. A jerk.

From the intercom speaker above them he heard a series of scratchy, incomprehensible prerecorded syllables—there was no flight attendant on this route— and he knew it was the message reminding them to have their tray tables locked in their upright positions and their seats fully forward, because they were about to land.

AT THE RENT-A-CAR COUNTER, while a good-natured wisp of a teen girl printed out the forms for the vehicle they were taking for the next week and a half—a minivan almost (but not quite) large enough for the extended family and their golf clubs—Catherine Seton-McCullough used her cell phone to leave a message on her mother's answering machine. She wanted to let her know that they had landed and would be at the house in about ninety minutes. Five o'clock at the latest. No doubt everyone was still at the club, taking whatever lessons Mother had lined up.

Spencer had apologized and she was grateful. But only to an extent. She still wasn't exactly sure what she should say because she was filled with a nauseating, almost debilitating sense of dread that her marriage was . . . winding down. And she was scared. She could no longer see anything behind Spencer's eyes but annoyance—and Lord knows how she hated this word—**issues.** She taught English and literature to high school girls at the Brearley School on the Upper East Side, and this spring the headmaster had brought in a consultant who called herself a corporate interdependence trainer and the woman had used that word—**issues**—as a euphemism for both actual crises and petty discontents. Instead of **challenge,** a word that Catherine knew other consultants depended upon as their substitute for weakness—as in "We have myriad strengths and a couple of small challenges to address"—this trainer savored the businesslike spitefulness of **issue**. Like **agenda,** it was a word that purported to sound neutral, but in truth was two syllables with inherently negative connotations: There really was no such thing as a **good** issue. It gave the woman the conversational upper hand with the school's teachers and administrators, implying at once that the faculty and staff had problems, while suggesting that she would never approach them in a manner that was overtly condescending. Patronizing? Yes. Condescending? Only if you thought for a moment about what the doctrinaire pedant really was saying.

Well, clearly, she and Spencer had **issues,** and they had only gotten worse since Charlotte had left for her grandmother's house in the country. Catherine had expected the time alone would give the two of them a chance to reconnect. They'd go to movies and dinner together, just the two of them, and perhaps he would relax and they would talk about . . . about everything. What demons were driving his temper. Why he could be as confrontational with his wife and daughter as he was with associations of big game hunters. Why he had become so focused on work that he could practically ignore Charlotte for weeks: He would jet to Washington (a presentation on the evils of biomedical animal research to the minions of some Senate committee) or Omaha (a press conference about the practices of a company that specialized in mail-order steak) or Sarasota (something about the treatment of circus animals) and then talk to his daughter when he returned home with about the same conversational involvement that he demonstrated with telemarketers. What happened to the days when he would whisk Charlotte off to a concert or museum or one of the Broadway shows that she loved? Patiently help her use the Internet to research school papers about the Montgomery Bus Boycott of 1955, the dolphin's glorious brain, or the reasons why we have seasons?

Likewise, he was neglecting her, too. His wife. In the two weeks that Charlotte had been in the country, Catherine had barely seen her husband before eight or eight thirty at night, an hour that felt particularly late because she was through with work until the middle of

August, when she would begin preparing her classroom in earnest for the fall. She saw friends and she played tennis and she read on the grass in Central Park. But she didn't see much of her husband.

Sometimes she found herself flirting. She would flirt with Hank Rechter, the fifty-five-year-old headmaster of a school on the West Side—not, thank God, Brearley—when she would see him jogging near Belvedere Castle late in the afternoon. It was an amiable flirtation because he was a neighbor in their building who was as happily married as everyone supposed she was, because his smooth business suits fit his wondrous shoulders like slipcovers, because he never seemed to sweat when he ran. Because he always found a way to touch her with his fingertips that was at once chummy and rakishly inappropriate. Sometimes when he would see her in the park he would sit down on the grass beside her, and she sensed that she was speaking to this man in the sort of breathless, whispery voice her husband no longer heard.

On occasions, she knew, she had flirted that spring as well with Chip Kinnell, the widower father of her fourteen-year-old Brontë scholar, Lindy Kinnell, stretching out their parent-teacher conferences and their visits in the hallways on those mornings he would bring his daughter to school. Kinnell was a rarity in the arbitrage circles in which he traveled: He read fiction that didn't have spies and submarines in it and could talk with Catherine—abstractedly fingering a purple Hermes tie patterned with, of all things, baby ducks—about the books he was reading now and the books he had read aloud to his wife while she was dying.

At least once, she feared, Charlotte had watched her in a conversation with Chip and grown suspicious. But suspicious of what? She was doing nothing wrong. One afternoon Charlotte had eavesdropped on a discussion she was having with Eric Miller, another English teacher (a **younger** English teacher; Catherine was almost certain that Eric hadn't hit thirty yet) at Brearley, and it was clear that her daughter hadn't understood that sometimes a harmless flirtation only enhances a friendship. Deepens the camaraderie.

It was, however, completely innocuous. All of it. All of them. At least that's what she told herself.

And she couldn't help but believe that if Spencer hadn't become so damn mercurial, she wouldn't have begun taking small comforts from the attention that Hank Rechter, Chip Kinnell, or Eric Miller paid her. She wouldn't have paid so much attention to them. She wouldn't have talked to them about . . . meat. Yes indeed, Hank and Eric and Chip were carnivores, and they knew what her husband did (everyone knew what her husband did) and they would tease her about it. They would make jokes about souvlaki and shish kebab, and Eric would try to interest her in the Sabrett hot dogs that were sold from a cart outside on the street.

She hoped this coming vacation would offer a meaningful reconciliation with Spencer, though she had to wonder how you could reconcile with somebody who didn't even know you were apart. Earlier this week she had imagined that with Spencer away from work in Sugar Hill—in a corner of the world that he loved—she would be able to talk to him. Perhaps he would talk to her. Perhaps they would finally work through their . . . issues. Now, however, she doubted that would happen, at least in quite the way she had supposed. Now she guessed if they talked about anything, it would be because she had chosen this week to see if dread could be transformed into something like relief when she broke the news to him that she simply could not continue any longer as she was—as they were—and she wanted change. Counseling, perhaps, though even counseling was a capitulation, a collapse of her adolescent imaginings of what her marriage would be. And maybe she wanted something more than counseling or change. Maybe she wanted out. Yes, that was it, all right. At the moment, at least, after his appalling behavior when they were packing this morning—the clock, the coffee, his retreat to their cats—she absolutely could not stand what their marriage had become and she wanted out.

Reflexively she picked her tennis racket up off the top of her suitcase so she would have something to do with her hands now that she had stowed her cell phone away, and much to her surprise she found herself volleying in slow motion. She'd played a lot of tennis that summer with her friends who were women, and she realized that she was looking forward to playing now with her brother and—if they were speaking—with Spencer. She was looking forward to playing with men. When she'd been younger she'd been an exceptional player: a high school standout in New York, ranked in Massachusetts when she was at college. She'd learned to play summers as a child at that goofy club her own grandfather had helped found near their country home in Sugar Hill, hitting balls for hours at a time with the different young adults who would parade through there year after year masquerading as tennis pros. Most of them were college students—and, she knew now, mediocre tennis players at best—but to a nine-year-old they seemed the height of glamour and sophistication and talent, and she had only fond memories of her afternoons on the clay courts in her shorts.

Her first summer here with Spencer, when the two of them were working at area restaurants, she'd destroy him on those very courts at least every other day before they'd go to work in the late afternoon, and the fact that he never seemed to mind endeared him to her. He could volley with her to help her keep her stroke in shape, but he rarely took more than a game from her each set they played, and she didn't believe that he ever once broke her serve.

It was funny: The man could not bear to lose an argument—**would not lose an argument**—but he was perfectly content losing to her at tennis. To his brother-in-law at golf, to his mother-in-law at badminton. Suddenly, she found this athletic acquiescence of his disturbing. Suddenly, she found all of him physically less attractive than she once had. He seemed wide-faced these days, especially now that his hair had rolled back to the top of his head, and his ears looked like uncooked Chinese dumplings. He was heavier than in college (but weren't all men?), and sometimes she thought the dark hair that once had fallen across his forehead had migrated to his back, his shoulders, and the insides of his ears. She knew he was fierce at work—spirited with politicians, feisty with the press—and though all too often he brought that fierceness home with him, he never brought it to the tennis court.

A thought came to her: She did things with Spencer that didn't interest her—such as that vegetable garden—for the sad reason that it was easier to do things she disliked than to bicker. This couldn't be healthy, and it struck her as yet another indication that her marriage might be over. It was possible, wasn't it? Maybe that's what happened to some marriages: They just ran out of energy and forward momentum, and both halves of the equation no longer saw the future as any more promising than the present. This notion made her even more queasy, and she tried to tell herself that she was wrong, that she didn't really want out, that this was all just a bad patch. All marriages had them. Still, she wondered if Spencer's motivation for playing tennis was similar to her involvement in his vegetable garden: He did it despite little enthusiasm because playing was easier than arguing.

No, that couldn't be right. Tennis for Spencer was an element of the world of Sugar Hill, an important component of the spell the place held for him. She knew he associated it with their first summers there together, his introduction to New Hampshire.

Maybe, she decided, focusing now with real effort on the week and a half before her instead of on the bigger problems posed by her marriage, if her brother and sister-in-law were willing to drive back to the club after dinner, she and Spencer could squeeze in an hour of doubles tonight—or, perhaps, they could even get in a game before dinner if she could catch John and Sara before they left the pool for the day. Maybe on vacation Spencer would find it within himself to care about something other than the plight of a bullhook-pricked circus elephant and actually play to win for a change.

She guessed she'd have a better chance of rounding up a match if she asked her brother (with any luck he'd even have a fresh can of balls, a real novelty for the Seton family when they were together in New Hampshire) than if she bounced the idea off Sara, who she presumed was still bleary-eyed by her five-month-old. And so she retrieved the cell phone once more and left a message for her brother with a woman who happened to pick up the phone at the clubhouse. If he got the message before she and Spencer reached Sugar Hill, then they could drive directly to the Contour Club instead of straight home.

Her mother would be proud: Going directly from the plane to the tennis court. Now, **that** was vigorous.

Inside the shoulder bag in which she kept her cell phone and her computer were four unopened Slim Jims. Spencer, of course, knew nothing about her secret stash of beef jerky—about, in truth, any of her secret stashes of meat. She hid them along with her

Altoids and those potent Listerine PocketPak strips of paper-thin mint that melted instantly on your tongue and she presumed were designed more to encourage better oral sex than oral hygiene. She considered whether she should tell Spencer she had to run to the ladies' room so she could scarf down one of the Slim Jims, but her secret desire for meat wasn't as powerful as a smoker's need for nicotine. She was not uncomfortable and she could wait.

She told herself that she needed to approach the coming ten days with a good attitude. Or, at least, not a bad one. She would play tennis, a little golf, she would swim. And there were worse ways to spend fifteen or twenty minutes in the morning than weeding a vegetable garden or deadheading rows of annuals. Had it been all that unpleasant to plant the gardens in the first place? Not really.

Moreover, soon she would get to see her daughter—though, these days, Charlotte was as likely to be a source of anxiety as she was emotional quietude or maternal pride. She adored the girl, but she didn't look forward to the way she and Charlotte could fight over nothing. Charlotte knew precisely how to push her buttons: which slang annoyed her the most, which music she found the most offensive. She was like her father in that anything could lead to a confrontation, any interaction could become a power struggle: which bathing suit to wear, when to go to sleep, whether it was appropriate to read **Cosmopolitan** in the orthodontist's office waiting room—whether an orthodontist should even have **Cosmopolitan** in his office waiting room. The child knew exactly where to leave her drool-swaddled retainer to cause her mother the most discomfort (the mouse pad beside the living room computer one day, atop whatever magazine Catherine was reading the next), and exactly which cosmetics were absolutely off-limits and therefore she simply had to use (the lids of which she would be sure to leave askew on her mother's vanity).

Before she had left for her grandmother's home for the summer, she'd even begun to challenge the antimeat, antileather, antizoo dictates of their household. She wanted a leather skirt. Leather shoes. Catherine suspected that she'd been to McDonald's. Hormones were starting to course through the girl like river rapids, and Catherine hoped they wouldn't transform a difficult child into an ungovernable adolescent.

When Spencer had finished with the forms for the rent-a-car, they each grabbed their suitcases and carry-ons, their tennis rackets and golf clubs, and labored their way through the tiny concourse and out into the small parking lot. The sun was still high and the air was warm. She thought it irrational that with a week of tennis and gardening and after-dinner family badminton challenges before her she was still so filled with anxiety.

But, of course, she also understood why that disquiet was there.

Six

Spencer stood in front of the vegetable garden, dinner behind him and the sun at the very tip of the highest of the scalloped foothills to the west, and considered going inside to boot up one of the laptop computers that sat inside the house in their nylon ballistic carriers. Perhaps the Internet held a solution to this problem with the deer. Sure, there had been no way to stop them in Connecticut, but that was both because there were so many and they were so comfortable in the Long Ridge suburbs. One time when he was inching along in traffic just south of exit 34 on the Merritt Parkway—exit 34, barely thirty miles from his office near the Empire State Building—he counted nineteen in a single, mile-long stretch nibbling the delicate April buds that grew on the trees just beyond the asphalt. The animals would pause, raising their heads so he could see clearly their great black marble eyes and their eyelashes—as long and lovely as human bangs—and then they would resume eating.

The only predator he knew of in Fairfield County was his neighbor Rick Salieri and his Ford Expedition: Salieri had managed to slam into deer on three separate occasions.

Spencer was sure there couldn't possibly be as many

deer here in this part of New Hampshire, and they couldn't possibly be as sassy or fat. Not with all the hunting that must occur in the fall. Not with winters here so much colder and longer than in southern Connecticut. The snow pack so deep. This herd had to be a reasonable—a **manageable**—size. Plus, here Spencer knew he had that lupine to work with. Clearly deer hated lupine, and as big as the garden was, it was still a small island in the midst of a sea of the stuff. It grew like grass, except that it was waist high and the roots were like vines. If only he could find the right Web site for gardeners or wildlife management . . .

Perhaps he could somehow build an impenetrable tangle of lupine, a barrier that would keep the animals at bay.

He was imagining exactly such a wall—a hedgerow made of lupine, the enclosure creating a secret garden of almost Victorian sensibility—when he realized his brother-in-law, John, was standing beside him, holding two bottles of beer by their long, thin necks. He'd already pulled the tops off them both, and he handed one to Spencer.

"You're depressed," John said to him with mock gravity and earnestness. "I understand."

Spencer took a swallow. "I'm not finished."

"You plan to sleep out here?"

He smiled. "I won't go that far. But I am shocked. How could everything have been thriving only yesterday?"

On the other side of the house they could hear the squeals from their girls as they played badminton in the yard against Grandmother and Catherine. Catherine wasn't as proficient at whacking birdies as she was tennis balls, but she was a Seton and thus had a genetic ability to swing things—rackets and golf clubs and, in the summer she'd lived at home immediately after college and thus wound up a part of the Brick Church's co-ed softball team, a baseball bat— with hereditary competence. Sara was nursing Patrick on the porch.

"Well, I presume it was only yesterday when the deer discovered what kind of good eating we'd put in the ground for them," John answered.

"They'll be back tonight, you know."

"And they'll bring their friends. Yes, I do know."

"I remember one year in Connecticut—the first year we tried to have a garden—they devoured the whole plot in two nights."

"It will take them more than two to finish off this one. Unless there's a whole herd that's interested."

"I know they're just acting like deer . . . but I really didn't think this would happen."

"Personally, I figured we'd lose the garden to rabbits. Or raccoons."

"It's like a car accident."

"Oh, it's not that bad. You sound like one of your news releases."

Above them a bat darted past in the twilight, then another. The bats lived in the room Nan used for storage above the garage, and when Spencer was leading the charge to get the seeds in the ground he took comfort in their presence: A tiny pipistrelle bat, he knew, ate as many as three thousand mosquitoes on a warm summer night; a colony of brown bats—say 150 animals strong—would consume eighteen million rootworms in a year. He squatted now and ran his fingers over the ravaged tendrils of one of the rows of what would have been snow peas. His mother-in-law's golden retriever had wandered outside, and when the dog saw him the animal ambled over and put a front paw on his knees. He scratched the back of the dog's ears and stroked his neck. Then he wrapped an arm around the canine's strong chest and allowed the creature to lick the side of his face.

It was already too dark to see the yellow and black **POSTED** signs at the bottom of the field, but John looked in that direction and thought about them. He had a vision of himself and a ten- or eleven-year-old boy, Patrick in a decade and change, marching one crisp November morning off into these woods in search of a buck: the offspring, perhaps, of one of the animals that had had dinner last night in this very garden. The signs, by then, would have been gone a long time, pried from their trees with the hooked end of a hammer.

John's father had never hunted, but his grandfather had. His great-grandfather, too, a man he had never met but the architect—literally—of this house on the hill behind them and the elegant carriage barn that once had stood beside it. John knew that barn only from black-and-white photographs and a painting that hung in the hallway on the second floor of the house, because his grandfather had replaced it with the

less sophisticated, more functional two-car garage long
before he'd been born.

He watched Spencer stand and wondered exactly
what kind of tirade would be triggered in his brother-
in-law if he mentioned that he had gone hunting last
November and planned to go again in another three
and a half months. If Spencer knew that he found
himself browsing Web sites for hunters and purchas-
ing magazines about tracking. If Spencer somehow
discovered that most days in a locked cabinet in the
guest bedroom in their house in Vermont was a rifle
and two little bottles of buck urine that—sometimes
John couldn't believe this himself—he had doused on
his legs last year every time he went into the woods in
search of deer.

Lord, how large would be the explosion if Spencer
knew that the only reason there wasn't a rifle in that
cabinet right now was because it was currently in its
gun bag in the trunk of his car, stashed there because
he was taking it to a gunsmith on Monday morning?
He thought of those fifteen-thousand-pound Daisy
Cutter bombs the United States had dropped a few
years back in Afghanistan. Spencer, he decided, would
be Daisy Cutter mad. His brother-in-law was thirty-
eight and change, and every single day of his adult life
he had worked for the likes of the Animal League, the
Wildlife Partnership, and, for the last six or seven
years, FERAL—each group more extreme than the
one that preceded it.

Actually, the part that would truly have disgusted
Spencer wasn't the notion that his brother-in-law, the

lawyer, was capable now of firing a bullet into a deer: That would infuriate him, all right, but it wouldn't sicken him. The part that would send ol' Spencer over the edge was the reality that when he was in the woods he carried with him a knife with a massive handle and a four-inch blade to field-dress the deer once it was dead. Cut away its penis and its genitals, cut through the breastbone and yank up its windpipe. Extract the heart, the entrails, and the liver.

In truth, John wasn't completely sure he could field-dress a deer without vomiting. He hadn't gotten a deer yet so he hadn't had to eviscerate one. But he had studied the manuals, and in his knapsack was a set of instructions with the sort of photographs that only a pathologist, a medical student, or a hunter could love.

He considered whether things might be different if Spencer had a son, too, but he doubted it. Spencer was meant to have a daughter: a child he could take to **Oliver, The Phantom of the Opera,** and—two times that John was aware of, so Charlotte could see how different actors handled the lead role—**Annie Get Your Gun.** John knew he could try to explain to his brother-in-law his vision of days alone in the woods with his son—the two of them occasionally whispering as they walked through the brush, sharing the sorts of intimacies he never shared with his own father— but he knew that none of it would register. You don't sing show tunes with a boy in the woods. Besides, all Spencer would hear was the fact that John wanted to take his son into the forest to kill something. The sense of independence—the feel of the tall trees that constituted the canopy and the small ones around which was built the understory—would never make sense to him. Nor would he ever acknowledge that hunting was a sport that demanded genuine skill. The hard reality was that Spencer would be appalled by what he would see as a betrayal . . . and then deeply disappointed.

Almost as if he knew that someday in the future he would be holding a gun at the edge of this very field and would thereby have earned Spencer's wrath, he thought he should top off the well of goodwill that existed between the two men—at some point he might need the water in that well to be lapping at the brim—and so he finished off his beer and wandered to the far side of the garden.

"What do you say?" he called back to Spencer. "Should we try to scare the piss out of a couple of uppity deer with some good old-fashioned human pee?"

"Damn right," his brother-in-law agreed, gently squeezing the dog one last time before rising himself, and there in the gathering dark the two men urinated along the edge of the lupine.

IN THE BRIEF MOMENT between when she unsnapped a cup on her nursing bra and brought her son's mouth to her nipple, Sara Seton felt a rush of the crisp twilight air on the sensitive skin on her breasts and she shivered. Then she gently pressed her son's face upon her, his wet maw a lamprey attaching itself to the areola, and she felt her nipple stretching like toffee and then disappearing into the infant's needy mouth. She held her son against her like he was a blanket against the chill, and with her fingers she stroked the down on his head that passed for hair.

"Fourteen-ten," Charlotte shouted gleefully, holding the birdie in one hand and the racket in the other. The girl was preparing to serve what she and Willow clearly expected would be the game-winning point. Across the net Nan and Catherine stood with their rackets raised as if they were saluting royalty, and while Sara understood that in badminton this was the proper position to await the birdie, she thought they looked ridiculous.

She wasn't happy here on the porch, but she didn't want to go inside with Patrick: Everyone else was outside, either playing badminton or inspecting the gardens. Although this house was extraordinarily cheerful when the sun was high, on cloudy days or at night she found the place capable of inducing a Zoloft-resistant depression. The place was over a century old, and its best feature was the simple fact that it existed at the very top of a ridge of foothills near the White Mountains and it had a wraparound porch facing east, south, and west that allowed one to savor the location. The clapboards, not yet in desperate need of fresh paint but certainly looking a tad tired these days, were dove gray, and the latticework along the bottom of the porch was a long series of diamond-shaped cross-checks. There was fish-scale trim on the first floor and a massive cupola bedroom—Nan's—on the third. The house had three more bedrooms on the second floor and a fourth off the kitchen on the first, but other than Nan's third-story empire—adjacent to her bedroom was a small study, her own bathroom, a walk-in closet, and a nook she used to catalog a lifetime's worth of photo albums and handwritten correspondence—most were oddly shaped and difficult to furnish despite their size. They had knee walls or dormers or the side of a chimney exactly where you might want to place a bureau. Moreover, the bedrooms—again, Nan's being a notable exception—were dark because the window frames were strangely thin, the curtains upon them were heavy, and the shades had springs so tired they never went all the way up. There were no ceiling fixtures in any of the rooms but the kitchen and the dining room, and every room could have used an additional outlet and a third (or, in some cases, a second) floor lamp. Clearly, the Setons—and Spencer, too—loved the dusky aura of the myriad ill-lit, melancholic rooms that made up the house, the narrow corridors that groaned underfoot, but most of the time she found the place merely gloomy.

The girls and the women in the yard batted the shuttlecock back across the net at each other six, eight, ten times, and each moment when her niece or her daughter would strike the red rubber tip Sara thought for sure they would finish off their older relatives, the game would end, and they would all go inside together. Nan was always indefatigable, however, even now at seventy, and Catherine was nothing if not competitive. Just when Sara was certain that the children had put the previous two generations away, Catherine raced back and hit a long, high lob from the very edge of the baseline that sent Charlotte reeling backward. And though the girl was able to return her mother's desperate shot, her own comeback was soft and Nan was waiting for it at the net, where she slammed it into the grass at the feet of her lunging granddaughters. The old folks were coming back, and Sara feared now that she might be outside with her son on her chest until it was too dark for any living creatures but the bats.

Seven

There was chaos in the kitchen Saturday morning, the very last day in July. Some of it was a simple result of the reality that the household had swollen from three people to eight, two of whom were planning on attending a funeral that day before going to the club. But part of it was due as well to the nature of Nan Seton: The woman had the vigor of a cruise director when it came to outdoor activities and organizing her brood, but her energy level deflated like a blood pressure cuff—you could almost hear the hiss of escaping air—when she was faced with a task that demanded long-term coordination, concentration, and planning. It was one thing to get her granddaughters into age-appropriate swimwear (though Nan was confident that Charlotte's choices in swimwear were inappropriate for any age) and then to the club; it was quite another to redo her kitchen. As a result, the room was in serious need of a makeover. The oven door that summer didn't quite close (which meant that the plastic dials for the burners on the stove had started to melt like images from a Salvador Dali painting); the dishwasher door did close but it demanded two hands and a back that was sturdy; and Nan insisted on keeping the electric skillet in a section of the counter that meant she had to wind the long cord around a blender with chunks of calcified water clinging to the rotor blades like barnacles, a toaster with sufficient bread crumbs in its base to stuff a turkey, and the baby bottles that had appeared in the night with the speed of button mushrooms in a wet summer. And, of course, because the telephone in the kitchen still had a receiver that was tethered to the wall unit with a plastic-coated wire, it was not uncommon when two Setons or McCulloughs were trying to cook for one inadvertently to trip or tie up the other.

This morning, moreover, Spencer was making waffles. Consequently, the waffle iron—an antique that looked more like a device the secret police in a third world nation might use to extract a confession from a political prisoner than a kitchen appliance—was taking up space on the counter as well. The batter, made with soy milk and without eggs, was runnier than regular batter, and so the waffle iron had glacierlike daggers of camel-colored globules running down three of its four sides.

Spencer suspected this morning might not be the best time to be making waffles because his mother-in-law and John were trying to get out the door for a nine thirty funeral. But he told himself he was making the waffles for Charlotte and Willow. He understood this justification wasn't quite true—he guessed he probably would be making waffles now even if he was the only person in the house who was going to eat them—but he felt like waffles, and wasn't this his vacation, too? Besides, he had checked the vegetable garden as soon as he had woken up, and he'd seen that the deer had returned to continue the job they had begun Thursday night. Worse, they had discovered the strawberries, which had arrived weeks late but now, finally, were just about ripe for the picking, and then ravaged the leaves on the raspberry bushes. This meant there would be no strawberry shortcake—or strawberry soup or strawberry smoothies or strawberry pasta—made with their very own strawberries while he was here this week, and there might be no raspberries ever this summer.

Spencer hadn't anticipated a huge crop from the transplants this season, but he had expected enough for the family. And so now he was repressing his profound disappointment with food. With waffles.

Around him there was chaos: Mrs. Seton was telling her daughter that the girls' suits had to be hanging outside on the line, but still no one could find Charlotte's suitable Speedo (including Charlotte); John was emptying day-old coffee grounds from the stovetop percolator his mother had used since the Eisenhower administration into the paper grocery bag (already tearing at the bottom from something gooey and wet that had been deposited there the night before after dinner); and his nephew was howling like a police siren while Sara, reduced almost to despair, walked the baby back and forth in the living room. Willow, according to fast-developing family lore the only antidote in the world to a full-blown Patrick Seton tirade, was outside somewhere, searching with Charlotte for the missing swimsuit.

Spencer knew that if he focused on anything other than the physical act of cooking, he would become involved in the bedlam around him and grow angry. Angrier, actually: Already he was exasperated, maddened by the sheer disorganization, by the annoying way everyone was speaking at cross purposes, and (most certainly) by the mess.

Finally Willow appeared, rescuing her mother from her younger brother—a child who had been sobbing for so long with Sara that although he had stopped crying, he now had hiccups that were heart-wrenching—and Spencer was able to concentrate on breakfast. With a decided effort to be serene, he pulled up the top of the press, trimmed away the half-cooked stalactites of batter from the sides, and deposited onto an antique china plate a waffle at once so perfectly square, evenly browned, and supernaturally fluffy that it looked like it belonged in a gourmet cooking magazine. There was not a corner of this house that did not hold for him a memory of what it was like to be a teenager, away from home and college for the first time in his life, making real money—or what seemed like real money at the time—and spending his days hiking and swimming and hitting tennis balls with the lovely young woman he knew even then he would marry. Why, he told himself as he savored the sight of this oh-so-perfect waffle, should a little chaos here trouble him now?

Willow brought Patrick over to the plate on the counter and said to her brother, "This, little man, is what a waffle is supposed to look like. Pretty good, huh?"

The baby hiccupped then gurgled.

"Then this one has to be yours," Spencer said. "I picked up some Soy-garine at the health food store on the way home from the club yesterday afternoon."

"The waffles my parents make always pop out of the toaster, and they look like burnt toast," she said.

"Please, enjoy it. Ask Charlotte if she's ready for one, too, okay?"

The girl nodded, stepped around the dishwasher door that hung open like a shin-level metal shelf—a bruise-inducing ledge from another era—scooted past her grandmother, who was saying something about everyone's lack of time if they wanted to get to the club at a decent hour, and called out the front door to her cousin.

JOHN STOOD in the lambent sun of the morning before the vegetable garden in his wing tips, holding a paisley necktie in his hands. He was relieved that he and Sara had planned on his going straight to work after breakfast on Monday, because it meant that he actually had a decent pair of shoes with him this weekend and therefore would not have to attend Walter Durnip's funeral in either golf cleats or sneakers.

He really wasn't surprised that the urine he and Spencer had showered around the edge of the garden last night had done so little to prevent the deer from dining at Chez Seton. Nevertheless, it struck him as a bit of an irony that a little human pee near your tree stand in the woods during rifle season was a way to make absolutely certain that you came home without a buck. When he was out with Howard Mansfield last year and his friend took him up on the U.S. Forest Service's land high on the mountain, they sat for hours in the primitive tree stand Howard's brother had built the year before. They finally moved for the simple reason that they both had to urinate, and rather than hoofing a quarter or half mile away through the snow and then wandering all the way back, they just decided to keep on walking until they found some fresh tracks.

Which they did. Actually, they came across something even better: They found the beds where only moments before deer had been resting, two ovals each the rough size of an automobile tire, the snow melted in the shape of eggs and the newly exposed oak and maple leaves on the forest floor still warm to their touch. Nearby were the piles of small pellets the deer had deposited before settling in. Howard had explained these had been left by a doe and her fawn, and they'd probably been watching the two of them before leaving. A few minutes later they found the tracks where the deer had actually crossed their own path— small divots in the snow and the spongy mud, some in the much larger prints from their own boots—and then they discovered what Howard really was after: the scrapes on the ground left by a buck in full rut and fresh hooking on the bark of a small beech tree. The exposed pulp was moist and almost as bright as the snow.

Deer were one of the few things that Mansfield, a

justice a decade and change older than John who had
been a partner in John's firm when he first moved to
Vermont, found more interesting than law. It wasn't
merely that he thought they were beautiful (though he
often said that he did) or that he was awed by their in-
stincts and reflexes and speed (though he would talk at
length if you didn't stop him about particular deer he
had witnessed race uphill through boulders and brush
with a grace and agility that seemed to put a bullet to
shame). It wasn't the grand racks on the bucks he had
killed or the deep eyes of the does he had spared. It
wasn't the meat, though he did love venison. It was their
work ethic. Mansfield was among the most disciplined
lawyers John had ever known, and now that he was on
the Vermont Supreme Court he was one of the most
well-prepared justices. The amount of effort that a
deer put into eating—into surviving—awed him.
"Imagine," he had said to John that time he had taken
the younger man hunting with him, his voice barely
more than a whisper as they rested on a small outcropping of stone with a good view of a deer path, "a 150-
pound animal has to consume six to eight pounds of
food a day to survive." Then he pulled off one of his
hunting gloves and ripped the end of a twig off one of
the maple saplings beside them, and showed John the
tiny, quiescent bud. "How much do you think that
weighs? A couple milligrams? A tenth of an ounce? Just
think of how much sweat it takes a deer to find his six
or eight pounds of food. Especially in the winter."

John knew that a big part of the reason why
Mansfield shot a deer every year in Vermont—and, if

his schedule permitted, another in New York and then a third in Maine—was because he believed it was the most merciful way humans had to manage the herd. The reality was that in much of America, the only predator left to keep the deer population at a number the habitat could support was man. Without hunting, the thousands of deer that hunters killed pretty close to instantly would overpopulate and then either die slowly of starvation when the heavy northern winter set in, or weakened by malnutrition they would be eaten alive—their haunches and legs and their bellies consumed first—by coyotes.

John watched Mansfield track the deer for the rest of the day, following the animal's rubs and scrapes and his prints, but they never saw him. There was no doubt that he saw them, but he always kept just enough distance that neither of the men even flipped off the safeties on their rifles or brought their Redfield scopes to their eyes.

Still, it had been a wonderful day and John understood why Howard loved hunting. With the exception of the occasional squeals from the blue jays, the woods were completely silent when they stood still or were sitting in Mansfield's brother's tree stand. They were hunting in a part of the forest where there didn't seem to be signs of any other hunters—no gunshots in the distance, no spots where leaves had been cleared so a hunter could move his body without making a sound if he saw a buck he wanted to shoot—and John couldn't imagine a setting more peaceful. His mind

wandered, but then he would watch Mansfield running his dry fingers over a beech leaf or he himself
would catch a glimpse of the peak of the mountain behind them through the trees, and he would remember
why he was there, his focus would return, and he
would experience an almost trancelike contentment.

He'd tried to describe it to Sara that first night, and
she observed that a part of the sensation probably had
just been fatigue. For nine-plus hours he had either
been hoofing around in the snow or sitting on a rock
or a tree stand in the cold, and he was exhausted. He
thought she might have been right, but that didn't
change the fact that the sensation had been pleasurable. And that night, just as Mansfield had promised,
he had eaten like he had a hollow leg and slept more
deeply than he could remember.

The next day, when John was back in his office,
Howard Mansfield went back up on the mountain
and bagged a 195-pound eight-pointer. John was not
exactly envious, but he was disappointed. The day before he had lugged his eight pounds of rifle through
the woods and hadn't fired it once. Those brassy missiles he'd loaded so carefully into his rifle when they
first exited Mansfield's truck—and then unloaded
with equal caution when they returned at the end of
the day—had never once exploded down the barrel
and brought down a deer or even taken a little bark off
a tree. Twice more that season he'd ventured into the
woods, and though he enjoyed his time slogging
through the wet leaves and the thin crusts of snow, he

still hadn't gotten his buck. It was on that last excursion, when he'd been alone, that for some reason he'd been unable to eject the bullet from the gun.

"Are you ready, John?"

He turned and saw his mother was beside him. "Yes. Absolutely."

"After the funeral, let's stop by the Grangers' farm stand on the way to the club," she said. "They have wonderful zucchini and string beans right now, and we don't."

He nodded and pulled his tie through the collar of his shirt. It saddened him that their vegetables that night wouldn't come from their own tilled bit of earth.

INSIDE THE HOUSE Willow pushed a small square of Soy-garine off the top of her waffle, having decided that the butter substitute tasted even worse than it looked. There was a reason this stuff didn't have people at Land O Lakes quaking in their boots. Her younger brother sat watching her in his blue canvas baby seat, occasionally plugging his small mouth with parts of his fist. The seat was in the middle of the table, as if Patrick were a centerpiece.

Through the dining room window she and Charlotte saw John and Nan leaving for Walter Durnip's funeral in Grandmother's antique gray Chevrolet. Willow wasn't sure how old the vehicle was, but she knew that Grandmother had bought it well before her own parents had gotten married. It wasn't simply pre–air bag; it was pre–CD player, pre–cassette player, pre–seat belts with a strap across the chest. It didn't even have an FM radio.

Charlotte, Willow observed, didn't seem to mind her father's butter substitute, or even the fact that although Uncle Spencer's waffle looked perfect, it had a strangely bitter aftertaste that Willow presumed had something to do with the soy milk. Her cousin sat in her skimpy white shorts with her bare legs underneath her in one of the antique ladder-back chairs around the dining room table, happily cutting the waffle apart with her fork, occasionally reaching down to peel a bit of burned skin off her thigh.

Abruptly she looked up at Willow and said, "Some teenagers are going to have a bonfire and their own party tonight at the club." That evening they were all going to the annual midsummer blowout at the Contour Club, which was one of the reasons why Grandmother wanted everyone here this particular weekend: She liked to show off her family.

"Are you going to go?"

"I might. Connor told me about it," she said. Connor, Willow knew, was a fifteen-year-old who came to the club under duress, but when he was there Charlotte didn't take her eyes off him. He never went near the pool, had no interest in golf, but twice in the last week the two girls had watched him play tennis. It was clear he was one of the few members of the Contour Club who might have been able to give Aunt Catherine a little competition. He had green eyes—though the girls had only seen them one time, because he almost always wore sunglasses—a little dark fuzz above his lip, and hair as black as Charlotte's string bikini.

"When were you talking to Connor?"

"He called."

"Really?"

"Well, he called across the grass."

"To you?"

Charlotte shrugged, and Willow guessed that small shoulder spasm meant that Connor had yelled across the grass by the Contour Club's terrace to some other teenager about the bonfire on Saturday night, and Charlotte had overheard him.

"Anyway, I think I might go," Charlotte murmured.

"You can't have a bonfire until it's dark out, and Grandmother will want us to go home by eight or eight thirty."

"My dad will pick me up in that case," she said, and then she called into the kitchen where her father was still at work beside the waffle iron, "Right, Dad?"

"Right what, honey?"

"Some of the kids are having a bonfire tonight. Can I go?"

"You mean at the club?"

"Uh-huh."

He strolled into the dining room with a dishtowel slung over his shoulder. "I think a bonfire sounds nice. Can grown-ups go, too?"

"Nope. Just kids."

"Too bad. How old will the kids be?"

"Oh, my age—and some older kids, too, of course, so the adults don't need to worry."

He smiled. "The presence of teenagers is supposed to make me worry less?"

"Well, you know, in terms of the fire. There will be older kids there so you don't need to fear we'll, like, burn down the woods."

"Gotcha."

"So we can go?"

"I don't see why not."

"The thing is, it might go on a little later than the cocktail party you and Mom will be at," she said.

"I understand. We'll obviously have a couple of cars. I don't mind hanging around so I can drive you girls home."

"Thank you, Dad."

Willow watched her uncle, and she thought that he might have been about to lean over and kiss his daughter on her forehead, but then he seemed to think better of the idea. Maybe he thought he'd embarrass her. Instead he bent down and kissed his nephew on the boy's cheek, oblivious to the long tendrils of drool that were hanging off the infant's chin or that linked his mouth and his hand like filaments from a spider's web. Then Uncle Spencer returned to the kitchen, where Willow heard the waffle iron scrape along the counter as he lifted the metal lid.

"See how easy that was?" Charlotte said. "My dad usually says yes to the things that don't involve any work, so he can say no to the things that do. We can go."

"You can go. I'm not sure I want to hang around with a bunch of teenagers."

"Suit yourself."

"Won't you be nervous?"

"I'm sure there will be thirteen- and fourteen-year-olds there, too."

"And sixteen- and seventeen-year-olds."

"Doubt it. Anyone around here old enough to drive has better places to go on a Saturday night than the Contour Club."

Willow heard her mother pad lightly down the steps from the second floor. She had been upstairs showering and getting dressed.

"Ask your mom if you can go," Charlotte said to her now. "Tell her my dad said it was okay with him, and he'd drive us home."

Reminding herself that she could change her mind that afternoon if she didn't want to tag along with Charlotte while her cousin lied about her age to a bunch of tenth- and eleventh-graders, she nodded, and when her mother wandered into the dining room—her hair in a towel because it was wet, but her eyes more refreshed than they'd been before she had climbed into the shower—she asked if she, too, could go to the bonfire.

Eight

Catherine stood at the baseline of the northern-most of the four courts at the Contour Club Saturday morning, a wire basket of yellow tennis balls at her feet. The sun was behind her, and she allowed herself a hearty grunt with each serve into the ether on the other side of the net, the exhalations conjuring like a faint breeze across her tongue the dim but pleasurable memory of that single slice of her mother's bologna she'd eaten surreptitiously before leaving with Sara and the girls for the club. She could feel sweat trickling down her shoulder blades and puddling in the small of her back. The grunts, she knew, were making the older men on the court beside her uncomfortable. At the Contour Club, people did not grunt—especially when they were practicing their serve all alone. Even those few members who actually lived in New Hampshire year-round knew enough not to grunt. Grunting, as her mother would say with a sniff, was awfully animalistic. And though Nan was preternaturally athletic for someone her age, she also believed it was inappropriate—unseemly, she would have said—to be **too** competitive. Grunters, it was clear, were people who tried way too hard.

The first time her mother had watched her play in

a tournament in college—just after Catherine had discovered the power grunting added to her game—she
had pulled her aside after the match and asked her
what sort of unladylike gremlin had taken over her
mouth. Catherine knew instantly what her mother
was referring to, but she had won that morning
against a high-seeded girl who was two years older
than she was, and so she wasn't about to stop grunting.

"UNNHH!" she cried out now, as she felt the wind
from her swing on her legs.

She wasn't exactly sure why she was taking such
pleasure this morning in her grunts—each sharp, ab-
breviated syllable sounded downright melodious in
her ear, and she loved the feel of her teeth against her
tongue as she finished—but she understood that on
some level this was (as her sister-in-law the therapist
would say) a hostile gesture. Still, why she should be
feeling hostile here and now was not entirely clear to
her. After all, Charlotte and her niece seemed happy
enough at the pool, her brother was holding up their
generation's honor at old Walter Durnip's funeral, Sara
was dozing on a blanket in the shade with Patrick, and
Spencer was off at some garden nursery, seeing if there
was anything at all the experts there could suggest to
buffer the sad remains of the garden from the deer.

The deer. She paused with the tennis ball in her
hand and rolled her thumb over the fuzz. She wondered if she was actually angry right now at the deer
for devouring the garden. Her husband's garden. It
was possible, she decided. But it wasn't likely: She
viewed the garden with the same benign distance that

she tolerated Charlotte's glitter cosmetics. It demanded a tad more of her attention than she cared to invest, but it was essentially harmless.

And despite the ruination brought about by the deer, Spencer had seemed happy enough this morning when he'd made the girls all those waffles. (She had been relieved to see that for all her daughter's neuroses and burgeoning adolescent angst, it was highly unlikely the kid was ever going to have an eating disorder. She'd wolfed down three of her dad's waffles before leaving for the club.) On the other hand, those waffles had annoyed her. The last thing her mother needed this morning was more commotion in the kitchen. Sara, of course, would probably remind her that her anger had nothing to do with the way Spencer's cooking had added to the Saturday morning confusion; rather, her sister-in-law would speculate—gently—that perhaps she was jealous because the waffles had allowed Spencer to further endear himself to the girls. There she was trying to appease her mother and organize the children, while her husband was (uncharacteristically) the anarchist who was reaping the children's approval.

She tossed the ball high over her head, and with the loudest, most atavistic grunt yet sent the orb in a clothesline-straight stripe into the far court. "UNNHH!"

No, she decided firmly, as the ball bounced against the chain-link fence in the corner, whatever pebble was wedged inside her soul right now had nothing at all to do with either those waffles or the deer in the garden. It was something else: her frustration with

Spencer throughout the spring and summer, perhaps, or the way they hadn't found time for each other while Charlotte had been here in the country. That's what it was.

Maybe this afternoon they would have some time alone together to talk and she would tell him. **Something's wrong between us,** she heard herself murmuring to the man in her head. **We can't go on as we are.** They'd go for a long walk like they did when they were younger, when they were in college, and she would tell him, **We've grown apart. I'm sorry to say it, but it's true. We've grown apart.** If not today, then maybe tomorrow. Maybe she'd tell him on Sunday.

Or, perhaps, the week after next. When they were home in Manhattan.

And maybe she needed to begin with something softer in any case: **Something is troubling you. Something is troubling us. We need counseling.** Counseling was a reasonable step, wasn't it? They had almost seventeen years of marriage and a daughter who would turn thirteen in a month.

Maybe they'd simply married too young. Certainly everyone had said so at the time. They'd married a mere seven months after finishing college, convinced there was no reason to wait because they'd been dating since they were freshmen. And less than four years after that she'd gotten pregnant, and she had been thrilled because she loved children—it was why she became a teacher—and he was thrilled because he seemed to love everything. Monkeys. Cats. Babies.

But they never did have another child, did they?

They talked about it. And they thought they would. They **assumed** they would, especially when they were planning their brief, failed foray into Connecticut. But that experiment had left them all miserable, and so they'd moved back to the city and, somehow, the idea of another child was left behind in the suburbs. The timing, they told themselves, just hadn't been right.

Same with the dog that Charlotte had wanted. It just didn't seem to make sense to get one—at least not to Spencer—once they returned to Manhattan. He worried that the apartment wasn't big enough for the kind of dog their young daughter desired (one, naturally enough, like Grandmother's), and, besides, they already had a pair of cats.

"You have one hell of a serve."

She turned and wiped her brow. There on the grass stood a young man in sneakers and baggy khaki shorts—one of the lifeguards, she believed—with a tennis racket and a can of balls in his hand. Something was sparkling on his left earlobe, and she couldn't tell from this distance whether it was a stud or a legitimate rock of some sort.

"It's not what it was fifteen years ago," she said.

"It looks mighty fine to me." She had the sense that he was making a leap from her serve to . . . to her.

"Trust me: It isn't what it once was. Nothing is."

"Can I join you? I was looking for a game."

She gazed at the nearly empty basket at her feet. She'd planned on heading back to the pool soon, and diving into the water and splashing around with her daughter and her niece. Moreover, if this young man was a lifeguard, then the old guard on the courts to her left—the conservative codgers who disapproved of her grunts—would be miffed that she was playing tennis with him on a Saturday morning. He was, in their opinion . . . the help.

That, of course, was reason enough to play with him in her mind. Not unlike her own daughter, she took great satisfaction from the torments she inflicted on the older generation. Besides, he was awfully cute.

"You don't honestly think you can keep up with me, do you?" she asked, raising a single eyebrow.

He smiled. "I think I can try."

There didn't seem to be anybody else waiting, and so she nodded. "Okay. A couple games," she agreed. "What's your name?"

"Gary. Gary Winslow. My grandfather is—"

"Your grandfather is Kelsey Winslow, of course," she said, and she understood instantly why this life-guard was so comfortable wandering around the courts right now looking for a game. Gary was work-ing here for the summer, yes, but he was also a mem-ber. His parents had died in the attack on the World Trade Center, when the two of them had had the mis-fortune of being on one of the early-morning planes out of Boston that were plunged into the towers like missiles. Gary's father was an anesthesiologist and he was on his way to a symposium in San Francisco. Gary's mother was accompanying him for no other reason than the fact that the conference was in north-ern California and she'd never been there. Ever since then Gary and his sister (whose name, at the moment, escaped Catherine) had been raised by Kelsey and Irene Winslow.

"And you're Nan Seton's daughter, right?" he said, vaguely mimicking the sudden recognition that had marked her own voice. "Charlotte McCullough's mom?"

"I am."

"Charlotte's a terrific kid. Wants to be nineteen, but she's a sweet girl. Good little swimmer, too. I keep a close eye on her, of course—on both her and her cousin. But I can assure you: She's a real water rat."

Catherine found herself nodding, and two unattractive thoughts simultaneously filled her head: The first was incredulity that anyone would ever refer to Charlotte McCullough as "a sweet girl"; the second was the realization that before she had understood that Gary was a Winslow—no, before she had understood that he was that **orphan** Winslow—she had seen him only as a cheeky young lifeguard with very nice arms, more hair than her husband, and an apparent interest in her despite the fact she was the mother of one of the girls he was watching that summer. He was, she guessed, not quite half her age. She was acting like Mrs. Robinson, for God's sake! Usually the men with whom she flirted at least had finished college.

Still, he had been the one to approach her, hadn't he? What the hell?

A sweet girl.

That orphan.

Mrs. Robinson.

Quickly she grabbed a ball, hurled it into the air, and then slammed it as hard as she could into the far court. The ball passed so close to the white ridge along the crest of the net that the plastic fluttered just the tiniest bit, and in her head she heard the echo of her grunt: **Unnhh!**

"Let's go," she said to Gary, and the young man smiled and jogged to the other side of the court.

YOU CAN'T SHOOT a buck out of season, and you can't shoot a doe ever. Not in Vermont, not here.

That was what John had said to Sara in the small hours of the night—no more than eight or nine hours ago, now—after he had changed Patrick's small diaper and she was nursing the baby back to sleep. It had come up because their bedroom window was open, and once Patrick had settled down they could listen to the wind in the lupine and John thought he might have heard animals rustling just outside the house. In the garden, perhaps. He wasn't exactly talking to himself as he stood before the screen, but she knew that he didn't expect an answer, either.

Still, with her son lolling against her breast she had felt compelled to remind him that she couldn't imagine him shooting a deer over Spencer's kohlrabi or green beans, anyway.

No, he'd said. **Of course not.**

She sat now in the cool shade in the grass near the swimming pool with Patrick in his baby seat beside her and wondered why her husband would even be thinking of such things in the middle of the night. She watched the two girls dive, and it made her forget the deer and the garden for a moment. She was impressed with their grace and their courage. How Charlotte had learned to stand on the board with her back to the water, throw her hips high into the air, curl her body back toward the fiberglass, and then dive into the water—the rear of her skull so close to the board that Sara flinched the first time her niece demonstrated an inward—was beyond her. The fact that her own daughter, still two years younger than Charlotte, had learned to do a somersault over the past two weeks was equally as amazing. She knew they had been taught by the young woman who was the lifeguard this morning, a plump girl between her junior and senior years at the high school in Littleton. She never expected overweight teens—boys as well as girls—to be sufficiently comfortable with their bodies to thrive in any activity that involved limited amounts of clothing. This girl, however, was an apparent exception. She seemed to wear a towel around her waist like a skirt when she wasn't actually in the water, but otherwise she seemed completely at ease with the bulk she had wedged into her spandex. And she dove, Sara thought, like the small kestrels and falcons she'd seen darting through the air from the cliffs off Snake Mountain.

She politely clapped when Willow showed her a forward dive in the pike position. Her baby's eyes followed her hands and then he cooed.

"Yes," she murmured to him, leaning over to press

her nose against his, "someday I will clap for you, too. Yes, I will."

Her daughter emerged from the water and raced across the grass to her, wrapping herself quickly in a towel. "At the bonfire tonight," Willow began, her sentence choppy because she was bouncing on one foot with her head angled to the side, "Charlotte said I can borrow her eye shadow. May I?"

"The stuff she was wearing last night at dinner?"

"Uh-huh."

"Why would you want to? It's purple, isn't it?"

"No. It's lavender."

"Oh."

"So it's okay?"

"I don't know, honey."

"Is it that you think ten is too young or you think I shouldn't wear eye shadow to a bonfire?" She had stopped hopping, but her teeth were chattering now.

"It's probably a little of both," she answered, and then said—her change of mood so abrupt that Patrick looked at her and clucked—"Oh, of course it's fine. Of course you may."

Willow smiled and then made Sara's morning more perfect than she had supposed it could be: The girl leaned over and kissed her warmly on her cheek, despite the nearby presence of Cousin Charlotte and the teenage lifeguard who had taught them to dive.

CATHERINE PADDED ACROSS the grass toward her sister-in-law and her nephew like a cat. Not a timid house cat: a feral cat, a mouser, the sort of strong and lithe feline that kills for a living. Her tennis sneakers barely touched the ground as she walked, and though she was sweating—it had taken her more effort to dispose of young Gary Winslow than she had expected—she wasn't tired and she moved with an undulant allure.

"That's Willow's mom, right?" Gary said to her as they approached Sara.

"Yes, indeed."

"A shrink?"

"Therapist," she answered, and as she said the word she wondered what her sister-in-law the therapist would think when she turned around and saw her striding across the grass with this young buck of a teenager. The truth was that Gary was simply going to introduce himself to the woman who was Willow's mom and then change into a swimsuit for his shift at the pool (and, suddenly, she thought of the swimsuit she had with her in her canvas bag and feared that it would seem matronly to this . . . boy). That was the only reason he was coming this way with her, after all, it wasn't really like the two of them were . . . together. But Catherine wondered if someone less perceptive than Sara might presume there was something vaguely untoward about her spending time with a strange teenager, the two of them glistening with sweat.

Sara looked up from the baby at her side and held her hand flat over her wild eyebrows like a visor. And the woman did indeed have big eyebrows. Sara was attractive, but with her eyebrows in need of attention, her coffee-colored hair the length of a teenager's—hair that was growing now the first telltale filaments of white, a few strands sprinkled in amid the brown just above her ears—and those eyeglasses even more dated than the ones worn by her own brother, John, she looked a tad too earthy for Catherine. Especially today in those sandals with clunky straps and those shorts the color of army fatigues.

Catherine remembered when John had first brought Sara to Manhattan to meet their mother and her and Spencer. John had discovered her while skiing in Vermont—within weeks, actually, of her and Spencer's own wedding—and unlike almost everyone else in the lodge that afternoon she was actually from the Green Mountains. Had grown up in a town northeast of Burlington. Her father taught at the University of Vermont, in the College of Agricultural and Life Sciences, and he was one of the country's leading experts on a bug with the appalling-sounding name of the pear thrip. Being an expert on the pear thrip mattered in Vermont, because pear thrips liked to eat maple tree leaves. Sara's mother was the secretary at the village's elementary school, but she had recently retired. In any case, when Sara first saw the courtyard and the columns in Nan Seton's Manhattan apartment building, the cobblestone circle into which the town cars and taxis would travel while awaiting the privileged who lived in the great monolith of a structure, the doormen—there was not a single doorman, not here; there was instead a cadre of wizened old men and enthusiastic young ones scattered throughout the courtyard and standing vigil inside the elevators, some in blue uniforms and some in gray, all of whom had thick, lyric Irish accents—and then the endless sprawl that was the apartment itself, she seemed ill at ease. She had been quiet when she was getting the tour, and when she finally said something more than a mono-syllabic murmur of appreciation, she had shaken her head and announced in a voice—playful, yes, but the awe, it was clear, was real, too—"Imagine. And to think I'd thought that everybody in New York City (at least everybody I'd ever meet) lived in those teeny-tiny studios where you slept on a convertible couch by the kitchen." Catherine remembered that her mother had been charming: She laughed and with a self-deprecating shrug explained to John's girlfriend that she and her husband had bought the apartment in the mid-1970s, when Manhattan real estate was worth a little less than property along the Love Canal. Nevertheless, Catherine thought that while there had been wonderment in Sara's reaction, there had also been a slight whiff of disapproval—as if Sara saw something decadent in the plates with the gold leaf in the breakfront or in the notion that although there wasn't a live-in maid, there really were two small bed-rooms in the back of the apartment near the kitchen that were referred to as the maids' rooms. Catherine recalled experiencing an unpleasant quiver of guilt, and suddenly the Japanese screens and the Italian floor tile seemed ostentatious. Showy. Dissolute.

Yet Sara never seemed to manifest any particular bias toward either the proletariat or the rustic sugar makers, loggers, or beleaguered dairy farmers in her own corner of the country, and so over time Catherine decided that she had read more into Sara's reaction than was there. Still, Sara's upcountry lack of refinement had made an impression on Catherine, and though Sara had since earned a series of postgraduate degrees and then joined a large and thriving counseling practice, in some ways Catherine still viewed the woman—even though she and Sara were in fact the same age—as a younger sister who would always need a bit of her guidance.

Behind Sara, Catherine saw their two girls sitting on towels on the cement on the side of the pool. Her daughter was wearing a tank suit today, because— bless her own mother's heart—yesterday Nan had accidentally left the two strips of black that Charlotte had chosen as her summer bathing suit in the trunk of the car overnight, and when they finally found them this morning they had still been damp and they smelled like a tire iron. Even her daughter had had the common sense to see that she couldn't wear the string thing today, and she had donned her green and yellow Speedo without a fuss.

"Sara, this is Gary Winslow," she said, and quickly Gary squatted like a baseball catcher so that he was eye level with her sister-in-law. She hadn't expected this sort of impulsive graciousness on the lad's part, and she was impressed. "Gary is a lifeguard," she added. "His grandparents are Kelsey and Irene Winslow."

"It's nice to meet you," Sara said.

"I've had a wonderful time watching over your

daughter this month. She's terrific," he told her, and Catherine felt a twinge of jealousy, a small spasm of resentment. This was awfully similar to what he had said to her about her own daughter when he'd introduced himself at the tennis court not forty-five minutes ago.

"She's having a nice summer," Sara said. "Thank you."

"And this must be her brother. Patrick, right?"

"Uh-huh."

He smiled at the infant, and then with a teenage boy's complete unease around babies—a discomfort that actually bordered on fear—he quickly turned back to Sara. Patrick reached out a hand toward him, batting at the air, and he might have cried out for this new person to pay him the attention he was accustomed to receiving, but he seemed to like the swishing feel the air made on his skin when he sliced his arm like a sword. "Has Willow showed you how well she can dive?" Gary asked.

"She has. It was one of the first things she did when we got to the club yesterday. She and Charlotte have been at it again most of this morning. They only stopped a couple of minutes ago."

"Gwen is teaching them. I can't dive to save my life, but Gwen is awesome. She's got the girls doing somersaults and inwards. Amazing."

"I saw."

"Mrs. McCullough just destroyed me on the tennis court. You play?" he asked.

Catherine found herself looking away, slightly relieved that he had called her Mrs. McCullough in front of her sister-in-law. At the tennis court, when they were changing sides after their fifth game, he had referred to her as Mrs. McCullough with such obsequiousness that she had told him he could call her Catherine. And, for the rest of the match, he had. Now, however, she was glad that he understood instinctively that around Sara a certain deference was in order.

So long, of course, as he didn't overdo it.

"I only play when I'm here," Sara replied, and she made it sound as if she played under duress. As if someone—a Seton, a McCullough—put a gun to her head.

"We just had an awesome game—me and Mrs. McCullough."

Catherine rolled her eyes for Sara's benefit. Now he was overdoing it: One "Mrs. McCullough" was appropriate; two, especially in such close proximity, made her sound geriatric.

"Oh, so that's what you were doing," Sara said, as if she hadn't known. As if she thought the tennis rackets they were holding were mere props. She was smiling when she said it so Catherine would know she was kidding.

"Yup," Gary said, and then his eyes trailed down Sara's legs to her ankle. "I like your tattoo."

"Ah, yes. I got that years ago."

"It's pretty."

"Thank you."

Catherine understood why men found tattoos on a woman erotic: It suggested she enjoyed forbidden things, was excited by taboos. It meant that she thought about her body as an object of ornamentation (or that she simply thought about her body at all). Still, Catherine didn't see how a wraparound tattoo of a little ivy could compensate for such dowdy shorts.

She was about to say something now to pull Gary's eyes away from her sister-in-law's legs, and her mind was trying to finalize the thought: perhaps note that Sara was married to her older brother. She didn't have to open her mouth to divert the young man's attention, however, because in the sky in the distance they all heard a small engine, and they looked up at once and saw an ultralight plane—a hang glider with an engine, really—moving in slow motion against the hulking silhouette of Mount Lafayette. Gary stood so he could see it better, and even the pair of girls by the pool left their towels on the cement and ran over so they, too, could watch the strange, birdlike machine motor high above them in the crisp, cloudless air.

FROM THE PARKING LOT of the garden nursery Spencer could also hear the steady rumble of the ultralight, but he had no interest in the craft. He stood before the minivan for barely an additional second before climbing inside and slamming the door. Slamming it so hard the four thousand pounds of rented metal actually rocked back and forth on the wide radial tires. He had bought nothing, and he was frustrated. No urines, no pepper sprays, no magic deterrent that would keep the deer at a distance. He was going to drive now to the club with absolutely nothing to show for his visit to the garden center—or, for

that matter, for the hour and a half he had spent surf-
ing the Web that morning, enduring the nightmar-
ishly sluggish download of each image onto his laptop
computer's screen.

He wondered what the ancient Stoics did to protect
their produce—or the Essenes or the Manicheans.
Actually, he had a dispiriting feeling he knew what the
Manicheans did: They probably posted their slaves in
their gardens. Clearly that wasn't an option here.

Nevertheless, it infuriated him that the only thing
even the owner of the nursery himself could suggest
was a fence.

"Make it six and a half to ten feet high, and you
should be in business," the guy had said. "You'll be
safe from most deer if you make it six and a half feet
tall, but you'll be safe to the max if you go for a ten-
footer. No deer is going to jump three yards and
change to get a little Swiss chard."

The owner had long, jet black hair that he tied back
in a ponytail, and the reddest eyes Spencer had ever
seen at ten thirty in the morning. Or, at least, the reddest eyes he had seen at ten thirty in the morning since
college. He was so thin that he looked almost gaunt,
and he was wearing a sleeveless T-shirt with a silk-
screen of a massive, fully open crimson peony on the
front. Spencer could almost see real ants attempting to
climb among the two-dimensional petals. The owner
had a smaller, less vibrant tattoo of a flower on each of
his biceps. One looked to be a faded purple pansy, but
Spencer couldn't quite tell what the other one was.
Monkshood, maybe. Foxglove, perhaps. Maybe it

wasn't even a flower at all: Maybe it was a biker's helmet of some sort. Either way, it was rough-looking—both the tattoos were—and nothing like the delicate, almost genteel bit of latticework that his own sister-in-law had had needled into the skin around her ankle when she was eighteen.

"I don't want a fence," Spencer had told him.

"Then get a great big thorny thing."

"A great big thorny thing?" Spencer asked. He expected more precision from the owner of the nursery than "a great big thorny thing."

"Rows of them. Build walls and walls of big thorny things. Deer hate thorns. Me, too. Don't carry a whole lot that has thorns—other than roses, of course. No one likes thorns, you know?"

"I do know. Certainly I don't like them."

"Evergreens, then? How about evergreens? I got two or three Fat Alberts you could take with you. Three seventy-five apiece," he said, and Spencer knew enough about trees to know that he meant $375.

"I doubt three would be enough."

"Oh, you got that right. I just meant to get you started. How big is your garden?"

"Maybe a third of an acre."

The man whistled, shook his head, and then allowed himself a laugh that sounded a bit like a snort. "You'd need a hell of a lot more than two or three trees. You got to build a fortress with them, you know!"

"It was your idea."

"I didn't realize your garden was . . . was a farm."

"It's not a farm."

"You hunt?"

"No."

"I was going to say if you started—"

"I don't hunt. I don't even eat meat. I work for FERAL."

He nodded. "Oh, yeah, I've heard of FERAL. You're the folks who hate dairy farmers, right?"

"We don't hate dairy farmers. Why would you think such a thing?"

"My nephew's in college, and one year he and his roommate had this poster on their wall. It said something like 'You don't have to milk barley and hops.' It was a picture of a giant hop, and it had all these suction tubes and—"

"I know the poster. The point wasn't to say that anyone hates dairy farmers—"

"And wasn't there some farmer in a leather mask? One of those creepy executioner's S-and-M hoods you see in . . . well, you know, you see some places?"

"No!"

"Oh."

"There was one very stylized photograph of some natural barley being treated like a dairy cow," Spencer told him, struggling to keep his voice even. He remembered well the fallout from the "Milk Is Cruel Food" disaster. It had kicked off late summer, almost two years ago now, and its purpose was to educate college students—huge milk drinkers—about the inhumanity of the corporate dairy industry. The vacuum pumps that were attached to the cows' udders, the male calves that were sent away to be slaughtered. The shadowy growth hormones that increased production.

"Because you wanted the college kids to drink beer instead of milk, right?" the nursery's owner asked.

"The point was simply to educate them that cows are mistreated, and when they drink milk—which is actually so bad for you that if I had my way my own daughter wouldn't drink it—they're supporting animal torture," he answered. The result of the campaign had been angry letters from practically every mother and father who had ever lost a son or daughter to a drunk college-aged driver, as well as mountains—no, mountain **ranges**—of bad publicity for FERAL. Spencer had wound up on **Nightline,** enduring a withering battery of statistics from a representative from MADD about the numbers of people in this country who were killed or maimed every year by drunk drivers. On one syndicated radio talk show a woman had called him the Antichrist, and (her voice breaking) informed him that her beautiful vegan, non-milk-drinking FERAL member daughter had drowned diving amid the coral reefs of Grand Cayman when the girl's boyfriend (drunk on beer) had improperly attached her regulator to her oxygen tank.

"Anyway," Spencer continued now, drawing a long breath, "I'm not about to shoot a deer."

"Or have much of a garden, I just guess." The owner was grinning mischievously when he spoke, and Spencer could see that the moment he had told the man he worked for FERAL, the fellow had written him off as a fanatic. This happened all the time, and it drove him crazy. He was an activist, he believed, but he wasn't an extremist. And if anyone wanted to talk about killing animals, the reality was that for better or worse he had finished off a great many more animals than most people you met on the street. One December evening when he was driving home from college with a friend for the winter break, he had tried to calculate in his mind the number of lobsters he had cleavered the previous summer by multiplying the average figure he killed in a night by the number of nights he had been the second chef at the Steer by the Shore. The bus tours, he understood, were what made him a statistical killing machine, and he guessed there were two of those each week. Those evenings he might have baked and stuffed as many as seventy lobsters. The other nights he presumed he killed about five an hour, and maybe twenty all told.

Still, he was able to come up with a figure that he supposed was a pretty good ballpark: 2,200.

That same car ride he had also calculated the pounds of ground beef he had consumed as a freshman, since he had eaten two cheeseburgers a day for lunch seven days a week and at least another six or seven either at dinner or at the snack bar when he was tired of the library late at night. At the time he didn't know exactly how much a cow weighed, but he guessed at a quarter pound per burger he'd eaten all the meat off at least one steer that school year.

As he sped from the garden center's parking lot, it didn't seem fair that it was actually animals that were keeping him from his vegetables. It was as if the deer had known the exact day he was coming and descended on the garden literally hours before he arrived. He was quite sure that his family—John and Sara and his mother-in-law, perhaps even Catherine—was secretly laughing at him.

He decided the first thing he would do when he got to the club was grab a swim with his daughter. Spend some time with Charlotte and Willow, the two people who would be least likely to see any humor in the way a couple of deer had undone his big plans. He knew he wouldn't dare say a word to Catherine, because although she had absolutely nothing to do with this debacle, he would be unable to speak of his experience at the nursery just now without sounding as if he were furious with her. Taking his disappointment out on her. Which, obviously, he wasn't. But, still, Catherine would get defensive. And he would grow sarcastic. And either they would stew separately or they would squabble together. He didn't want that, not here.

Maybe when he'd calmed down he would see if John wanted to play nine holes of golf.

Then, when he was more serene at the end of the day, perhaps he could get in a game of doubles with Catherine and Sara and John. He'd be so tired by nightfall that he wouldn't care—or, at least, he wouldn't care quite so much—that the greens he would eat this coming week wouldn't come from the seeds he had planted back in May.

As he drove past Gerta's Edelweiss Garden (the Steer by the Shore was long gone, replaced by a store that sold home medical equipment), he decided that what he actually found most disturbing was the notion that even a guy with tattoos of flowers on his arms thought he was a kook because he didn't want to bring down a couple of deer—in season or out—with an assault rifle.

Nine

Walter Durnip's funeral was worse than Nan Seton had expected. At least a dozen people with absolutely no background in public speaking had felt compelled to share stories, most of which were so pointless and dull that not even a seasoned orator could have brought them to life. The man's principal legacies were the meaningless facts that he loathed golf carts but enjoyed his tractor; that he disapproved of modern antilock brakes on automobiles and remained till the day he died a firm proponent of pumping ("No one could drive on snow like Walter," said Lida Barnum with great solemnity); and that for the last half century of his life he had used the putter that had been given to him by Phillip Cole Jr., the president of the Contour Club from 1947 to 1963 and the son of one of the revered institution's founders.

When she and John reached their car, when she was safely settled in the passenger seat and her son was behind the wheel, she turned to him and said, "In the name of God, John, no funeral for me. At least no unscripted recollections. If you have any respect for your mother's memory at all, you will not allow those people to babble over my dead body."

"You really don't like these things, do you?"

"No. They remind me of how little we do with our lives."

"I thought some of the stories were rather nice. Revealing."

"Yes. They revealed just how boring Walter Durnip really was. Now, drive, please. I want to go by the Grangers' and get some string beans and early zucchini. And then I can't wait to get to the club and go for a swim. If I thought you had your suit—"

"I do, Mother. It's in the trunk."

"Oh, good. In that case, let's go to Echo Lake before the club. A brisk swim will clear our heads."

She looked over the couch into the backseat of her car to make sure she had an extra beach towel back there and was relieved to see that she did. She was impressed that her son had remembered his bathing suit, but she knew there wasn't a prayer in the world that he would have remembered to grab a towel, too.

"How cold is Echo Lake this summer?" he asked her.

"It's warm as toast. Sixty-three degrees the other day. I'm sure it's up to sixty-five by now."

"Sara calls Echo Lake a big frozen slushie."

"Are you tattling?"

"No, I agree with her. I think it's funny."

"And to think she grew up in Vermont," Nan said with a sigh. Sometimes she couldn't believe how soft this next generation was. "Really, now, John: It's lovely. Invigorating."

Though the two-lane road to the highway was little wider than a cow path and filled with the sorts of switchbacks that made her granddaughters nauseous

(Nan honestly didn't believe it was her driving that was the cause, because she reasoned then she would be nauseous, too), a beaten-up sports car appeared out of nowhere behind them and—ignoring the double yellow line—passed them. Its engine roared like a jet, and she noted inside the vehicle the mangy young men with their sleeveless muscle shirts and cigarettes dangling from their mouths.

"If we were in Vermont, I would guess they were your clients," she said.

He smiled. "If we were in Vermont—in Chittenden County, anyway—they probably would be."

She wasn't sure how to show it (and so she never did), but she was proud of her son. When he had chosen to leave that tony law firm in Burlington to become a public defender, he had demonstrated to her that he understood the importance of service. A responsibility he shouldered for no other reason than the simple reality that his family had advantages. Nan didn't focus much attention on the nuances of Democratic or Republican policy toward the urban poor she saw in Manhattan or the rural poor she saw here in the country, but she did have the sense that policy in both cases revolved largely around throwing money at the problem: In the case of the Democrats it was tax money and in the case of the Republicans it was tax-deductible contributions. But it was never, in Nan's opinion, about time. It was never about giving what she deemed a human being's most precious commodity: the hours and days one had on this planet. It was especially important to be generous with your life if you had one as cushy as she had, which was why she had volunteered for years and years to help children learn to read at public schools in Harlem and Chinatown and the South Bronx. When her privileged son had realized he had certain responsibilities in his early thirties and moved his career in a different direction, she had been pleased.

"Have you had a busy summer?" she asked John. "At the office?"

"No worse than usual. But it seems more out of control since Patrick was born. Everything does. These days I'm constantly treading water and still getting waves and waves up my nose."

"Do you ever regret leaving private practice?" she asked him—a reflex she couldn't restrain.

He turned briefly from the road to her: Clearly he was as shocked as she that she had asked such a personal question, one so rife with the possibility for honesty and confession and delicate revelation. Then his eyes went back to the road and he answered, "Not a bit. These people need me. Sometimes they have no one else in the world looking out for them."

She found herself smiling because her son was happy and doing good work, but also because he hadn't allowed their conversation to grow intimate with the sort of disclosure that just might have made them both uncomfortable.

LATE THAT AFTERNOON, Willow listened as the grown-ups sat on the porch at the house on the hill sipping iced tea and talking about the deer and Walter Durnip's funeral, or teasing Aunt Catherine for playing tennis with a hunky teenage lifeguard half her age. She listened as they talked about golf and tennis and swimming in Echo Lake and as they made jokes at her and her cousin's expense about how tough the Seton New England Boot Camp really was—and how difficult it must be for them to keep up with their grandmother. And while Charlotte defended herself with enthusiasm, Willow was content to sit on the outdoor rug on the wood beside Patrick, painting her toenails and watching the baby loll on his back and pedal his small feet in the air. She was happy because soon they would be going back to the club, where she would be only briefly on parade for Grandmother's friends. Then she and Charlotte would be allowed to join the older kids—teenagers, really—at their own barbecue and bonfire at the edge of the golf course. She was still nervous, but in the course of the day she had also grown excited.

She thought her uncle's rant about his visit to the garden center was unintentionally funny, especially the way he would seethe when he would bring up the nursery owner's suggestion that he hunt the deer down. She didn't know if the owner meant now or during deer season, but the whole idea of her uncle even holding a rifle was laughable.

"There must be something you can do—something we can do," Charlotte said at one point, and Willow was touched by her cousin's uncharacteristic solicitude—her desire to help her father with his cause.

Charlotte rarely volunteered to help anyone with anything, and Willow attributed the girl's longing to be of assistance to the reality that before yesterday she hadn't seen her parents in almost two weeks.

"Sure there is," John Seton told his niece. "Replant the garden and turn the property into a petting zoo. If you can't beat 'em, feed 'em."

Willow knew it was a family secret that her father had taken up hunting. When he'd started to speak, for a brief second Willow had presumed with no small amount of astonishment that he was about to admit to the McCulloughs that he owned a gun and bullets and those water-repellent army fatigues. The whole deal. She had never told Charlotte about her father's new hobby, and a couple of times when deer had come up in the last twenty-four hours, her mother had looked at her with raised eyebrows, a gentle reminder that Uncle Spencer and his family did not need to know that Dad now owned a gun.

"Anyway, I think we should all have dinner tomorrow night at Gerta's," her father was saying. "See if the busboys are still wearing lederhosen and the waitresses still have to wear those bib things with the push-up bras. You just loved that costume, didn't you, Sis?"

"We did not wear push-up bras," her aunt Catherine said.

Grandmother looked up from the biography as thick as a brick in her lap and said, "When Marguerite had dinner there two weeks ago, she said that one of the busboys started playing the piano after the kitchen had stopped serving."

"They have a piano there?" Aunt Catherine asked.

"They do now. And the busboy started playing and three of the young waitresses started singing. And they sang the most lovely songs from **The Sound of Music.**"

" 'Edelweiss,' I suppose," her father said.

"Yes, absolutely. Marguerite said it was beautiful, and they all looked adorable in their little outfits."

"As I recall, Mother, when I worked there you weren't wild about my little outfit. You thought it showed too much cleavage."

"You're my daughter."

"If we're going to go out to dinner, let's go to Polly's instead and have pancakes," Charlotte said, referring to a nearby pancake parlor. She glanced over at Willow and added, "After all, most of us can eat pancakes. We went to Gerta's last summer, and everything was meat."

Uncle Spencer smiled sardonically. "Ah, yes. Remember the Alpine Meat Tray? A lazy Susan with a bit of cow, a little pig. Some chicken."

"There was something else," her father said. "I swear there were four kinds of meat."

"Werewolf?"

"You're thinking too eastern European, Spencer. Too Romanian. Austria was never known for werewolves," Grandmother said.

"Well, there's a huge salad bar, so if we want to go to Gerta's, it's fine with me. I could live on spaetzle and a salad bar."

"Spaetzle has eggs, Spencer. It's loaded with eggs."

It was her aunt Catherine telling her uncle this, and Willow thought she sounded a bit like she was talking to a toddler.

Uncle Spencer turned to her and said—speaking so slowly it was as if every single word were a chore—"Fine, then. I will stick to the lettuce and the carrots and whatever soy protein they have at the salad bar."

"There is no need to get huffy," Aunt Catherine said. "I was only pointing out for you—"

"Correcting me, you mean."

"No. I wasn't sure if you knew—"

"I was simply trying to make all of your lives easier. I was trying to be agreeable. Truth is, I really don't give a—" He paused for the briefest of seconds before finishing his thought. "I really don't care where we eat."

"Why don't we all see how we feel tomorrow," her mother said suddenly, her voice a tad louder than usual, and she got up from her chair and lifted young Patrick into her arms. When she sat back down, she discreetly opened a few buttons on her blouse and started to nurse. Normally Willow didn't feel strongly about her mother nursing in public, but because she knew it made Grandmother uncomfortable she found herself looking away. She concentrated on her toes, dabbing polish on the tiny squares of her nails. Once she looked up and stared for a moment at the white plastic spikes in the ground that marked the outer edges of the badminton court and at the grass in the yard, so verdantly green this time of the day that it shimmered. She noticed that Charlotte was glancing back and forth between her parents, a hint of nervousness in her eyes, and she wondered if Uncle Spencer and Aunt Catherine fought often.

As she resumed her work on her feet, she wished there were fewer silences in the grown-ups' conversation so everyone would not have to hear Patrick savoring his early dinner with the gluttonous abandon of a baby.

BY DESIGN, the Contour Club—the name an homage to the contour of the Old Man of the Mountain, the massive rock profile that once jutted out from a granite cliff a mere three miles to the south—was not physically impressive. Its founders, including patriarch James MacGregor Seton himself, wanted to be sure that the establishment had a rustic flavor to it. Consequently, the clubhouse, though spacious to the point that it sprawled, was only a single floor. It was shaped roughly like a croissant, with thin white clapboards that were repainted at least every other year and reflected the sun like fresh snow. The inner arc looked out on the first hole of the golf course and the practice green, and the outer walls faced the Presidential Range and Mount Lafayette. The tables in the dining room belonged in a hunting lodge—the pine had been stained the brown of old acorns, and the legs were stocky and straight—and the oak chairs with their massive cushions appeared capable of swallowing small children whole. The bar had the heads of deer and moose and black bears on two walls (though the animals without exception had been killed by generations long gone), and a series of shelves with the taxidermal remains of a fox, a mink, and a bobcat (again, all brought to the club years and years earlier). Another wall had the plaques with the names of the annual champions in golf and tennis and bridge, and twice there appeared Catherine's name: Her one summer after college when she was still Catherine Seton, she won the women's singles championship handily; then, after she was married, as Catherine Seton-McCullough, she and Eleanor Morrison had taken the women's doubles cup.

Most of the Contour Club members were families like the Setons: Either they lived in Manhattan or Boston (or the suburbs of Manhattan or Boston) and only spent small parts of the year in the White Mountains at their second homes, or they had retired to the area after successful careers in New York or Massachusetts. Certainly there were some members who were actually born in New Hampshire: lawyers and doctors and accountants, and some of the developers and builders of the nearby ski resorts. But they were outnumbered and most felt vaguely second class because they had never worked in the Prudential Center or ridden subways twice daily to and from Wall Street.

The bonfire for the teenagers was lit around eight thirty, when there was still a purple gauze to the west and—if the girls had been back at their grandmother's house now—just enough light for a few more minutes of badminton. But the mountains to the east were almost invisible now, just one more part of the distant night sky. Occasionally a gang of moths, hobolike, would approach the blaze before disappearing either into the night or the flames, and the girls saw fireflies that looked like stars.

For the past hour, since the teens had started to congregate with their cans of soda (and, so far, no one was drinking anything stronger than soda), Willow and Charlotte had been looked after largely by Gwen—the lifeguard who was teaching them how to dive. It had crossed Willow's mind that either her parents or her aunt and uncle had probably asked the young woman to keep an eye on the two of them, but she wasn't sure. It might just have been that Gwen had taken pity on them: Charlotte was at least two years younger than everyone else, and Willow was four. Gwen wasn't with them every moment, but periodically she would wander by to see how they were and hand them some marshmallows or point an open bag of popcorn in their direction. A couple of times other teenagers had come with her, but they always seemed to view Willow and Charlotte as small, pleasant animals that could be stroked briefly and abstractedly and then left once more to their own devices.

As the evening progressed it seemed to Willow that Charlotte's biggest disappointment wasn't that she was younger than the rest of the crowd. After all, she had expected this. Rather, it was that Gary, the lifeguard on whom it was obvious to anyone who cared to notice such things she had a serious crush, was actually hanging around with the grown-ups back at the clubhouse. Here Charlotte was with the teenagers at the bonfire, and the teenager she was most interested in had chosen to be with the adults. Worse, when they had first started down the hill with Gwen to the site of the great mound of long dead limbs and dying tree branches, Gary had been chatting with Aunt Catherine. The two of them were on the terrace with those old-fashioned highball glasses in their hands, and they were talking like they were old friends.

Charlotte had been furious. Furious and confused. Why would Gary want to be with the adults when he could be with normal people his own age? she had asked Willow and Gwen rhetorically as they wandered across the fairway. Where was her father? she had wondered, as if there was something inappropriate about her mother chatting with the lifeguard.

Willow had expected that her own parents would leave early with Patrick and Grandmother, but they hadn't. Patrick had fallen asleep a little after seven in a corner of the clubhouse in his canvas baby seat, and her mom had decided it was best to let him rest. Normally her mom didn't seem to like the crowd at the Contour Club—at least not the way her dad and her aunt and uncle did—but she seemed to be having a pretty good time tonight.

Someone had brought a portable CD player to the bonfire, and a few of the older girls were trying to convince a couple of the boys to dance. When Charlotte realized that Gwen was leaving them once again— when she saw the girl put an arm casually around Connor Fitzhugh's shoulders and then start to move him around like an immensely supple marionette—

she sat down in the grass and pulled Willow down with her. Connor, though younger than Gwen, was handsome and athletic and the very same lad whom Charlotte had implied at breakfast had suggested that the two girls come to the bonfire in the first place. So far he hadn't said a word to either of them.

"In my school in New York, by now someone would have gotten the party going with a little beer," Charlotte murmured, and her voice was dripping with condescension.

"The party seems to be going just fine . . . if you're fifteen," she answered, and immediately she regretted what she had said. It had sounded clever to her in her mind, but when she saw Charlotte look down at the grass between her legs and start ripping at the small strands as if they were weeds in the vegetable garden, she realized it had only been hurtful.

She wondered briefly why Charlotte hated being twelve so much, why she desired so madly to be older. "You know," she went on, "we don't have to stay."

"You can go any time you want," Charlotte said.

"I know."

Connor was moving a bit on his own now, and sometimes he was holding Gwen's hands as they danced and sometimes there was a wide corridor of air between them. Gwen was wearing a sweatshirt and baggy shorts, and she didn't look nearly as heavy as she did in only a bathing suit.

Behind them they heard a small group of boys arriving, three of them with baseball caps on backward, and they were laughing a little too loudly. When the boys got closer to the circle Willow saw why: They were holding open bottles of beer in their hands, and two of them had cases of beer under their arms. They put the cases down on the grass—one of the boys nearly dropped his, which caused everyone around them to laugh even more boisterously since those beers would now erupt like geysers when they were opened—and the teenagers descended on the cartons as if they were burlap sacks of grain at a refugee camp. A moment later the crowd dispersed and the music began to seem strident and angry to Willow.

Beside her Charlotte stood. She watched her cousin brush the grass off the back of her shorts and then stroll casually over to the ransacked cardboard cartons. There she bent over, pawed briefly among the bent and torn flaps—and among something near the cartons as well, a bag or a large purse of some kind—and then seemed to find amid the pillaged boxes what she was searching for: two bottles of beer that had been overlooked when the hordes had started seizing the alcohol. She glanced briefly, nervously, around to see if any of the teenagers cared that she was procuring a little beer, but no one was taking any interest in her.

When she returned to her spot in the grass beside Willow, she smiled knowingly and offered her one of the bottles.

"No, thanks," Willow said.

"Suit yourself."

"You're not really going to drink that, are you?"

"What do you think, I just got it for show?"

As a matter of fact, I do, Willow thought, but she kept her mouth shut this time. She didn't want to challenge her cousin, to dare her in essence into consuming the whole bottle. Perhaps Charlotte's big plan was simply to hold the bottle in her hands, either so she could feel older or so that one of the teenagers would see her with the beer and start paying her some attention. A lot of what Charlotte did, in Willow's opinion, was about getting people to pay attention to her.

"No, I didn't think that," she said simply.

Still, Charlotte unscrewed the top and took a small sip and then, after pausing for just the briefest moment with the lip of the bottle at the edge of her mouth, she took a second one. Willow realized that as bad as the beer probably tasted, Charlotte planned at the very least to polish off that first bottle—and maybe, if the opportunity presented itself, that second one, too. She didn't think that was a good idea at all, and so she reached over for the unopened bottle in the grass between Charlotte's legs and said, "Here. Let me have that one."

It was more difficult to unscrew the lid than she had expected—she saw in the light from the bonfire that she had given herself a sliver of a cut on the inside of her thumb, and a little blood was just starting to puddle in the small split in the skin—but the beer didn't taste quite as horrible as it smelled. She told herself that it would be better for everyone if she drank one bottle than if her cousin drank two.

"You like it, don't you?" Charlotte asked.

She shrugged. "It's okay."

"Only okay. Yeah, right. I got something else, too."

"Food?" Willow asked hopefully. "I'm starved."

"Better than food," she said, and then she told Willow about stumbling just now across the canvas bag beside the cartons of beer in the grass. It was Gwen's bag—the small sack the high school student carried around with her like a purse—and it was on its side on the ground, the contents spilling haphazardly out onto the manicured fairway lawn: A lipstick, Gwen's bathing suit, a small can of lavender-scented aerosol body spray. A disposable lighter. Tampax. A plastic Ziploc bag with loose flakes of marijuana and three thick, tightly rolled joints. Charlotte said that she had set the large canvas bag upright, and carefully put everything back inside it except for one of the joints. Now she cradled the dope in her hand like a rolled hundred-dollar bill.

"I can't believe Gwen would do drugs," Willow murmured, at once appalled and entranced. She had never before seen an actual joint. Certainly she had seen images in health class and on antidrug commercials on TV, but never before had she glimpsed an honest-to-God spliff up close and personal.

"It's not drugs," Charlotte said, correcting her. "It's just marijuana. Cancer patients and people with AIDS smoke it all the time. And, if you want, we can, too."

"Charlotte!"

Her cousin mimicked her, repeating her name in

the singsong voice of a little girl crybaby: "Charrrrrrr-lotte!"

"Come on . . . don't be like that."

"Gwen had three of them. She won't miss one. It's okay."

Charlotte patted the pockets of her shirt and her shorts, and Willow wondered what she was looking for. Then, without saying a word, the girl stood up again and walked casually back to Gwen's canvas bag. She reached in, and Willow presumed she was taking a second (or even a third) joint, but then she understood that her cousin was swiping—**borrowing,** she imagined Charlotte would say—the teenager's matches or lighter.

When she returned, Willow saw that the girl had indeed brought back a lime-colored Bic, and she was flicking the striker with her thumb. She considered teasing Charlotte about that ridiculous bit of pantomime she had performed a moment earlier: patting herself down like she actually expected to find a lighter of her own in her pockets. But she restrained herself, and then she found herself watching enrapt as Charlotte proceeded to light the joint. She inhaled, hacked loudly and powerfully, rasped . . . and then inhaled again. This time she didn't cough, and then slowly she exhaled. The smell was sweet, vaguely reminiscent of both blueberries and an exotic herb she had once smelled at an Indian restaurant. She liked it, and when her cousin turned toward her and raised her eyebrows invitingly, she accepted the joint and took a drag, too. Then she took another. And there in the grass the two girls proceeded to smoke and sniff and rasp until the burning paper scorched the tips of Charlotte's fingers, and she dropped it onto the ground as if it were a wooden match that almost had consumed itself.

Ten

N an Seton wanted desperately to glance at her watch, but she knew if she did this nice but dull Martin and Cecilia Dallmally from Scotland would presume she was either tired or bored (or both). Still, like an itch the desire to know whether it was nine or nine fifteen was growing insufferable. Finally, just when she thought she was going to have to pull back the straw-colored linen on her wrist to look at her watch and make some pretext to leave, she felt a small breeze on her neck. When she turned toward the terrace door, she saw Charlotte and Willow approaching. For a brief second they looked a tad unsteady on their feet—Charlotte seemed to be touching every table and chair within arm's reach as she navigated her way through the crowded clubhouse—but Nan couldn't imagine why that would be and decided her eyes had played a small trick on her.

"Oh, look," she said to the Dallmallys, "there are my granddaughters now. Will you excuse me?"

"They're adorable! You'll have to introduce us," Cecilia cooed.

"Oh, sometime, certainly," she murmured, pulling away from the couple like a sailboat that has at last snared the wind. She put a hand on each of her granddaughters' shoulders and was pleasantly surprised to find the girls smiling up at her.

"I'll bet you want us to meet some more people, don't you, Grandmother?" Charlotte said, her words giddy and playful. Given the rare and uncharacteristic good cheer that filled the child's voice, her eyes were not as wide as Nan would have expected. But she was so pleased to see Charlotte in such fine spirits that she didn't think anything of it, and she concluded that if she weren't already so anxious to get home she actually might have chosen this moment to show off her granddaughters some more.

"I always want you to meet people," she answered. "And you were both so charming earlier. But we're through for tonight. It's late."

"It sure is," Willow agreed, nodding, and then she giggled as if she found something funny in the fact it was after nine.

"Let's find your parents—"

"There's Mom," Willow said, the words a chipper little cry, and she pointed at Sara as her mother was lifting Patrick from his canvas chair, the baby's head swaying on his shoulders as if it were a poorly attached pumpkin on a scarecrow. John was beside her, gathering into his arms the diaper bag with its bottles and lotions and wipes.

Nan nodded and felt a surge of relief at the idea that—almost miraculously—everybody was preparing to go home at exactly the same moment, and that moment was now: Her granddaughters had returned as happy as could be from the bonfire, and her daughter-in-law and her son were collecting little Patrick and his accessories. Any minute now she would spy Catherine and Spencer, and they all would be off.

"I don't see my mom," Charlotte said, craning her neck.

"I saw her a few minutes ago," Nan said. "She was talking to Gary Winslow."

"Where was Dad?"

"He's around, too."

"Was **he** talking to Gary?"

"I don't recall who he was talking to, Charlotte. Now, do you have your shoes? Where **are** your shoes?" She had happened to look down and saw that Charlotte's feet were bare.

"Oh, yeah. My sneak-sneaks."

"Your what?"

"My—oh, don't worry, Grandmother, I know right where they are," she said, and suddenly she and Willow were almost doubled over in laughter.

"Well, I don't see what's funny about misplacing your sneakers. Go get them so we can go home. Shoo, now!"

"They're . . . they're . . ."

"They're down by the golf course, I suppose? At the bonfire?"

"Uh-huh."

"Okay. Willow, why don't you go help your parents with Patrick? Tell them Charlotte and I are just getting her sneakers."

"But call them sneak-sneaks!" Charlotte called after her cousin, and once again the children succumbed to a burst of hilarity at the word.

She took Charlotte's hand and led the girl through the crowd. Her granddaughter was unusually pliant, and Nan attributed this to the lateness of the hour and the idea that the child had apparently had a nice time with the teenagers. The older children had not let her down: They'd taken good care of her granddaughters.

There were people on the terrace and the soft grass surrounding the practice green, and the tiki torches were sending small plumes of jet black smoke into the sky. Here she could hear the music from the clubroom, something slightly jazzy, as well as the rock music from the bonfire down the hill. As she and Charlotte approached the teenagers she thought she smelled something sweet and herbal and unfamiliar, and she wondered if the teenagers had thrown pinecones or cloves into the blaze to give it this scent.

"They're over by those cartons," Charlotte said, as they stood in the shadows at a short distance. "I see them."

"Are those beer cartons?"

"Oh, no! Soda. They're the soda cartons."

She nodded, though she didn't believe for a minute those cartons had ever held anything but beer. Still, she wasn't upset: Certainly John and Catherine had snuck a few surreptitious beers when they had been teenagers, and there were worse places for these teens to drink a beer or two than a bonfire no more than 150 yards from their parents. Generally, these were pretty wholesome kids. She watched some of the girls and boys dance, while others sat in the grass in small groups of three and four. She guessed there were twenty or twenty-five teenagers here. None of them seemed to pay Charlotte much attention as she rounded up her sneakers, and Nan was glad: She didn't want to delay their departure any longer than neces-sary. She wanted to return to the clubroom with Charlotte, find Catherine and Spencer, and then head home. Tomorrow was Sunday, and she wanted every-one to get plenty of sleep tonight so they could spend a healthy chunk of the next day swimming at Echo Lake, before returning to the club for some late-after-noon tennis. Activity would be especially important if, as discussed, they all went to Gerta's Edelweiss Garden for dinner.

"Got my sneak-sneaks," Charlotte cooed, and she held them high in the air, one in each hand, by their laces.

"Come on, then."

"I'm come-on-ing."

It took them a tad longer to climb back up the hill than Nan would have liked because Charlotte seemed to be dawdling—one moment she was lifting her legs in slow motion as if they were cranes and staring down at her knees in rapt fascination, and the next she was stopping still in her tracks to gaze at her fingers—but finally she managed to herd her granddaughter back to the terrace. She sighed, but her relief was short-lived because there she saw Catherine and Gary at the very edge of the terrace. They were not exactly alone, but they were not exactly a part of the festivities, either. They were buffered from the rest of the crowd by the massive stone barbecue Gary's own grandfather had paid to have built after some other club member had used the sand dune on nearby eighteen for a clambake. The barbecue was at least seven feet tall and that many feet wide, the individual stones the size of lamp shades and basketballs. At first Nan couldn't imagine why Catherine and Gary had felt the need to carry on their conversation behind the barbecue, but then almost instantly she could. She saw Gary's free hand, the one not holding his glass, reach behind Catherine's head, brushing her daughter's ponytail with his fingers and (surely she had not seen this part correctly) stroking briefly the back of her neck. With the reflexes of a mother bear protecting both a cub and a grand-cub, in one smooth motion Nan moved herself between Charlotte and Catherine so the girl couldn't see her mother and guided the child forward onto the cold slate of the patio. Then she looked back over her shoulder and called out in a voice that she was confident sounded completely normal, "Catherine, Charlotte and I are rounding up Spencer and heading home." She thought it was important now to remind Catherine that she had both a daughter and a husband and they both were present at the club.

She listened for a moment, but over the sounds of the music and the conversation and the clinking of ice against glass she heard nothing from either Catherine or Gary.

"Did you see Mom?" Charlotte asked her, and

the girl suddenly looked young and small to Nan, almost tiny.

"Yes, dear," she said. "Here she comes now." From behind the barbecue they watched Catherine emerge. She was alone, she looked vaguely uncomfortable, and Nan noticed that the glass in her hands was empty. A moment later Nan saw Gary strolling down the hill toward the bonfire, away from the cocktail party, his hands in the pockets of his shorts. If she hadn't known that he, too, had been behind that massive wall of stones, she would have presumed that he'd materialized out of thin air.

THEY WERE DRIVING HOME in a caravan of two cars, the minivan that Catherine and Spencer had rented, followed by John and Sara's navy blue Volvo. Nan was riding with John and Sara, sharing the backseat with baby Patrick, while the girls went ahead in the rental. Nan didn't mind sharing the backseat with the baby, but he was a tad fussy right now because he smelled like a Dumpster, and it was taking a lot of work to keep him from howling. Still, if she wished she were in the other car it was primarily because she would have liked to have watched her daughter and son-in-law up close to see if there was any tension between them. When they were assembling in the parking lot of the club a few minutes ago, Spencer had wondered aloud whether they'd arrive home and actually witness deer racing away from the yard when their headlights washed over the garden, and with a real edge in her voice Catherine had asked him to let go of the deer—**Get over it,** she had said—and to please move on.

Nevertheless, her distance now from Catherine and Spencer proved calming. Reassuring. By the time they pulled into her driveway, she told herself that she hadn't witnessed anything inappropriate when she and Charlotte had been returning to the clubhouse from the bonfire. She had seen Catherine talking to a teenager at a cocktail party. Maybe Gary had been swatting at a mosquito near Catherine's ear or pulling a bug from her hair. There were a million innocent reasons why the two of them might have been standing behind a barbecue rather than, say, by the glass doors or the tiki torches or—along with almost all of the other adults who were outside at that moment— near the long tables with the finger foods and the booze. For all she knew, Gary was regaling Catherine with stories about how her daughter had been spending her days at the club. What a dolphin the child had become in the pool. How nicely she dove.

The cars arrived back home together, and while John and Sara took the baby upstairs she watched her granddaughters and Catherine and Spencer climb from their vehicle. She noticed that the two girls still seemed to be giggling, and they were strolling to the edge of the garden with Spencer. Catherine walked past her to the front door of the house, moving, Nan observed, with her head down as if she were an embarrassed teenager. She recalled the time Catherine had been fifteen years old, and she and some summer fling had managed to fog up the windows in Catherine's bedroom upstairs. It had been a chilly, rainy August afternoon and they had closed the windows against the cold. When Nan had gone upstairs to tell the young man it was time to go home, she discovered that he and Catherine had been petting with such vigor that the glass panes looked like a shower stall. Catherine had the same guilty expression on her face now.

After she heard the screen door swing shut, she joined Spencer and the girls at the perimeter of the garden. Even in the moonlight, they couldn't see much. They could distinguish the corn plants that Spencer had returned to their upright positions, gently showering the roots with clay and dirt, and they could make out the potato hills. They could see the twine that had been stretched like tightropes over the rows of carrots and the stakes that were nearest them. But that was about it.

Spencer sighed so loudly that Nan and the girls heard him, and then mumbled something about a short walk.

"Dad is really bummed out, isn't he?" Charlotte said, once he had started off into the night.

"Yes, he is," Nan said. "But he'll get over it." She hadn't meant to sound unsympathetic, but she could tell by the way her granddaughter was looking at her—her lower lip drooping slightly, her eyebrows raised into a dome—that she had. All she had meant to suggest was that, like most men, her father was overreacting. Men made a big deal about pain and a big deal about disappointment. Then they got over both. At least they did if they had any character, and she knew Spencer certainly had some. He had a temper and that annoying eccentricity about meat, but otherwise he was pretty solid.

"Don't stay out here too long, girls," she continued after a moment, when neither Charlotte nor Willow said anything. Charlotte had turned away from her, and—not unlike her father a moment ago—was staring into the dark. It dawned on Nan suddenly that her two children and their spouses were so focused on other things that they had all gone into the house or into the fields without a single word to their daughters: not a word about the evening, not a word about getting ready for bed. John and Sara had raced inside with Patrick, Catherine had gone inside with her tail between her legs, guilty over . . . Nan didn't know what, but guilty over a desire, a word, perhaps even an act. (No, it hadn't gone that far, Nan quickly reassured herself.) And Spencer had gone for a walk, unable to think about anything but his distress over this ridiculous garden.

She felt a slight rush of annoyance at all four of them, both for their dereliction of parental duty and for taking her for granted. They were all so absorbed in their own lives that either they hadn't thought for a moment of their daughters or they had presumed that Grandmother would take care of the pair. Get their teeth brushed, their hair combed. Get them into their nightgowns. Settle them down with their books.

Did they—John and Sara, Catherine and Spencer—

have any idea how complicated it was to settle the two girls down at the end of the day? Of course they didn't. Last night, everyone's first together in the country, the girls had stayed up till eleven thirty with their parents, showing them what they had learned about bridge, telling them about their nature hikes, and regaling them with their stories of their days at the club. The children (and, Nan reminded herself, they **were** children) had collapsed into their beds, exhausted. It wasn't usually that easy.

She paused with her hands on her hips and stared at the house. She was torn between her belief that these girls needed a grown-up right now and her sense that her own two children were taking advantage of her—as, in truth, they did for weeks at a time with the Seton New England Boot Camp. She loved her grandchildren, she loved them very much. But she was a glorified babysitter, that's what she was.

She could hear her breath steam from her nose, and she shook her head. Then, convinced that any second she would stop herself and turn around and herd the children inside, she started toward the front door. She did not stop herself, however, not this time. She went through the front hall and past the living room, up the stairs—pausing briefly on the second-floor landing where she heard John and Sara down the hall whispering as they arranged Patrick's crib and started preparing the baby for bed, saw the shut bathroom door and understood that Catherine was inside there running a bath—and then to her own sanctum sanctorum on the third floor. She sat on her bed with her hands on the edge of the mattress, vexed by her children. When she would recall this moment in the coming days, she would wonder if that sensation of pique had in actuality been apprehension.

THE TWO GIRLS collapsed into grass already damp with evening dew and gazed up at the stars.

"We don't have stars like this in New York, you know," Charlotte said.

"I do know," Willow said. "How are you?"

"What do you mean, how am I?"

"You know."

"If I knew, why would I ask?"

"I'm still pretty buzzed. I know that. But the giggles are gone."

"Personally, I think you're more drunk than buzzed. There's a difference."

"What about you?"

"Mellow. Mellow stoned."

"How does your throat feel?"

"My throat feels fine."

"Not sore?"

"It was at first. But then the buzz began and it went away. Poof."

"I still can't believe you did that."

"I can't believe **we** did that," Charlotte said, and she chuckled.

"I mean your taking the pot in the first place."

"It was no big deal."

"I think it was: You took something that wasn't yours."

"Gwen wouldn't have cared. I told you, I've smoked pot before—two times. If I'd asked, she would have shared some with me," Charlotte said.

"No way. There is no way Gwen would have let a twelve-year-old kid smoke her pot."

"Why does everyone keep saying I'm twelve—"

"Because you are!"

"No, I'm not! I'm almost thirteen. If people want to round my age, they should round it up to thirteen!"

"Fine, you're thirteen. There is still no way that Gwen would have let a thirteen-year-old smoke her pot—or anyone's pot!"

"She wouldn't have had a choice," Charlotte said, and she lowered her voice slightly. "Maybe I would have pointed out to her that I could tell the grown-ups there were kids at the bonfire with dope if she didn't let me have some."

"You would have done that to Gwen?"

The older girl shrugged her shoulders. In reality, Willow knew, Charlotte wouldn't have dared. She wouldn't have wanted to anger this young adult whose friendship she cherished or do something as decidedly uncool as rat on a teenager.

"I guess I wouldn't have," Charlotte said after a moment. "But I still don't think Gwen would have minded all that much. I'm sure she would have given us a couple of puffs."

Willow found herself nodding. Sometimes this was

about as close to acquiescence as you got with Charlotte. "I think my mom had a good time," she said, consciously changing the subject. "Sometimes she says she gets a little shy at parties. But I think she thought this one was fun."

"My mom sure thought so," Charlotte said, but she sounded annoyed.

"What? You don't want your mom to have a good time?"

"I want her to have a good time with Dad."

"I don't understand."

"You wouldn't. Your mom . . ."

"My mom what?"

"It doesn't matter."

"No, tell me."

Charlotte draped her arm over her eyes. "I'm hungry," she said. "I think I have the munchies."

"Tell me what you meant!"

She took a very deep breath, and when she exhaled it sounded a bit like the wind. "I was going to say that my mom is this really huge flirt—even though she's married. It's pathetic."

Willow was stunned. She couldn't imagine thinking such a thing of one's mother, much less verbalizing the notion aloud. She told herself this was some idea that had popped into her cousin's head because of the marijuana.

"And my dad doesn't know it," Charlotte continued. "He's completely clueless."

"They seem happy to me."

"Yeah, right. You saw Mom with Gary at the club

this morning, didn't you? And then tonight at the party?"

"Your mom and Gary played tennis. What's the big deal?"

"And she's done this before," Charlotte went on, ignoring her.

"Your mom?"

"Uh-huh. I get it from her. I've seen how she is with men at parties at our apartment and at school, and I've heard her on the phone. I've even picked up the phone and listened. One time—"

"You've listened in on her phone conversations?"

"Twice. One time she was talking to a teacher and another time it was this headmaster, but I could tell there was more going on than just school stuff."

Willow realized this disclosure was not merely making her uncomfortable, it was scaring her. She felt cold suddenly and wanted to go inside, but—as if she were watching a desperately frightening movie—she couldn't bring herself to leave. "Are they going to get a divorce?" she asked, and her voice sounded tiny to her.

"I wouldn't be surprised if they did someday. You know that one out of every two marriages ends in divorce. So it wouldn't be a big deal."

"Yes it would."

"You don't understand because your mom doesn't drool over other men, and your father isn't so caught up in all the other stuff he does—cows or monkeys or something—that he doesn't even notice."

"Charlotte, divorce would be horrible."

"You just think that because you live in Vermont. Divorce is a lot more normal—"

"Divorce is never normal!"

"It happens, Cousin. You deal. Anyway, the thing that really gets me is the way she doesn't take Dad seriously. Like this garden. Dad really wanted it to work, but Mom just didn't care. I mean, if my boyfriend—"

"Husband—"

"You know what I mean. If my boyfriend or husband really cared about something, I'd take it seriously. Wouldn't you? I'm only his daughter, but I still wish I could do something to save the garden—and not because I love radishes or beets."

"No one loves radishes."

"Sometimes I get pissed at both of them. I don't think Mom would be the way she is if Dad wasn't this public wacko. You want to know something? You've been to the Bronx Zoo more times than I have."

"I think I've been once."

"Well, that's one more time than me. FERAL doesn't approve of zoos."

High overhead Willow saw the blinking lights of an airplane, but it was so far away that she couldn't hear it. If she squinted, it looked a bit like a slow-motion shooting star. She decided right then that she wished Charlotte hadn't told her any of this, because it was information she didn't need, and then she decided she would never drink beer or smoke pot again—and, if she could, she would prevent her cousin from dabbling with either. She blamed this whole conversation—and, especially, Charlotte's revelations—on the beer and the dope.

Over her shoulder she heard a noise from the house, and when she turned around she saw her father in the lit frame of the window of the bedroom that her parents and Patrick were sharing. His hands were on the sill and he had pulled up the screen so he could lean outside. He looked around, and she realized he couldn't pinpoint them in the dark. He was already wearing the blue T-shirt in which he slept, and she could see the check plaid of his summer pajamas around his waist.

"Willow?" he called in a stage whisper, his voice carrying well through the tranquil night air. "Willow?"

"We're out here, Dad," she yelled back, trying to make her voice project without shouting. She guessed Patrick was either asleep in his crib or settling down with one of Mom's breasts in his mouth.

"There's an unopened packet of diapers in the trunk of the Volvo," he told her from the window. "Could you get it, please? There are none left in the diaper bag."

"Sure."

He nodded, closed the screen, and disappeared back into the room.

"Babies are very high maintenance," Charlotte said.

"They are," Willow agreed, relieved that her father had already gotten into his pajamas and hadn't felt like going outside for the diapers. It had taken Charlotte's mind off her own mother and father and given the two of them an excuse to get away from this conversation about divorce. Together they stood up, the two of them still wobbly, and when Charlotte nearly toppled over like a toddler Willow grabbed her around the waist and suddenly they were both laughing hysterically once again. They walked across the yard to the car after they had caught their breath, moving gingerly because it was dark and because their feet seemed strangely detached from their legs. There Willow managed to pop open the trunk, though it seemed considerably more difficult than usual to find the button and press it.

At first Willow didn't think anything of the contents. She saw the diapers and she saw the jack, and she saw a moldy towel and an empty plastic bottle that once had held mineral water. But then, at the exact moment that Charlotte was opening her mouth and asking what that thing was that was shaped a lot like a rifle, she saw her dad's lambskin gun bag. Before she could stop Charlotte—her own hands were too busy hoisting the plastic-wrapped cube of diapers as big as a television set—her cousin was reaching into the trunk and lifting Dad's Adirondack into the air, feeling its shape through the leather and the fleece and the long metal zipper.

"What the heck is this?" Charlotte said, and though Willow dropped the diapers onto the grass and ripped the gun bag from her cousin's hands, she knew it was too late.

"It's nothing," Willow said, the words useless.

"It's a gun is what it is. Why does Uncle John have a gun?"

"Maybe it's evidence in some case."

"Yeah, right."

"I'm sure that's what it is."

"Then why did you grab it out of my hands like . . ."

"Like what?"

"Like you knew what it was."

"It's Dad's. Leave it alone." She dropped it back into the trunk and slammed the trunk shut. She wished she had a key so she could lock it.

"Seriously, tell me: Why does your dad have a gun? Is he, like, in trouble?"

"What do you mean?"

"Is some criminal after him? I know he represents some real scary characters."

"No!"

"Then why?"

She rubbed her eyes, and then reached down for the diapers. She picked the plush cube up, cradling it against her chest as if it were a massive stuffed animal, and said, "If you must know—and before I tell you this, you have to swear on your life you won't tell your mom and dad, okay?"

"Fine. Whatever you want."

"You swear?"

Charlotte rolled her eyes. "I am way too old for this sort of thing. But sure: I swear."

"Since you must know, Dad sometimes goes hunting. Deer hunting. He's not superserious about it, but he started last fall."

"Has he killed anything?"

"Not yet."

"But he hunts," she said, her voice an odd combination of incredulity and wonder.

"Yes. He hunts," Willow said, and she took the diapers and started toward the house. Before she had gone inside, however, a thought crossed her mind and she called out to her cousin, "I'll be right back, you know. So just leave my dad's stuff alone, okay?"

WHEN THE SINGLE GUNSHOT blistered the night quiet, Catherine's ears were under the water in the bath and she was only vaguely aware of the sound. She imagined something had fallen over in the kitchen, and she guessed her mother's dog had toppled the metal trash can in the corner near the sink. She didn't even pull the back of her head up from underneath the bubbles and the foam, and she continued to breathe in slowly through her nose, which was barely a fraction of an inch above the surface of the water. She was wondering which of her divorced friends she should call to get the name of a marriage counselor and then whether a divorcée was really the best route to a person who might actually be capable of preserving her and Spencer's marriage. It was only when she heard footsteps pounding down the stairs and her nephew's shrill cries a moment later that she pulled herself from the water, listened carefully, and then threw her nightgown over her damp body and ran to investigate.

Two rooms away young Patrick heard the blast loud and clear, and he started with his mother's nipple in his mouth, biting down so hard with his lips and small, sharp teeth that Sara yelped—an echo, almost, of the gunshot's lingering ping, the higher, less angry sound following the initial, concussive explosion—and she pulled her baby away from her breast. Then he let loose with a yowl. John knew instantly what the bang was, and he turned from his wife and his son, dimly aware of the milk and a tiny bit of blood puddling across Sara's reddish brown arcola, and raced to the window with the cube of diapers still in his hands. For a split second his heart had stopped, but now it was pounding so hard and fast in his chest that each thump sounded as loud in his head as the rifle's discharge.

Upstairs on the third floor Nan heard it, too, though her first reaction was that a large vehicle had backfired. It was as if she were back in Manhattan and it was, say, early May, and a bus or a garbage truck had just passed by her apartment and she had heard the bang through an open window. But then she realized that this had nothing to do with a bus or a truck, because she was in Sugar Hill and the house was too far from the road for the sound of a vehicle backfiring to have been so disconcerting and brutish.

And, of course, Spencer heard it, as he wandered out from the lupine that bordered the remnants of the vegetable garden, but he had no time to understand what the sound was because the bullet—the Menzer Premium that John, so new and green, had been unable to remove from the chamber back in November—slammed into his upper body and sent him flying into the air in much the same way as his daughter when she was doing an inward dive (hips thrown back high and hard, arms spread wide to the sides). He landed with his legs in the lupine and his chest and his arms and his head atop the ruined tangles of peas, and though he had heard the gunshot he did not hear the scream of the child, even though the scream—then a shriek, then a wail that sounded to anyone who was listening carefully like the word **No!**—followed the blast by no more than a second or a second and a half.

Part II

LOBSTERS

Eleven

It was after two in the morning when John and Nan and Charlotte and Willow finally left the hospital in Hanover to return to Sugar Hill, where Patrick was sleeping and Sara was sitting in the chair by the window, wondering just what she would say to her husband if Spencer died and what kinds of things Charlotte would say a decade from now to (it was inevitable) her therapist, regardless of whether her father survived the night. She was scared, she realized, and she was feeling left out. She didn't normally feel left out when she managed to avoid a game of golf with everyone else or a hike through the woods of Franconia Notch to the flume. Usually she felt relieved. But not this night. As she had looked through the slightly grimy screen window at the driveway and the vegetable garden, she felt—as she had at different points when she was a child and even in college—that she was on the outskirts of some place or some clique of which she wanted sincerely to be a part. She had known the feeling since the second or third grade, when her mother was the school secretary and sat right outside the principal's office. She knew that other children in her class had secrets that they kept from her simply because of who her mother was.

Consequently, she was grateful when well past three in the morning she saw the headlights coming up the long driveway in the dark, and downright euphoric when she saw that Catherine did not emerge from the car with the rest of the family. It had to mean that Spencer was still breathing, because she believed that no wife would have left her husband at the hospital at that time of the night unless her husband had died.

There had been moments in her vigil by the window when she had wished that John or Nan would call her from the hospital, but she hadn't thought that was likely. Everyone was hoping that she and the baby would sleep, and everyone was so stunned by the accident that they weren't thinking sufficiently straight to realize that even a catnap was going to be impossible.

She watched her husband with particular interest as he walked from her mother-in-law's car to the house. She wanted to see whether she could detect what he was feeling, because she wanted to be able to comfort him. Comfort them. Charlotte, Willow, her mother-in-law, too. They all had to be reeling.

She presumed John was still numb, but there was also remorse because he had never bothered to deal with the jammed bullet. He'd mentioned it off and on over the past eight or nine months, but it simply hadn't been a top-priority errand—especially after their lives were thrown into turmoil with the arrival of Patrick. She'd told John that she didn't like the idea of a loaded gun in the house, but he'd reassured her that the safety was on and the gun was locked away. And

Willow, they both knew, would never try to break into the gun cabinet.

Tonight the fellow from Fish and Wildlife had informed her that in some states keeping a loaded long arm in the trunk of a moving vehicle was a misdemeanor offense, but her husband was lucky because neither Vermont nor New Hampshire was among them. In response she'd said that her husband hadn't a choice: He couldn't unload the weapon, because the bullet wouldn't come out! She was afraid that she'd sounded defensive—almost abrasive—but she thought she detected something vaguely ominous in the uniformed man's remark, and she wanted it known that while John should have dealt with the bullet in the chamber, this wasn't completely his fault. She presumed—as she had since that November afternoon when John had returned from his day in the woods—that there was some minor defect with the gun, because otherwise he would have finished unloading it.

Though she still didn't understand exactly what Charlotte had said to the state trooper because the girl had been sobbing so hard, from the conversation she overheard it sounded as if the child didn't realize there was a bullet in the rifle. This didn't excuse her taking the weapon from the trunk of the car and playing with it, but it did make her behavior less foolish.

Still, as frustrated as she was with her husband for failing to take the rifle to a gunsmith, she was also saddened for him because she knew that John viewed Spencer more as a very good friend than a brother-in-law. She understood that he was going to be writhing in a deep, deep trough of guilt and self-loathing. Yes, she and John both considered Spencer a trifle extreme when it came to animal rights, but it was a pretty harmless eccentricity. At the moment, in fact, it seemed to Sara as substantially more harmless than her own husband's recent interest in hunting—an ample eccentricity in its own right.

She noticed in the porch light over the garage that her husband advanced alone along the blue gravel to the slate walkway with the tentative steps of a very old man, leaving their daughter and their niece to Nan. They were a few paces behind him, and the whole group was inching forward without saying a word. She heard the jingle of his keys, but their steps were oddly soundless on the stones, as if they were walking on tip-toe.

A few seconds after they had rounded the corner of the house and were no longer in view, she listened for the worn-out wheeze of the screen door as it opened. Then, glancing once at her sleeping baby—his chest raising the small comforter ever so slightly as he breathed—she went down the stairs to see exactly how Spencer was doing and what she could say that might help.

Twelve

Late Sunday morning Willow discovered strawberrics the deer had neither devoured nor trampled. Her inclination was to kneel down and eat them, but she squatted instead because she didn't dare get dirt on her knees—not this morning. The air felt heavy, and it was as eerily silent here at the edge of the yard as it was back in the house. Somewhere, she knew, there were birds, but they too seemed to understand that they didn't dare make a sound. The high gray sky was creased with curlicue wisps of cirrus clouds, and the heat seemed to Willow as if it were rising up from the ground. She twisted the first strawberry she found from its vine and bit into its moist, cuneiform tip. She hadn't had breakfast—her father had insisted on getting out the English muffins and boxes of dry cereal for her, but then the phone rang yet again and he was lost to a male voice at the other end of the line, and she hadn't wanted to sit alone at Grandmother's dining room table—and now, hours later, she was hungry. The strawberry was delicious, and not simply because she hadn't eaten a thing since she'd gotten a candy bar from the vending machine at the hospital last night. She finished it off in a second bite and then tossed the cap stem into the weeds at the edge of yet more lupine.

When she'd been younger, her mother had read to her a children's picture book about an old spinster who wanted to make the world a more beautiful place, and so she had spread lupine across some island. The spinster was called the lupine lady, and the lavender, blue, and ruby-colored flowers she planted were her gift to the world.

Grandmother's lupine had largely peaked by the time she and her cousin had arrived here, and so the wildflower struck her as more of an aggravation than a present. It made it difficult to wade through the fields. She remembered how it had been torture to uproot it over Memorial Day Weekend.

She ate a second strawberry, this one smaller than the first, in a single bite. Then she started to paw through the plants and the flattened leaves for additional berries, and saw a whole cluster the deer had missed. It was pretty clear to her that no one in the house felt like eating, and so she figured if she wanted she could finish off the strawberries and no one would care. But she decided that certainly wasn't what her uncle had had in mind when he'd placed these plants in the ground one by one. He'd envisioned them having feasts of berries together—as a family.

On the porch she saw her mother approaching the balustrade and leaning over the rail. She was pressing one of her feet abstractedly through the spindles and scanning the fields to the south. Any second she would turn her gaze to the west and see her. Willow knew there wasn't time to race into the lupine—or, better still, the nearby cluster of white pine—and hide, but she wished there were. She didn't want to be seen. She wanted to be invisible.

No, that wasn't quite accurate. It wasn't that she wanted to be invisible; it was that she wanted it to be nighttime again and to hear her father in the upstairs window, asking her to bring in some diapers for Patrick. If she could do it all over again—and, of course, she couldn't—she would get the diapers while Charlotte wasn't hovering over her shoulder, because then her cousin would never have discovered the rifle. She heard once again the colossal blast in her head. She had delivered the diapers to her parents and already come down the stairs. She was about to round the corner in the hall that led past the kitchen. Reflexively she ran toward the gunshot rather than away from it, because she knew immediately it was Charlotte. Her first thought, however, was that her cousin might have hurt herself—not someone else— but she didn't really believe even that. When she thought back on those last precious seconds before she knew what in fact had occurred, she recalled racing outside convinced that Charlotte had accidentally fired the rifle into the air and somewhere in the distant fields a bullet was falling harmlessly to earth.

But then she heard the girl's wail, almost at the same moment that she saw Charlotte standing in the grass near the garden with her hands empty at her sides. Already she had dropped the gun. Later that night she would learn from Charlotte's interviews with the man from Fish and Wildlife and the state trooper that the rifle's recoil had actually knocked her back onto her rear end—which was when she had dropped the Adirondack—but she had bounced back up as if she were a child's inflatable, bottom-weighted punching bag. It was Aunt Catherine, arriving maybe a minute later, who'd heaved the gun against the nearby apple tree.

Willow was the first person to reach Uncle Spencer. She'd simply continued to run in the direction that her cousin—the other girl's eyes wide with hysteria and insensible grief—was facing. Dimly she understood Charlotte was shrieking, "I thought it was a deer! I thought it was a deer!" but she hadn't yet realized that the girl was actually referring to her own father. **It.** Later, when they were at the hospital, Willow guessed by **it** Charlotte had meant also the movement. The physical presence that emerged from the lupine at the edge of the garden.

Willow knew that everyone—the state trooper, that fellow from Fish and Wildlife, those two EMTs— seemed worried that what she had seen would leave her scarred. The body. Her uncle. No kid should have to see such a thing, she overheard the trooper murmuring to the officer from Fish and Wildlife. But the truth was, it wasn't that bad. It wasn't good, either, that was for sure: She saw the deep burgundy stain spreading across her uncle's sport shirt like an overturned glass of tomato juice—the red indeed as viscous and thick as tomato juice, especially by his shoulder and collarbone—and she had seen the faraway look in his wide-open eyes. She was scared for her uncle, and for a moment she'd been so hot and dizzy that she thought she might faint—something she'd never done before in her life. But, she realized, she had seen far, far worse things in horror movies. Every kid had.

Still, she had no plans to visit the vegetable garden on the other side of the house for a very long time. Certainly, if she could help it, for the rest of the summer.

Above her she saw a bird, the first one she had noticed since she had ventured out here to the strawberries. It was a crow, that massive black bird that Charlotte had suspected was a raven when they'd first mentioned it to Grandmother three days ago. Three days. How could things possibly have changed so much in only three days? As she watched the bird's silent flight over the house, she guessed that it had emerged from the top of the pines—from exactly where Grandmother had said its nest was. It circled the house and the garage and then descended abruptly to a spot she couldn't quite see. Maybe it had landed in the garden. Or seen something beside the apple trees or on the driveway. She wished she and her cousin had tried that experiment with the dime her grandmother had suggested. It would have been interesting to have come home from the club on Thursday afternoon and seen whether the coin was gone.

She supposed that Uncle Spencer would live, if only because she couldn't imagine a world in which he could die. Yes, things could change in three days, but she couldn't allow herself to believe they could change that much. It was going to be difficult enough for

Charlotte to go through life with the knowledge that she had shot her dad, and so she was giving little credence to the possibility that her uncle wouldn't be out of intensive care in a couple of days and back home in a couple of weeks.

Her mother saw her now, pulled her sandal in from the bulbous porch spindles, and started toward her across the grass of the badminton court. She was walking slowly, almost gingerly, her hands casually in the front pants pockets of her shorts. **How are you feeling? How does that make you feel?** Her conversations with her mother—the serious ones—seemed to begin with her mother asking her one of those questions, and already Willow heard the words in her head. Other children, she knew, were jealous of her mother's apparent placidity in the midst of either crisis or misbehavior. And, she decided, they had every right to be. The way Sara actually asked how she felt about things sometimes drove her crazy—especially when she didn't yet **know** how she felt about something—but it was also one of the many reasons why Willow loved her so much and knew the woman was different from other moms.

She sighed and stood up, as if she'd been caught red-handed doing something wrong. She noticed a drop of pulpy red juice on her fingertips, as well as a dimpled bit of the fruit itself, and she thought once again of her uncle.

Thirteen

While the two EMTs, the sergeant from the state police, and the officer from Fish and Wildlife continued to wonder on Sunday what the hell kind of moron flatlander would fail to unload his thirty-ought-six and then leave the damn thing in the trunk of his car, Nan Seton had a pressing question of her own: Where in the name of heaven were the baby wipes? John was on his way back to the hospital and Sara was outside in the strawberries with Willow. Charlotte was the only other person in the house with her and Patrick, and she was still sobbing behind closed doors.

Normally Nan would have disturbed the pair in the strawberries without hesitation, but she hadn't seen her daughter-in-law and Willow sit still together—just the two of them—for more than ten minutes since Patrick had been born. She guessed the girl needed her mother, and she didn't want to intrude on them.

Patrick, alas, had turned a once spongelike disposable diaper into an oozing jellyfish so sloppy that no one—not even Sara—would have been able to compact it into one of those neat little softballs that were so easy to throw away. Worse, the baby had somehow managed to coat even his little light switch of a penis with waste. He smiled up at her now from his perch on a towel on the bureau where she was changing him, and she interpreted that smile on his face to be one of pride. His diaper sat dripping on a century-old cherry dresser.

Finally, when it was clear that the wipes were not beside the opened block of diapers on the floor or anywhere on the dresser, when it was evident there were none in the medicine cabinet, she decided she'd have to do something drastic. Hoisting the infant into the air in the towel, using it like a hammock, she carried him into the bathroom. There she filled the sink and started bobbing him up and down in the water. He clucked with pleasure, and she found herself clucking back. She'd have this lad swimming with her in Echo Lake in no time.

WHEN SARA AND WILLOW wandered inside twenty minutes later, Nan didn't tell them of her resourcefulness, but Sara noticed the clean diaper and the baby's contentment. She kissed Patrick's toes, which Nan guessed must have tasted agreeably clean. Then Sara brought the baby onto the porch to nurse him, and Willow collapsed into the thick couch in the living room. Nan sat down beside her and started to rub her hand in wide, slow circles along the child's back. It felt thin and tiny to her, almost too fragile for a child less than two months shy of eleven.

"Did you have a nice chat with your mother?" Nan asked.

"Uh-huh."

"You sound pensive."

"No. Not really. Just tired."

"No more questions?"

The girl turned toward her. "Well, maybe one."

"Go ahead."

"How angry are people going to be with Charlotte?"

She thought about this for a moment. "It was idiotic of her to do what she did. But she's a child and she made a mistake." Then she surprised herself by adding, "As for my son . . . that's another story."

"Mom thinks you're pretty mad at Dad."

"Your mother is right. Thank God your uncle is going to live. If he weren't . . . well, if he weren't I think as bad as things seem now, they'd be a thousand times worse. A thousand times. Really, I have no idea how a man as smart as your father—as smart and as organized as your father—could have done such a thing."

"He thought the gun was broken," the child said.

"Oh, I have no doubt about that. I'm sure it was. What I can't fathom is why he didn't get it fixed before now. Something like this was bound to happen."

"Is Charlotte still upstairs in her room?"

"Yes. Still crying, I believe. Have you two spoken this morning?"

"Uh-huh. She was pretty upset. Mom talked to her, too—and I guess she will again before we go to the hospital."

Nan nodded. There were advantages to having a therapist in the family, even if sometimes it made them all more comfortable discussing their feelings than she'd like. "Good. Has your mother said when she would like us to go?"

"No."

"After lunch, I'd imagine," she murmured, and then decided to broach the question that was really on her mind. "Tell me, Willow: What exactly was Charlotte thinking? Do you know? Did she honestly believe she could just take her uncle's rifle and shoot a deer?"

Willow took a deep breath because she wanted, she realized, to tell Grandmother—to tell **anyone**—that Charlotte probably hadn't been thinking at all (at least not particularly clearly) because she'd had a beer and helped smoke a joint. She wanted to say that she wasn't exactly sure **what** Charlotte had believed. But she knew that Charlotte didn't want her to tell anyone what they had done at the bonfire, because then things could get really nasty. All of a sudden drugs and alcohol would be involved, and Charlotte had managed to sniffle to Willow at the hospital in the middle of the night that she didn't want to get Gwen in trouble, too.

"I don't know what she was thinking, Grandmother," she answered simply.

"No idea?"

"Nope. None."

Nan gave the girl's shoulder one final squeeze and then stood, exhaling a long, slow breath through her nose. She gazed out the window for a moment and finally announced, "Well. We should get some food in you—and, perhaps, in your cousin. Before we know it, it will be time for us all to go to the hospital."

THERE WERE LOTS of reasons for pointing Uncle John's rifle at whatever was moving at the edge of the garden, and with her head buried underneath her pillow on her bed Charlotte could see them all. There were those hideous plastic shoes she had to wear to school, because her father wouldn't let her wear leather ones; there was her ugly vinyl wallet and change purse; there was her dream of visiting the circus when it came to Madison Square Garden one time—once, that was all she desired—before she was really too old; there was her frustration that again this year Grandmother hadn't been allowed to take her to the county fair in Haverhill, because among the games of chance were the baby racing pigs, and inside the 4-H tents there would be beef cows and dairy cows and the full-grown pigs that might be only days away from their slaughter. Depending upon what day they would have gone to the fair, there might also have been a milking exhibition or a horse pull—the spectacle, evil in her father's mind, of a couple of draft horses competing to see which could pull the greatest weight across a dirt arena.

There was even this pillow itself, a flat, poly-filled sack that was nowhere near as soft and fluffy as the goose down pillows on which Grandmother, Uncle John, and Aunt Sara slept. She'd felt their inviting plumpness, she knew the difference. Willow, too. She knew that the only reason Willow didn't have one of those comfortable pillows was because Grandmother tried not to give one granddaughter something she couldn't give both.

And there was the desire to make her own decisions about food and clothing and animals. About what was right and wrong.

And then last night, suddenly, there was that gun. Uncle John's gun. In her hands.

Her uncle was among the most reasonable—the most normal—grown-ups she knew, and if he hunted . . . well, truly, how bad could it be?

The truth was, she didn't expect to actually hit the deer. She never even expected to pull the trigger. She was just aiming and curling her finger, aiming and squeezing . . .

And the night was so quiet, she didn't think anything was out there at first.

Oh, but then she heard the movement in the lupine. The rustling. The sound of an animal pawing its way through the tall brush—perhaps one of the very same animals that had been pillaging the garden. That was when she first envisioned herself actually pointing the rifle at something and pulling the trigger. And if she did hit the creature, well, that would certainly show her parents. Her father. **See, Dad, it's one or the other,** she imagined herself saying. **It's either the vegetable garden or animal rights. You can't have both.**

Yes, she had been irritated last night when they got

home from the club. No doubt about that. Whether it was because of the beer or the dope or the reality that more times than not she was—she had to admit—an angry girl, she honestly didn't know. But she was feeling downright pissy by the time they got back to Sugar Hill, and here was this sleek and powerful and (yes) handsome gun in her grasp and the chance to cause some real havoc.

She remembered saying to someone—she couldn't recall now whether it was the state trooper or that other guy from the state animal department—that she hadn't even known the rifle was loaded, but that wasn't completely true. When she thought back carefully on all she remembered, she knew that safety button she kept flipping back and forth had struck her as a warning of some sort: Why would there be a safety if there weren't a bullet? Still, only when she was curling her index finger that one last time—that final time, the time she knew she would curl it until something happened—did the notion take firm root in her mind that if there was a bullet in the rifle this might be an inadvisable course of action. Until then, she'd operated on the premise that it didn't really matter if the gun was loaded or not, because she was just aiming it randomly out into the garden.

Until she heard that movement near the snow peas.

And continued her pressure on the trigger, this time not pausing until she heard the roar. No, she didn't just hear the roar, she felt it: The rifle exploded like fireworks in her arms, and she was heaved up in the air like a shot put ball, arcing back to the earth and onto her butt. Only later would she and Willow discover how badly her shoulder was bruised. It was indeed nasty: a massive yellow and black and blue paint stain on—and the irony was not lost on Charlotte—the very same shoulder in which her father had taken the bullet.

It's just a cry for attention. How many times had she overheard one of her teachers or one of her friends' parents or her aunt Sara telling her mom that over the years? Too many to count, that was for sure. According to some of the grown-ups around her, half of what she did in this world was a cry for attention. Someone was bound to say that about this disaster, too. **She was just doing it to get your attention.**

Well, not this time. This wasn't about trying to get her dad's or her mom's attention. This wasn't about trying to get anyone's attention. It wasn't **about** anything. It just . . . was. It was like a plane crash or a subway fire or a toddler who falls out an apartment window and dies. It was one of those nightmarish accidents that happened all the time because people were human and made mistakes. Yes, she'd been teed off at her dad for a decade of large and small slights—the way he believed that a Broadway show or one Saturday afternoon riding made up for three or four weeks of neglect—and maybe she did want to plug a deer to piss him off. Maybe she wanted to plug a deer to piss off both of her parents.

And maybe, just maybe, she wanted to help. Maybe she thought she was frightening the deer away and saving what was left of the snow peas. Now here was an interpretation of history that might get her through this disaster, an explanation of events that might allow her to actually rise from this bed and face her grandmother and her aunt and her cousin. Her mother. Her father. Hadn't she even told Willow last night that she wished there was something she could do about the garden? Certainly she had.

Oh, she was kidding herself. The truth was there was no design to this disaster, no conscious plan. At least she didn't think there was. It wasn't as if she **wanted** to shoot anything. Not a deer, not her dad. God, she couldn't possibly have wanted to shoot her dad. Could she? He may not have been a perfect father, but she knew in her heart that he did what he did because he loved animals, and there were worse faults to have in this world.

She had a vague sense that when her mom had picked the gun up off the ground and hurled it away from her like it was a live hand grenade—the thing had banged against one of Grandmother's apple trees before falling into the grass—she'd feared it was going to go off once again, and send a second bullet into whoever happened to be in its path.

She told herself now that all she wanted was for her father to survive and to forgive her. Her pillow was sodden with tears, and she wondered if she would ever stop crying.

SARA HEARD the state trooper's vehicle rumbling up the long rocky driveway before she saw it. She was making sandwiches for the girls and her mother-in-law—Willow and Nan were upstairs now with her niece—and her first instinct was that the car was owned by a friend of Nan's who was coming by to see what she could do. Instead, however, she saw a green and tan cruiser coasting to a stop before the garage, and the trooper they'd met the night before emerging from the vehicle. His name was Ned and he was a sergeant, and she thought his last name might have been Howland, but she wasn't positive. He was about forty, clean-shaven, and his hair was just starting to gray: There were patches of white along his sideburns. She presumed that he was returning John's gun, which he'd confiscated the night before. But she saw that he wasn't reaching into the backseat or venturing around the car to the trunk. He was simply heading up the slate walkway toward the front door, a clipboard and a pad under his arm.

Patrick had actually fallen back to sleep and his body was lolling right now in his little blue chair on the floor by her feet. She didn't want the doorbell to wake him, and so she raced outside to greet the trooper.

"Good morning, ma'am," he said, and he tipped his hat. "I hope you don't mind my dropping by. I meant to call first, but a young man rolled his father's pickup in Lisbon. I had to take care of that before coming here, and it threw my day off a bit. The boy's shaken—mostly because his father is furious—but otherwise he's okay. Still, I should have called. My apologies."

"That's fine."

"May I come in?"

She nodded. "Now I should apologize. My manners. I just wasn't thinking. Of course you can come in. I was making sandwiches. We were going to have something to eat and then go to the hospital."

"I understand your brother-in-law is going to live. That's good news."

"That's what they tell us," she said, and she opened the screen door and led the trooper into the living room. She motioned toward the couch, but Ned didn't sit down right away.

"I was wondering, ma'am, are the girls home? And your husband? I know Mrs. McCullough is still at the hospital with Mr. McCullough, and so I'll try and catch up with her a little later. But I would like to speak to Charlotte and Willow again—and to Mr. Seton, if he's here."

She felt a small shiver of alarm, and she made a conscious effort not to cross her arms before her defensively. She wanted to say, **You spoke to everyone last night!** but she was able to restrain herself. Still, Howland must have detected her sudden discomfort because he added quickly, "I just want to cross a few t's and dot a few i's, ma'am. Your niece and your daughter were pretty shaken after the accident—your husband was, too, of course—and so I wasn't as thorough as I would have liked."

She focused in her mind on the fact he had used the word **accident** and managed to force her lips into a small smile. "I understand," she said. "My husband is actually on his way to the hospital, too. But I can get Willow and Charlotte right now."

"One at a time, please."

"One at a time?"

"That's what I would prefer."

"May I be with them?"

"Absolutely."

She paused, wondering exactly how she should phrase the question that had formed in her mind and caused a quiver of anxiety to lodge in her stomach. Her husband was an attorney: Perhaps he would advise her to tell this Sergeant Howland that everyone would be happy to speak with him when they had a lawyer present. But not until.

"If you'd like a lawyer with them, I can come back," he said softly, and though she knew he couldn't possibly have read her mind it felt as if he had.

"Well. Let's see where this questioning is going, okay? We have nothing to hide."

"I didn't think so."

"Should I get my daughter? Or would you like to start with my niece?"

"Whichever, ma'am."

"Please: Call me Sara."

He smiled. "I'll try."

"Thank you."

"Truth is, I'd be happy to start with you."

"Me?"

"Yes, ma'am."

She felt there was something vaguely antagonistic about his relentless use of the word **ma'am,** especially after she'd just asked him to call her Sara. It was as if the word was a small sarcastic dig.

"All right, then. But may we do this in the kitchen? I would love to finish making the family lunch."

"That would be fine," Howland said. Behind her she heard Nan scuffling down the stairs. Her mother-in-law must have noticed they had company.

JOHN SETON stood paralyzed in a dim aisle in a natural foods grocery store. He was supposed to be on his way back to the hospital in Hanover to keep his sister company during her vigil in the ICU waiting room, but he had spontaneously detoured here to acquire provisions. He couldn't bear to think of Catherine trying to survive on either food from the vending machines or the hospital cafeteria. He realized now, however, that he honestly didn't know how extreme his sister's diet was or what she really liked to eat. And "like" was the guiding principle in his opinion, because whatever he bought was supposed to provide her comfort. He knew his niece consumed dairy products. Did her mother?

He looked at his watch and thought of the people he had left back at the house in Sugar Hill. He guessed it would be another few hours before they returned to the hospital, too. Now that Spencer was out of danger, he and his mother had agreed it was best if the whole clan didn't crowd into that bleak waiting room until Spencer was awake. Besides, his mother had observed, it was too nice a day to be inside.

He wondered how his niece was doing. He felt that he and Charlotte suddenly shared a very special bond: the bond of idiots. The two of them had nearly killed poor Spencer and probably disabled him for life. The difference between them, of course, was that a twelve-year-old girl was afforded the opportunity to sob alone in her bedroom or (last night) in those hideous Naugahyde orange chairs in the waiting room near the hospital's trauma center. A forty-year-old man was not. He had to rally, stifle that penitent urge to curl up in a closet where no one could see him. He had to answer questions, explain his monumental stupidity, make phone calls. This morning he'd spoken, it seemed, to half of Catherine and Spencer's friends, Spencer's sister, and a pair of top managers from FERAL.

The FERAL calls had actually been worse than the one to Spencer's sister. It was no easy task to explain to vegetarians and animal rights activists that one of their tribal leaders had been shot by his own daughter with a hunting rifle because he'd been mistaken for a deer. While he had been on the phone with the group's director—a stunningly telegenic woman named Dominique with a mane of raven black hair that fell almost to her waist and the greenest eyes he had ever seen on an animal that didn't use a litter box—he had feared briefly that he would be responsible for a second serious injury to a member of FERAL's senior management, by giving the director a stroke. He'd seen the woman before on **The CBS Early Show,** and so he knew how skilled she was at preventing anyone else from sliding a word of their own into a conversation, but he was still astounded at the way she proceeded to speak for five solid minutes without seeming to breathe after he had broken the news to her.

Nevertheless, the call to the deputy director was even more demeaning: Like John he was a lawyer, and he was very sharp. But it was clear on the phone that he was older than John, and he tended to speak with the slow-motion thoughtfulness of a grandfather in a family movie from the 1950s. It was only when the fellow was near the end of each deliberate, carefully considered observation or response to something John had said would he realize how coldly and precisely he had been diminished by this New York City attorney with a slight trace of a southern accent and how little this other lawyer thought of him. John felt not merely like the moron who had nearly killed his brother-in-law: He felt like the public defender from Mayberry, RFD.

The point that both FERAL officials wanted to make sure John understood wasn't simply that his negligence had almost slain their friend and associate, Spencer McCullough: It was that his **loathsome hobby** and his **shameful inattention** (the former were the high-minded words of the director, the latter the construction of her deputy) had the potential to humiliate FERAL. It simply didn't look good for the organization's communications director to have a brother-in-law who hunted. It made them all look like hypocrites. And—worse, in the opinion of the lawyer—it made the group look laughable.

"But I'm the one who hunts," John had said lamely to the lawyer, when the man had paused to consider how best to twist the knife next. He thought this was a point that should matter.

"Indeed you are, son. Indeed you are. On occasion, we've all made bad choices with our lives," the lawyer responded. "It's a particular shame, however, when those choices cause pain not simply to ourselves but to the people around us we love. Sometimes, you know, people seem sadly oblivious to the reality that their more irresponsible excursions into the realms of mis-behavior reflect badly not merely on themselves, but on their families, too. If the president's brother gets ar-rested for drug abuse, the president is tarnished as well. If the president's teenage daughter gets stopped for underage drinking, the president himself will be sullied. You, John, have not simply injured your brother-in-law; you may have left a deeply troubling blemish on this organization. Sad but true. You have some education—"

"I do not have **some** education," John heard him-self saying. "I have a law degree from—"

"Of course you do, son. Of course you do. That's why I am sure you can understand the way all of us with FERAL may look a tad disingenuous if we do not properly control how this information is dissemi-nated. Have you ever seen the op-ed pages of a news-paper? The section in which there is informed commentary? Well—"

"Yes, I have seen the op-ed pages of a newspaper. I may live in Vermont—I may **practice** in Vermont—

but I still read more than my horoscope and the comics!"

"Then I am sure you can imagine what could appear on the op-ed pages this week. Or what Jay Leno and David Letterman might be saying one day soon in their monologues. Vegan animal lover gets plugged by a deer rifle. A deer rifle, John—and fired by his own daughter. Our FERAL family would look deeply troubled. Perhaps even deceitful. At the very least, we would appear to lack the courage of our convictions and—"

"I'm sorry!" John finally shouted into the telephone, exasperated after having to listen first to Catwoman's rage and now to the sanctimonious diatribe of this lawyer. "I'm sorry my brother-in-law was shot! But lay off this goddamn condescending, holier-than-thou, meat-eaters-are-brainless-barbarians bullshit! I really don't give a rat's ass about your precious FERAL reputation! I care about my brother-in-law and my friend. The truth is, most people view you as a bunch of fanatic sociopaths who try to scare little kids away from hot dogs and want cats to become vegetarians! Okay? **That** is your reputation!" Then he hung up.

As annoyed as he was with the FERAL attorney, he still felt considerably more angry at himself. He **was** sorry! He vowed he'd never pull the trigger on a rifle again. He'd prayed while he was driving to the hospital the night before, while Spencer was in surgery, and then again this morning before he had gotten out of bed. He prayed not simply that Spencer would live but that he wouldn't be crippled when he awoke.

He remembered how the hardest part last night hadn't been having to look Catherine in the eye. It had been having to gaze at Willow—especially when she was looking back at him. At one point his daughter was in the chair beside Charlotte, who was crying. He and Catherine were leaning aimlessly against the walls, but he watched Willow as she patted Charlotte's bare arm. Her touch, in much the same way that it seemed to calm Patrick, soothed her: She put her head down on Willow's lap, and her crying grew silent.

He feared that for as long as he lived he would be an imbecile in the eyes of his daughter, and he couldn't imagine how he could possibly regain a semblance of the admiration she must once—a mere day earlier—have had for him. Sara would understand, he guessed, if only because she was a grown-up and whatever delusions she had of his competence had evaporated in all the years they had been married. She knew his strengths (and almost desperately he tried to remind himself that he did have some), and she wouldn't lose sight of them in this one mistake.

He thought also of his clients, the women and men—invariably guilty but invariably scarred—and their mistakes. The nineteen-year-old heroin addict who lifted cash from the convenience store where she worked and over the course of eight weeks was alleged to have stolen three thousand dollars. The carpenter who tried to make a quick score by bringing a couple blocks of hashish into Vermont from Montreal. The kid from the Northeast Kingdom who took the checkbook of an older neighbor who'd died and thought he could get away with using the checks to catch up on two months of back rent **and** treat himself to a couple new CDs.

There were the men and women who drove drunk (too many to count in his head) and the women who were nothing more than unemployable—uneducated or obese or mentally ill—and thus fell into mischief.

Most of these individuals didn't make one mistake, they made many: Their whole lives were studies in their own bad choices and someone older's unforgivable negligence. And, John realized with both clarity and sadness, they had grown up in broken homes or they had been abused as children or they had been seduced early by drugs . . . and he had no such excuse.

But then, he reminded himself, he hadn't done what they had. He had committed no crime in either the state where the accident had occurred or the state in which he lived. The state trooper and the officer from Fish and Wildlife were clear on this. Yes, the trooper had confiscated his weapon, but Sara told him that after the two men had inspected the gun by the light in his mother's garage she'd overheard them mumbling that perhaps something they called the extractor was faulty and would turn out to be the real culprit in this disaster.

Consequently, John told himself that he shouldn't be comparing himself to his clients. If he should be comparing himself to anyone, he decided, it should be to those myriad drivers who lead busy lives (he'd become a father again this year) and thus fail to get snow tires on their vehicles before the first winter blizzard and then careen off the road—though even this thought, in the end, offered precious little comfort.

He understood that if anyone other than Spencer had been wounded this way, the civil suit facing him now would be enormous. Gargantuan. Quite likely to test the upper limits of even the umbrella atop his homeowner's insurance policy. He and the gun company might even have wound up as codefendants. Consequently, he guessed that in a twisted, self-interested sort of way he should actually take some comfort in the fact this horror had occurred to his brother-in-law and not to an acquaintance or neighbor. Then he most likely would have been sued.

After all, though Charlotte had fired the weapon, it was he who had knowingly left a live round in the chamber for eight and a half months. What was he thinking? He envisioned the way the gun must have bounced around in the trunk of the car on the way here only two days ago, and he wondered what would have happened if somehow a first pothole had loosened the safety and a second had caused the gun to discharge. What if one of Willow's friends had decided to break one of the house's cardinal rules and had unlocked the cabinet in the guest bedroom in which the rifle was stored? Under normal circumstances this wouldn't have been cataclysmic because he kept his ammunition in a separate lockbox in his armoire. But what if some child—that rowdy kid in Willow's class who wound up playing at their home once in a while because he lived only two houses away, Gregg, for instance—had gotten a hold of the gun with the live round inside it? Willow had nicknamed the kid Little Hoodlum, and the boy took pride in the moniker.

John allowed himself a small shudder. What if something had happened to Willow?

He remembered the precise moment last November when he had expelled the ammunition from the gun—most of it, anyway. Before getting into the car to drive home from the logging trail on which he had parked, he had pushed the magazine release by the trigger guard and caught the four cartridges as they rolled into the palm of his hand. He'd taken his glove off, and the brass had been cold. Next he cycled the bolt in the action to remove the live round in the chamber, only this time nothing happened. He tried it again, and then a third time. He had a visual picture in his mind of flipping the safety to fire and back to safety—as if this were a computer problem, and he could remedy the situation by simply rebooting—but still the bullet remained stubbornly lodged in the gun. When the bolt was open, he could see clearly the grooves along the rear of the shell's casing, and he even tried freeing the cartridge with his fingers. It was evident quickly that he hadn't a prayer.

And so he had put the four cartridges from the magazine back in their small box and the small box back in his pack. He remembered flipping on the gun's safety and securing the rifle in the gun bag in his trunk before driving home.

He guessed if hunting and guns weren't so new to him, so frightening and foreign, he might have done what his friend Howard Mansfield had suggested and tried to dislodge the live round with a ramrod. Or if he understood more about guns, maybe he wouldn't have been afraid to simply fire the rifle into the sky in the woods.

Likewise, if he hadn't been so busy he would have had the cartridge removed by a professional. If he wasn't short one lawyer and down an investigator in his office. If he didn't have a caseload so big that half the time he couldn't keep his clients' names straight as they besieged him in the corridors of the courthouse during the Wednesday afternoon calendar calls, before they were paraded before the judge. If his daughter hadn't started piano lessons, while continuing ballet and after-school soccer. If his wife hadn't been pregnant. If there hadn't been a new baby in the house. If . . . if . . . if . . .

He shook his head, trying to clear from his mind the notion that he had been preoccupied this last year and therefore could sprinkle some portion of the blame on others. The idea was not simply ludicrous, it was pathetic. He was responsible, and he whispered the words to himself: "I am responsible."

Finally, when he realized that he'd been standing in the same spot in the same aisle for close to ten minutes, he made some decisions. He would bring Catherine a small loaf of freshly baked multigrain bread and local blueberry preserves, a container of vegan granola, and a batch of oatmeal cookies filled with carob chips. It wasn't his idea of comfort food, but he imagined it was the sort of thing Catherine would eat when she was troubled.

CATHERINE HELD THE BUN in which sat the flattened discus of ground beef with both hands— aware that this was precisely the recommendation this very fast-food chain had made some years earlier in its advertising campaign—and took a bite. The burger was delicious. She contemplated eating it slowly so she could savor each mouthful—the wondrously bedewed pickles and lettuce, the tomato slice lacquered with mayonnaise, and, of course, the patty itself, the pieces of meat crushed by her teeth into a glorious, spumescent paste—but the consideration lasted barely seconds. She ate it with the gleeful, rapacious speed of a wild animal who hasn't eaten in days.

When she was done, she glanced around the bright restaurant. The place was filled with the lunchtime crowd, and everyone around her who wasn't feeding French fries to toddlers was eating burgers or fish fillets or chicken nuggets with the same gusto she had evidenced only moments before. Quickly she dabbed at her mouth with the napkin, rubbed a quarter-sized dollop of jasmine-scented antibacterial hand gel into her fingers and palms (it was the smell that mattered more to Catherine than the cleansing properties), and left.

The hospital was three blocks away, and she presumed that Spencer would be unhooked from the ventilator by now. This was good news for a variety of reasons, not the least of which was that it meant there was less chance that Spencer's already sizable physical troubles would be compounded by pneumonia. He was going to spend one more night in the ICU before being settled in a bed in a regular hospital room, but she had been made to understand that it was an excellent sign indeed that they were already replacing the massive breathing machine that covered his face and his mouth with a mere nasal respirator. She had been surprised, in part because he was still so groggy with anesthesia and painkillers that he was only dimly aware of what had occurred: How close to dying he had come, the reality that he probably faced a crippling disability—possibly even amputation—when he was fully conscious. The fact that his own daughter had shot him.

She put on her sunglasses as she started to walk and popped an Altoids mint into her mouth. She knew she would crunch plenty more once she was in the hospital elevator.

She wondered why she wasn't furious, and why, in fact, she hadn't been furious once in the past fifteen or sixteen hours. Partly, she decided, it was because initially she had been frightened as hell. Then, once it was likely that Spencer would live, she was relieved. She had vomited in the ladies' room at the hospital, and at that moment she'd felt a twinge of anger at her brother; but once she emerged back into the waiting room and saw him leaning pathetically against the kiosk for the pay phone—not actually using it, but gripping the faux cubicle walls like they were the sides of a ladder—her hostility had evaporated almost instantly.

She was thankful that she and Spencer had never gotten around to having a serious discussion on

Saturday about their marriage—or, to be precise, her deepening sense that their marriage was in trouble. As complicated as her life with Spencer was about to become, it would be even worse if it were encumbered as well by his knowledge that she was unhappy. What kind of convalescence would that be for him? Imagine knowing that your caregiver, the person on whom you are completely dependent, would rather be elsewhere?

She told herself that this accident most assuredly did not mean she was now facing a life sentence in a marriage that hadn't been working or a lifetime of dinners in which she and Spencer barely spoke. It couldn't. Things would get better, or they would end. That hadn't changed . . . had it?

Charlotte, meanwhile, seemed to be vacillating between inconsolability and catatonia. As a mother she guessed this was normal, and any time Charlotte behaved in a manner that was outwardly normal and age appropriate Catherine took comfort. Still, Charlotte's eyes had grown so red so quickly last night that if her daughter had been a couple of years older Catherine knew she would have assumed that the deep color change was due more to dope than regret.

As she approached the hospital, she sighed. She thought of the floors and floors of pain in that building right now and the misery that awaited her own husband when he was—finally—completely awake.

SERGEANT NED HOWLAND had been a state trooper for nineteen years, and he had every expectation that he would be promoted to lieutenant within the next eighteen months. He was supremely competent, the principal chink in his armor being his inability to suffer fools gladly. Alas, most of his job was spent with fools, which was why he guessed he wasn't a lieutenant already. Either they were poor, rural fools who rolled their dad's trucks because they thought they could navigate a sharp Lisbon turn at seventy-five or they were wealthy flatlander fools who moved to northern New England and decided they wanted to bag themselves a ten-pointer but didn't have the slightest idea how to remove a cartridge from a thirty-ought-six when the bolt didn't extract it normally—and then, an even worse sin in Howland's opinion, they viewed themselves as so bloody busy and supremely entitled that they never bothered to take the damn rifle to a gunsmith and thus left it sitting around their house or in the trunk of their car. Loaded. Was it any wonder that some poor guy wound up spending the night on a ventilator at Dartmouth-Hitchcock? The miracle was that no one was killed.

And while he was fairly confident this was indeed just a stupid—SRS-stupid, as in stupid-really-stupid—accident, he figured he better make absolutely certain that there wasn't more going on beneath the surface here. Treat it like an attempted homicide until he knew otherwise. Be thorough. Maybe the daughter hated her dad and plugged him on purpose. Maybe that cousin was involved in some fashion. Maybe the great white hunter from Vermont had fabricated the

whole story and loaded the weapon only yesterday because he wanted to . . .

Howland couldn't finish the sentence, a further indication in his mind that while it was unlikely the
state's attorney would want to file criminal charges, it
was better to know too much than too little. That was
why he took the weapon with him last night and had
it stored safely now in the firearms locker. Picked it up
off the ground by that apple tree where he found it. If
they ever did want to send it to the state firearms laboratory, he wanted to be sure that they had it in their
possession.

Now he sat in the red wool easy chair in this Nan
Seton's living room, the woman's daughter-in-law and
older granddaughter sitting across from him on the
couch.

"So you didn't know the weapon had a bullet in the
chamber?" he asked the girl, Charlotte, one more
time.

The girl nodded sheepishly.

"But you did know the gun had a safety. Correct?"

"I guess."

"You had to switch it from S to F. At least according to your uncle, you did. Before he left for the hospital last night, he told us he was sure the gun was on
safety. Do you remember doing that? Switching a little lever from S to F?"

"Sort of."

He could see the girl had been crying, and he was
relieved. He really did want this interview now to be
nothing more than compulsive busywork.

"Sort of?"

"Uh-huh."

"Did you know that you were releasing the safety?"

"No."

"But Charlotte: You just told me that you knew the gun was on safety. So if you didn't know you were releasing it, what did you think you were doing when you switched the lever from S to F?"

"I was just . . ."

"Go on."

"I was just, I don't know, flipping it back and forth. I wasn't really thinking about what I was doing. Willow and I had just been at that party, and I was . . ."

"Yes?"

"I was tired. I'd never seen a gun before—a rifle, anyway—and I was just playing around. I know you shouldn't play with guns, but I wasn't thinking. I'm sorry, I'm so sorry about all of this," she said, and she shook her head and started to cry. Her aunt squeezed her bare knee reassuringly.

"Is there anything else, Sergeant Howland?" The woman's voice was soothing and serene. He wondered if she sang in a church choir.

"You're a vegetarian, right? Like your dad?" he asked the girl simply. He put his clipboard on the floor and leaned forward in his chair.

"Yes."

"Don't eat any meat?"

"None."

"You love animals?"

"Yes!"

"Then tell me something: Why were you even pretending to shoot a deer? I understand you presumed the weapon was unloaded, but why were you pointing it at what you thought was an animal in the first place?"

She heaved up her shoulders through her tears and said nothing.

"Why were you taking a rifle and aiming it at what you believed was a deer?"

She looked at the rug, at her aunt, and finally at him. She wiped at her cheeks with her fingers. "I guess I was thinking about the garden. I don't know. The vegetable garden. The deer were eating everything, and I just . . . I just . . ."

"You just . . ."

The room grew quiet, except for the girl's sniffles.

"You were just goofing, huh?" he asked her, unsure why he was letting her off the hook. He didn't have children of his own—he had a girlfriend, but in his opinion they were a long way away from even considering marriage, much less starting a family—but he did have a niece about this child's age. Maybe this was why he was throwing her a lifeline now.

"I guess."

He sighed. "That's about what I figured." Then, before another wave of mercy could overwhelm him, he asked quickly—almost abruptly—"Do you and your dad get along?"

There was another long pause while Charlotte gathered herself. He half-expected that the next voice he would hear would be the aunt, and he thought it very possible that she would end the interview right now. She was, after all, married to a lawyer. But then Charlotte was speaking, and she was telling him through her tears, "How can you even ask that? God, don't you get it? I will never, ever be able to forgive myself for what I did! Never!"

He nodded and picked up his clipboard off the floor. Regardless of what this kid really thought of her father, he decided that she hadn't meant to nearly blow off his arm. She'd simply been screwing around with a gun and accidentally wounded her dad. That was it, case closed. Yes, he would talk to Willow since he was already here, and at some point he would talk to the grown-ups. But he knew there would be nothing in his report that would suggest they file criminal charges, and in the next week or so they would return the gun to that idiot public defender.

At times like these, he concluded, the country didn't merely need stronger handgun laws: It needed laws as well that would demand a knucklehead like John Seton prove he could handle and store a firearm before being allowed to bring one into his home.

EVEN WITHOUT AN OXYGEN MASK covering much of his face, Spencer was still in an ICU bed that terrified both children when they arrived that afternoon, and looked especially horrific to Charlotte. He lay immobile on his back, his whole upper torso swathed in bandages, his wrecked arm encased in a plaster strip and draped across his abdomen. It looked a bit like he was supposed to be saying the Pledge of Allegiance but had gotten lazy with his right hand and hadn't brought it all the way up to his heart. His face, for reasons neither girl understood—the bullet had hit him just below his shoulder, right?—was oddly swollen, making even the catcher's mitts that posed as his ears seem just about the right size for his head. His heartbeat was monitored, there was a crystal clear tube uncoiling up into his nose—the fluid coursing inside it was a disturbingly gastric yellowish brown—and there were a pair of IV drips attached to the arm he could move. His left one. His right arm, it was clear, was in no condition even to scratch an itch that happened to crop up on the skin within half an inch of those fingers.

Spencer was still muzzy with painkillers and dazed by an anesthesia-born hangover. Apparently he wouldn't start hurting like hell for another couple of hours, and so the physicians had recommended that Charlotte and Willow come see him now. His eyes were open, but Charlotte had the distinct sense that he was only vaguely aware of the crowd that gathered around him in his glass-enclosed ICU cubicle. Aunt Sara and Uncle John and Grandmother were sitting somberly on the boxy radiator against the window, while she and Willow and her mom were standing like columns on the side of Uncle Spencer's bed nearest the massive glass wall that faced the nurses' station. Everyone, Charlotte noticed, had their hands at their sides, as if they were afraid they might brush against the metal bars that ran along the mattress like a guardrail.

She wanted to tell her father that she was sorry, but the very idea of apologizing seemed so pathetically meaningless and inadequate that so far she hadn't said a word. She feared she was behaving like a sullen teenager—a term she had heard her seventh-grade history teacher use with great frequency during the previous school year, as if a sullen teenager were the single worst thing in the world a person could become. Still, she couldn't bring herself to speak. She had barely been able to bring herself to inch to this corner so close—so very close—to her father's face and all those bandages and wires and tubes.

No one, in truth, was saying a whole lot. Her mother, her breath such a powerful windstorm of mint that it almost covered up the smell of antiseptics and her father's own sick-person dog breath, had kissed her dad gently on his damp forehead any number of times, but even she had said very little. Apparently she had talked to him a great deal when he was first beginning to surface from his chemical coma, but now she had grown quiet.

Charlotte wondered what would happen if she even tried to open her mouth and apologize, and she guessed there was a pretty good chance she would wind up weeping again. Moreover, there were so many things for which to apologize. At the top of the list, of course, was shooting her dad, even if that had been an accident. But that accident sprang from the fact that she shouldn't have been fooling around with the rifle while her cousin was bringing the diapers up to her aunt and uncle. And so perhaps she should begin by telling Uncle John that she was sorry for taking his gun in the first place. Clearly that had been a bad idea. A **very** bad idea.

Likewise, she could tell her cousin that she was sorry she had ignored her when Willow had asked her to leave the gun alone.

And if she really wanted to make amends, she could apologize to everyone for stealing Gwen's joint and smoking it and for getting herself and her younger cousin both tipsy and stoned.

It was a long list. She had really screwed up this time, no doubt about it. And while she was smart enough to know that a lot of people were going to blame Uncle John for leaving a loaded rifle in the trunk of his car, she was the one who'd smoked the dope, taken the gun, and foolishly fired it at the first thing that moved in the night.

You couldn't fix this disaster. No way.

Nevertheless, she had already started to make vows. She would never smoke pot or drink beer or say a rude word to her parents again. She would wear whatever bathing suit Grandmother wanted. She wouldn't steal her mother's cosmetics, she wouldn't complain about Grandmother's nature hikes. She would weed without complaint whenever—and whatever—her dad desired, and she would stop trying to flirt with older boys.

She would discourage her mother from flirting, too—at least with anyone other than Dad.

She would take pride in her plastic shoes, her canvas belts, her vinyl wallet. She would not dream of her own black leather jacket.

She felt the heat from the sun through the window, despite the chill in the room from the air-conditioning. She guessed they were facing west.

Suddenly her father's eyes turned toward her, and even his head rolled a degree in her direction.

"So," he murmured, and he started to smile. Then, his voice the shallowest of whispers, he rasped, "Guess . . . Annie . . . had it . . . right."

She tried to recall who they both knew named Annie, but could think of no one. Her mother, it was evident, hadn't a clue who he was talking about either.

"Annie?" she asked him simply.

"Oakley," he continued slowly. "You . . . know. You . . . can't . . . get a man . . . with a gun."

She stood motionless for another moment, absorbing his grin. He was referencing a show tune they had sung together for laughs when she'd been a little girl. Then she felt the long quivers deep in her nose that always preceded her tears, and before she knew it she had fallen against her mother's chest—she would have put her head atop her father but she was afraid she would hurt him or break something—and, once again, she was sobbing.

Fourteen

Spencer knew the button that would propel a burst of morphine down the intravenous drip and into his blood was within inches of his left hand, and he needed only to move half an inch on his back and then stretch his fingers and press. But the very idea of that first motion—sliding over barely the width of his pinkie in his bed—filled him with dread. He feared if he did he would feel once again those excruciating spikes of pain that had filled his shut eyes with omegoid bursts of white light, caused his back and shoulders and arms to recall in all too precise detail what it felt like to be pulverized—the bone ground to powder, the muscles and tendons shredded and whisked. He spasmed at the memory, whimpered like a terrified puppy. But he knew he could use some more drugs. As it was, even lying still in the middle of the night, he was in more agony than he had ever endured in his life, and he wanted either a rush of morphine pumped into his system now or a nurse to appear in the dim light in his hospital room with one of those tiny paper cups full of meds.

Moreover, every time his shoulder sent one of those throbbing tendrils of pain through his whole body (even his head, for God's sake: The back of his skull felt like there was a sinus infection festering there the size of a melting glacier), he would surprise himself by groaning aloud. Spencer viewed himself as many things, but a groaner had never been among them.

Occasionally, when he wasn't focused exclusively on how much he hurt—when the pain was merely a Rorschach that elicited other memories—he would think of the lobsters he'd killed and what he presumed was the torture he'd inflicted on them. In theory, if he cleavered the creatures properly and landed the edge of the kitchen hatchet squarely on the straight line along the animal's abdomen and carapace, in an instant the blade would slice through the body and down to the mass of brain and nerve that ran like a string along the inside of the shell, thereby rendering the lobster insensate. Of course, only rarely did he cleaver the lobsters with anything like that sort of surgical exactitude. Most of the time he was simply trying not to get gnashed by a claw that had broken free of its rubber band, and to get the damn thing into the oven so that the waiters—grown men who questioned silently (and, some days, not so silently) why a **kid** was in the kitchen—could get their dinners out to their diners.

And though Spencer did not view his situation now as karmic payback for the lobsters he'd cooked, there were moments (and he wasn't sure whether these would be considered lucid moments or the kinds of increasingly bizarre reveries he had come to call painkiller moments) when he saw his suffering as a reminder (God, he would think then, wouldn't a fucking Post-it note have sufficed?) of the pain that humans inflicted on millions of animals every day.

Then, more times than not, he would focus only on his own agony, and he would grow scared. He wondered if it was actually possible to die of pain, if the body could ever reach a point when it said **Enough!** and just shut down. The nerves grew tired of screaming and begged the guys running the show in the brain to start flipping off the switches that ran the lungs and the heart and everything else that kept this mass of flesh and bone (some of it suddenly gone) breathing. In his stranger painkiller moments, those guys in the brain were retro cartoons of site foremen in a construction zone. They were caricatures with the pencil-thin arms and legs and boxy torsos he recalled from the **Mad** magazines he'd read as a boy, and their hands had so little definition that they looked like they were sheathed in mittens. Then, for brief moments, he would be a boy again in the suburbs of New York City, and he would forget that he had just had a sizable part of his right shoulder pureed by a bullet.

Still, even these fleeting distractions were not without danger. At least one time the mittens on those line drawings in the control room behind his eyes began to look an awful lot to Spencer like . . . pincers. And the very notion that there were people with pincers running the show instantly brought him back to those nights at the Steer by the Shore, and because of his newfound affinity for the crustaceans—deep inside his brain, didn't **he** have pincers, too?—he would feel guilty. And then he would feel a cleaver the length of his body slamming into his own abdomen and chest, crushing the sternum and slicing his body in two.

Once when this happened he passed out. But other times his whimpering grew abruptly into a scream that sounded a lot to the nurses at their station like the word **No!**

Finally his need to be zapped by morphine outstripped his fear of moving the fraction of an inch that it would take to reach the button that would undam the drug in the plastic bag above him, and he prepared himself for the woe that awaited him when he slid his body a hair to his left. He gritted his teeth and was about to do it—really, really do it this time, he was going to make it, he was going to move—when he detected motion in the doorway. The light was changing. Someone was nearing his bed. It was that nice guy with the unruly mustache, the nurse who'd come on duty a couple of hours ago.

"You're awake," the nurse said, and he offered Spencer a smile.

He nodded, but he honestly wasn't sure if he'd spoken.

"Well, this will knock you back out," the nurse said, and he reached for the small dial—a wheel the size of a dime—that seemed to float on a tube that linked one of the intravenous bags to his arm. For the briefest moment Spencer thought that he was about to get what he wanted more than anything else in the world and he might have opened his mouth to say thank you if he hadn't opened his mouth to scream in-

stead—he was no longer merely a groaner, now he was
a screamer, too!—because the nurse was not reaching
for the dial with the fingers on his hand. No, where
there should have been human flesh and a wrist
emerging from his hospital whites there was instead a
lobster's massive, ocean brown crusher claw, and the
nurse was using its sharp-as-shell crushing teeth to
snip the clear tube that linked him with his morphine
and his fluids and everything else that was, apparently,
going to keep him alive.

HE WASN'T SURE whether this was a memory or a
dream, whether he was waking or sleeping, but here he
was now, once again jumping into a half-frozen creek
in Scarsdale as a teenager to rescue a raccoon. The animal had been hit by a vehicle a few moments before
the McCulloughs—his mother and his father and his
sister were in the car with him—passed it, the creature
a quivering lump at the side of the road. Spencer insisted they stop, and he climbed from the car. Not
only was the raccoon still alive, but as soon as he got
within three feet of it, the animal bolted into the thin
strip of snow-dusted bushes and shrubs along the asphalt and slid down the embankment into the icy
creek just below. Spencer slipped down the side of the
hill after it, his parents yelling for him to stop, falling
knee deep into the water and slush and thin skin of
ice. He grabbed the raccoon off the rock on which it
was cowering, wrapped it in his own snow jacket, and
the four McCulloughs drove twenty or twenty-five

miles to the only veterinary hospital in the county that
was open that late on a Saturday afternoon. The doctor lectured him about rabies. He called a Fish and
Wildlife officer. But the raccoon hadn't had rabies, and
in fact had escaped being mashed by a fender or tires
(or both) with a mere broken leg. The creature lived,
and a month later Spencer himself released the animal
back into the woods.

He couldn't have done any of it, he knew with a
dispiriting clarity, with only one hand.

SPENCER WAS A LITTLE better by midmorning
when he was settled in his new hospital room—a **regular** hospital room—and the Torquemada-like torture
of being transported on a gurney was behind him.
Around six thirty, almost at daybreak, they had informed him that there were a couple of bypass surger-
ies occurring that very moment, and within hours
there would be patients who would need his ICU bed
far more than he. Then they had sent him and his IV
drips packing.

Now that the sun was high in the sky, he was no
longer confusing his nightmares with reality. It was
Monday, someone had told him, and he thought back
on his family's visit the day before. He had a vague recollection that he had tried to cheer up his daughter by
saying something silly about **Annie Get Your Gun,**
but he wasn't sure if this, too, had really happened or
whether it had merely been a part of a dream. He
wasn't completely certain what had occurred Saturday

night when he'd wandered through the lupine toward the garden. He knew he'd been shot and that his daughter had pulled the trigger while aiming at what she supposed was a deer. But what he didn't understand was where in the name of God his daughter had gotten a loaded rifle in the first place and what in the name of heaven would lead her to believe that shooting a deer was a good idea. At one point Catherine had started to tell him something (maybe, he decided, she had told him everything), but whatever explanation she had offered had been swallowed up both by painkiller moments and the pain of the injury itself.

He guessed it was approaching ten o'clock (though he didn't dare turn his head to glance at the clock on the table by the bed), and so he figured Catherine and Charlotte would arrive any moment. A nurse—a woman this time who most assuredly did not have a lobster claw for a hand—had told him the surgeon would drop by this morning, too.

He didn't know whether his mother-in-law or John or Sara or Willow would be coming to visit. He understood that he certainly wasn't getting out of here today or tomorrow, and so he decided that what John and Sara did now would offer a barometer of just how serious this bullet wound was. If they went back to work in Vermont—perhaps after a brief visit this morning—that would be an indication that this injury might hurt like hell, but he was out of danger. On the other hand, if they planned on hanging around for a couple of days, then he might still have reason to worry.

About quarter to eleven he got his answer when the entire household arrived. He didn't get to see them all at once, because the nurses on this floor weren't allowing more than two people into the room. He recalled four and five people at a time crowding around him when he'd been in the ICU, and he wondered briefly if he really had been close to death yesterday and the hospital had wanted the whole family to be present—just in case. In any event, now his wife and his daughter were sidling into his room, and the first thing Catherine told him was that everyone was with them at the hospital. His mother-in-law and the Setons were downstairs in either the gift shop or the cafeteria.

She stroked the back of his hand and his good arm, and when she leaned over him he detected peppermint on her breath. There were many small things that he appreciated about Catherine, and one of them was the way her breath always seemed to smell like a candy jar. It never ceased to please him. Even now. He was grateful that they had removed those horrible tubes from his nose when they'd brought him here, and he was no longer having to breathe with a pair of clear prongs up his nostrils.

"What are . . . you girls doing . . . later today?" he asked, carefully enunciating each syllable both because his tongue felt like a large soggy English muffin in his mouth and because the mere act of forming a half-dozen syllables was exhausting. Catherine was standing beside him and Charlotte was sitting, thank God, at a safe distance from the odors—innards and antiseptic and simple sweat—that he presumed were oozing from his body and his wound. She had hopped onto the empty bed.

"I'll be with you, sweetheart. Right here. Maybe Charlotte and Willow will go to the club after lunch. We'll see."

He thought about this and was relieved. The club. Going to the club seemed a clear confirmation that there wasn't a deathwatch going on.

"How are you doing?" Catherine asked.

"I hurt."

"A lot?"

"Oh, yeah."

"Has the surgeon been here yet?"

"No."

He heard Catherine sigh.

"Vacation," he said. "It's our . . . vacation. So . . . sorry."

"Oh, God, you have nothing to apologize for," Catherine said, and she smiled down at him like one of those wondrous seraphs on the borders of the Christmas card the family received every year from a Unitarian minister in Connecticut who was also an animal rights activist: The borders had deer and sheep along with angels with great, dark doe eyes, and eyebrows—angels and animals alike, actually—that were raised in adoration, tenderness, and love. For a split second he forgot that his right arm was immobilized and he attempted to reach for her hand. He didn't get far. His arm didn't move, and the mere act of even trying caused him to squeeze shut his eyes and cry out in pain. A moment later when he could open his eyes—

when they were no longer being dazzled by the phantasmagoric light show on the insides of his lids—he detected movement behind his wife. His daughter was jumping off that other bed and running from the room. He heard a choking sob from the corridor and the sound of her struggling to breathe as she wept.

"I'VE NEVER SEEN HER like this," Catherine said, once more rubbing his unhurt forearm softly.

He wondered if he was actually in the midst of yet another waking dream. Probably not. Everything seemed to have the concrete tangibility he associated with full consciousness: soft pillow, firm mattress, solid aluminum rails. Certainly his daughter's inconsolable cries in the hallway sounded pretty damn authentic.

"Catherine?"

Her gaze moved from the window to his face. She arched her eyebrows and smiled for him. "Yes?"

"Gun . . . where she get . . . it?"

"It can wait, sweetheart. It can wait."

"No." How could it wait when it sounded like Charlotte's heart was breaking? As much as he hurt, as disabled as he was, he felt a tide of anger cascading up from deep inside him: a father's righteous rage. He wanted to know who'd given his daughter a rifle, and—here was a word he hadn't thought of in years, a word he guessed the painkillers had helped him to retrieve—**smite** him. Smite him into the ground.

"Oh, Spencer—"

"Charlotte . . . listen to her."

"I have. I have for two days." Now she sounded like she might cry, too. Her small smile faded as she glanced at the door. He sensed how desperately she wanted to be in two places at once. With Charlotte. With him.

"Then . . . tell me. Who?"

"Spencer—"

"Please."

"My brother," she answered finally, her voice muted and tired. A leaf on a languid breeze in November.

"John?"

"He's the only brother I have." She brushed an unruly wisp of hair behind his ear. "He left the gun in the trunk of his car. That's where Charlotte got it. But she had no idea it was loaded. She and Willow discovered it when they were getting Patrick more diapers on Saturday night."

His mind could barely process this notion, and his anger was swamped by incredulity: John Seton with a loaded rifle in the trunk of his Volvo. Was it possible it was there because one of his clients—that endless, frightening parade of alcoholics and thugs and drug dealers—was angry at him? Did John feel the need to protect himself? But if that were the case, wouldn't he use a handgun? Besides, what good would a rifle do John if he kept it stowed in the trunk of his car?

"Why?"

"Why was it loaded?"

"Why was . . . it . . . there?"

"My brother is a deer hunter. Was, I guess. I believe he's done now."

He noticed the light by the side of his bed was changing again, not unlike the way it had in the middle of the night: There was a shadow there now. It was his daughter—their daughter—returning from the hallway. Her cheeks glistened with moisture and he wanted more than anything to reach out and pull her to him. But he couldn't. She wiped her nose with the back of her hand and tried to smile. Then she nuzzled pathetically against her mother, her shoulders lurching up with one final sob.

CHARLOTTE WASN'T SURE where she'd first learned about cutting—a movie, a Web site, a conversation between older girls she'd overheard—but she did know that the word had come to her today in the hospital elevator. A doctor had used it, though clearly not in the context she had in mind. Mutilation.

When she'd been a toddler, apparently, she would sometimes send herself to the timeout chair after she had misbehaved. She had no memory of doing this, but her parents sometimes joked about it. **Of all the things to outgrow, why did she have to stop disciplining herself in so adorable a fashion?**

Well, she thought now, perhaps I didn't. Perhaps I just . . . evolved.

It was night and so she pulled down the shade in the bathroom window in case someone was out walk-

ing. Maybe Grandmother bringing in the dog. Maybe
her mother or her uncle pacing. Talking about her father. About her. Then she got out the Band-Aids and
the Bactine—the key was to cut yourself, not give
yourself tetanus or some gross infection—and those
old-fashioned razor blades she found in Grandmother's medicine chest. She pulled her nightgown
above her waist on the toilet, the lid cold even through
her cotton underwear, and spread her legs. She stared
for a long moment at the line of her tan, at the down
bleached almost white by the sun.

This was going to be more complicated than she
thought, because she had to do this in a spot that no
one could see—such as the insides of her thighs. But
Grandmother would continue dragging her to the
club or Echo Lake as her dad convalesced, which
meant she was going to have to wear a bathing suit.
This ruled out her legs. Quickly she pulled off her un-
derpants and stared at the patch of dark pubic hair and
at the outline of her pelvic bone. There wasn't room
there, either, she realized.

Her stomach, however, was another story. If she
wore only her Speedo tank suit for the rest of the summer, instead of her bikini, she could slice up her belly
as much as she wanted and no one ever would know.

With the hem of her nightgown in her teeth, she
stared for a long moment at the skin around her navel.
Then she sprayed some Bactine in a line just beside it
and pressed the razor against her flesh with her thumb.
She was crying, though not from pain. She would
have to saw or slice at the skin—or press much

harder—to feel pain. She guessed she was crying yet again because of what she had done, and how she was reduced by it to . . . to this. Well, she deserved it, didn't she? She pushed the edge deeper into her lower abdomen and then twisted her fingers. Reflexively she yelped, as a tiny red filigree the length of the blade filled quickly with blood. For a long moment she watched it bleed—the raspberry fluid dribbled down her hip and into the crevice between her legs, some getting caught in the thatch of curling hair there—and then abruptly she stood up on her toes and leaned over the sink.

"Charlotte?" It was Willow on the other side of the door. "You okay?"

"Fine," she answered, aware that her voice sounded strange and loud. "I banged my shin on the bathtub," she lied. Quickly she doused a tissue in cold tap water and pressed it against the cut. Almost instantly the paper grew red.

"Do you want some ice?"

"No. I'm okay."

When her cousin had retreated, she sat back down on the toilet seat. She realized that she felt as lousy as she had before she had carved a delicate little gash into her stomach, and she took some comfort in this. Mutilation might help some girls, but clearly it wasn't going to help her. She might be screwed up, but at least she wasn't about to become the Queen of the Band-Aids. She wiped her eyes and applied two of the adhesive bandages across the wound. Then she flushed the razor blade down the toilet.

Fifteen

Dominique Germaine had her doubts about a lawsuit Monday morning, but she wanted to hear more. She liked suing big organizations. In her tenure FERAL had sued dairy councils, meat packers, and public school systems that hung posters encouraging children to drink their milk; they had taken legal action against circuses and aquariums and a marine science museum; they had sued the U.S. Department of Agriculture to make sure that rats, mice, and birds would be afforded protection in the Animal Welfare Act, and then (just for good measure) they had sued the cosmetics companies, the drug companies, and a couple of shoe companies, too. It astonished her that it had never crossed her mind to have her group sue a gun maker or find someone with a reason—real or imagined—to sue one: After all, she loathed hunting. In this day and age it seemed to Dominique to be an anachronism that was at once barbaric and cruel. And it certainly wasn't a sport, since **sport** implied a competition of sorts, the certainty—or, at least, the likelihood—that each side had a fighting chance. Obviously no mallard or deer had a fighting chance against a human with a rifle. No elephant had any prospect of "winning" against a hunter armed with a

Holland & Holland .500 Nitro or one of those legal monstrosities that fired armor-piercing shells into the creatures. A lawsuit was an intriguing idea, regardless of whether Spencer McCullough had a prayer in hell of receiving a penny in compensation—in or out of court—because of the way FERAL could use the family's lawsuit to shed light on the mind-numbingly violent culture that surrounded guns and hunting and . . . **deer camp**.

The very term gave Dominique the shivers. She had grown up in Montreal and known children whose families owned hunting shacks in the province's eastern lakes region or in upstate New York, and so she had a pretty good idea of the way the men fell back innumerable steps on the evolutionary ladder when they were there. She doubted that they even continued to walk upright after a day or two of eating half-cooked doe meat (yes, she knew they illegally killed does the first day; it was a tradition with many hunting families).

Here before her now, some two and a half hours after he had first broached the idea of a lawsuit, was her deputy director and the organization's general counsel. Keenan Barrett was a tall and elegant southerner with a red cob for a nose, eyes the color of cornflowers in bloom, and a great shock of white hair he kept slicked back with Brylcreem. He was probably pushing sixty, and outwardly he had the demeanor of a good-natured but slightly ponderous headmaster for a private school long past its prime. It was only after he'd spoken for a few minutes and methodically slogged his way to his point that you got a sense of how sharp he really was—which was part of the reason why he had driven John Seton into such a fury on the phone Sunday morning. He tended to still his adversaries, lulling them so they let down their guards or giving them the impression that he was nothing more than a gracious old windbag. Then he would pounce. Dominique had seen him do this in meetings with Revlon and Gillette and a Quebecois fur company, first causing the eyes of the corporate denizens across the table to glaze during his courtly preambles and then causing their blood pressures to climb like Nepalese trekkers when abruptly he put FERAL's findings or demands (or both) on the table. He was patient as well as intelligent, and as a result he got things done. When Dominique was around him she always felt like a teenage girl who had an ill-advised crush on an older friend of the family.

He sat down in one of the four modern swivel chairs that surrounded the circular table she used for small conferences, and she emerged from behind her own desk to join him. Her office wasn't huge—they were a nonprofit—but it was far from shabby. It looked out on the northern entrance to the Empire State Building. On two walls there were abstract paintings of tropical birds she had found in a Miami gallery, all of which looked like vaguely erotic flowers, and the polished hardwood floor was the silky color of soy milk. If the room struck some journalists and visitors as a trifle tacky, it was usually because in her desire to make certain there were no animal-based or animal-enhanced products in her sight, there was a lot of hemp on the couch and the chairs, and the coffee table, the credenza, and the desk were made from postconsumer recycled paper. It was actually pretty expensive stuff, but it looked like you wouldn't dare put anything heavier than a paper cup of coffee or a yellow legal pad atop any of it.

"You know," Keenan began in his soft, patient voice, "there are myriad reasons why it is just so difficult to be a parent these days. A good parent, that is. My sense is that our friend, Spencer, is going to have a lot of conversations with young Charlotte over the next couple of months that can only be called intense. Same with this John Seton fellow and his little girl. Those conversations will be rather different in nature, as you can imagine, but they will share a certain umbrella reality that may have a good deal to do with what those families read about this story in the newspapers or happen to catch on the nightly news. My guess is that although it's unlikely we'll ever see anything that happened up in New Hampshire go to trial, we may be able to turn what I thought was going to be a public relations nightmare to our advantage."

"I don't think Spencer and Charlotte have intense conversations about anything. Spencer saves his intensity for us."

"Maybe you're right. Maybe Catherine and Charlotte will have to have the hard talks."

"Actually, I find it rather encouraging that you believe a gun manufacturer might even consider settling," she said. "I figured this was all, I don't know, nuisance material. Frivolous. After all, even if there is some tiny defect with the rifle, the man left it sitting around since last November with a bullet inside it. And we still don't know whether there was a flaw or if this brother-in-law is just an imbecile. Besides, the child shouldn't have been playing with the weapon. It's pretty obvious that if you pull the trigger on a gun, there's a chance that someone's going to get hurt. Wouldn't this be like suing a knife company because you cut yourself on the blade?"

"Oh, we can muddy things up a bit. Spencer's lawyers, that is. Especially if the extractor was defective. Then he's in pretty fine shape, though there won't be a doubt in anyone's mind that his brother-in-law should have gotten the darn thing taken care of last year. But even if the extractor doesn't have some little ding somewhere, Spencer's lawyers would have a shot. Pun intended. It comes down to the nature of most gun chambers and magazines. I had my assistant do a little research online this morning—intellectual curiosity, more than anything. I wanted to see the general shape of product liability with guns, and whether ol' Spencer would have a chance of getting his bad wing in front of a jury. Then I took a walk over to that sporting goods store by Madison Square Garden and looked at the hunting rifles."

"And?"

"Seems to me a lawyer could argue a couple of things. A strict product liability suit: the gun folks have been placing a dangerously defective product in the stream of commerce—"

"The girl fired the gun and it went off. Where's the defect?"

"It goes back to how you unload the weapon. Even after you empty all the bullets from the magazine, there is still one in the chamber. Can you imagine? You have to remove that one separately, using the bolt of the weapon. Now, someone could contend that's a design flaw. All you'd need is one expert—or, if we were very, very lucky, one seriously disgruntled ex-employee—who was willing to suggest that no one at the company ever bothered to link the magazine and the chamber more efficiently because it would cost too much."

"Don't most hunters know that?"

"About the bullet in the chamber? I expect so. But things happen. People forget. This is a route you might go if Spencer's gun experts don't find anything wrong with his actual weapon. If they can't claim his particular gun was uniquely defective, then—what the hell?—you take on the whole damn Adirondack thirty-ought-six. You argue that the magazine and the chamber should be able to be unloaded simultane-ously—or that there should be some sort of indication when there's a bullet in the chamber. A light, maybe, or a flag. Perhaps we contend that the weapon needed to be childproof—have a more secure safety device."

"And it's conceivable that the gun company might settle?"

"Gun companies—Adirondack, Winchester, Browning—have insurance for exactly this sort of thing. It's a cost of doing business."

"What if Spencer refuses?"

"To settle?"

"Uh-huh." Dominique was aware that she sounded hopeful. She could already imagine the publicity that would surround a trial.

Keenan wrote with a fountain pen, and for a long moment he seemed to be staring at the budlike gold nib as he formulated his answer in his mind. His fingers were elegant: not effeminate but as long and slender as a pianist's, and each nail was an immaculate seashell pink box with four rounded corners. He had, Dominique thought, the perfect hands for a fountain pen. Finally he answered her. "It goes to court in three or four years," he said, "and then Spencer wins or loses. Who can say? It would depend upon his experts—and theirs. And if Spencer's little girl is sufficiently telegenic, and if Spencer doesn't look downright evil to the jury—"

"Spencer, evil? I can think of many words to describe Spencer, but **evil** isn't exactly top of the list."

"Evil either because he looks like someone trying to recoup from an injury caused by his own daughter—that can certainly put off a jury—or evil because he works for us. Obviously we've never done anything as outrageous as, say, the Animal Freedom Front, but we've irritated our share of folks in this world who believe our opinions are a tad extreme. Who knows?

Maybe we'll get some doctor or scientist from that medical school on the jury—someone who still hasn't forgiven FERAL for getting their research labs shut down a couple years back."

"They were giving cats AIDS and crystal meth—and then killing them."

He shrugged. "And we might be surprised if somehow we could prevent his brother-in-law from coming across as a moron of Herculean proportions. After all, we'd have an attractive, remorseful teenage girl—Charlotte is what now, twelve?—whom we can portray as desperately traumatized by what happened and a small-town lawyer from Vermont. They might look pretty good to a jury."

"And even if the manufacturer does eventually settle, we still get three or four years' worth of media coverage, right?"

"Probably not that long," he answered. "At some point the judge puts us all under a gag order. Or they settle quickly to make this whole incident go away."

Dominique thought about this and wondered suddenly if Spencer might actually need a windfall settlement. She didn't think so: He came from some money, and Catherine was absolutely loaded. His mother-in-law lived in some massive Park Avenue apartment, and the Setons owned that baronial place on a hill up in the White Mountains. She'd seen Spencer's pictures. And it wasn't as if this injury—even if the poor guy did lose his right arm—was going to affect his ability to do his job. It wasn't like you needed two hands to rewrite an assistant's news release or plan a press conference or make catty comments about bunny-tested eyeliner on TV talk shows.

Besides, that was the McCullough family's decision to make, not hers. Her only responsibility was to FERAL. For all she knew, nothing would come of this, anyway. But she decided that she liked the notion of a lawsuit against a gun manufacturer. She liked it very much.

"It's too bad you can't be Spencer's lawyer," she said.

"Oh, product liability isn't exactly my specialty. But obviously I'd be happy to work with the right person."

"You know who that might be?"

"I'd recommend Paige Sutherland."

"I like Paige."

"Course you do," he said, and he slipped the cap back on his fountain pen. "Want me to call her?"

"And Spencer."

He raised his eyebrows mischievously. "Yes. We can't forget to tell Spencer."

"No."

"I'll call him right now," Barrett said. "Besides, I want someone to photograph his shoulder in the next day or two—before it gets any better."

"I don't believe there's much chance of that."

"Pardon me. Before it outwardly begins to look less repulsive. We want images that show Spencer at his absolute worst."

For a moment she tried to envision what the wound must look like and the sort of agony her communications director was probably enduring, but her mind kept offering images instead of the deer she had seen in the countryside beyond Montreal—upstate New York, the Laurentians—the animals shot and disemboweled and left hanging on the families' front porches. She wanted to be sympathetic to people, too, but the truth was that she just didn't have it in her.

Sixteen

Late Tuesday afternoon, while a photographer was taking pictures of her uncle Spencer in the hospital in Hanover, Willow Seton saw her first urinal. Urinals, actually. There were two of them in the men's room in the clubhouse at the Contour Club. She was showing them to Charlotte—seeing them for herself—because this pair had a unique adornment all the grown-ups knew about but the women (at least) never discussed and because this was the most gloriously anarchic activity she could think of at the moment to take her cousin's mind off her father. Since they'd arrived at the club her cousin had done nothing but continue to wallow in remorse. She'd sat, almost unmoving, in one of the big wrought-iron chairs that faced Mount Lafayette, and she hadn't even bothered to change into her tennis shorts or her gleefully inappropriate string bikini. She wasn't sobbing anymore, but she wasn't talking, either. She was, in fact, barely moving.

Now Willow had her up and about. This wasn't the sort of athletic, good-for-you activity in which her family usually indulged here at the club, but at least it was something. A project. She gestured for Charlotte to wait just outside the wood-paneled door with the

silhouette of a male golfer in knickers, while she slith-
ered in first to make absolutely certain it was empty.
Willow didn't believe there was a man in there because
she had been hovering in the pro shop for close to ten
minutes, carefully staking out the door. But she
thought she should check—just in case. Charlotte was
in no condition to be yelled at.

"Coast is clear," she said, once she had confirmed
that the room was empty. She had emerged partway
from the doorway and glanced quickly out the club
room's picture windows to make sure that her grandmother was still on the practice putting green and her
own mother was still reading a magazine with Patrick
beside her in his baby chair.

The girls had heard about these urinals and their
exceptional artwork—pictures, paintings, or photographs, no one would say—at the bonfire on Saturday
night. Willow had never before had any desire to see a
urinal because until then she hadn't even known such
a thing existed. In the last five or six years, whenever
she had traveled anywhere alone with her father and
needed to go to the bathroom—in shopping malls, in
airports—he had sent her into the ladies' room alone
and stood guard outside the door. Even when she'd
been three years old she was pretty sure that she had
been using the ladies' rooms (though in those days, ev-
idently, her father had ventured into the refuge with
her, standing beside the mirrors and the sinks as her
sentinel against abduction). She'd actually had to ask
Charlotte precisely what one was, and when her
cousin had described their design to her that evening

she wasn't sure whether the notion astonished her more because it meant going to the bathroom with nothing but air between you and the person beside you or whether it was the freedom to go to the bathroom so casually. With such remarkable ease. Now that young Patrick was in her life she saw a penis with frequency, and its advantages—at least when it came to urinating—were apparent.

No, she decided finally, it was the immodesty that fascinated her more than anything. It was the complete lack of reserve.

"You coming?" she asked Charlotte, and the older girl nodded. She liked this reversal of roles. And so with one last glimpse around her to make sure no adults were nearby, she drew her cousin with her into the men's room, scooted past the corner wall into the bathroom area itself, and saw before her the urinals. There they were, mounted against the far wall, the two of them surrounded by a delft blue tile that looked more interesting or impressive than the pink tile that adorned the ladies' room. Still, the urinals themselves were disappointing: She saw nothing that resembled artwork, no glorious beautification, no flourishes that might elevate them beyond their purpose.

She looked at Charlotte and saw the girl was nodding, a tiny smirk at the edges of her lips. Her arms were folded across her chest, as if she were trying to understand a painting at one of the grand museums across the park from her apartment in the city.

"A guy from Franconia College did it years ago," Charlotte said finally, her voice even now a tad shaky.

"One of those hippie guys who went to the school before it closed."

Willow had gotten the sense from her parents that **everyone** who went to Franconia College before it closed was a hippie guy—or girl.

"You know the painter. We both do," her cousin continued. "He's the man with that Rip Van Winkle beard in the bookstore in Littleton." Willow nodded. She knew exactly whom Charlotte was talking about. Every other day Grandmother took them to the nearby town of Littleton on errands of one sort or another, and inevitably they went to the bookstore. Willow guessed she knew it as well as any of the bookstores near her home in Vermont. There was a fellow who worked there in his late fifties, and he had a bushy beard the color of cigarette ash that fell to the middle of his chest. He was a quiet guy, but when you asked him a question about a book he knew exactly where in the store to find it, and whenever he recommended a novel to Willow there was a very good chance she would like it.

She glanced back at the urinals, wondering exactly what she was missing—what the fellow had painted. She could tell the urinals were made of the same kind of porcelain as a regular toilet, and she'd never before thought about whether a toilet actually had to be painted. Individually painted, that is. The notion crossed her mind that perhaps urinals weren't usually white. Maybe they were some other color. Something that made them even more repulsive than they already were.

No, that wasn't possible. They couldn't be more repulsive.

"Did you think the bugs were real?" Charlotte was asking. "I did when I first saw them."

"Bugs?"

"The flies!"

She turned back to the urinals and understood for the first time what those black smudges were that hung slightly below the midpoint of each smooth-hollowed porcelain wall. They were so perfectly centered that she'd presumed they were merely a manufacturing logo of some sort. She took a step closer, and then another. Sure enough, the black marks were flies—rendered, she saw now, with the exactitude of a naturalist, right down to the tiny hairs on the bugs' legs and the intricate lacework on the insects' wings—one on each urinal.

"Why a fly?" she asked Charlotte. "Do you know?"

"Uh-huh. Aim."

"Aim?"

"Aim. Some people at the club wanted to keep the men's room a little cleaner and they figured out that all men—even my dad, I guess—are hunters at heart."

Willow looked down at the ground around the urinals and then at the walls beside them. Some men, she knew, were better hunters than others, and suddenly she was desperately glad that she was wearing her sandals.

JOHN WAS UNSURE if he was pleased that he was about to be alone with Spencer for the first time since the accident. The photographer was finishing up now, and Catherine was taking a short walk in Hanover to clear her head. Hours earlier his mother and Sara had brought the three children back to Sugar Hill . . . or, if he knew Mother, back to the Contour Club. Just because her son-in-law had just had half his shoulder blown away was no reason that she and the two girls couldn't grab a quick swim or sneak in a brief golf or bridge lesson. By now, he guessed, his mother was on the practice putting green or the driving range, and the girls were doing something equally as wholesome and lively.

There was a lot that John felt he had to say to Spencer, most of it apologetic and self-flagellating, though he did want to discuss as well FERAL's plan that he turn a lawsuit against the gun manufacturer into a public spectacle.

Once the photographer had packed his camera bag and left, John sat down on the empty bed across from his brother-in-law and said, "You must be exhausted. That looked excruciating." The photographer had taken some shots with film and some with a digital camera, and twice he had insisted on showing John in the viewfinder the image of his brother-in-law's shoulder that he was preserving for the lawyer—a woman from New York City named Paige. Paige was flying to New Hampshire first thing Wednesday morning, along with that pompous attorney from FERAL. Keenan Barrett.

"Excruciating is . . . 'bout right," Spencer said quietly. The nurse had replaced his bandages and the splint that held his arm flat against his chest. It had been evident that despite the painkillers, the process had been almost unbearable.

"So," John began, deciding now was as good a time as any to ask the question that was standing in the room with them like an uninvited and slightly malodorous third person, "how angry are you?"

Spencer considered his response for a moment before answering vaguely, "Don't know."

"But you know how sorry I am, right? How desperately and sincerely—"

"You're . . . sorry. I know that."

"You have every right to be angry."

Spencer swallowed and then gave him the tiniest of nods in agreement. John had noticed in the course of the day that Spencer was not merely speaking softly, he was answering in as few words as possible (and sometimes with no words), as if even the act of speaking was at once painful and exhausting.

"May I ask you another question? Are you angry because—"

"Just angry, 'kay? I am . . . just . . . angry."

"Because I hunt."

"Yes."

"Because I left a bullet in the gun."

"Yes."

"Because—"

"Because I may . . . be . . . crippled. That seems reason . . . enough." It was the longest response he had heard from Spencer all afternoon, and the length—as well as the wheezy rasp—caught John off guard.

"They don't know that for sure," he murmured, and he feared he sounded blindly—illogically—optimistic.

Spencer rolled his eyes and then grimaced. "When did you start?"

"Hunting? Last fall. I got interested in the summer, around the time we got Sara's amnio results and we realized we were going to have a little boy. A son. I've known lots of people in Vermont who hunt, of course, and I guess I'd always been intrigued. And so I took a course and some lessons—"

"Not enough . . ."

John sighed, knowing there was nothing he could (or should) say in his defense.

"No. Apparently not. Anyway, I took lessons and I took the safety course and before I knew it, I was"— and he felt himself shrugging, as if he were commenting on a subject as innocuous as which necktie he had worn to work—"hunting."

"You kill something?"

"No. Not yet. Never, now."

Spencer breathed in and out through his nose. It sounded a bit like a small plastic whistle.

"When you feel a little better—and only when you feel better—let's talk about FERAL, okay? About what they want you to do."

"I don't think so."

"You don't think so?"

"When it comes to . . . to that, we should talk . . . through lawyers."

"God, Spencer, you know how sorry I am, don't you? I am—"

"Go. Please."

"You want me to leave?"

"Yes. Thank you."

"Look: I went hunting a couple times last November. I was one guy with one gun. I'm sorry about that. But it's not like I was electrocuting minks or sending the ham hogs up the chute at Tar Heel. I'm—"

"John: Not now . . . okay?"

"Okay," he agreed, stunned, and he stood. There was so much he wanted to explain to his brother-in-law—about why he hunted, what he had once (though no longer) hoped the sport someday might give to him and to his son. He wanted to explain to Spencer what was really in store for him—and, alas, for his daughter—if he made a public circus of a lawsuit against Adirondack. It would be more than just depositions and investigations. There would be thinly veiled threats. His daughter in news stories on television, in print, on the Web. He himself defined solely in terms of his disability. The media coverage might serve FERAL's agenda well, but it certainly wouldn't make his family's life any easier.

And did he want to risk seeing his wife's brother drawn into the suit by the gun company? That, too, was a possibility, depending upon the state in which they brought the action. The legal wording was "contribution among joint tortfeasors," but in lay terms it simply meant that the gun company might drag him into this disaster as a codefendant.

Currently the rifle was with the New Hampshire State Police. Assuming that the state's attorney decided not to file criminal charges (and John desperately reassured himself that no New Hampshire "live free or die" prosecutor, even if he were the sort of unforgiving Draconian sociopath he'd dealt with on occasion in Vermont, would charge either him or his niece with a crime), Spencer's lawyers would want it. And, he knew, he would give it to them before they subpoenaed it, because this was Spencer they were talking about. Then his brother-in-law's lawyers would have the rifle examined by experts of their own in a laboratory somewhere—probably that one in Maryland—and he would know once and for all just how incompetent he was.

Or, to be precise, just how incompetent he would be made to appear to the world.

Still, it wasn't the fact that he was about to leave without having discussed the lawsuit that most distressed John: It was that he had asked Spencer, his brother-in-law and his friend, if he had known he was sorry, and the experience had proven completely unsatisfactory. He understood now that he wanted to fall on his knees on the hospital room floor and actually beg his brother-in-law's forgiveness. He wanted, he realized, to weep. But he wasn't the sort of man who cried—at least in front of other people—and Spencer wasn't the type of man who would want to see such a spectacle. Nevertheless, he desired nothing more in the world right now than the chance to go back in time to Saturday afternoon and remove his rifle from the trunk of the Volvo. He would get that bullet out of the chamber—to think he could have fired the gun into the sky all along!—and then he would bury the weapon as deep in the fields of lupine as he could. He never wanted to touch a rifle again or venture into the woods with a gun. His brief excursion into the great northern forest as a hunter was over.

Spencer, he saw, had turned his eyes toward the window and was still waiting for him to leave. And so he did. He mumbled that he'd be back in the morning, and then he left. It was only when he was in the hallway that he realized he couldn't go home yet—he couldn't, in fact, go home for hours—because he had to drive his sister back to Sugar Hill. He couldn't leave until she was ready. Until she had said good-bye to Spencer for the night. And so he sat alone in one of the chairs with the carrot-colored vinyl that squeaked near the nurses' station on Spencer's floor and rested his head in his hands.

SARA LAID PATRICK on the towel in the grass in the shade and pulled off the zippered bodysuit he was wearing so she could change his small diaper. Once it was off—the outfit had a large patch of an ostensibly playful-looking automobile to the left side of the zipper, with wheels that resembled eyes—she contemplated her son's tiny shoulders. As if he were a doll, she gently lifted his right arm like a lever, then spun it slowly in its socket. The baby cooed and smiled up at her. She smiled back. She didn't want to pull Patrick's arm over his head and replicate the movement he would make someday soon when he threw a cereal bowl onto the floor for the first time or heaved Drool Monkey from his bed, because she was afraid she might hurt him. But she saw the exact movement in her mind: She saw the shoulder moving under a shirt, the denim strap from a pair of overalls rising up off the cotton just below it. She saw those petite fingers coming forward with a whoosh.

She couldn't imagine her brother-in-law, Spencer, not striving to be—and here was that word again, as much an adjective as a family moniker—**vigorous.** A part of that small but oh-so-vigorous Seton tribe. He was disabled now, that was a given, but she doubted that his physical therapists would ever understand that among the greatest handicaps confronting poor Spencer would be his inability simply to hang around with Catherine and John and, yes, Nan on their level: the level of people in perpetual motion, people who are constantly busy so they never have time to reflect on . . .

On anything.

At least when they were in New Hampshire.

Sometimes she wondered what demons lived with them here that drove them to the golf course and the tennis court, the bridge table and the vegetable garden. To cocktail parties at the Contour Club, to nature walks up and down Sugar Hill. Nan was a particular mystery to her. Exactly what was it that she didn't want to think about? Nan was, apparently, somewhat better when she was home in Manhattan, but even there, Sara knew, she was always relentlessly busy—and she always had been.

Over the years John had revealed to her much of his childhood, but other than the death of his father at a relatively—though not horrifically—young age, there was little there that seemed likely to scar either him or his sister or their mother. Unlike so many other Manhattan childhoods (or marriages) of the era, there wasn't any boozing or drugs (at least not to bacchanalian excess), there didn't seem to be any adultery. Obviously there was no wrenching divorce. It was actually a life so full of privilege and entitlement it was uneventful.

No, not uneventful. Sara knew that behind its locked front door no home was routine. Not the house of her childhood, not the apartment of her husband's, not the world they were building together with Willow and Patrick. All households had their mysteries, their particular forms of dysfunction. She knew that John was going to suffer profoundly over what he had done to Spencer, and his anguish would transcend normal guilt in large measure because it was his own daughter who had first reached Spencer's body out there by the snow peas. John's father had been so completely irrelevant to his own childhood that he was intent on being a dad who was both present and perfect, and the fact that Willow had seen the grisly ramifications of the most egregious mistake he would ever make in his life was going to cause him serious pain.

She remembered one time John offered her a partial litany of all the moments in his life that mattered to him that his own father had missed, either because he was at work or because he was dead (the former, in John's opinion, leading directly to the latter). There was the Saturday morning when he was eight when the county swim team time trials were actually held in the Contour Club pool, a grand morning in which he placed first in the twenty-five meter crawl, first in the twenty-five meter backstroke, and was a part of the second-place one-hundred-meter medley relay team. There was his fourth-grade transition ceremony from Cub Scouts to Webelos and the tie racks the boys had made from plywood and coated with oil paint for their fathers, all of whom were present to accept the gifts that June evening . . . but one. There was the eighth-grade citywide debate competition in which his school's team won a variety of prizes for both eloquence and good-natured feistiness. There were all the birthday parties that did not occur on either a Saturday or a Sunday, there was the first half of his high school commencement (thank God the family name began with an **S**), as well as the only high school musical in which he actually had a part with a solo and lines. And though John's father was present for his son's college graduation, he missed John's induction into the Phi Beta Kappa society the day before. Richard died months after John started law school and so he had a valid excuse for missing the moments when his son received his law degree, got married, and became a father for the first time himself. But that

didn't mean that on some level John wasn't bitter—
and determined to do better with his own children.

Except, strangely enough, when he was here in
Sugar Hill.

Here it was more important to be vigorous in the
eyes of his mother—and, yes, in his own eyes when he
shaved or combed his thinning hair in the mirror—
than to spend serious time with Willow or Patrick.
That man who had spent all Friday morning rolling
around on their living room floor with his son while
she'd packed had barely seen the boy since they'd arrived—and that was true even before their lives had
been thrown into turmoil on Saturday night. That father who once took three planes home from a conference in Minneapolis after his original flight was
canceled and then ran like a madman between terminals D and B at Logan Airport—terminals usually
linked only by shuttle buses—so he could sprint onto
a plane to Vermont that was going to give him at least
a fighting chance (if he sped all the way home once he
landed) of arriving in time to witness his daughter's
transition ceremony from Daisy to Brownie, didn't say
more than a few dozen words to the girl on Friday and
Saturday. (And, Sara feared, most of those words involved appeals to Willow to try to pacify Patrick—as
well as, of course, that now infamous request on
Saturday night that she bring into the house the new
block of diapers from the trunk of the car.)

She pressed the Velcro tabs on the corners of
Patrick's fresh diaper together and left him on the
towel—blowing him a kiss and reassuring him that

she would be right back—and started toward the green garbage can against the side wall of the clubhouse with the dirty one. As she walked, she watched her free arm sway with her body. It was a good thing that Catherine and Spencer didn't seem likely to have another child, because there was no way that Spencer would ever be able to change a diaper. It was one of the many tasks that Sara was beginning to realize were completely unmanageable with one hand.

She guessed Spencer's energy would be a real asset to him now. That quintessential drive to be hale and hearty and strong. His nostril-flaring frustration at being disabled would help him with the tortures of physical therapy—though it would also, alas, make the indignities of having to have someone else button his shirts and zip up his fly yet more irksome.

At the garbage can she heard the chirping of girls through a glazed window into the clubhouse. The window was open only an inch or two, but the children were giggling and she knew instantly that the voices belonged to Willow and Charlotte. She took a step back and gazed at the building. She'd always presumed it was the clubhouse men's room that was against this wall and that the casement before her was therefore one of the windows into the men's room. For a moment she decided she must have been mistaken all those years, and this was actually the ladies' room. After all, why in heaven would the children be in the men's room? Then she knew. The flies. They were drawn into the men's room by the flies that hippie bookseller had painted years ago on the urinals.

Somehow Willow and Charlotte had heard about the bugs and they had to see them for themselves.

She considered going into the clubhouse to extricate the cousins from the men's room since it was only a matter of time before someone (no doubt, someone cranky) walked in and discovered them, but she had an idea she liked more. The last thing either child needed right now was to be chastised. And so she crouched just below the windowsill, took a deep breath, and proceeded to buzz. She placed her tongue just behind her front teeth and tried her very best to imitate the loud, annoying drone of the insect.

Instantly the girls went silent. And barely ten or fifteen seconds after that, Sara saw them racing around the side of the clubhouse toward her, their eyes wide, determined to catch the culprit who had sent them scurrying from the two urinals with their meticulous renderings of a pair of black flies. It was, as far as Sara knew, the first time her niece had run playfully—a spontaneous smile on her face—in almost three days.

Seventeen

Catherine never viewed herself as the sort of girl—
now woman—who thought she could smother
her troubles beneath frozen moguls of ice cream or
half-thawed clubs of freezer-case cookie dough. There
was the secret meat thing, of course, but she presumed
this had more to do with the body's natural desire for
animal protein than an attempt to overpower her anx-
ieties with junk food.

Nevertheless, Wednesday afternoon as she sat
around the table in the bar at the Hanover Inn with
these two lawyers from New York, she realized she
wanted nothing more right now than a cheeseburger.
No, make it a hamburger. Screw the cheese. Make it
meat and nothing but meat. Like the burger she'd had
at the fast-food restaurant on Sunday afternoon, but
bigger. Thicker. Juicier. She guessed this was because
she was scared. She had no idea anymore what sort of
future awaited her or just how debilitating Spencer's
injury would be. Every time she tried to get even the
smallest glimmer of hope from the surgeons or these
lawyers, however, they were cruelly adamant in their
prognoses. Her husband was going to be severely disabled, and he was going to find his "floppy arm" so annoying and unattractive (they kept talking about the

way the muscles would shrink from disuse) that he might choose to have it amputated in two or three years. Apparently, most people with this sort of injury chose exactly that path.

She had begun to wonder if she would even be in the classroom in September and—if indeed she weren't—what a September without students would be like. She almost couldn't imagine, because she'd been teaching in one capacity or another since her very first autumn after college. Over a decade and a half now. The only year she hadn't been in the classroom in September was the year that Charlotte was born.

And though she knew she hadn't thought about school a whole lot in the last couple of weeks, July was an exceptional month: It was the one period in the course of the year when she didn't focus on her students and her lesson plans and the simple presentation of her classroom—what it looked like, what decorated the walls. The truth was, she enjoyed teaching. She liked children: It was why she had gone into teaching in the first place. The only reason Charlotte was an only child was because for a decade now she and Spencer had always concluded, for one reason or another, that the timing was wrong for a second child— a decision that in hindsight probably had more to do with the subterranean fissures in their marriage than the busyness of their lives. Moreover, Catherine knew that she especially liked high school girls—their insights and their angst, the way their desperate insecurities waffled with their profound self-absorption—and she enjoyed the relationships that she had with their parents (and, yes, especially the relationships that she had with their fathers). Though she worried on occasion that she wasn't doing a very good job with her own daughter, she knew that the older girls in her classes listened to her; likewise, they knew that she listened to them and cared about what they had to say. She was confident that she helped them as much with their self-esteem as she did with Brontë and Austin and Dickens, and in this world that was an undeniably meaningful contribution.

It dawned on her that this coming autumn, however, she might be trapped in the apartment with Spencer. She felt bad that the word **trapped** had come to her, but there it was, a blinking neon warning light in her mind. Trapped, these days, was precisely how she would feel if she were alone for weeks at a time with her husband. All afternoon Catherine had sensed the way her fear was being compounded by resentment, and now at the bar she felt that bitterness pounding away at the insides of her temples. Yes, she remained grateful that she hadn't yet told Spencer how tired she was of his fussy correctness, of the way he put anonymous animals before his wife and his daughter. But she also wasn't sure she could find it within herself to be the crutch and the cheerleader he was going to need in the coming year. This . . . this mess . . . was her brother's fault, and if anyone should become Spencer McCullough's nursemaid and whipping boy (good Lord, she thought, how did crutch and cheerleader become nursemaid and whipping boy so fast?), it should be John.

"Catherine?"

She turned to Paige Sutherland, the attorney her age who had flown to New Hampshire that morning with Spencer's friend, Keenan. The woman had honey in her voice and seemed capable of making any subject sound lewd. She was petite and her hair had a tam-o'-shanter wave rising up from the side of her horseshoe-shaped headband. She looked elfin, but Catherine knew the type: She was a barracuda.

"Catherine, you need a drink," Paige said to her, resting two of her cold-blooded fingers gently on her wrist.

She nodded. A few moments ago when they'd been handed what the young waitress called the café menus, she'd stared at it eagerly. In theory, they weren't going to eat now because it was four in the afternoon. They were just going to drink. Besides, she couldn't possibly order a burger in front of these lawyers. Certainly she couldn't in front of Keenan. She'd known him for years. And so she decided that if she couldn't have meat then she'd have something powerful to drink and ordered a martini.

"Spencer can be very, very focused. You know that as well as anyone," Keenan was saying as the waitress smiled and left the table. She realized she, too, needed to . . . focus . . . and so she apologized and asked him to repeat what he was explaining. She saw that he had scribbled some notes on a paper cocktail napkin with a fountain pen, and some of the characters looked more like inkblots than letters.

He smiled at her sympathetically. She knew she was

going to see that sort of smile a lot in the coming months.

"I was describing secondary gain. You know the concept?"

She shook her head.

"Normally when you get hurt, you try to get better. Right? Real basic notion. Well, that's not always the case with folks when there's a lawsuit and they see the chance for some reasonable recompense for all they've endured—and perhaps will endure for as long as they live. Sometimes the unconscious seems to take over, and the body doesn't seem to fully heal until the trial is done or there's a settlement. It's as if an important part of the brain knows it's in the body's best interest to look a little disabled, a little sickly, until the money's safely in the bank."

"Spencer's a fighter," Catherine said simply.

"Yes, he is. He is a very determined individual. And I know a lot of trial lawyers who believe the whole idea of secondary gain is a myth. Course, it's in **their** best interests to believe that."

"Spencer will want to get better as quickly as possible. He'll want to get back whatever movement he can."

"Catherine, that is certainly what he's going to believe on a conscious level. I am quite sure of that. Paige and I were merely saying that with some individuals in this situation—perhaps even with Spencer—it's only when the legal tumult is completely behind them that they regain their health."

"Spencer wouldn't even be considering a lawsuit, if you—"

"I think we're beyond contemplation," Paige said, and Catherine felt just the tiniest, not unpleasant pressure on her wrist. She looked down and saw Paige's fingers were still there.

She sighed and tried again. "Spencer wouldn't be planning to sue the gun company if you hadn't come up with the idea in the first place."

"Then he would have sued your brother," Paige murmured, in the tone of voice that Catherine knew the younger teachers in the school used with the younger students at recess. **Marissa, do you really think it's a good idea to put the hermit crabs inside the printer? No, Brandy, let's not play fifty-two card pickup with the phonics flash cards.**

"I don't think the word **sue** had crossed his mind until it crossed yours," she said, taking back her arm.

"When Spencer is feeling a little better and you can worry a little less about him, you'll be glad we're doing this," Paige said. "After all, it doesn't sound like it was your brother's fault any more than it was your daughter's. The bullet was just stuck in the chamber!"

"You've contacted the laboratory, haven't you?" Keenan asked Paige.

"I have, but they can't do much until the state police release the gun. Still, one engineer I spoke with there is going to see what they know about the extractor on John Seton's model—if they've come across any problems before with that type of gun."

"The laboratory?" Catherine asked.

"I—excuse me—we," Paige said, "hope to learn

why your brother was unable to extract the cartridge. We want to know if there was a tiny flaw in the gun."

The waitress returned with their order and doled out the drinks like party favors. When she was gone, Paige took a sip of wine and then said, "Besides, Catherine, there are financial realities here. A lawsuit makes sense for that reason alone."

"Obviously we have insurance," Catherine snapped. "And, if we must talk about such things, my family has"—she paused for just the briefest of seconds while she found the right euphemism—"assets. We have insurance and we have assets."

"Injury like this? You'd be amazed how much you're going to need," Keenan said. "And we all want Spencer to have the very best care."

"Besides, why should your assets have to cover the costs of something that wasn't your fault and should never have happened in the first place?"

"I only want what's best for my husband. And I understand you believe that either the gun or the gun's design has a flaw. But there is another issue here. Another person," Catherine said, and she took a sip of her drink. **Cleaning fluid,** she thought as the alcohol tumbled over her tongue and burned the back of her throat. **This is cleaning fluid and I could use it to clean toilets.** "I have to look out for my daughter. All that publicity, having to testify before strangers about what she did: None of that will do anything but make her feel worse. A lot worse. I think once Spencer and I really talk about this, he'll agree. He's not himself yet."

Keenan sat back in his seat, crossed his legs, and wrapped his hands around his seersucker-clad knees. He looked like a college professor from Mississippi. "Oh, Spencer's himself. He sees the opportunity here."

"He sees an opportunity for your organization! Once he—"

"Your husband is a very dedicated man. Very dedicated."

She wasn't sure what to make of his repeating the words. Was this irony?

"And your little girl will be fine," Paige was saying, "especially when she understands that this is all about punishing the company that disabled her daddy. Your little girl—"

"Charlotte is not a little girl. She is fast approaching thirteen."

"All the better. All I meant was that this lawsuit will actually help Charlotte because it will show her that we don't believe she's responsible. This tragedy is the fault of a company that makes a product that's inherently dangerous."

"It's a gun. Of course it's dangerous!"

Paige leaned toward her and purred, "It's a gun that—even when it functions properly—leaves a round in the chamber when you empty the magazine. And this one, it sounds like, was broken."

"Catherine, we know you love animals, too," Keenan added. "We know you love them as much as your husband. Don't forget, this lawsuit will help FERAL with its efforts to educate people."

"How could I forget that? It's the whole reason you're doing this!"

"We're doing this because we care for Spencer. Frankly, the Spencer I work with would want to talk about the accident with Harry Smith or Ted Koppel—especially if the network had some talking head lawyer from the rifle's manufacturer on-air to argue with him. No one is, forgive my choice of words, putting a gun to his head to make him do this." He reached for his drink and his expression grew unreadable behind the glass, but she had the distinct sense that he was completely oblivious to what her family was suffering. Suddenly, despite having been acquainted with this man since her husband had joined FERAL, she realized that in fact she didn't know him at all.

SARA GUESSED NO ONE had set foot on the badminton court since Saturday afternoon. That was four days ago now. It almost defied belief.

On the other side of the house she heard the lawn mower. Her mother-in-law, despite driving to Hanover to see Spencer—an hour-plus drive each way—playing nine holes of golf, and swimming laps across the roped-off section of Echo Lake, was now cutting the grass. Sara was quite sure that Nan was the only seventy-year-old woman she knew who actually pushed a lawn mower through the thick field grass that passed for lawn here in northern New England. Certainly her own mother and her own mother's friends weren't about to. When John had offered, she had shooed him away, reminding him that she cut it herself when he wasn't here. In a desperate stab at normalcy, he had decided then to take Willow to the club for a swim.

She sat down now at the end of the chaise lounge on which her niece was curled up, half under a small quilt Nan had made some years earlier. The sky was a heavy gray sheet shielding the mountains, but it was really quite humid: She sensed that Charlotte's need for the comforter had more to do with a yearning to cocoon than a craving for warmth. She stroked the child's back.

"Can I get you something to eat?" she asked the girl. "It's almost five. I was thinking of getting myself a glass of wine. Would you like a soda? A ginger ale?"

Charlotte shook her head and gnawed at the cuticle of her thumb. The tips of her fingers were flecked with dried blood and raw splinters of skin. Other than visiting her father, she hadn't left the house today. She hadn't even been willing to join her uncle and her cousin for a quick dip in the pool a half hour ago. Yesterday, when Sara had caught Charlotte and Willow sneaking into the men's room to see the painted flies on the urinals, she had begun to hope that perhaps the girl was emerging from the shell of self-hatred and guilt that was enveloping her, but she understood now that wasn't happening. Only briefly had the flies taken her mind off what she'd done, only briefly had even Willow—sweet, serene, magical Willow—been capable of soothing her grieving, disablingly penitent cousin. The child was little better now than she'd been Sunday morning, when she'd spent hours sobbing on her bed in her room. She had made a half effort at showering last night, but she'd forgotten to rinse the conditioner from her hair and so today it was greasy and flat and she looked like a waif.

"Really, nothing? Have you eaten anything at all today?"

"I'm not hungry."

"You still should eat."

"I don't know. Grandmother probably would be afraid if I ate now it would spoil my dinner. She'd want me to wait."

"I think most rules are off these days. If you want something, I'd be happy to bring it out to you. Some good bread and jam? A banana?"

She seemed to consider the notion before rejecting it. "No. But thank you, Aunt Sara. I think I'll just wait till dinner."

Her mother-in-law's dog ambled around the corner and up the steps onto the porch. He smelled of the fields in which he'd been wandering, an aroma that was sweet and clean. Abstractedly, Charlotte dangled one of her hands and rubbed the top of his head when he nuzzled her fingers.

Finally, in a voice as neutral as Sara could make it, she turned to the subject that had brought her to her niece in the first place: "You know your father isn't mad at you. Don't you?"

The girl pressed the side of her face deep into the vinyl chaise pad and pulled the edge of the quilt up to her chin. "That only makes me feel worse. I wish he'd get pissed at me. I mean, I'm sure pissed at myself."

"Oh, he doesn't blame you at all."

"Well, he should."

"Not necessarily. Obviously you shouldn't have been playing with the gun—"

"I know that!"

She continued placidly as if her niece hadn't interrupted her. "But you didn't know it was loaded. You didn't mean to hurt anyone. You mustn't lose sight of those two facts, Charlotte. We all make mistakes—small ones, huge ones—and I've always felt it's important to distinguish between those mistakes we make when we mean to be hurtful and those we make simply because we're human. This—what happened Saturday night—falls so completely into that latter category. You weren't trying to be hurtful or to hurt anyone. Do you see the difference?"

The girl wiped at the corners of her eyes with her pinkies. She was a beautiful child, Sara thought, but almost overnight—less than four full days, really—her cheeks had begun to hollow. Despair, almost before their eyes, was making the girl appear sickly.

"Charlotte?"

"I see the difference."

"I'm glad."

"But that doesn't make things any easier for anyone. Not for my dad, not for my mom. I really did it this time."

She heard the lawn mower as Nan pushed the old

machine back and forth in the side yard, the noise growing closer and then receding. It was actually louder than the ride-on mowers that most people used in the rural corners of Vermont in which she always had lived.

"But you're still his daughter. And Catherine's daughter. And my niece. No one loves you any less—"

"I love me less!"

"You shouldn't feel that way. I understand why you would. Really, I do. But I wish you wouldn't even think such a thing. Your father and mother will need you a lot in the coming months, and one of the best things you could do for them is to get on with your own life. You're going to need someone to talk to—"

"I figured," she said, a tiny twinge of disgust coloring her voice.

"You make seeing a therapist sound like, I don't know, having to wear a burlap sack to a prom."

"That would be kind of cool, actually."

"I'm going to give your mom the name of someone I know in Manhattan. Her practice is on the East Side, not far from your school. She's wonderful. And you can always call me, too. You know that, right?"

She offered a small, almost imperceptible nod.

"Make no mistake: It's okay to be sad. I'd be worried about you if you weren't. But don't let it become incapacitating. You were going to audition for some show in September, right?"

"The Secret Garden," she murmured. "It's a musical. Our school's doing it at the end of November."

"Your mother told me something about that. Well, you should still audition. Moping does no one any good."

"God . . ."

"What?"

"You just sounded exactly like Grandmother."

Abruptly she jerked upright. In her head she could indeed hear her mother-in-law saying precisely those words. **Moping does no one any good.** She saw her niece was looking at her and she wondered if it had something to do with the air or this house. Maybe vigorousness was contagious.

"I did, didn't I?"

"Yeah. You did," the girl said, and she raised her eyebrows. Sara had the distinct sense that on another day in another place—if they weren't on this porch, perhaps, if Spencer weren't in a hospital to the south—the two of them right now would be howling with laughter. She thought of what Willow had accomplished yesterday with the painted flies. Though her own imitation of Nan Seton had been completely unintentional, she was absolutely delighted with the gentle ripple of pleasure it had given her niece.

WHEN, YEARS LATER, people spoke of the accident at Nan Seton's house in Sugar Hill, Melissa Fearon—a.k.a. Missy Fearless—knew she would be a part of the story. A nameless footnote, perhaps, but she had been an EMT long enough to realize that her and Evan Seaver's rescue of Spencer McCullough was a very impressive save.

That was not, however, why she went to the hospital to see him Wednesday afternoon. She felt no need to pat herself on the back. She drove to Hanover because she didn't want her last memory of the man to be his glazed eyes and clammy skin and the way his shoulder the other night had been transformed into stew. She wanted instead to see him flipping the channels on the TV from his hospital bed with the remote. She wanted to watch him savoring the simple fact he was alive.

She had done this three times before in the past, each time after a scoop-and-run had been particularly gruesome (and the prospects for survival discouraging) but had learned in the following days that the patient was actually getting better.

Like Catherine, Missy was the sort of schoolteacher who didn't trouble herself with her classroom and lesson plans until the second week in August, and so she spent most of the day gardening. She left for the hospital a little after four, confident that her husband, the manager of the Agway in Haverhill, wouldn't mind if their dinner was a little late tonight. Roger Fearon was nothing if not flexible from his years of living with a part-time EMT. By the time she'd parked her car, gotten her visitor's pass and wound her way through the labyrinthine corridors to Spencer's room, it was close to five thirty. Nevertheless, she was surprised to find the room empty but for Spencer. She had expected the whole Seton clan would be present, that multigenera-

tional throng she had seen Saturday night from the
corners of her eyes while she was trying to prevent
Spencer McCullough's blood from spurting into the
lupine like water from a garden hose.

It looked like Spencer was asleep, and so she
reached into her purse for a pen and a piece of paper.
She thought she would write him a note. From the
doorway he appeared better than the other night, but
that didn't take much. The mere fact that the massive
hole in his shoulder had been patched and he wasn't
hemorrhaging whole pints of blood was a sizable improvement.

"You looking for Paige?"

She glanced up and saw he had opened his eyes.

"I woke you. I'm so sorry."

"I wasn't sleeping."

"I was going to leave you a note."

"Me?"

"Uh-huh." She took a step farther into the room,
but without his wife or his mother-in-law present, she
felt as if she were intruding. She dropped the pen back
into her purse and pulled the strap over her shoulder.
"I was just going to write that I was glad to see you're
getting better."

"You can come closer. I don't bite. Lord, I don't
move. I don't dare." Though his voice was subdued—
almost muted—she could sense right away a distinct
scrappiness in every syllable. This guy was a fighter. It
was probably a big reason why he was still alive in the
first place.

"Honest: I don't bite," he murmured again, and so

she strolled all the way into the room and stood at the foot of his bed.

"You're looking for Paige?"

She shook her head. "I don't know any Paige. I was coming to see you."

"I thought you were looking for my lawyer."

She didn't like the sound of that: a lawyer. That couldn't be good for the family. She understood that the gun belonged to John Seton, and she wondered if he was actually planning to sue his brother-in-law.

"Nope," she said. "Just you."

"Forgive me, please, but . . . do I know you?"

"I didn't expect you'd remember me. I'm Melissa Fearon. I'm with Franconia Rescue. I'm an EMT."

"God, you saved my life, didn't you?" His voice was slightly more animated now, and she was pleased.

"I had help."

"Well. Thank you. God. Thank you so much."

She saw a line of flowers along the window and atop the dresser. Some had been sent by a florist, but others had been picked by whoever had brought them—especially the twin vases of pink and white phlox. The last thing she had been focused on at the Seton house Saturday night were the flowers in the garden, but she decided those probably came from Sugar Hill. Maybe the guy's gun-toting daughter had cut them herself. Or that niece.

"You can sit on that other bed," he said to her. "People use it like a couch."

She agreed and pulled herself up onto the mattress. "How are you feeling today? You look pretty good."

"I look better than"—he paused for a wince and then continued—"the last time you saw me. But I don't look good."

"I've seen much worse four days after an accident. Trust me. Have they told you when you go home?"

"Won't be this week. Maybe early next week."

She nodded. "How is everyone doing?"

"You mean my family?"

"Uh-huh."

"They're worried. Upset."

"I guess they were all here today."

"They were. Catherine—my wife—just left. I'm supposed to be . . . resting now."

"I should go, then. You **should** rest. I just wanted to check in."

"Stay. Please. Today's the first day I've really been able to talk."

"Okay, then."

"And I don't want to nap. I don't know which drugs do it, but my dreams are filled with . . . lobsters. Really big . . . lobsters. They're nightmares. Complete and utter nightmares."

"Do you not like lobsters?"

"I like them fine," he said quietly.

"I love them. There used to be this restaurant on the road to the notch in Franconia. It's closed now, but it was called the Steer by the Shore, and they had this baked stuffed lobster. You would have killed for it. They said the lobsters were one and a quarter pounds, but they always seemed bigger to me. Delicious. And the stuffing was this buttery, crackery—I know that's not a word, but you get my drift, it was kind of like a Ritz—paste. It just melted in your mouth. The lobster, too. My husband and I used to go there at least two or three times during the summer, and we always ordered the baked stuffed lobster."

She began to fear she was talking too much. The color was receding from Spencer's face, visibly plummeting like the water line in the bathtub once the drain has been opened.

"You probably don't have much of an appetite yet. I shouldn't talk so much about food."

"It **was** Ritz," he muttered.

"Excuse me?"

"The stuffing. That was the secret ingredient. Ritz crackers. Whole stuffing was nothing but Ritz crackers and margarine. And it wasn't even very good margarine. It was the supermarket brand. One time I tried to spice it up with celery salt. The chef saw me, and I thought he was going to have a stroke. Made me throw"—there was that wince again, his nose crinkling up toward his eyes, and his forehead a series of furrows in a newly planted vegetable garden—"the whole batch away and start again."

"You used to work there?"

"Yeah. I did," he said. "You know, I never told anyone that."

"You never told anyone that you used to work at the Steer by the Shore?"

"No. About the Ritz. I never told anyone that the secret ingredient in the stuffing was Ritz. It was all so important to them. The chef. The owners."

"It was good!"

He grunted, a lone rumble of disgust from deep in his throat. "It was appalling. The stuffing, the lobsters . . ."

"You said you like lobsters!"

"I did. I didn't say I liked to eat them."

"What? You're a vegetarian?"

"Uh-huh."

"Fish, too?"

"Anything with a parent."

"I guess you don't eat whatever venison your brother-in-law brings home in the fall. Personally, I don't like venison. You're not missing anything."

"I agree. And as for my brother-in-law . . ." He sighed. "I am hoping this appalling interest of his is just . . . a phase. Temporary insanity."

"Yeah, I guess I heard somewhere that he hasn't been hunting very long," she told him. She wanted to ask him how his daughter had gotten his brother-in-law's gun in the first place or what she thought she was doing when she pulled the trigger on Saturday night. But then that part of her that was a mother—though both of her sons were grown men now in their twenties—and a teacher wanted to know something she decided was infinitely more important: She wanted to know how the child was feeling four days after the accident.

"So," she said, drawing the vowel out into a rope as she tried to figure out how to begin, "what's your daughter's name?"

"Charlotte."

"Charlotte McCullough. That sounds very regal."

"Charlotte is many things . . . but regal is not among them."

"She's playful?"

"She's . . . she wants to be a teenager."

"How old is she?"

"Twelve. About to turn thirteen."

"Then she's there. Is she badly shaken by what she did?"

"**She** didn't do anything!" he answered, and Missy noticed the way he almost hissed out the pronoun in his desire to make it clear that his daughter was not responsible for what had occurred.

"I'm sorry. I didn't mean anything. I was only wondering how she was doing."

"It's my brother-in-law who should be shaken. It's John Seton who has to live with this."

She nodded because she didn't want this intense man in the bed to get any more upset than he already was. But she didn't completely agree with him. Although she was confident that Spencer's brother-in-law felt enormous responsibility for what had occurred, she was also quite sure that his daughter was going to struggle with the fact she had nearly killed her father for a very long time. Probably forever.

"You see a lot of gun accidents?" he asked her suddenly.

"A few."

"I'm suing the gun company." He said this as if he were informing her that he had just changed the oil in his car or eaten a grilled cheese sandwich for lunch.

She was relieved that it was a manufacturer he was su-ing and not, as she had feared when she first arrived, his brother-in-law. "Maybe you should talk to my lawyer," he added.

Reflexively, as if he were pointing a gun at her, she threw her hands up in the air. "Oh, I don't think so. I'm happy to tell the lawyers what I saw on Saturday night. But I'm not your expert witness on guns or bul-lets or accidents. Okay?"

"Just a thought."

She lowered her arms and tried to smile. "Really, I don't believe you should be thinking about lawsuits and money right now. I think you should be putting all your energy into getting better."

"I'm not suing for the money. I'm suing because it's a great . . . opportunity to bring attention to the plight of hunted animals. Deer, especially. But moose and birds, too. Perhaps even elephants."

She considered telling him that in her opinion things might be worse if people didn't hunt. In places like northern New Hampshire the herd would grow too large for the browse. She didn't say anything, how-ever, because she hadn't come here to argue.

"I'll bet you hunt," he continued, his tone slightly accusing.

"No."

"But your husband does."

"No, he doesn't, either," she answered, though this was a lie. She couldn't believe that on Saturday night this guy was spewing so much blood into the clay soil of Sugar Hill that she had knelt in a puddle when she had arrived at his side—an oozy bit of bog that actually made a sucking sound as she lifted her knee the first time—and now he was proselytizing against hunting. He really was feisty.

"Ah, but you eat meat. You told me you eat lobster. You—"

"Look, I have two sons. One is a vegetarian, one isn't. It isn't a big deal to me, it isn't a big deal to anyone. These days, lots of people are—"

"You ever think about what you're eating when you eat a lobster? When you eat any animal?"

In the past these spontaneous visits had been pleasant for both her and the patient. That's why she did it. The man or woman in the bed went on and on about how grateful they were to be alive, and she was able to go home with an image in her mind of a person on the mend. Not this character. He actually wanted to lecture her. And so she looked at her watch and expressed surprise at the time. She heard herself telling him how glad she was to see him alive and how she was sure that he would dazzle them all with his recovery. She spoke quickly so he couldn't get a word in, and then she backed out of his room, waving as she retreated, until she was safely in the hallway.

As she raced down the long series of corridors that led to the elevators, she thought of Spencer McCullough's twelve-year-old daughter once again. She decided if this guy were her father, she might have shot him, too. Anything to shut him up.

HOURS LATER, as Spencer was lying alone in bed, he kept thinking back on something the EMT had asked about Charlotte, and the way she had phrased the question: **Is she badly shaken by what she did?** It was dark now and it was raining outside, and he thought of his daughter and his niece in the room with the twin beds they shared here in the country and he wondered what they were talking about tonight. He imagined their light was still on, and in his mind he saw them in their summer nightgowns and he heard the rain drumming against the slate roof. He pictured them alone, just the two of them. In all likelihood, their grandmother was already safely ensconced in her turret for the night, John and Sara were focused on baby Patrick, and he guessed that Catherine either was soaking in the tub or curled up in bed with a book.

He worried that over the past couple of days he hadn't told Charlotte—really made the point crystal clear—that she hadn't done anything wrong. How could she have known there was a bullet in the gun? She was twelve, and while he had been absolutely sincere when he told the EMT that Charlotte wanted nothing more in the world than to be sixteen or seventeen, the reality was that in so many ways she was still a child. She had no idea the rifle was loaded, she had no idea her father was out walking at the edge of the garden. On some level, he decided, he was probably suing the gun company precisely because he wanted to make clear to the world that this travesty was not his daughter's fault.

He made a mental note that in the morning when Charlotte came for a visit, the very first thing he was going to do was explain this to her. Maybe he'd ask everyone else to leave so he could have a moment alone with her. Then he would make absolutely certain that she knew she was blameless.

Well, not completely blameless. Twelve might still make her a child, but even twelve-year-olds should know not to play with guns. But then, she'd never seen a rifle before! None of their friends in Manhattan had guns lying around the house—at least that they knew of.

He imagined Charlotte and Willow were sitting together on the twin bed against the wall right now, the one that was Willow's, and he saw the girls playing gin rummy with one of his mother-in-law's shoe box full of bridge decks, the rain cooling the night so the windows were open only an inch. As they played they were talking about . . .

He realized he couldn't begin to conceive what they were talking about, and this lapse troubled him. He told himself it was the painkillers he was taking, but he knew this was different. Deeper. He couldn't concoct a conversation for them in his mind because he didn't know how badly his daughter was hurting. That EMT might have been onto something.

He felt a small freshet of fear ripple through him: He was scared. There was nothing he loved more in the world than his wife and his daughter, and alone in this bed he had to admit he was probably losing his wife. Had been for months. These days, they could fight over what to pack, where to eat, which vegetables they'd plant in the garden. Whether they should even have a garden.

Well, in this case Catherine had been right. No good had come from the garden, that was for sure. Next year they'd let the lupine return to the patch of earth they had tried to make their own. Allow all traces of the vegetables to disappear. It was ridiculous to believe they—he, this was all his idea—could maintain a garden when he and Catherine lived in Manhattan and John and Sara lived two hours to the west in Vermont.

He hoped he wouldn't lose his daughter now, too, especially since the accident really wasn't her fault. He thought of the little girl who once raced for hours at a time amidst the stuffed animals on the first floor of the old FAO Schwarz, that preschooler entranced by the cotton- and poly-stuffed snakes and chimpanzees and giraffes. He couldn't lose the girl who, when she was seven, was capable of belting out "A Lot of Livin' to Do" in a children's cabaret as if she were Ann-Margret, or the child who on occasion could be so wondrously giving that at nine she'd taken a booth at the church rummage sale and sold all her old puzzles and Barbies and books and raised $273 for FERAL's special fund for abused circus animals. Yes, right now she was going through a rough period. Right now she was subjecting everyone around her to her preadolescent angst . . . but this was the same child who would run into his and Catherine's room when she was in the second grade for one last good-night kiss or who would lean against him for hours as they sat on the beach in Florida and watched seagulls and talked.

Spencer decided he hadn't been very nice to that EMT. He wasn't proud of his behavior, and he wondered why he had been so testy and sanctimonious with her. All she did was save his life. Was it because of his injury? The fact that he would, in all likelihood, be disabled? Or was it more basic than that: Was he cranky simply because last night he had slept poorly again—woken twice by the lobsters in his dreams—and now he was tired?

He had asked for and been given a different kind of sleeping pill tonight, but he was still wary about what sorts of dreams might await him when he dozed off. Last night there had been a couple of doozies, including one in which his hands were bound with belt-wide rubber bands, and he was trapped on his side in a crate in a walk-in refrigerator. He woke up in a sweat as he was being grabbed by a giant human hand to be either cleavered or dropped into a pot of boiling water. It was only a dream, but it had still been a pretty hideous experience.

No doubt tonight he'd start dreaming of deer. Inadvertently Catherine had put the idea into his head when she'd been commiserating with him this afternoon, trying to cheer him up. Trying to elicit a smile from him, she'd suggested that tonight he'd probably start dreaming of Bambi: The fawn would emerge from the garden, beet greens and kohlrabi on the young buck's breath.

Well, deer were beautiful animals: graceful, athletic,

and lithe. They were completely unlike lobsters, which Spencer believed were among the most vile-looking creatures on the planet. What in the name of God had the first person to eat one been thinking? He decided he was mistaken when he had told Melissa Fearon that he liked lobsters. He didn't. He tried to appreciate all animals, and most of the time he did. But not lobsters. He couldn't appreciate a lobster.

He stared into the blackness out the window, watching the designs the raindrops made on the glass. He would have to get the address of that EMT from someone at the hospital so he could write her a note. He wanted to apologize for being short with her, as well as, yes, to thank her for saving his life. He would be unable to write the note himself, of course. At least in the foreseeable future. He guessed eventually he would learn to write legibly with his left hand, but that day was almost unimaginable to him at the moment. He could barely lift his left arm right now because of the way any upper-body movement at all sent tectonic shudders of pain across his right side. But he would thank her. Somehow. And he would do more than write a note, because sixty or eighty dictated words were insufficient when someone has brought you back from the dead.

He told himself he shouldn't lose sight of that. It was certainly a temptation to read more into this second chance than was most certainly there—to see it as an opportunity to make resolutions and vows, promises that he knew in his heart he would never keep for more than a week or a month—but the undeniable reality was that he very nearly had died. Bought the farm. Augured in. If the bullet had been a few inches higher, he would have been all but decapitated. A few inches in another direction, and his heart would have become a ragout. Either way, he would have been dead before his body landed back in the snow peas. As troubling as his future looked to him tonight—the considerable handicap that loomed before him, his daughter's almost crippling remorse, the damage he had inflicted on his marriage before this accident had even occurred—the truth was that he was alive. Just about four days ago there was no reason to believe that he would be.

And so while he wasn't about to see more of a spiritual second chance here than was probably warranted, neither would he forget that he still had a future. It might not be the future he once had imagined. But when the sun rose in the morning over the mountains just east of his mother-in-law's house in Sugar Hill, he would still be around. Tomorrow—and the day after tomorrow and the day after that—he would try to be less careless with his time.

IN THE HOUSE IN SUGAR HILL, Sara stood above the crib in which Patrick was sleeping and watched the small blanket rise almost imperceptibly off his chest with each inhalation. She wondered if he was going to have her husband's elegant, patrician slide of a nose. People said they saw as much of her in the baby as they did John, but she knew they were just being polite. Right now the child looked like nothing more than a John Seton clone. She closed the window completely and for a moment gazed out into the garden. The rain had resumed a few minutes ago, soon after her husband had left for a walk. She didn't think John had brought an umbrella with him. She thought she saw something move in the dark and the mist, guessed it was probably the deer, and decided to go outside to turn on the floodlights by the garage. Scare the creatures away: frighten the hell out of the animals that, inadvertently, had brought so much pain on her family.

At the top of the stairs she could hear the murmurs of Willow's and Charlotte's small voices, but she couldn't make out what they were saying. She'd kissed them good night and turned out their lights perhaps fifteen minutes ago. She hoped they were talking about something silly—not the accident or poor Spencer's injuries. As she passed the kitchen, she saw Nan glancing at the catalogs and the bills and the solicitations (did no one write letters anymore?) that somehow had managed to amass in the few days her mother-in-law had been shuttling her brood back and forth between the hospital in Hanover and the Contour Club.

The house was linked to the garage by a path made of slate, and the slabs tonight were cold and slippery and wet. Sara's feet were bare, and despite the rain she walked slowly. It wasn't simply that she didn't want to fall: Suddenly she wanted to catch the deer in the floodlights and watch them freeze before fleeing. The light switch was just inside the side door to the garage—what Willow had referred to as the people door when she'd been younger, her means of differentiating it from the massive overhead doors for the vehicles, which even now she had to struggle to lift.

Sara found the switch with her fingers, and turned toward the garden before flipping the lights on. She wanted to be sure she had the patch of badly mauled vegetables fixed in her gaze.

In the instant of illumination she spied not deer, however, nor a dog or raccoons or even a black bear. She saw instead John, his hair plastered so flat on his head by the rain that it looked as if he had just emerged from the pool at the club. He wasn't wearing a shirt, and before she saw he was still clad in his khaki shorts she thought he was naked. He had a pair of metal tomato cages in one hand and the cherry tomato plants that moments earlier had been growing inside them—easily three feet high now—in the other, their stalks and roots dangling in the air like the spindly legs of unimaginably giant insects. On the ground beside him she observed that he had upended the other tomato cages as well, and ripped those plants from the ground, too. She wasn't sure, but it looked as if he had yanked up the corn plants the family had meticulously replanted on Friday and Saturday, and savaged the peas, the string beans, the beets, the pumpkins, and the squash. It appeared as if he had ripped up everything the deer hadn't already nibbled to death in the garden.

She couldn't tell if he could see her—if he could determine exactly who it was who had just turned on the lights—both because she was in the dark and because at some point he had taken off his eyeglasses (perhaps, she worried, when he had ripped off his shirt). He looked unsteady on his feet, but he squinted and stared in her general direction.

"Mother? Sara? Who's there?" he cried, and it was indeed a sob that he was offering up through the wind and the rain and the night.

She tried to answer but her voice caught in her throat. She tried one more time but was struck dumb by the sight of her husband and the half-mad waste he had inflicted on the vegetables and—now she glimpsed the edge of the cutting garden, partly illuminated by the floodlights—the flowers the family had planted Memorial Day Weekend. She was incapable of offering anything but a desperately sad little whimper.

"Sara?"

She wiped the rain from her eyes and nodded though he couldn't see her, and then she ran to him across the driveway and soggy carpet of lawn.

Part III

EAT WHAT
YOU KILL

Eighteen

On a Tuesday in early September, a full five weeks and three days since he'd taken a .30-caliber bullet in his shoulder, Spencer began the time-consuming ordeal of getting ready for work. Catherine and Charlotte both wanted to help him, as they had in different ways throughout the entire month of August and those still-balmy days of September. They had each felt a particular desire to assist him this morning since today he would be returning to the FERAL offices for the first time since before their disastrous family vacation in New Hampshire. But Spencer made it clear that this Tuesday he wanted to be completely on his own. He wanted to be a free agent: Capable. Confident. Independent. He understood that this image lacked a certain fidelity to his actual circumstances, since Charlotte had been tying his sneakers for him for most of the last month and slathering his plaque-fighting gel on his toothbrush. Likewise, it had been Catherine who had been pulling up his socks and his pants (it was almost impossible, he had discovered, to get a pair of slacks on without his right hand, because the fabric along the waistband kept bunching up just below his right hip), and opening the small prescription bottles with the Allegra he depended upon this time of the year for his allergy and the Percocet he needed these days like air. But it was an image toward which, he told himself, he could aspire.

Spencer knew his independence would not be a pretty sight and would take mind-numbing amounts of time, and so he'd told Dominique on the phone the previous Friday not to expect him until midmorning. And because he wanted no witnesses to the embarrassing struggles that loomed before him, he was still in bed when his wife and his daughter ventured into the bedroom one last time to kiss him good-bye before leaving for their separate classrooms at the Brearley School across town. They asked—for, he guessed, the hundredth time that morning—what they could do for him.

"I'm really okay," he said, feigning a self-assurance he didn't feel. He was, after all, about to try to conquer Everest. "Go, go, go—I'll be fine!"

He wasn't at all sure this was the truth. Still, he reminded himself that today might not be quite like his other days of pathetic incompetence, his right arm and hand completely useless, his left hand mesmerizing him with its weakness and palsylike lack of dexterity. This morning he was going to christen the tools that his physical therapist, a square-shouldered young man with hands that were at once muscular and soft named Nick Trigiani, had brought him over the weekend. Between grueling reps to build up the muscles on his left arm and hand and to prevent the ones on his right from atrophying completely, the two of them had pored over the catalogs Nick had brought with him from his office at Roosevelt Hospital, each one filled with myriad wonders to help the sick and the lame survive in the modern world. Spencer managed to run up a thousand-plus-dollar tab with items that cost between five and fifty dollars apiece, uncaring whether his insurance would cover the cost of a single one. These were things he had to have, and now they were here, unpacked and ready to use.

Catherine had done the unpacking and unwrapping over the weekend and pulled the items from their cardboard boxes and clear plastic sarcophagi. This work demanded two hands, one of which more times than not was using a pair of scissors or slashing strapping tape with a kitchen knife. He had done nothing as each device was unveiled other than watch the two family cats paw delightedly through the papers and climb inside the now empty shipping cartons.

In any case, as soon as Spencer heard the front door to their apartment glide shut Tuesday morning, he swung his legs over the side of the mattress and used his one good arm to push himself to his feet. Even getting out of bed had become a chore, because he had three-plus decades of muscle memory using both hands for leverage. Now he had only his left. He still slept with his right arm held to his chest with his shoulder immobilizer, a sling with a strap that wound around his rib cage, and so he knew intellectually that his fingers and his hand would tingle like they had gone to sleep if there had been any functioning nerves remaining. There weren't, and so he felt nothing. His shoulder, of course, was stinging fiercely because it was only a few minutes ago that he had swallowed his first Percocet and his first three Advils of the day—a Percocet and Advil cocktail didn't quash completely the hot branding iron he felt every waking moment in what remained of his shoulder, but at least it made the pain bearable—and the pills hadn't kicked in yet.

His plan was to endure the agony that came with removing the sling so he could shower, dry himself as best he could, climb back into the sling and run an electric razor over his face (never before his injury had he even contemplated using an electric razor to try to mow down the stubble that covered his cheeks and his neck like shards of steel wool), and then brush his teeth. If he accomplished this without falling back onto the bed in the torturous pain he had endured in his shoulder only yesterday when he'd forgotten that his arm would flap the moment he first removed it from the sling—he was much better off when he rested it on his lap while he pulled apart the Velcro clasps with the fingers on his left hand—he would get dressed and make breakfast on his own.

AND HE DID INDEED manage to shower (though, as always, he was almost completely incapable of an undertaking as simple as drying his left underarm) and shave and brush his teeth—this last task proving particularly difficult because he had to hold the handle of the brush with his teeth like it was a cigar so he could apply the aquamarine gel with his one functioning hand. When he was done he gave himself license to leave the cap off (he vowed the next tooth-paste they bought would have a flip top), because he figured if he held the tube in his teeth the way he'd just held the brush he would send a stream of gel spurting out onto the bathroom counter. Abruptly one of the cats, Emma, appeared on the Formica out of nowhere, saw the cap as a toy and swiped at it with her paw. Much to her apparent amazement she sent it hurtling into the wastepaper basket. Spencer knew that even if bending over weren't an exercise in excru-ciating torment, he wouldn't have bothered to re-trieve it. Toothpaste caps were a luxury that was now beyond him.

He didn't floss, but he made a mental note to ask Nick about ordering a device that would allow him to floss with one hand. A few times Catherine had tried to floss for him, but not only had the experience been demeaning, it had been physically unpleasant: The amount of blood Spencer spat into the sink when she was through and the way his gums felt like they'd just been worked over with the tip of a box cutter were tes-timony to the reality that it took genuine skill to floss someone else's teeth, and they should have more re-spect for the dental hygienists who did it daily.

For a moment before getting dressed he stared at his shoulder in the mirror. He was long past squea-mishness at the sight of the injury, and the tissue was actually healing quite nicely. Dr. Palmer, the self-pro-claimed "upholstery guy" back in Hanover, had done a wonderful job and the wound—both the chasm where the bullet had entered his shoulder and done its dirty work, and the ravine made by the surgeons when they had climbed inside him to try to return a semblance of order to the shattered bone and twitching muscular slush—itself no longer repulsed him. Certainly it had in the second and third week in August, when he was back in Sugar Hill and that portly home health nurse who always smelled slightly of onion was changing his dressings twice a day. The first couple of times he'd showered with his sling off (**Just get the soap and water right in there, don't worry,** Palmer had told him), he'd practically vomited in the stall.

Now it was starting to look like the glossy, hairless skin of a burn victim. Though his shoulder would never heal to the point where you couldn't tell it had once suffered a colossal assault—there would always be scarring—eventually it would appear as if it had endured a trauma no worse than, say, rotator cuff surgery. Maybe rotator cuff surgery with complications that had been manageable. In any case, it wouldn't be grotesque.

What would be grotesque was the subluxation that would occur over the next year or so. It was inevitable. Because there was no bone linking his arm to his torso—and no reason to bother with a metal shoulder because there were no working nerves—it would be largely scar tissue fusing the appendage to his body. As a result, the joint would slowly come apart. It wouldn't be violent like a dislocation; it would be a slow, steady, inexorable separation so that a year from now there would in all likelihood be a two-finger-width indentation—a pothole, one doctor had called it—between his shoulder and the uppermost bone in his perpetually dangling right arm. The very idea left Spencer sickened, and no amount of physical therapy could prevent the subluxation from occurring.

Too bad they couldn't share that hideous deformity with the world at the press conference Paige was planning for the week after next. No, he thought, maybe that wasn't too bad. At some point people would have to see how scarred and disabled he was, but he wasn't prepared to reveal that just yet. Even for deer. Especially for deer.

He realized that he didn't particularly like the animal. Deer and lobsters. He loathed them both, he decided, and for the briefest moment he wondered if he was in the right business. The notion passed quickly, however, and he started a litany in his mind of all the animals in the world that were abused and that he did love. He tried telling himself that if he'd been shot because people went monkey hunting in the fall, he'd be downright excited by all of Paige's plans, but he didn't quite believe it.

Still naked (he was no longer capable of cinching a towel around his waist the way he once could), he wandered back into his and Catherine's bedroom and surveyed the tools he had lined up the night before along the top of his bureau. There they were, the Good Grips Button Hook he would use to grasp his shirt buttons with the end of a dolphin-nosed wire and pull them through the thin slats in the fabric, and the generic dressing stick with the C hook at the end he would loop through a belt loop to pull his pants over the strangely unconquerable ledge that was his right hip. Gently he fingered the rubber handle on the crowbar-long shoehorn and then gazed down at his brand-new loafers. He hadn't worn loafers since college, but he would be wearing them when he went to the office today. They were black and they were ugly, because he refused to wear the brown calfskin ones his mother-in-law had ordered for him as a get-well gift from Brooks Brothers. He had to admit, the ones Mrs. Seton had sent him were softer than any shoe he'd slipped onto his foot in the last decade and change . . . but he still wasn't going to wear them.

These were made of something called vegetan suede, and they looked more like a pair of bedroom slippers for some unintentionally comic British fop than shoes for an ostensibly media savvy spokesperson for an organization headquartered in Manhattan. In the past he had always worn leather-free hiking boots or black canvas sneakers and felt rather hip. He sighed: He'd have to find the time when he returned to work to search out a decent pair of pigskin-free Merrells. Then he sat down on the bed, catching his breath before beginning the task—rich, he knew well, with petty humiliations—of getting dressed.

O H , B U T A S D E M E A N I N G and time-consuming (and painful) as it was to stuff his right arm into the sleeve of his shirt or use his dressing stick to hoist up his khakis, getting dressed was a picnic compared to making his breakfast. Catherine had left everything out for him on the counter, but he still had to craft his meal by himself. The breakfast he envisioned would demand effort both in the preparation and the consumption. The menu? Bran flakes with soy milk, coffee, and fresh honey wheat bread from the bakery around the corner topped with the homemade blueberry jam that one of his mother-in-law's New Hampshire friends, Marguerite, had given him before he returned to New York.

Spencer sensed that an eight-year-old with two hands easily could make this breakfast—replacing the coffee, of course, with a more appropriate beverage. Apple juice, he decided. Hell, a reasonably resourceful six-year-old could make this breakfast if the bread were already sliced and the soy milk was in a quart container the kid could lift. Nevertheless, Spencer knew he would need the brand-new kitchen tools for the disabled he and Nick had picked out.

He began with the easy part and actually allowed himself a small smile when he managed to open and pour his cereal without spilling more than a dozen flakes around the outside of the bowl. Then he unscrewed the top of the soy milk, and left the container open on the counter. He understood that the real problem he would face with the cereal would come only when he tried to eat it. Though he was now the proud owner of a Good Grips easy-to-hold spoon that was supposed to make it easier for a right-handed person to eat with his left hand (the shaft was as wide and round as a hammer handle), he'd discovered yesterday that he still dribbled more cereal onto the table and into his lap than he managed to bring to his mouth. His left arm and hand still weren't very strong—despite the hours he'd already spent squeezing his hand exerciser—and their utter lack of coordination continued to fascinate him.

The more difficult part of his breakfast preparation would be slicing the bread, and then spreading that jam with one hand. He would try out his Spreadboard for the first time, a device that resembled a baseball diamond's home plate, with a pair of plastic guards along the apex against which he would place his bread to hold it still while slathering on the preserves and (perhaps) a little Soy-garine.

Even before he did that, of course, he would have to wedge the jar between his knees and then hope he could unscrew the lid with his left hand. Given the reality that these preserves had never been opened, he had a pretty good sense that the lid would be snug. He shook his head: He should have had Catherine open it for him before she and Charlotte had left for school.

Nevertheless, he had cereal in a bowl and a loaf of bread on the cutting board. **Even I can slice fresh bread,** he thought to himself, **and make my own breakfast.**

HE WAS, ALAS, MISTAKEN. In the cab to his office he tried not to focus on the degrading spectacle he would have made if there'd been any witnesses: the bread crushed instead of cut, crumbs on the counter and the floor and (somehow) the dish rack three feet away, soggy clumps of cereal flakes everywhere but in his bowl, the jam jar completely impregnable until finally—half in rage and half in despair—he'd thrown it into the sink, the container banging off the faucet and then (much to his horror) shattering against the white porcelain sides. He honestly wasn't sure whether it was the faucet or the sink that had actually broken the glass.

Finally he just put his left hand into the box of cereal and grabbed a few fistfuls, and then wiped a wad of bread against the Soy-garine that was starting to melt on the counter. He was astonished at how tired his left arm had become in the failed effort and how much his right side had wound up hurting. The pain, exacerbated he knew by anxiety and exhaustion, was a soaring, white hot stinging in his shoulder and upper back, that—unfortunately—was now so pronounced that his head was starting to ache, his ears were ringing, and he wanted to put his head down in the cab that very moment and vomit.

He took in deep breaths through his nose and tried to concentrate on the sports radio talk station the cabbie was listening to softly on the radio. God, was Don Imus already off the air? Was it already after ten? Had it taken him that long to get dressed and make the kitchen look like a chimpanzee had just tried to make breakfast? When the cab braked abruptly before a red traffic light, he conked his head against the insufficiently padded rear of the front seat, and—despite the sling—his right hand swung forward just enough to cause the pain in his shoulder to slide off the charts for a moment. He heard himself cry out "Shit!" with such a pathetic shrillness to his voice that he grew embarrassed.

But even that embarrassment paled a moment later, when the cab jerked forward with the green light and he was pushed back in his seat. The cattle prod of pain deep inside him simultaneously pressed downward from his shoulder to his back and upward from his neck to his head, and though he brought his left hand to his mouth with impressive rapidity there was no stopping the vomit that was spewing up from his stomach, burning his throat and his mouth and his tongue, and spraying through his fingers like water sent full blast through a partly plugged faucet.

"What the fuck?" the cabbie was saying, "I can't stop here! What the fuck are you doing?"

He opened his mouth—the acid on his lips a minor annoyance compared to the spikes of agony everywhere else in his body and the humiliation and disgust he felt when he looked down and saw the vomit on the knees of his slacks and the front of his shirt—and heard himself murmur, "Just turn around please. I want to go home."

Nineteen

Charlotte understood that her father was in excruciating pain most of the time and that he was trying to hide it from her: He didn't want her to feel any worse than she already did. But she knew how much he hurt. She knew he was popping Percocet and Advil like they were M&M's, and she doubted fifteen minutes went by when she herself didn't think in some way about the accident and what she had done. She might recall the blast of the gun—and the feeling that she was flying backward—with a vividness that would cause her to flinch while performing a task as habitual as setting the dinner table or brushing the cats, or while in the midst of an endeavor that demanded serious concentration: reading through the scene from **The Secret Garden** that she was going to use in her audition for Brearley's fall musical or trying to decide exactly which of her blouses were appropriate now that she was in the eighth grade and had a full year's distance from that nightmarish elementary school jumper. She thought her father's tolerance for pain was downright heroic.

This morning, however, on what they presumed would be his triumphant return to work, she had come across a photo of him in a magazine and for the first time since the accident she had grown angry. Furious. The magazine was four and a half years old, and she was really only skimming it to kill a minute or two while her mother made absolutely certain that Dad didn't need anything before they left together for Brearley. She'd found the periodical wedged upright into the mass of glossy pulp in the brass magazine rack in the den, the one that sat beside the fireplace they never used.

In the journal was a photo essay about reading in America, in which dozens of photographers had captured all kinds of people reading in one twenty-four-hour span. Some were authors giving readings at universities or bookstores, and some were cameos of actors or politicians holding in their hands whatever book they happened to be enjoying at the moment. There were a few of small book groups gathered in suburban living rooms to discuss a novel they had just read together. And there in the midst of it was one of Molly the gorilla in her five-thousand-square-foot Woodside, California, pen with—of all people— Spencer McCullough beside her.

Over and over Charlotte read the photo caption:

> **Molly, a thirty-one-year-old female gorilla, and Spencer McCullough, the thirty-three-year-old communications director for the animal rights organization FERAL, savor one of both Molly's and McCullough's favorite children's books,** Maurice and the Magic Banana. **Though McCullough read**

the popular children's book aloud to the western lowland gorilla, Molly is capable of reading about Maurice's adventures with the enchanted fruit on her own. Molly understands well over two thousand words.

"Molly's and my DNA are 97.7 percent identical," says McCullough, an obvious fan of both the very real gorilla and the fictional Maurice. "Should it really be all that surprising that the two of us share a taste in children's literature, as well?"

No one had ever told her about the picture and when she saw it instantly she guessed why: When Maurice had enjoyed his brief stay atop the children's best-seller lists—nudging aside Harry Potter and Violet Baudelaire—her father had refused to read it aloud to her because he said it was completely idiotic and (in some way she didn't understand at the time) vaguely obscene. Certainly he hadn't viewed **Maurice and the Magic Banana** as "children's literature" when she'd been younger. Here he was, however, reading it aloud quite happily with some gorilla because he could use the opportunity to get some ink for FERAL. To make a point that gorillas were smart and should be respected.

Initially she had been hurt, and she had felt betrayed as she had ridden the bus across town with her mom. She had wandered into the school like a sleepwalker, and it was only after she had said good-bye to Catherine and arrived at her homeroom did the pain become transformed into resentment. Then irritation.

Then, finally, disgust. She was well aware of the cyclical nature of her relationship with her father—or, to be precise, of her father's relationship with her. She knew that he would go through phases in which he would be absent: Sometimes he would be literally gone, traveling to whatever dolphins or bunnies or baby elephants needed him that month, and sometimes he would be home in body but his spirit would be with those creatures great and small, all of whom, it seemed, were more interesting to him than his family. And then, almost as if he had suddenly discovered that he had a daughter (or a wife), for an all too brief period he would spoil her with whatever she wanted and do with her whatever she liked. She had grown accustomed to the pattern, savoring the waves when she could and accepting the barrenness of low tide when he was preoccupied with animals other than the mammals with whom he lived.

Including his cats. For an animal lover, he didn't spend a heck of a lot of time with the family's own cats, an irony that she discovered wasn't lost on her father when she brought it up to him one time when she was in the sixth grade.

"They don't need me," he'd said simply, shrugging, when she confronted him. "They're anything but mistreated. Besides, they have you and your mom."

And when she'd gone through that phase when she wanted a dog desperately, a big and gentle golden retriever like Grandmother's, her father had adamantly refused to subject a dog to the confines of their city apartment.

"Grandmother's dog is happy, and Grandmother lives in an apartment," she'd argued.

"No, your grandmother lives in a private Park Avenue wing of the Metropolitan Museum of Art. We just call that massive sprawl an apartment to be polite," he'd responded, smiling. But he hadn't budged.

Now in algebra, her last class of the day, she was still unable to push the image of her father and Molly and the banana-touting Maurice from her mind. Her ire was so great that she thought she might cry, and she vowed that before going home—after school and the information meeting for the kids trying out for **The Secret Garden**—she would stop by the bookstore near their apartment and buy a copy of **Maurice and the Magic Banana.** When her father came home from FERAL (and she had no delusions that he would leave work early this afternoon, not on the day of his triumphant return), she would paw at the air like a gorilla, and she would grunt, screech, and ululate like the monkeys she had seen on TV. (**Of course** she had never seen a monkey at a zoo like a normal child, a source of periodic bitterness for her—including this very moment.) Then she would toss the book into his lap and demand that he treat her as well as he had a big, hairy gorilla he'd probably met one time in his life.

PAIGE SUTHERLAND would never tell Dominique Germaine or Keenan Barrett what she thought of the FERAL offices, because she valued their business and people were entitled to their tastes—however misguided. Still, whenever she dropped by for a meeting it was always disarming to see so many framed images of rabbits intentionally blinded by cosmetic companies and chickens trapped in what looked like hatbox-sized cages and monkeys with wires up their . . . well, in every orifice on their bodies, it seemed. Dominique's office didn't have those sorts of photos, of course, because she had those massive paintings instead of birds whose plumage looked more than a little to Paige like human vaginas. She thought they would have been great in a New Age gynecologist's office.

There was also a massive, framed presentation of the Ovid poem that FERAL used parts of almost everywhere, the lettering in this case a pretentious cross between wedding invitation calligraphy and the ninth-century script of the monk of Saint Gall:

> **He who can slit his calf's throat, hear its cries**
> **Unmoved, who has the heart to kill his kid**
> **That screams like a small child, or eat the**
> **   bird**
> **His hand has reared and fed! How far does**
> **   this**
> **Fall short of murder? Where else does it**
> **   lead?**
> **Away with traps and snares and lures and**
> **   wiles!**
> **Never again lime twigs to cheat the birds,**
> **Nor feather ropes to drive the frightened**
> **   deer,**

Nor hide the hook with dainties that deceive!
Destroy what harms; destroy, but never eat;
Choose wholesome fare and never feast on meat!

Moreover, because so much of what FERAL did revolved around publicity, many of the employees' cubicle or office walls were covered with posters of the organization's recent campaigns against leather and ice cream and the running of the bulls in Pamplona. Most of these were pretty unpleasant, though she did notice an exception this morning: On a wall in the reception area hung a nice new poster of fashion models posing nude to protest fur. It was taken in one of the Greek statue galleries at the Metropolitan, and she couldn't imagine how Dominique or Spencer (or one of his minions) had convinced the museum to let them do a photo shoot there. She was mightily impressed. She thought the group would be a lot more successful if they did more with nudity and less with Ovid.

Nevertheless, Paige, too, was a vegetarian, though she still had her share of leather in her wardrobe and accessories. Oh, she'd been a bit of a phony when she'd first agreed to help FERAL with a complaint to the Federal Trade Commission about New York State's "Lucky Cow" campaign: a series of television commercials the state's dairy board had produced that suggested Empire State dairy cows were the luckiest bovines on the planet. In Dominique and Keenan and

Spencer's opinion, the ads took the notion of permissible puffery to an altogether new pinnacle of deceptiveness, since they suggested a dairy cow led a long and bucolic life, and stood around grazing and nursing her young in green fields with small coppices of shade trees most days. This was complete malarkey—but, alas, not everyone knew it.

What pushed her over the line firmly into FERAL's camp occurred the following year, during an outbreak of foot-and-mouth disease in Europe. She watched on the television news a pyre made from the carcasses of three-hundred-plus sheep on a farm near Inverness, a tiny fraction of the ten million cows and pigs and sheep being shot and burned and buried all across Great Britain and the continent across the channel—most of whom weren't even sick. Suddenly she was sobbing uncontrollably, since she knew from her work with FERAL that foot-and-mouth disease wasn't lethal either to people or animals and was actually treatable with appropriate veterinary care. Instead of trying to heal the animals, however, humans were obliterating them, and all because their value as food was in jeopardy and the slaughter was viewed as a reasonable way to restore confidence in meat.

Bottom line? Paige considered most of the individuals who worked for FERAL a tad fanatic and their behavior more times than not a bit extreme. But she was glad they were out there fighting the good fight, and she was happy to help—especially given the serious pile of money this particular case was likely to be worth. An injury this terrible? Her share of the contingent fee alone might well approach seven figures, given her firm's policy that you "eat what you kill." (Now, there, she thought, was an expression she was unlikely ever to share with Keenan or Dominique.)

She guessed altogether that somewhere between twenty-five or thirty people were employed in FERAL's New York office and another ten or twelve in Washington, D.C. Somewhere in central Connecticut the organization also rented space in a warehouse, where they stored the FERAL shirts and mugs and canvas totes, the Pleather cat suits and skirts, and the myriad trinkets people could buy to show their support for the group. Most of the New York employees seemed to be involved in what FERAL called its "campaigns"—education and publicity, which included everything from sending a "humane instruction trainer" into one of the few public schools on the planet that would actually allow a FERAL staffer onto the premises, to getting Spencer or Dominique on **Good Morning, America**—while most of the employees in Washington assisted with the legislative lobbying efforts. FERAL had five full-time attorneys, but Keenan and his young assistant were the only two based in New York.

This morning Paige expected to meet with Dominique and Keenan and Spencer, and she was neither surprised nor flattered that on Spencer's very first day back in the office she was on his agenda. She knew that what she did was important.

Consequently, when the receptionist, that strange young woman with the twin piercings in both eyebrows (four thin rings altogether) and the metal stud in her tongue told her (the stud occasionally clicking against her teeth as she spoke) that Spencer wasn't coming in after all, she began to wonder exactly what had happened to the poor man. She wasn't worried, because in the long run it could only make her life easier if he was physically falling apart. But in the short run it might complicate certain tasks. After all, they were planning to have a press conference the week after next, and one of the things she wanted to discuss today—and Spencer was critical to this part of the plan, both because he was the victim and because he was in charge of FERAL's communications programs—was the timing of their various announcements.

Still, it was clear that she and Dominique and Keenan would meet anyway, and the receptionist made it sound as if one of Spencer's assistants would join them as well. She guessed it would be that sweet Randy Mitchell, a young woman who had wanted originally to be a model but was just not quite beautiful enough: She was a tad too short, her face a bit too round, and even in long sweaters and those blouses of hers that were meant to remain untucked it was evident that she was little too wide in the hips. But she was certainly pretty enough to pose in many of FERAL's promotional pieces, and in the course of three and a half years she had gone from being one of the FERAL Granola Girls—the young women who wore little but strategically draped garlands of granola while handing out vegan granola bars for free outside of Taco Bell, McDonald's, and Kentucky Fried Chicken—to being Spencer's principal assistant. She was, Paige knew, on a first-name basis with the producers of all the morning news programs and afternoon talk shows, and Paige had a pretty good sense that Randy was capable of getting the attention of the lifestyle and science reporters at most of the nation's premier newspapers.

She emerged now from the glass doors behind the receptionist's half-moon of a desk, wearing a peasant dress that fell almost to her ankles and black sandals that looked like they were made from old tires. She was smiling, however, and Paige had to admit that the woman had a beam that was downright telegenic.

"I hear Spencer isn't returning to work today," she said to Randy as they wandered down the corridor to Dominique's office. "Has something happened?"

"He wasn't feeling well."

"He hasn't been feeling well since the accident."

"He got sick in the cab."

"Vomit sick?"

Randy nodded sympathetically.

"The flu?" she asked.

"I didn't talk to him. Dominique did. But it didn't sound like the flu. It sounded to Dominique like Spencer was trying to do too much too soon, and his body was rebelling. He didn't offer to do this meeting by speakerphone, and Dominique didn't even suggest it."

She saw that Keenan and Dominique were already sitting at the circular table in Dominique's office, and

she guessed they'd been meeting for a few minutes already because both of their paper cups—it looked as if
his had held coffee and hers had held herbal tea—were
nearly empty. Dominique was curled inside a clingy
black sweater dress most women Dominique's age
(even women who jogged as religiously as Dominique
and worked out as strenuously with a personal trainer)
would never even pull off a rack, but it seemed to
work on the FERAL executive: Even at forty-some-
thing, she moved with the confidence and grace of a
tiger. Keenan, she saw, was wearing the sort of pin-
striped suit that the lawyers in her own office wore. If,
in fact, he hadn't been wearing those hideous plastic
wing tips, he could have passed for an attorney in her
own tony firm.

She took the seat beside Keenan as a lawyer-to-
lawyer courtesy, and Randy sat between her and
Dominique. Once they had dispensed with the pleasantries and Dominique had made it clear that she had
told Spencer not even to try returning to work for the
rest of the week after what he had endured that morning in the cab, Paige started pulling her notes from her
briefcase (the ballistic nylon one she reserved for her
meetings with FERAL, not the leather one she still
preferred to use with the rest of her clients). She began
by passing stapled stacks of paper a quarter inch thick
to the three other people, keeping the copy well
marked with her notes for herself.

"Here, essentially, is where we are on the lawsuit,"
she began. "I'm still expecting we'll be able to file in
two weeks and announce the action with a press con-

ference at my firm. I've also attached some very rough thoughts on the sorts of things I'll be asking Adirondack for in the interrogatories later this fall. Obviously, I'll want all the materials and documents that refer to the bolt and the extractor on John Seton's model, as well as any prototypes. I'm also going to ask for gross sales, gross profit, net profit, managers' salaries and bonuses, the contributions they make to hunting organizations and the NRA, and their expenditures for safety engineering and research. Don't worry: If that last figure isn't in reality paltry, we can certainly portray it that way—especially if we compare it to, say, their gross advertising expenditures."

"Will they have to answer all that?" Randy asked.

"Oh, if a judge says so, they will," Keenan said in his soft, slow voice. "And they'll have to answer it all under oath."

"Will it come to that?" the young assistant continued.

As much as she liked Keenan, Paige wanted complete control of this meeting (the truth was, she wanted complete control of all meetings), and so she quickly jumped in: "Their lawyers will object to the financial questions. And, I have to admit, some of the information is irrelevant and some will only become important if we request punitive damages. But, yes, depending upon the judge, we'll be able to get most of it."

"You plan on deposing Morton Knapp?" Keenan asked, referring to the Adirondack CEO, carefully uncapping a fountain pen as he spoke.

She hadn't decided yet, but she guessed it couldn't hurt. The CEO probably wouldn't know much about the mechanics of the extractor on any one rifle, much less about obscure design specifications, but all those "I don't knows" and "I wasn't involveds" would make him look arrogant and removed, and that could only help. Besides, these days most people loathed any executive who had the letters CEO or CFO attached to his name. "Yes, definitely," Paige heard herself saying now, as if she'd planned on deposing Knapp all along.

"I've also decided that Spencer must see a psychiatrist," she went on, "and I've picked out two we can consider, both of whom would be very . . . sympathetic. We already have plenty of experts who can talk to the physical disability, but I want it clear that there is profound psychological trauma as well."

"How about for the little girl?" This was Keenan again, and she nodded—nodded sincerely, this time.

"You may know this already, but the girl's aunt is a therapist. Seton's wife. And so she was all over that. The kid is going to see a doctor in Manhattan named Warwick. A woman. She sounded very nice."

"You've spoken to her?" Randy asked. She sounded incredulous.

"Yes. I wanted to make sure we could work with her." Keenan smiled. "And?"

"If we can't, we'll simply have the girl see someone else. My sense is we don't have a lot to worry about: The child sounds pretty disturbed by this little disaster."

"Does all this have to happen before the press conference?" Randy wondered, flipping abstractedly through the papers Paige had handed her. It was clear she thought the task was impossible—which, if they needed it all when they filed the lawsuit and held the press conference, it was. Fortunately, they didn't need most of it anytime soon. So far there had been very little media coverage of the accident outside of some brief stories in small newspapers in New Hampshire and Vermont. Nothing had been picked up by the majors on the wires, however, because none of the short articles from northern New England had mentioned what Spencer did for a living. Keenan's initial fears that Leno and Letterman would make FERAL out to be either a group of morons or a group of hypocrites (or both) before the organization could put its spin on the story had so far proven unfounded. As a result, Paige was confident they still had the upper hand and were in control of how they disseminated the information.

Now she patted Randy's wrist (Paige wasn't precisely sure why she liked this gesture so much, but she told herself it was compassionate and theatric at once) and reassured her, "No, it doesn't have to happen in the next two weeks. We can embarrass Adirondack quite badly with what we have already. The basic facts of this story."

"What about the deer?" Dominique asked, and the woman ran the fingers of one hand gently over the lobe of her ear, skirting the tiny silver dolphin that dangled nearby. Her nails were long, and today they were painted a deep cardinal red. "I want to be sure we get to the deer at the press conference. Let us not forget that Spencer's lawsuit is merely our means to the animals."

Randy reached for a manila folder of her own. "We'll have all sorts of surprises."

"Such as?" Dominique said. It was obvious to Paige that this was the part that really interested the director.

"Well, for starters, hunting actually may cause wildlife overpopulation, because those buck-only laws leave six to ten does per male. If hunters were honestly concerned about keeping the herd the right size for the environment, they'd be shooting does instead of bucks. But that just doesn't seem very macho—or **sporting**—does it? Human predators are also less likely than natural predators to kill the weakest deer—hunters want that really big rack—which over time diminishes the strength of the species. And, of course, hunting inflicts enormous stress on deer, and that limits the animals' ability to eat and digest properly, so they don't have the fat they need to get through a tough northern winter."

"And the numbers? The media love a good statistic," Dominique said.

"I do, too. Spencer taught me that. First of all, it's clear that hunters kill a lot more deer than the records claim. For every animal that's slaughtered, easily another one or two are only wounded and die agonizing deaths in the woods from infection, starvation or blood loss. We can also present the numbers of cows and horses and dogs and people—yes, people—killed by hunting: 191 last year. One fellow in Maine took a stray bullet in the head while watching a football game on a Sunday afternoon in his living room. Ironically, he was a hunter, too, but he stayed home that day because he's a real Patriots fan."

"Will we have pictures?" Dominique asked.

"Of deer or people?"

"Deer. I really don't care about a couple hundred dead hunters."

"Yes, we'll have pictures of deer. We'll have them after they've been shot and disemboweled, and some that were left to die in the woods and were found by people who happened to live nearby. We'll even have a few of motherless fawns that starved to death in the snow."

"Good. Well, not good. But helpful."

"You bet. And I came across one more study that's really surprising. A report by the Erie Insurance Company showed that insurance claims for car accidents involving deer are five times more common during hunting season in Pennsylvania than in the rest of the year."

"Meaning?"

"Well, hunters claim that by thinning the herd, they're doing drivers a favor: fewer deer, fewer car accidents. But this study says they're actually chasing panicked animals onto highways and streets, thereby causing more accidents." She smiled with satisfaction at the link she had found, and Dominique nodded appreciatively.

"Do we need to address the understory?" This was

Keenan, and Paige instantly felt a small chill descend on the table. The understory was going to be the weak link when FERAL defended deer, because it would make the animals appear to be predators themselves. In areas where there wasn't any hunting, especially places like Westchester and Fairfield County, the ever-increasing size of the herd was transforming the very ecosystems in which the animals lived as they devoured the plants that grew beneath the forest canopy and on which a sizable ark of smaller creatures depended. It was not uncommon for biologists to find foot-high cedars that were actually twelve and thirteen years old. Among the ramifications were fewer places for birds to nest or stop over in their migrations, as well as great ensuing swings in the numbers of insects.

Dominique, however, simply waved off Keenan's concern. "No, we don't. This is about hunting."

"There are scientists who contend that the only way to keep some ecosystems from falling into complete chaos is hunting—"

"And there are scientists who turn flamethrowers on pigs so they can look at burns on live tissue. If you really believe we need to be prepared for a discussion of ecosystems, we'll just trot out the birth control studies."

She watched both Keenan and Randy nod patiently. They both knew that birth control only worked in places like Fire Island, worlds so small that individual deer could be tracked annually and darted with contraception. Still, this was about racket, not reality, and Dominique probably was right. And so Paige sat forward in her chair, a palpably physical need driving her to be back in the center of the conversation. "Now," she began, "even though the point of the press conference is to announce the lawsuit—"

"And call attention to the moral horrors of hunting," Dominique said.

"Yes, of course. But from the perspective of the lawsuit, I want to be sure that we do not reveal too much about our case or our plans. I don't want any of Spencer's doctors or his physical therapist talking, I don't want a psychiatrist there if one happens to evaluate him in the next week or two, and I don't want any ballistics experts present. The only people on the dais with me should be Dominique and Spencer. Are you okay with that, Keenan? I just don't want three people from FERAL up there, because technically FERAL isn't even a party to this suit."

"Oh, I've spent enough time in front of cameras in my life. And I know I speak too slowly for the younger folks in broadcast. Give me a judge and a jury anytime," Keenan said. Then: "When is the last time you heard from Adirondack?"

"Thursday of last week. They want to start talking, but I'm not interested in negotiating since we're not interested in settling. At least not yet."

"At least not until we know more about the gun, right?" Randy asked.

"And John Seton only got the gun back from the New Hampshire authorities on—" she glanced at a note on her pad—"the eleventh of August. And by the time we got it back from him and down to the lab, it was the fourteenth."

"The state's attorney made our public defender friend sweat for ten days before deciding not to press charges? Isn't that something? That alone must have taught him a lesson," Keenan said.

"And with people taking their summer vacations and Labor Day and the laboratory's own backlog of work," she continued, "they haven't gotten to our gun. Nevertheless, they should have something for us any day now. And that's one of the very last gaps we need to fill in before we file the suit: the concrete specifics of our theory of liability. But the fact is, even if the people in Maryland can't find anything wrong with the extractor, there is still the issue that when you un-load the magazine, a bullet remains in the chamber. It would be more difficult to win with that in front of a jury, but we could certainly threaten to make enough noise that Adirondack might say uncle. Now, I haven't spoken to Spencer today, but you have, Dominique. I presume he still wants us to drag this out as long as possible before settling."

Dominique took a deep breath and then said—her voice a human purr—"Spencer is ailing. I don't hon-estly know for sure when he'll be back. But I believe I can speak for him when I tell you that, yes, he wants to drag this out for as long as the media is interested." She looked at Keenan. "You agree?"

"I do. And I also believe that he'll stay mad at his brother-in-law for as long as needs be, and his shoulder will continue to torment him until this is behind him. And he'll bear it all, because he is, like each of us, a true believer. I think ol' Spencer would be more than willing to—pardon the pun—take a bullet on behalf of the deer of the great northern forest."

AT LUNCH THAT DAY in the teachers' lounge, Catherine finally asked Eric Miller exactly how old he was. It was a spontaneous question, triggered, she guessed, because she had just spoken to Spencer on the phone and heard that he'd thrown up in the cab and had to return home. She felt her husband's setback acutely, experiencing not merely the disappointment he was enduring at their apartment across town but also the harrowing sense that her own life's opportunities were continuing to dwindle. To herself (and only to herself) she could admit the truth: She, too, was trapped by her husband's disability. Yes, she was back at school, and in the days immediately after the shooting she had seriously doubted such a thing would be possible. But there was a far bigger issue in her mind: She certainly had not admitted to Spencer that had he not been crippled by a bullet and nearly died, she would have told him she was dissatisfied with their marriage—with **him,** to be honest.

"Twenty-nine," Eric said, after taking a sip from his bottled iced tea.

She nodded.

"Why?" he asked her, and even his eyes seemed to be laughing. He was sitting below the window, and the sun was pouring in on the back of his head and his hair seemed to shine like a freshly buffed pumpkin pine floor. Sometimes she thought his hair was only blond. Today she decided it had splashes of a red—not unlike her own hair—especially in his sideburns and the long, unruly swath of bang he had to keep pushing back off his forehead. This afternoon he looked more like a surfer than an English teacher. He had spent much of the summer on Nantucket, and his skin was the sort of deep tan she herself hadn't had since she was a child and her mother was still oblivious to sunblock.

"I was just wondering," she answered. "I didn't think you'd hit thirty."

He smiled. "Is that a good thing or a bad thing?"

"Sometimes it's nice to see a man who still has a little puppylike awkwardness. That hubris that's really just optimism. Innocence. On the other hand, sometimes it's also nice to see a man who's a little more calm. Not wizened—but chastened, perhaps."

"You didn't answer my question. Is it good or bad that I haven't reached thirty?"

"It isn't either. It was just that I didn't know."

"Are you suggesting I'm puppylike?"

"Hah!"

"And if I were to ask you your age?"

"I'd tell you."

"Okay: How old are you?"

"Thirty-eight."

"No. Really?"

"Don't try to flatter me. I know how old I look.

And we both know that I have a daughter who turned thirteen last month."

"You don't look thirty-eight. Honest to God, if I met you in, say, a bar, and didn't know Charlotte was your daughter, I would peg you for my age."

"I doubt that."

"I'm being completely sincere."

"Any man who even tries to **peg** a woman's age in a bar is completely incapable of sincerity."

"Hey, you were the one who just admitted you were wondering about my age!"

"Because you're a good teacher and I know you're younger than I am. I was curious."

"People get curious in bars, Catherine."

They were alone at the moment, and suddenly she wanted them to be beyond this conversation about age before another teacher strolled in. As one certainly would. She wished she hadn't asked him his age now in the first place, because it made her feel disloyal to Spencer. Sometimes she thought the only subject she should talk about was her husband: his disability, his pain, his attempts to regain a semblance of control over his life.

But it was hard. Often she wanted to talk about anything but his injury, especially if she was around people who knew about the way FERAL was going to make the lawsuit a cause célèbre. She never wanted to think about that, much less discuss it. It made her feel at once like a bad mother and a bad sister.

And so with an almost guilty quiver to her voice— guilty both because she hadn't been speaking of

Spencer sooner and because she was speaking of him now largely out of obligation—she brought up her husband. The transition was awkward, clunky. She guessed it was obvious to Eric that she was changing the subject because she didn't want to flirt with him at the moment.

"Spencer tried going back to work today," she said. "He didn't make it." And then she started describing for this tan younger man with a teacher's playful smile the assortment of tools that Spencer had lined up on his bureau last night, and the hope that an item as small as a dressing stick or a button hook would give him these days.

"God," Eric said simply when she was done. "What can I do?"

"Nothing."

"Surely there's something. Can I bring you guys dinner tomorrow night?"

"We don't need dinner."

"But you have to eat."

"And you can cook? You?"

"Come on: Couldn't you cook when you were twenty-nine?"

"I had been married for six years when I was twenty-nine."

"Wow. You really did get married young."

"Yes. I did," she admitted, and then—concerned that her voice had lacked the angry defensiveness she had once felt whenever someone even hinted that she and Spencer may have married too young—she said quickly, "I was very fortunate. Some people have to wait half a lifetime to find a soul mate."

He nodded. "And some people never do."

"Indeed."

They both were quiet for a moment, and then Eric continued, "So: dinner. How about I bring it by tomorrow night around seven?"

"People have been bringing us meals for the last couple of weeks. Neighbors in the building, our friends, people from FERAL. Since we got back from New Hampshire, I don't think I've made dinner more than four or five times. Seriously: You don't have to do this."

"Ah, but I **get** to. There's a difference. Okay? Is anyone bringing you dinner tomorrow night?"

"Not that I know of."

"Good. Then I will. I won't stay, but I'll drop off a small feast—no animals, of course. Is dairy all right?"

"Not if you want Spencer to eat."

"Very well, no cream sauces."

"And no soup."

"No soup?"

She shook her head. "It wouldn't be pretty. Spencer has a very long way to go with his left hand."

CATHERINE WAS ACTUALLY PLANNING to play tennis this afternoon for the first time since the accident. She and her friend Angie Merullo were going to meet in the park and play an hour of singles.

But once Catherine had heard that Spencer hadn't made it to work she had called Angie and canceled and gone straight home after school. Charlotte would be a couple of hours behind her, because she had an information meeting about the autumn musical.

She got to the apartment soon after four and found Spencer sitting up in bed with Emma the cat on his legs. The cat glanced up at her when she entered the bedroom, then gazed back at Spencer. Whenever anyone in their house was ill, it was Emma who would seem most desirous of providing solace and comfort and warmth. She liked to sleep on the sick.

Spencer was wearing tennis shorts and what she presumed was the beige short-sleeved sport shirt he'd put on first thing in the morning, but then she remembered he'd thrown up in the cab and must have changed as soon as he'd returned home. The **New York Times** was a wad of crinkled papers on the floor by the bed. Before the accident, Spencer read the newspaper with meticulous care, and even on those days when she would read the paper after him she always found it looking as if it were fresh from the newsstand. No more. It was simply too difficult for him to fold the paper with only one hand.

"Hi, sweetheart," she murmured, and she sat gently on the bed beside him.

He turned to her and sighed, but otherwise he didn't say a word. His hair, she realized suddenly, had started going gray at the temples. There they were: white threads from a sewing box. Had this happened only this morning, or had it been changing throughout the summer and somehow she hadn't noticed? He looked exhausted, and she wondered if he'd been doing his exercises. Nick wasn't scheduled to be here today, but perhaps Spencer had called him and the therapist had had a free hour. Perhaps Spencer had done his reps on his own.

"You were doing your range-of-motions, weren't you?" she said.

"No."

"Nick wasn't here?"

"It's not his day."

"I know. I just thought . . ."

"I'm too tired. And right now my shoulder hurts too much."

She stroked his leg, because even now she was afraid to touch his back or his neck. She feared she would jostle him and cause him yet more pain.

"I saw you bought some of that cheddar-flavored soy cheese," he said quietly. "Thank you. Around one thirty, I tried to grill some in a sandwich."

"Good for you!"

He shook his head and said—his voice the sort of fatalistic monotone she wasn't sure she'd ever heard from him—"Oh, it wasn't good." With his eyes he motioned down toward his right hand, still slung against his chest in its sling. The skin there was mottled with a series of deep red welts and watery blisters, and she saw that a line of the tawny fur along all four of his fingers was shriveled and black.

"Oh, God, Spencer," she said, "let me get some lotion for that! Have you called the doctor?"

"It's not that bad. In fact, I don't feel a thing . . . obviously."

"What happened?"

"I was leaning over the stove and I didn't realize that my hand was resting along the edge of the frying pan. I only looked down when I smelled something burning. The hair had already curled up, and the skin may actually have been smoldering. I don't know. It looked pretty nasty. I put cold water on it. At least I think it was cold. Who knows?"

"I think there's some medicated lotion in the bathroom. It may be as old as Charlotte, but—"

"It doesn't hurt."

"No, but we need to get something on it so it heals," she said, and she carefully rose from the bed. "Some lotion or something. Let's call the doctor."

He breathed in deeply through his nose. "No, let's not."

"You've already called him?" she asked, a litany of names forming in her mind as she verbalized the question. Did she mean Dr. Tasker, the orthopedic and trauma surgeon they'd been referred to at Roosevelt, or Dr. Leeds, the cosmetic surgeon at Lenox Hill? Or did she mean Spencer's primary care physician, Dr. Ives, the guy he'd been seeing for his physical exams and minor aches and pains ever since they'd moved back to Manhattan from Connecticut? She realized she wasn't sure whom she had meant.

"No, I didn't call anyone. And, please, let's not bother. Okay? It's a burn. It happens."

"It just . . ."

"Yes?"

"It just looks so painful," she murmured.

He took his index finger on his left hand and rubbed at the raw skin and the scorched follicles of hair. "Well, we both know that's no longer an issue," he said, and then she watched him do something he had begun to do with increasing frequency. He stopped touching the burn and brought his left hand before his face, no more than six or seven inches away, and he spread wide his fingers, palm toward him. And then he seemed to run his eyes over each finger, occasionally flexing one individually or curling all of them together as if they were petals on a flower that was closing for the night. Sometimes she wasn't sure he was even conscious that he had developed this tic, and she'd considered asking him over the weekend why he did it. But she thought she understood. He was, pure and simple, amazed at the dexterity that he—most of us, she knew—always had taken for granted. He might not have anywhere near the control with his left hand that he once had with his right, but it was still an astonishing bit of machinery.

"Where's Charlotte?" he asked, as he bent his left index finger toward him again and again, as if he were plunking a piano key.

"At school. Audition information meeting for **The Secret Garden**." Her eyes were beginning to cross as she tried to look into his face through the cobweb of his fingers.

"Have you ever noticed how limited the ring finger is in comparison to the index finger?" he asked. "I'm not even sure it's as helpful as the pinky."

She looked down again at his burn. Some of the blisters looked particularly nasty: They could become infected and Spencer might never know until it was too late—though too late for what she wasn't sure. Still, she nodded and then carefully rose from the bed. She decided she would go to the kitchen and call Dr. Ives, Spencer's regular physician, and ask him what he thought Spencer should do.

Twenty

John and Sara and Willow had breakfast in silence—most of their meals were silent these days, unless Patrick was awake and felt the need to contribute. When they were finished, John stood, grabbed his attaché off the floor by the coatrack, and walked Willow to the end of their driveway. The bus stop was about fifty yards farther down the road. He kissed his daughter once on her forehead and then climbed into the Volvo (the one that would always hold for him his memories of an Adirondack rifle in the trunk), and turned the silver key in the ignition. He hadn't spoken to Spencer since he and his family had left his mother's house in Sugar Hill a month ago, and he guessed it might be years before they'd speak again. He glanced in the rearview mirror before starting to back the car from the driveway, and paused for a moment when he saw how bereaved and haggard the eyes were that gazed back at him from the glass.

HE WENT STRAIGHT to the courthouse this morning, because his caseload today showed a welfare fraud, a pair of unrelated larcenies (one petty, one grand), an unlawful mischief, and a sexual assault on a minor. It was almost lunchtime now as he sat in the basement of the building in an eight-by-eight-foot room made almost entirely of cement blocks painted light yellow, listening to a twenty-three-year-old named Brady Simmons tell him across a thin table, "It's a long story, see" (arguably the most common construction any of his clients ever made with five words), before launching into his explanation as to why he had sex with a fifteen-year-old girl.

Abruptly his cell phone started to ring, and he saw by the number that it was his brother-in-law's human attack dog of a lawyer. Paige Sutherland. She had been trying to reach him for days now to update him on her plans for the lawsuit and discuss how she'd want to prep him for the deposition later that autumn. He decided he might as well get it over with—agree, at least, to a date they could meet once the lawsuit was filed—and so he asked Simmons for a minute and rapped on the door for one of the guards to let him out.

"Hello, Paige," he said, reaching into the front pocket of his blazer for his Palm as he spoke.

"You're a hard man to reach," she said, and though her voice was sweet he detected the slight edge of chastisement.

"Oh, you know the drill," he murmured. "A lot of clients who are, well, not as reliable as we might like."

"No, actually I don't know. The sorts of people I represent are extremely reliable."

"Uh-huh."

"Oh, don't take offense."

He ignored her and tried to find a time on his calendar when he could subject himself to the torture of a morning or afternoon discussing his role in this disaster with her.

"I've left a couple messages for you on your voice mail," she went on when he was quiet. "So I guess you know why I'm calling."

"Yes, let's get this over with."

"Get this over with? You make it sound like you're the one being sued! You make it sound like we're not on the same side. You're helping your brother-in-law by doing this. You're helping to make a gun company take responsibility for—"

"Paige, please. My brother-in-law doesn't even speak to me anymore. We haven't said a single word to each other in five weeks. You know that."

"Time heals all wounds—"

"Except Spencer's."

"That was exactly what I was thinking right after I said it! Too funny. Do you have representation yet? Why don't I schedule a meeting through them? Really, we have so much to go over."

"I . . . haven't finalized my choice for a lawyer yet."

"John, really. What would you do if one of your own clients were behaving this way?"

"My clients always behave this way."

"It will be painless. Trust me."

"I promise you: Reliving that night will be anything but painless. Maybe if you weren't planning on making such a big deal about this in the media, I would—"

"It's what Spencer wants."

"That press conference? It's not what my sister wants. Or what I believe is in the best interests of my niece."

"First of all, it's Spencer's life we're dealing with. He is the one who has to live with this trag—"

"We all have to live with this tragedy!"

"Well, yes, but some of you have two functioning arms to help you cope. Spencer doesn't. And as for young Charlotte, well, Spencer is her father. You're merely her uncle. I believe you should defer to his wishes. Don't you?"

"If Spencer and I could just talk about this."

"Spencer and I don't make a practice of discussing your relationship, but as you yourself just pointed out, it's pretty clear that he's not quite ready to resume communications with you."

He considered briefly asking her to give Spencer a message, but his brother-in-law wasn't listening to his pleas through Catherine—the man's own wife—so there was no reason to believe that Spencer would listen to whatever Paige said on his behalf.

He sighed so loudly on the phone that Paige murmured, "Oh, John, it's not that bad," but he had the distinct sense that she was smiling.

"Where do you want to do this? In New York or Vermont?" he asked.

"I thought we could do it in your neck of the woods. I'm going to be in New Hampshire the last week in September with the surgeons and those EMTs, and I could scoot over to Burlington on that Wednesday—the twenty-ninth. What does your schedule look like that day?"

"I don't have to look at it to tell you that I can't do a Wednesday. Not ever. Wednesday is the weekly calendar call, and—"

"And you have dozens of your little DWIs and pickpockets to parade before the judge. I understand."

"Please do not demean—"

"People who drive drunk and pick other people's pockets? Honestly, John, they don't need me to demean them. They do a pretty good job of demeaning themselves. How about that Tuesday instead—the twenty-eighth?"

"Fine."

"Ah, progress! Bless you, John Seton. How is midmorning? I could fly up on the first flight out of—"

"I have to go," he said, not because he felt an overarching desire to return to a conversation with a young man who actually believed that he'd behaved responsibly (or, at least, not unreasonably) when he'd had consensual sex with a fifteen-year-old girl, but simply because he couldn't stand to speak for another moment with Paige Sutherland.

"Get a lawyer!" he heard her shout into the cell phone, and he had the sense that she was going to add something more, but he was already pressing the small button with his thumb that ended their conversation.

A PARTNER IN SARA'S PRACTICE had asked her once in August if her niece had begun to process why in reality she had shot her father.

"She shot him because she thought he was a deer,"

Sara had answered simply, hoping that she hadn't sounded defensive. The partner—a woman whose three teenage children behaved so outrageously that Sara had always considered this other woman's parenting skills more than a little suspect—had merely nodded and smiled.

Most of the time, what Sara had told her partner was exactly what she believed: Charlotte indeed had presumed she was shooting a deer. That's all there was to it. Sometimes, however, the idea that her vegetarian niece—the daughter of the communications director for FERAL—was either planning or pretending (who could ever know for sure?) to shoot a wild animal suggested to Sara that her niece might actually have some unresolved conflicts with her dad. And then she would have to admit to herself that this other woman in her practice, despite her apparent difficulties raising her own children, may have been onto something.

Now, as she and Willow drove from her daughter's elementary school to ballet practice, the September sun highlighting the first orange leaves at the very tips of the sugar maples and the dying, knee-high remains of the cow corn, she asked the child the question that off and on had passed through her mind.

"Willow?" she began, and she turned down the volume on the radio. She was careful not to turn the radio off, because she did not want her daughter to view the conversation as ominous.

"Yes?"

"Can I ask you a question about your cousin?"

"Sure. What about her?"

"Oh, it's nothing serious. I've just always wondered . . . I guess I've been curious . . . does Charlotte ever wish their family ate meat?" **There,** Sara thought to herself. **A perfectly innocuous opening.**

"No, I don't think so. Why?"

"I was just thinking about the accident."

"Plenty of people are vegetarians. I don't think it's a big deal for anyone in the whole world except Grandmother."

"Oh, I know. But her dad . . . Uncle Spencer . . . what he does for a living makes it all so . . . so public. That does make it a big deal."

"Charlotte actually likes the taste of things like his awful Soy-garine."

"Well, what about the other parts of her life? All the things that I know she doesn't get to do because of Uncle Spencer?"

"You mean like the time we all went to Sea World, and she wasn't allowed to come with us?"

"Yes. Exactly."

"Maybe sometimes she misses that sort of thing. But I also think she's kind of proud of her dad."

"You do?"

"Oh, yeah. At least she used to be. She thought it was incredibly cool when he was on **The Today Show** a couple years ago. She's into that sort of thing."

"So she never gets angry at him . . ."

"At her dad? Oh, she does. But as far as I can tell, mostly she gets mad at her mom."

"Yes, we have gotten to witness Catherine and Charlotte go at it over the years, haven't we?"

"Sure have. And Charlotte and Grandmother in the summer."

"And heaven knows all mothers and daughters can have pretty dicey relationships, especially when the daughter is an adolescent—or almost one," she said. Then she added quickly, her voice light, "Now, don't you get any ideas, Willow Seton."

"I can't be a brat?"

"I'd rather you weren't."

She glanced back after she spoke, and Willow seemed to be pondering seriously the notion that heretofore unchallenged behavioral boundaries might be worth exploring. When she returned her gaze to the road, she asked, "Do you think there's anything in particular that Aunt Catherine does that might trigger all that anger in Charlotte? Anything specific she does around your cousin or your uncle? Or maybe just around other people?"

There was a long silence, so long that Sara was about to repeat the question. Finally: "Nope."

"Nothing at all?"

"Mom? I just told you: No. And it's not like Charlotte and Aunt Catherine spend their whole lives fighting."

She wasn't sure why, but she sensed there was something here that Willow wasn't telling her about Aunt Catherine and Charlotte, the silence not so much the filing cards in the girl's brain riffling for an example as it was the quiet of a child trying to avoid a potentially unpleasant conversation. But she knew also not to push the girl. The important thing, she decided, was that in Willow's opinion Charlotte wasn't harboring any special hostility toward her father.

Or, at least, she hadn't been venting constantly to Willow that July and August.

"Can I ask you something else?"

"Go ahead." There was a twinge of exasperation in her daughter's voice now.

"Actually, it's something I need to tell you."

"What?"

Initially Sara hadn't planned on bringing this up for days, but then John had phoned her this morning with the news that he and Paige Sutherland had set a date to begin his preparation for his deposition. That meant they would have to start prepping Willow, too. And so Sara decided that she had better tell her that, like her father, soon enough she would have to start speaking to lawyers.

"You've heard your father use the term **deposition** before, right?"

"I guess."

"Do you know what it means?"

"No. Not really."

Carefully she pulled into the left lane to pass a lumbering manure spreader and waited until they were back on the right side of the road to continue. "It's like an interview. But the person asking the questions is a lawyer instead of a reporter."

"Uh-huh."

"And you're supposed to tell the truth—just like a witness in a courtroom, you swear an oath—because the lawyer uses the information from the interview to try to figure out what happened at the scene of a . . . at an event. It's not a big deal. We'll go to someone's office and we'll—"

"I do not want to talk to a lawyer! No way!"

Only briefly was Sara surprised by how quickly Willow had determined where this conversation was heading. Her daughter was sharp, and she and John had never treated her like a baby: They'd tried always to respect her intellect and talk to her like a grown-up.

"Well—"

"No! I didn't do anything but open the trunk to get Patrick's diapers! How was I supposed to know there was a gun in there? And—"

"Willow—"

"And you know I told Charlotte to leave the gun alone! I told her not to touch it! I've told you that, I told the trooper guy that, I—"

Already Sara was braking to a stop in the patch of grass along the side of the road, grateful that the ground was flat and the farmer hadn't put his fence too close to the asphalt.

"I've told anyone who will listen that! And now I'm done talking about that whole night, okay? I won't talk to anyone anymore!"

She put the vehicle in park and turned around. "Willow? Are you finished?" she asked, her inflection, she hoped, playful and soft.

"I'm just telling you: I'm not taking any oaths and I'm not talking about that night with any lawyers."

"A second ago you said you won't talk about that night with anyone. Now I'm hearing it's the presence of the lawyer that's the deal breaker. Can you help me understand a little more why—"

"You're using your therapist's voice. I hate it when you use your therapist's voice with me. I'm your daughter, not one of your patients!"

She considered offering Willow a small, sympathetic smile, but she feared if she did her daughter would see clearly parental condescension. The truth was that she **was** using her therapist's voice. "Fair enough," she said, evening her tone. "Tell me why you're getting so upset about this, without—"

"It's because—"

"Without interrupting me. It's my turn to speak now, okay? Here's what I want to know: Are you getting upset because you don't want to talk about that night anymore or because you might have to talk about it with a lawyer?"

Willow cupped her hands in front of her nose and mouth like a gas mask.

"Willow? Please? Why did my mentioning the lawyer bother you? The truth is, we've talked about that night a fair amount over the last month and it never seemed to trouble you before."

"How do you know that? Why would you think that? Of course it troubled me! You don't know what I saw, you don't know what I'm feeling!" the child said, speaking through her hands. Sara considered prying her fingers from her face but figured this, too, would only antagonize her daughter further. She decided there was a fair amount of disingenuousness going on here: Yes, Willow had been the first to reach Uncle

Spencer, but until this moment Willow had never once behaved in a manner that might suggest the vision had been traumatizing. They'd talked about that night at length when they were in New Hampshire, and—usually when John wasn't in the room—they'd talked about Uncle Spencer's likely disability when they were home in Vermont. They'd talked about what Charlotte may or may not have been experiencing in terms of guilt, and what John clearly was enduring in terms of self-loathing. At least between mother and daughter the accident certainly had not been a forbidden subject.

No, Sara decided now, this wasn't about the shooting. This was about . . . the lawyer. And when she analyzed what had just occurred between the two of them in the car, she was pretty sure that it was precisely when she had said to Willow that she would be expected to tell the lawyer the truth—as if she were a witness in a courtroom—that the child had suddenly gone nuclear. And that might mean there was more to the accident than she knew.

Than anyone but Willow and Charlotte knew.

"You're right, sweetheart," she said, stalling for time while she tried to think. "I don't know what you're feeling."

The hands came down from the mouth, but her daughter wrapped them around her chest and stared angrily out the window. In the field they could see Holsteins clustered in groups of four and five, some of the animals grazing lazily near a trough.

She decided that she should probably get Willow to

ballet and not force the issue right now. But with a pronounced ripple across her stomach and a slight fuzziness in her eyes—a sensation reminiscent of the very first wave of seasickness—she understood that she had just learned something important: She might not know as much about what had occurred that night in Sugar Hill as she thought she did.

She took a deep breath to calm herself. Then she smiled at her daughter and put the car back into drive. She told herself that while Willow was dancing she would try to figure out exactly what to do next.

ANDRE NADEAU, avid sportsman (Translation? Deer hunter) and single father of two, Andre Nadeau with a misdemeanor assault on his record (a fine, probation, but no time to be served), called John late that afternoon in his office. Awash in guilt John took the call, because he hadn't spoken to Andre since before he had left for New Hampshire on the second to last day of July—where he had then remained far longer than planned. Consequently, it was no thanks to John that Andre received a mere fine and probation, despite smashing a glass beer mug on the head of one Cameron Gerrity to the tune of thirty-four stitches. Andre could thank Whitney Bowerman, one of John's PDs who had pinch-hit for him while he had driven back and forth between his mother-in-law's and the hospital in Hanover those first weeks in August.

Andre understood that John hadn't represented him because an "accident" had befallen his lawyer's

brother-in-law, but he did not know the details.
Consequently, he was calling now to ask simply—simply because he was decent, simply because he was a
dad, simply because he still presumed that he was going to mentor John Seton in the woods that
November—why he hadn't bothered to bring his rifle
to that gunsmith in Essex Junction.

"You really should take care of that bullet in the
chamber," he said to John. "Something could happen."

He wondered what he should say to Andre, how
much to tell him. He did not miss the irony that one of
his clients was now offering him the sort of obvious
counsel—you can't drive when your license has been revoked, even if it is your own car; you can't forge someone else's name on someone else's check, even if the guy
has passed away—that formed such a high percentage
of the wisdom he himself volunteered daily. He was also
touched that one of those women and men at whom
Paige Sutherland sneered, her nose crinkled in distaste,
was calling for no other reason than because he cared.

KEENAN BARRETT walked up Fifth Avenue to
Grand Central at the end of the day, and the train that
was waiting to take him home. With each block the
crowds grew thicker, and the city—despite the fact
Labor Day was behind him—felt increasingly equatorial. He was perspiring, a rarity for him this far north
in September, and he decided he had to slow down.
His train didn't leave for twenty-three minutes.

He was sorry to hear that Spencer had burned himself while trying to fry a soy cheese sandwich, but he also knew the additional injury—minor as it most likely was—could only help at the press conference. If the wound was still visible in two weeks, a reporter invariably would ask whether the marks on his hand had something to do with the shooting, and then Spencer could answer yes, indirectly, and talk about what the disability meant in terms of nerve damage: the reality that once the sling was gone the limb would dangle like a plumb line, knocking over teacups as he wandered through restaurants, getting caught in elevator doors, and banging with such frequency into door frames and desktops that his knuckles forever would be black and blue.

Alas, the new wound probably wouldn't look like much the week after next. It might not even be noticeable. And they certainly couldn't move the press conference forward, even if they had the results from the ballistics lab, not with this Saturday the eleventh of September. He knew from experience that in the week before and the week after 9/11, with the exception of breaking news, it was difficult (and, he felt, inappropriate) to get the media to pay attention to anything that didn't commemorate the people who had died in the attacks in New York and Washington or the people who rose to the daunting task of carting away the literal mountain of rubble where the World Trade Towers once had stood. It was an annual media frenzy that Keenan found at once moving and numbing: profiles of the medical examiners and laboratory technicians who helped identify the tens of thousands of body parts, of the bond traders who were in the towers and survived, of the Baptist volunteers from Vermont who replaced the windows that were blown to pieces in the nearby apartment buildings. There would be an endless parade of images on television—the altered skyline, the twin towers, the Pentagon, the living, the dead, the missing who never were found—a ritual that was now as much a part of the memorial mores as fireworks on the Fourth of July or fighting for drumsticks on Thanksgiving.

It was, of course, a supreme testimony to the resiliency of that great oxymoron called American culture that the anniversary of the tragedy was still observed each year with an avalanche of new books, special-edition magazines, newspaper extras, and exclusive television programming that was never in reality all that unique. Even FERAL always found a way to get into the act. This year Dominique would be photographed in Long Island on Friday with the Suffolk County SPCA at a ceremony honoring rescue dogs, some of which had wandered deep into the World Trade Center wreckage that awful September in search of survivors and then for victims throughout that nightmarish fall. She would be giving the animals a lifetime supply of vegetarian dog biscuits and poly-filled dog beds, each item embroidered with the name of one of the dogs who'd sustained an injury that had forced him to retire—usually respiratory disease or blindness from the powder and dust.

He wasn't proud of what FERAL was doing, but he also believed that the organization was exploiting 9/11 for a good cause and that the dogs wouldn't mind the treats and the beds. Besides, profits and nonprofits alike would be taking advantage of the moment. He hoped the anniversary would never become an excuse for retail sales bonanzas the way Washington's Birthday and Memorial Day had, but you never knew: Perhaps in fifty years 9/11 would be commemorated always on the second Monday in September, so there would be back-to-back three-day weekends at the end of the summer. The very notion made him shudder, but he knew in this world it could happen.

He was jostled by a young man in a blazer with a mandarin collar talking with great animation into his cell phone, and the bump brought Keenan's mind back to the press conference. Spencer, he concluded, should not be the one to discuss the ramifications of the nerve damage. A surgeon should. Spencer would sound like a medieval monk if he himself cataloged the likely future mortifications to his flesh. But a physician wouldn't be on the dais, both because Paige didn't want to risk revealing too much of her hand and because Paige had a very healthy ego—healthy even by the Rushmore-sized standards of most big-time litigators. Consequently, in addition to announcing the lawsuit, Paige should explain to the press the petty indignities that awaited Spencer McCullough—petty, of course, only in comparison to the complete loss of function. There was really nothing petty about accidentally slamming a car door on your hand and not having a clue that you've just shattered half the phalanx bones in your fingers.

Still, Keenan guessed that Spencer was the sort who might never allow the arm to be amputated. The man was both too vain to walk through life without it (and given the complete destruction of the bones and muscle in his shoulder, he understood there was no point in a prosthetic replacement) and too in love with his daughter to subject her to a visual reminder for as long as he lived of what she had done. If he were in the same situation, Keenan presumed he would keep the arm, too.

So, the press conference would feature Spencer, Paige, and Dominique. Keenan decided he could live without a surgeon, if Paige felt comfortable explaining the medical carnage (and he sensed that Paige would savor every gruesome detail). That team was sufficiently capable of embarrassing the hell out of Adirondack and getting Spencer on-air with the morning news anchors if the right people were in the audience. Dominique, too.

A key, obviously, would be to make sure that those right people were there. And that was something that Spencer himself often handled. Certainly his assistants were quite capable, especially Randy Mitchell. Randy, too, knew the key producers and some of the more powerful editors. But it was Spencer who had the special rapport with them and knew which freelance writers had the clout to convince the **New Yorker** to let them write about the horrors of the beef industry or were capable of selling the **Atlantic** on the idea of an exploration about what really went on in the university labs that experimented on animals. These people

were particularly important because broadcast followed print. That was the rule. And sometimes it took
a few timely magazine and newspaper features to get
the network news and their prime-time news-
magazines to produce those glorious exposés with
their computer-generated graphics.

Already Keenan could see in his mind the computer-
generated blues, blacks, and golds of an animated cut-
away diagram of the Adirondack thirty-ought-six, a
moving, fluidlike image that showed the placement of
the bolt, the extractor, and the ejector. He heard the reporter's even tones in a voice-over, as an image of a hook
failed again and again to fasten itself into the groove in
the back of the bullet in the chamber, until . . . until finally the computer zeroed in on the round. Maybe the
designer would cause the bullet to flash red now, like
the defective part in a passenger jet that caused the
plane to crash.

He sighed, contributing his small moan to the sul-
try crush on the street. Depending upon what the ballistics lab told them, the angle would be either that
John Seton's individual gun had a faulty component or
the contention that even used properly his Adirondack
brand of rifle needlessly left a bullet in the chamber after the magazine was emptied. Either way, Keenan believed, they would make the firearms manufacturer
look bad. Very bad. And they would portray hunting
as the barbaric, irresponsible hobby that it was.

As he made his way through the throngs pressing
their way into the station, he wondered if Spencer was
capable of calling select members of the media himself,

or—even if he was—whether he should. It might be unseemly. Spencer, after all, was the focus of this tragedy. He guessed they would have to depend upon Randy Mitchell or Joan Robbins or Turner Smolens— Spencer's staff. He tried to imagine their phone presence, to recall what he could from their conversations with him and the numerous times he had overheard them on the telephone as he strolled past their cubicles.

Then it hit him, and he actually stood still for a moment on the platform beside the very rear of his train while the thought registered: All Randy or Joan or Turner had to say to these people was that Spencer McCullough had been shot by a hunting rifle, and they would be at the press conference in a heartbeat. It wasn't that they cared so deeply for Spencer; it wasn't, in truth, that they cared for him at all. Rather, it was that same ghoulish irony that had led him to fear back on the first day of August that FERAL would wind up the butt of jokes by Jay Leno and David Letterman. How could they possibly miss getting the story on this one?

The answer? They couldn't. They wouldn't.

The difference now—unlike his worries in early August—was that FERAL was going to control how the information was presented.

When he started moving forward once more, it was with a gait that was brisk and confident and—for a man of his age and reserve on a sweltering train platform in the bowels of Grand Central Station—downright effervescent.

Twenty-one

On Thursday afternoon Charlotte came home from school before her mother, radiant with the news that she had gotten one of the leads in the autumn musical. She was the only eighth-grader with a part—the only student, in fact, with a role who wasn't at least in the ninth grade. She understood that she was going to play a ten-year-old girl surrounded by grown-ups, and so it helped that she was younger (and shorter) than the rest of the cast. Still, this was a real coup, and when she saw the cast list outside the drama teacher's classroom at the end of the school day she'd raced down the Brearley corridors to her own mother's room, demonstrating exactly the sort of unfettered enthusiasm that usually she disdained.

Now when she opened the front door to her family's apartment across town, she was no less cheerful. She saw her father was dozing in a pair of sweatpants and a T-shirt in a chair by the window, and initially she was disappointed that she couldn't tell him the news that very moment. She was still annoyed with him over what she considered the **Maurice and the Magic Banana** slight, but he had seemed so pathetic since Tuesday that she never had confronted him with either the book itself or the magazine photo she had discovered of her father and the gifted gorilla. Now she thought she would burst if she didn't tell someone her news and so she was delighted when he opened his eyes and stared at her. His hair hung lank down his temples and he looked rather tubby. Uncharacteristically slovenly. Until Tuesday, when he had failed to make it to work, he had tried to keep up a semblance of hygiene and fashion normalcy. No more. Over the last couple of days, he had lived in sweatpants, tennis shorts, and bulky T-shirts a size too large. He hadn't even tried to shave, and his face was covered with the gray and black stubble she associated with the homeless along Riverside Drive. She noticed that his small weights were out by the couch, and though she hoped it was because the physical therapist had been at the apartment earlier that afternoon, she was pretty sure the weights had been there for days.

"I'm really sorry if I woke you," she said, "but I'm glad you're awake. Guess what?"

He used his left arm to push himself up in the chair, visibly wincing, so he wasn't slouching like biscuit dough. "Go ahead."

"I got the part! I'm Mary Lennox!"

"Wow, that's pretty big news. Congratulations!" He raised his eyebrows as he spoke, taking in the information.

"Yup. Can I use the phone, I'm going to call—"

"Hold on, hold on. Tell me all the details. I want to hear everything."

"Do you really have time?" she asked, a reflex before she could stop herself. In the past, her father never

had time for details. Before the accident, she either
would have left this news for him on his voice mail at
FERAL or told him at dinner between his own anecdotes about the ponies, dolphins, or lab rats the organization was working that moment to save. She
knew he would be happy for her—and yes, proud that
she was his daughter. But unless he was in one of his
infrequent phases of almost manic parental involvement, the very last thing he would want would be the
details. Now, of course, time was less of an issue. He
seemed to have plenty of it.

"Yes," he said with almost dreamlike serenity. "I
have time."

And so she sat on the pouf between the dormant
fireplace and her father's chair and told him all that
she could remember about the audition yesterday: The
high school boys from another school who were asked
to audition for the parts of Archie and Neville, the
songs she had been asked to sing, the dancing that was
required. The number of girls she had to beat out for
the part. She told him in a chirping voice that gathered momentum as she spoke, as she remembered specific details.

When she was done he surprised her yet again by
asking what the rehearsal schedule would be and
whether he could help her learn her lines.

"Won't you be back at work next week?" she asked.

"I guess."

"Then how can you help me?"

"I can fit your school play in. Parents do it all the
time. Work. Play. Parenting. They do, don't they?"

She agreed in her head that they did, and as a courtesy to her ailing father she nodded. But she couldn't imagine him actually running her lines with her or helping her memorize song lyrics.

"It's really incredible what you did," he murmured when she remained silent. "But you know what? I'm not surprised you got the part. I'm not surprised at all. You'll be stupendous. Absolutely stupendous."

WILLOW ALREADY KNEW that her birthday this year fell on a Monday, but she checked the calendar in the kitchen again now because she had a feeling it was going to be the day before her parents expected her to talk to that lawyer—or, perhaps, lawyers. She saw she was correct: It was. She would officially be eleven then. Barely eleven years old, she thought, and already she was being (and she hated the very phonetics of this new word) deposed.

Her father came into the kitchen, a couple of rattles he'd found on the floor in the den in his hands. The dinner dishes were in the sink, and she watched him stare at them for a long moment—as if he were actually surprised to find the remnants of their meat loaf and mashed potatoes and spaghetti squash still present. He seemed to do this a lot these days: He would simply stop and stare for a long instant at something as if the object or the panorama (it happened outdoors as frequently as it did inside the house) were new and unfamiliar. Then he tossed the rattles in a wicker basket on a shelf below the cookbooks where he and her mother tended to toss all of the small, nonessential items that belonged to Patrick: Toe puppets. Pacifiers. The flat plastic shells in which they packed wet wipes when they went out.

Her brother was upstairs sleeping and her mother was working behind closed doors in the living room. Whenever she worked in the evening she tended to close the door, because there was a chance she was listening to a tape of a patient. Sometimes she used a headset, but as often as not—even before Patrick was born—the headset disappeared under a couch or deep in a crevice in her shoulder bag.

"A busy schedule, eh?" he murmured when he saw her looking at the calendar.

She sighed and sat down on one of the stools at the L-shaped counter around which they ate breakfast. She was already in her nightshirt, and she could feel the cool wood against the backs of her legs. "My birthday is the day before I have to talk to the lawyer," she said.

"Oh. I'm sorry, sweetheart. It is going to be a hard month, isn't it?" She knew he was referring to the litany of bad dates before them. Saturday was the anniversary of the attacks on the World Trade Center and the Pentagon, which was at least part of the reason why her mother was working right now: She had had extra office hours today and would have them again tomorrow. Then the week after next was the FERAL press conference that her parents and, she knew, her aunt dreaded: Even though none of them would be present, it was going to generate the media attention her uncle desired and make them all more public than they liked—especially, of course, her father and Charlotte. Her aunt had warned her father that reporters would try to reach him (and, Willow knew, they would succeed). And then the week after the press conference she and her cousin had to start meeting with lawyers to prepare for their depositions. Her first appointment was on Tuesday in Vermont and Charlotte's was on Thursday in Manhattan.

She decided she was going to call her cousin over the weekend. She needed to know exactly what Charlotte was going to say and—perhaps of more importance—what she wasn't. They hadn't spoken since her own family had left for Vermont the day after Uncle Spencer had returned to Grandmother's from the hospital, and that had been more than four weeks ago now.

Everything had grown much more complicated the moment her uncle had struggled back into the house in Sugar Hill. He was refusing to talk to her father, which was the reason why her own family had left the next day. The house was big, but not big enough for the two brothers-in-law once they weren't speaking. She knew the two men hadn't spoken since then, and she guessed on some level this was why she and Charlotte hadn't called each other, either. It was awkward now.

"It's going to be a very bad month," she agreed.

Though her father had loosened his necktie before dinner, the rope of fabric still hung around his neck. He nodded and sat down on a stool beside her and finally untied the knot completely and pulled the long strip of silk through the collar of his shirt. He wrapped the tie around his hand as if it were a roll of Scotch tape.

"You want to talk about it?" he asked.

"You sound like Mom."

"Thank you."

"No, I guess not."

"Really? You seem to want to—and we can talk about it right now, if you like."

It. She thought about the word, and wondered exactly what he meant. Did he mean the shooting? That was usually what they meant these days when they used the word **it**. Or was her dad merely referring to her deposition? That was what had led him to sit beside her just now. Or perhaps he meant the whole litany of unpleasant dates that loomed before them in the coming month.

"When do you think you and Uncle Spencer will start speaking again?" She surprised herself by asking this question first. The words just slid from her mouth the moment she parted her lips.

"I'd talk to him now, if he'd talk to me."

"I know."

"I hope soon. He can't be angry with me forever."

She almost disagreed with her father: Everyone always talked about how stubborn Uncle Spencer could be, and if anyone could decide to be mad at someone forever, it was probably him. She knew her uncle blamed her father for what happened—as would a lot of people once the press conference was behind them. She knew how much her father blamed himself.

But the truth was, she didn't think it was her dad's fault. She blamed this nightmare on Charlotte—which, she understood so suddenly that she actually sat up a little straighter on the stool, may have been another reason why she hadn't felt an inclination to phone her cousin over the last month. Everyone was so focused on the idea that her father hadn't gotten around to bringing his gun to a repair shop to have a stubborn bullet removed that they were forgetting—or ignoring—the fact that it was Charlotte who had taken the gun from the trunk of the car even though she'd been told explicitly not to touch it, switched off the safety, and fired it into the night. She knew the people at FERAL and her uncle's lawyer were going to portray her cousin as a victim, and she knew also that this was a complete fabrication: Her cousin—two weeks beyond her thirteenth birthday now—had been stoned and a little drunk when she'd pulled the trigger.

"You and Aunt Catherine are talking, right?" she asked her father. "Mom says Aunt Catherine's not mad at you."

"Yes, your aunt and I are talking. And while I'd say she's not as mad at me as your uncle is, she still wishes I had . . . behaved more responsibly. After all, she loves Uncle Spencer."

"I'm not so sure about that." She hadn't planned to say this, either, but she realized there was indeed a lot that she'd kept inside her for almost six weeks now. She wondered how much she was about to reveal.

"What do you mean?"

"Charlotte . . ."

"Yes?"

"Charlotte thinks her parents might someday get a divorce."

"What? When did she say such a thing?"

"This summer. The night of the accident."

"Have you told your mother this?"

She shook her head.

"Why does your cousin think that?" Her father dropped his necktie into his lap and rested his temple against his fingers and stared at her.

"Because . . ."

"Yes?"

"Oh, a lot of reasons. She says her mom flirts all the time, and her dad isn't really interested in Aunt Catherine. He's so busy with his animal causes."

"Your aunt Catherine has always been a flirt," he said, and although his eyes looked tired he was smiling. "Trust me. When we were growing up, I don't think I had a friend she didn't flirt with—especially when she was the age Charlotte is now. I think it would have killed her if I'd gone to Exeter, which your grandmother and I discussed pretty seriously, instead of staying in the city at Trinity. She wouldn't have been able to bat her eyelashes at my friends when they came by the apartment. And as for your uncle Spencer . . ."

He paused and took off his eyeglasses. This was, Willow knew, one of his courtroom gestures. But it also meant that he was about to say something that mattered to him greatly. "And as for your uncle

Spencer: He may be self-absorbed, he may be fixated on monkeys or dolphins or whatever . . . but he adores your aunt. I know that. I know Spencer. He loves your aunt Catherine very much."

"But what if . . ."

"Go on."

"What if she doesn't love him? Charlotte doesn't think she does. She says her mom and dad are always fighting, and it's usually over nothing."

"Your mom and I argue sometimes—"

"No, you don't."

He thought about this and nodded. "We don't, do we?"

"Not like some parents I hear about. Not like Loree's parents. Or Mr. and Mrs. Hall." Loree King and Kristin Hall were two of Willow's classmates, and the squabbles Willow had witnessed when she was playing at Loree's or Kristin's house were legendary around the Seton dinner table.

"But most parents have their arguments," her father continued. "Just like most siblings and most friends. And most cousins."

"Charlotte thinks this is different."

"Your mom really doesn't know any of this? You haven't told her?"

She felt the sides of her eyes start to quiver. She still had math homework that was due tomorrow, she hadn't done her required thirty minutes of reading for the day, and it was clear that her father and she were still a while away from going upstairs so he could read to her while she curled up in bed. She didn't want to cry, and she didn't quite understand how her innocuous peek at the calendar had led to this. But she was afraid she was about to start sobbing—not hideous Patrick-like howls, but real tears and whimpers and sniffles, nonetheless. And a lot of them. A month-and-a-half's worth. Tears for her uncle who couldn't ever use his right arm again, for her cousin who—even if she wasn't getting blamed for this the way her dad was—still had to live with herself, for her aunt and uncle who might someday get a divorce, and (perhaps most of all) for her dad who she decided firmly now had done nothing wrong but was being treated like he had and always seemed sad. She felt her body starting to shake and gave in. Before she knew it she had climbed onto her father's lap on the stool as if she were a girl half her age, her shoulders heaving with sadness. She cried into the cotton shoulder of his button-down shirt, only vaguely aware of the smell of the deodorant he wore to work and the coffee that was still on his breath, and completely unconscious of the fact that her father's eyes had begun to water, too.

CATHERINE PUT THE NOVEL she was reading on her nightstand and was about to turn out the light. She glanced at Spencer, hoping he was finally asleep, because his breathing had been even and soft for at least the last two or three pages. He wasn't: He looked up at her, his eyes alone moving. He was, as he was always now when he tried to sleep, flat on his back—a position that, in the month and a half since the accident, he still had not grown accustomed to. In the past, he had fallen asleep on his right side, his body facing hers. Not only did he now have to try to nod off in what was still a new and uncomfortable position for him, the two of them had switched sides of the bed: For twenty years, since they'd been freshmen in college, he had always slept on her left. No longer. She couldn't be on his right because it meant his wounded shoulder was near her, and she couldn't bear the thought that she might pain him further by rolling against it in her sleep.

She leaned over and kissed him on his forehead. "You've taken a sleeping pill, right?" she asked him. "If not, I can get you one."

"I took one. It will kick in soon enough."

"Okay."

"I keep wondering about something . . ."

She had been sitting up with her knees making a tent of the sheets, but now she lay on her side so he wouldn't be looking up at her like an invalid. Something in his tone suggested he might want to talk about his disability and his future. "Yes?"

"I keep wondering: Should we have a surgeon at the press conference? Paige says we shouldn't because—"

"You want to talk about the press conference?" she asked. She realized she sounded shrill, but she couldn't contain her surprise—and her disappointment. Even now, at ten thirty at night in their bed, he was thinking about the press conference. Even though he knew how much she detested the very notion of the press conference—and FERAL's whole involvement in a

lawsuit that, as far as she was concerned, was absolutely none of their business—he was bringing it up
as if she supported what he was doing and was willing
to discuss its particulars. She couldn't believe it. She
simply could not believe it, and reflexively she sat up
again so she could have some distance from him. If
they were going to have a discussion that involved
FERAL, she didn't want to be that close.

"Yes," he said. "I was thinking—"

"No you weren't thinking. That's the problem. You
know my opinion of that press conference, you know
how unhappy it makes me. Your animal-obsessed
friends want to humiliate my brother and make a spectacle of our—yes, our—daughter. I will not discuss
this right now, Spencer. I'm sorry."

"The lawsuit will benefit us. This family. That's
why I'm doing it."

"No you're not! You don't need FERAL to sue
Adirondack. You could sue them without all this
ridiculous animal rights nonsense, without trotting
out my brother—"

"No one is going to trot out your brother."

"You could do this without Dominique or Keenan.
I like Keenan fine, but lately Dominique . . . before
the accident, you and Dominique . . ." She shook her
head: This wasn't about Dominique. She knew that
Dominique had no romantic interest in her husband,
but sometimes it seemed Spencer had an almost slav-
ish devotion to her. The two of them shared an obses-
sive interest in beleaguered prairie dogs, whales, and
chinchillas. They were soldiers together in their fanat-

ical cause, and—in New York and on the road—they were often together. She wondered why, suddenly, she was jealous of Dominique, and all she could think of was that she was angry at the woman for all the hours she had kept Spencer away from his family over the last five or six years—and, yes, used him. And now she was using him again. Using his disability. Keenan was, too. They all were. That whole hideous organization that cared more about pandas than people.

"What about Dominique?" he asked.

"Nothing about Dominique."

"No, something's going on in your head. What?"

"Look, this isn't about Dominique. It's about Charlotte. It's about John. You know how I hate this whole thing. I'm only having breakfast with Paige tomorrow morning because I don't want her alone with our daughter. I shudder when I think of the ideas she'd put into Charlotte's head."

As if she hadn't spoken just now and explained herself, he said—still staring straight up at the ceiling— "If this isn't about Dominique, I don't know why you brought her up. We're friends. Just like you and Eric."

Eric, her associate from Brearley, had been at their home for dinner the night before. He'd brought with him a French green salad with basil shiitake mushrooms, a pasta dripping with a pesto he'd made of pine nuts and roasted red peppers, and a peach cobbler which he admitted he hadn't baked himself but he assured everyone had not a drop of cream or butter in it and was built largely of soy flour and substitute eggs. He hadn't planned to stay and eat with them, but she had insisted he remain. How could she not? He'd brought with him a small feast, every element of which (even the faux cobbler) was delicious. Had she and Eric flirted last night in front of Spencer and Charlotte? She thought not: She had been courteous and appreciative and (she hoped) charming and funny. But she didn't believe either of them had crossed any boundaries. Sometimes, she knew, Charlotte thought she saw things that weren't there. Her daughter didn't realize that sometimes men and women flirted simply because they **were** friends, but there wasn't anything to it. It was all part of being a grown-up. Everybody did it.

At least she presumed everybody did.

She wasn't sure how she should respond to what Spencer had just said. Should she be defensive, or should she simply ignore the innuendo? She was angry, that was for sure. But it was also late and he was in pain. It was one thing to argue about the press conference, an issue that affected her child and her brother. It was quite another to squabble right now over . . . flirting.

"You're right," she said simply. "You're absolutely right. And as for the press conference, I couldn't tell you whether a surgeon should be there or not—especially since, in my opinion, there shouldn't even be a press conference."

He seemed to think about this, but he didn't say anything. She considered simply turning out the light without another word, but she couldn't bring herself to be that antagonistic. Not with him like . . . this.

And so she leaned over and kissed him once more, a sisterly peck on the forehead. Then she curled up in a ball under the sheet, reached for the knob on the bed-side lamp, and murmured a distant good night.

NAN MOVED CAREFULLY up the trail in the woods, watching for tree roots and rocks with every step. She'd been careful to park her car at the edge of the lot at the trailhead so that it was visible from the road, but this little hike had been such a spontaneous decision that she hadn't even told Marguerite she was going. No one in the world knew she was here. She'd driven to North Conway first thing in the morning to buy bed linens at the outlet mall—some of her sheets had been in need of replacement for a very long time, and the ones in which Spencer had slept (and sweated and oozed) in his convalescence were beyond salva-tion—and on the way home she had surprised herself by pulling into the parking lot at the base of Artists' Bluff, a little peak across the street from Echo Lake. Why not? she had asked herself. It wasn't quite noon, she had sneakers in the trunk of her car, and it felt like sixty or sixty-five degrees outside. Other than the short nature walks around Sugar Hill on which she had taken her granddaughters, she hadn't gone on a single hike this summer and already it was the second week in September.

It was only now, however, when she'd been walking alone in the woods for half an hour and begun to feel a bit winded that she began to question whether this agreeable little hike was wise. She worried suddenly (and uncharacteristically) that she might trip and break an ankle or, worse, her hip. She might be stranded here for hours. Perhaps even overnight.

No, not overnight. There had been another car in the parking lot, and so there had to be somebody else somewhere along the trail. Still, it would not be pleasant to sit for hours in the woods with a broken bone, and she was glad she had parked her automobile where people could see it.

She pushed aside a branch and continued upward. The end of the trail, perhaps fifteen or twenty minutes farther, was a bluff with a panoramic vista of Cannon Mountain, Echo Lake, and, looming to the east, Mount Lafayette.

She wondered if this modest ramble had been inspired in some fashion because on the way home she had driven past the cliff on which the Old Man of the Mountain had once resided. Never had she supposed she would outlive him. Never. But she had. For only the second time since he had slid down the crag to his death—and the first since the days immediately after his collapse—she had actually pulled into the viewing area off the interstate to gaze up at the spot where ledges of red granite had once formed the face of one very tough hombre.

Tough even by her standards. The Old Man of the Mountain had never been a gentle grandfather. In Nan's mind, he had always been the sort of character who, with a bit of bombast and a cantankerous hiss, really would have insisted that he would live free or die. Maybe that was why she liked him. In the last years of his life, of course, he'd been a little long in the tooth. Everybody knew it. He'd been forced by his mere flesh and blood caretakers—young pups a tiny fraction his age—to don steel cables and turnbuckles. To smooth epoxy on his visage like face cream.

But she still hadn't ever expected that she would live to see him gone.

It pained Nan to admit it, but she was scared of dying. She had absolutely no confidence that anything awaited her once the old ticker broke down. And though some people, such as Walter Durnip, were fortunate enough to glissade away in their sleep—none of the pain or mess or dreadful inconvenience that came with a long illness—most were not. Most people went slowly, their vigor sapped from them bit by bit in small, degrading increments.

For all she knew, a year from now an impulsive jaunt such as this to the top of Artists' Bluff would be impossible. For all she knew, a year from now she would be dead.

When the Old Man had first crumbled, she had scoffed at the sentimental outpouring she had witnessed. The memorial service, the obituaries. The hundreds of e-mails of condolence that in the days after his demise people sent to the Web site for the state's Division of Parks and Recreation. At the time, it had struck her as more than a little ridiculous.

It seemed less absurd to her now, and she guessed this had something to do with the way her own family was ailing. Aging. Separating. She understood that

some pieces of earth transcended mere rock and vista
and were capable of summoning a particular place in
time. A precise memory, an echo of a season in one's
life. She knew that the view that awaited her at the end
of this walk would conjure for her a picnic from thirty
years ago, when she and Richard and their two young
children had eaten egg-salad sandwiches on boulders
on the summit. She would recall the August afternoon
when from this peak they had seen a mother black
bear and her cub saunter contentedly across a ski trail
on Cannon. She would see clearly those bears in her
mind, watch them amble once more across the lush
green trace in the side of the mountain opposite them.

Apparently, all that remained of the Old Man was
a part of his right ear. If she had brought binoculars,
she might have been able to see it. Then again, maybe
not. Besides, a bit of ear is not very interesting.

She was glad that her granddaughters had seen the
Old Man over the years, but it grieved her that Patrick
had been born too late. She didn't, she decided, mourn
the Old Man so much as she mourned the memories
he evoked.

She stepped gingerly over a sprain-causing crevice
in a stone and wiped the sweat away from her brow
with the sleeve of her sweater. Then she stopped and
took her sweater off and tied it girlishly around her
neck. She was seventy years old, and she was alone.
She was tired. Very, very tired. She had raised her children and most of the time she thought she had raised
them well. She was proud that one was a public defender and one was a teacher. Oh, there were certainly

moments when they disappointed her or when she questioned their abilities as parents: She recalled her feelings that awful last night in July. Usually, however, she looked upon them with quiet satisfaction.

But she was nonetheless left wondering: Was this all there was to her life?

She considered whether she would live to see John and Spencer—the McCulloughs and the Setons, her children—reconcile. She doubted it. She seriously doubted it.

She stood absolutely still in the path, because she was experiencing an emotion so alien to her that it took her a long moment to understand what it was. When she figured it out, she only half-believed it: dread. Nan Seton knew from many things, but dread had never been among them. It was almost incapacitating. She had the unmistakable feeling that she was dying and a fear that it was not going to be pretty.

She couldn't possibly stand still, not for a moment more. She considered turning around and returning to the car, but nearly seven decades' worth of persistence and intractability made that impossible, too. And so she did the only thing she could, the only thing she had ever done with her life. She continued forward. She remained on task.

But the anxiety was with her the rest of the day.

PAIGE WATCHED CHARLOTTE slather blueberry preserves on her scone and then she noticed Catherine glance at her sideways, and so she smiled. She knew

Catherine despised her, but she really didn't care. Spencer liked her and Keenan liked her, and that was all that mattered right now. Hell, it really didn't matter if even they liked her. Besides, it was natural for Catherine to feel conflicted: Though her brother wasn't a defendant, he might wind up looking pretty foolish.

The three of them were sitting in an elegant little restaurant with great waterfalls of ferns and white linen napkins not far from Brearley that was open for breakfast, because she wanted to discuss with Charlotte—with Charlotte and Catherine, actually—the reality that after the press conference, there might be eager beaver reporters who would want to get the girl in their sights. And she wanted to prevent that. She guessed that Catherine would be her ally on this one, and she was glad: She needed the woman to take on the role of mother lioness. If she were a reporter and the child's parents consistently refused an interview—which Spencer and Catherine had been instructed to do—she might consider making an end-around and try meeting the girl at school for a comment or two. Fortunately, both mother and daughter were at Brearley, so even that would be difficult if Catherine had her guard up.

Outside it was raining, and the showers had broken the heat wave. It was the tenth, and Paige thought the gray skies and mist might actually make tomorrow's anniversary easier for New Yorkers to bear: There weren't the cloudless, cerulean blue skies everyone associated with the attacks or the image of silver planes hurtling unfettered through the air just above the long, polygonal lines of skyscrapers. She could overhear the diners at the other tables discussing the anniversary— playing the game of one-upmanship that colored so many conversations, the contestants each trying to find personal connections to the tragedy that all too often were as tenuous as they were insulting to the people who'd suffered real loss—and she was glad the three of them were focused largely on FERAL's plans and where this child fit in. She felt almost admirable.

"So, suppose some guy shows up after play practice? I have one of the leads in the show we're doing. Can you believe it? Eighth grade, and I have one of the two or three best parts. It's **The Secret Garden,** and I'm Mary Lennox—the little British girl who is so **very** contrary."

Paige smiled, at once appreciating the irony that Charlotte was already typecast as a little bitch and that the kid was going to play a girl saved, in part, by a garden.

"Anyway," the child continued, "suppose there's a reporter waiting for me outside the auditorium. What am I supposed to do, give him a judo chop?"

"Go find a grown-up. And don't say a word."

The girl took a healthy bite of her scone, chewed it, and then said, "Be rude?"

"As rude as you like."

"No, sweetheart," her mother said. "You don't need to be rude. Ever. You can simply tell the reporter that you have nothing to say, and ask to be excused."

"Now, Catherine—"

"Now, Paige. First of all, she doesn't need to be rude. She can leave graciously. Second, given what my husband does for a living, the last thing he would want would be for his daughter to alienate a reporter."

She started to reach across the tablecloth to touch Catherine's arm, but she had a sense the gesture would be unappreciated right now.

"What are you so worried about? What do you think they would ask me?" Charlotte said.

There was a silver pot of coffee between her and Catherine, and so she refilled her cup. "They might ask you about the accident, they might ask you about your father. They might ask you about being a vegetarian."

"And why don't you want me to talk about that? It's not like I have any secrets, you know."

"Of course you don't."

"Then why all this cloak-and-dagger stuff?"

"I want you to save it for the lawyers."

The child paused with her scone in the air and surveyed it for a moment. Then: "Someday I want restaurants to have butter it's okay for me to eat. I don't like my scones with just jam."

"You can have butter, sweetheart. Butter's not meat, and—"

"You know Dad doesn't want me to have dairy."

"And you know your dad and I don't completely agree on that. I want to be sure you get enough calcium."

Charlotte put the scone down and looked at her nails. This morning they were painted a robin's egg blue that Paige thought looked quite nice with the navy skirt the child had to wear while in the middle school at Brearley.

"These conversations with lawyers," the girl said. "I've wanted to ask you about that. Will they be in a courtroom?"

"Maybe down the road. Far down the road. But at this point I just meant in an office. Probably my office. It's all part of the process: your way of helping people to learn how dangerous guns are and how evil deer hunting is."

"The thing is," the girl began, turning toward her with eyes that were wide and slightly bewildered. "I don't think deer hunting is all that evil. Really. I think Uncle John is a pretty normal guy."

Paige looked quickly at Catherine, but the girl's mom, it was clear, may actually have agreed with the child. "I wasn't aware you felt that way about hunting, Charlotte. Thank you. You're entitled to your opinions. I'll be sure not to ask you for your thoughts on that subject. And I think we can assume that Adirondack won't either. Mostly the lawyers will want to know exactly what you recall about the night the accident occurred," she said, resorting—as she did always—to the passive when discussing the shooting. She did not believe she had ever used the construction "when you shot your father" or "when your daughter shot you" or even the vaguely innocuous "when Charlotte inadvertently discharged the firearm" around any of the McCulloughs.

"They'll just ask me what happened?"

"Uh-huh. They'll want you to reconstruct what occurred that night. Exactly what you did at the country
club, exactly what you did when you got home. There
will be other questions, of course. Other things will
surely come up. General things, like I said. But most
of it will be about the night your father was injured."

The girl's gaze returned to its normal eighth-grade
pout. She wiped at her lips with her fingers. "Will
there be a lie detector?"

"A lie detector?"

"You know, one of those things that tells people if
you're lying. It monitors your heartbeat or your sweat
or something."

"I know what a lie detector is. I was only repeating
the question because I was surprised you'd even worry
about such a thing. There will most certainly not be a
lie detector. I can promise you that."

"Good."

"You sound relieved," Paige said, her antennae
now up.

"No. But I still wouldn't take one."

"Any special reason why not?"

"I just wouldn't," she said. "And I'm pretty sure
that's, like, my constitutional right or something."

Slowly Catherine turned toward her daughter, and
she was looking at her with apprehension: as if the
child were a stranger on the street whose intentions
were suspect. Paige knew that if this girl were her
daughter, she would be reacting exactly the same way.
It was the way the kid had snapped "Good" a moment
ago and then announced that she wouldn't take a

lie detector test. Paige began to wonder if she really did know exactly what had gone on that night in New Hampshire. If, for that matter, any of the grown-ups did.

And maybe that was the problem: These parents—Spencer and Catherine, Sara and John—farmed their daughters out to Charlotte's grandmother for a major chunk of the summer, and maybe that was indicative of their parenting attitudes in general. Paige had no delusions that she would be a better parent than any of these people, but then she also didn't have any expectations that she would have to try . . . at least not in the foreseeable future. Nevertheless, she liked to believe that educated people who chose to become parents would not become so absorbed in their own lives that they would grow oblivious to whatever it was their children were thinking. Or doing. Especially if they were going to leave loaded weapons in the trunks of their cars.

But, of course, they became less mindful over time. It was inevitable. Often people like the Setons and the McCulloughs were particularly impressive when it came to finding interests other than their own children: Their careers—clients and causes, patients and students. Their marriages. Gardens. Guns.

Nevertheless, Paige decided now there was definitely something curdling in the back of this kid's head that her parents weren't exploring with sufficient resolve, and something had occurred that last night in July that no one knew about except this girl. Perhaps this girl and her cousin.

"It is my constitutional right . . . right?" Charlotte was asking her.

"I'm not a constitutional lawyer," she answered carefully, not wanting to lie but still hoping to plant a small seed of fear in the child's mind. "Nevertheless, I don't believe the men who framed the Constitution even envisioned such a device as a lie detector machine."

"Well, I won't take one."

"Charlotte?" her mother said, a nervous tinniness to her voice. "Did something else happen that night you haven't told us about? Is there something more we need to know?"

"No."

"You're sure?"

"Like what? You think I shot Dad on purpose? Is that what you're thinking? Well, I didn't, and I can't believe you'd even accuse me of such a thing!"

"I didn't accuse you of anything. That idea hadn't even crossed my mind," Catherine said, but Charlotte clearly wasn't listening. The girl pulled her napkin from her lap and heaved it in a messy ball on the tablecloth.

"Isn't it bad enough that I shot him by accident? Isn't that horrible enough?" she said, barely choking out her second sentence before storming off in the direction of the ladies' room.

After a long, awkward moment, Catherine said quietly, "I can't believe she would fear for even a split second that I would think such a thing. I just can't believe it." Then she took a breath to compose herself and followed after her daughter.

Paige nodded in agreement as a courtesy, but the truth was that the notion had come to her before, and now, she knew, it was going to remain lodged in her mind whenever the subject of that night in New Hampshire came up. Thank God the kid never would have to take a lie detector test. Who the hell knew what the child really had done—and why? Certainly, Paige understood, she didn't.

And, as a lawyer, she was glad.

Twenty-two

The next day, Saturday, Spencer sat alone in a living room chair late in the afternoon and cataloged all the precise ways he and his wife would never make love again, all the small ways he needed both arms—and both hands—when they had sex. It was a sort of negative Kama Sutra, a litany of sexual impossibilities. Some of the losses were pretty basic: Unless he became real proficient at the one-handed push-up, he was never going to be atop Catherine in any manner that wasn't pathetically smothering—and certainly not in the variant of the old-fashioned missionary position that Catherine preferred, her legs on his shoulders, her ankles behind his head. Other losses were more idiosyncratic to the two of them, the sorts of physical eccentricities any couple with a long history together discover about one another, many of which demanded that he have the use of two hands and plenty of functioning fingers.

And in addition to all the things he no longer could do, there was the reality that whenever he moved his body back and forth with anything that resembled an energetic motion, his arm was going to sway accordingly. Now that was sure to be an aphrodisiac for Catherine: her husband's increasingly thin and stunted arm banging against her hip, her side, or the back of her leg as he moved inside her.

He and Catherine hadn't made love since the accident. Of course, they hadn't made love a whole lot in the months before the accident, either. They'd never talked about it, but something was happening—or, to be precise, not happening—even before his brother-in-law had left a loaded rifle in the trunk of his car. He had gotten a reminder of it the other night in their bed when he brought up the press conference.

He was pulled from his unpleasant little musings when he heard the metallic thud of their copper-core soup pot being dropped onto the burner on the stove. At the moment, Catherine and Charlotte were preparing dinner and setting the table while he sipped a gin and tonic. So far the gin wasn't doing a whole lot to help buttress the work of the Advil and the Percocet. He still hurt like hell. At least the combination of alcohol and drugs hadn't sent him spiraling down into a coma, though he did wonder whether a painless coma might actually represent a small improvement over his current circumstances.

The glass was cold from the ice, and he held it gently against the back of his right hand. His arm was still swathed in the sling and cradled tightly against his chest. He didn't feel a thing, even when he pressed the glass very hard against his knuckles. He didn't expect he would feel anything, but still the absolute nothingness fascinated him, especially since at the other end of his arm, the sensation—none of it good—was pretty near ceaseless.

He knew he looked a bit scruffy—no, that wasn't right; he looked exceedingly scruffy—and he considered trying to shave before dinner. It had been days. He gazed at the russet brick wall of the apartment building across the street and the cement skirts of the windows, his mind on the logistics of shaving with his left hand with that electric razor he loathed, and quickly gave up on the idea. He'd never get an electric razor through the scrub pine growing now on his cheeks and chin.

A moment later he heard the phone ringing in the kitchen, and then Charlotte was scooting through the living room with the cordless phone pressed against her ear. She waved at him, and he thought she had mouthed the name "Willow" as she continued past, apparently taking the phone with her to her bedroom at the very end of their apartment's thin corridor.

WILLOW WAS HAPPY to hear that her cousin had gotten the part she wanted in the play, but it wasn't why she had phoned her. As soon as she could she brought up the depositions that loomed before them.

"And that's why you're calling?" Charlotte was asking her now, and Willow could hear the disbelief in her cousin's voice. "They're still months away!"

"Charlotte, I don't want to lie."

"Look, if you're so worried about getting caught, do what I did: I simply told them I wouldn't take a lie detector test. I said it was my constitutional right. And

Paige—she's my dad's lawyer—she said I wouldn't have to."

Willow was sitting outside on the front steps of their home in Vermont, savoring the early autumn chill in the air. It wasn't quite seven, but already the sun was behind the mountains to the west, offering only a strip of red against an otherwise colorless dusk sky. She'd brought the phone out here so her parents wouldn't overhear her conversation.

"I'm not worried about getting caught. I'm worried about having to lie in the first place. We're going to have to take oaths, you know."

"So, what are you saying?"

"I'm saying we should tell them everything."

"No way. Why would you want to get Gwen in trouble?"

"Charlotte—"

"Look, they probably won't even ask us the sorts of questions where we'd have to lie. What are they going to do, say, 'Willow, were you smoking marijuana the night your cousin found a loaded rifle in the trunk of your dad's car?' I don't think so. They have no idea we did that."

"But we did. And that's important. We were both stoned. You wouldn't have shot your dad if you weren't stoned."

"Don't put it that way. It makes me sound dreadful. And I feel lousy enough as it is. Besides . . ."

"Yes?"

"Besides, none of this would have happened if your

dad hadn't left a loaded gun sitting around in the first place."

"I realize that. He feels terrible, too, you know."

"Well, so do I."

"Look, Charlotte, I didn't call to fight. I called because I'm scared. I'm scared I'm either going to have to lie under oath or I'm going to have to tell the truth— and I don't know which would be worse."

"I do. Trust me: Lie."

"But I don't want to, this is too important. My dad's a lawyer and I know about oaths. I know how these things work. And . . ."

"Yes?"

"And it would be wrong. That's all. It would be wrong."

"Telling the truth would only make things worse. I know that doesn't seem possible, but—believe it or not—it is. Things actually could get worse. A lot worse."

Willow sensed someone was standing behind her in the mudroom just inside the screen door, and when she turned around her mother held up two fingers to signal that dinner was about two minutes away. Her mother was smiling, and Willow thought she had mouthed the sentence, "Say hi to Charlotte for us."

"Look, I don't believe this accident would have happened if you hadn't been a little bit tipsy and a little bit stoned," she said to her cousin when her mother once more was out of earshot. "And maybe more than a little bit."

Charlotte sighed, a gust of wind she heard in her ear. "I don't know about that."

"What?"

"I said, I don't know."

"What do you mean you don't know?"

"This week I start seeing a psychiatrist—a friend of your mom's, I guess. And I'm really glad, because sometimes I wonder if I have even the slightest idea of just how screwed up I am. Sometimes I think I'm keeping it together really well, and then when I'm alone I'll just lose it completely. And while most of the time I'm only mad at myself, there are other times when I'll find myself mad at my dad, and then I'll wonder . . ."

"You'll wonder what?"

"I'll wonder if I would have taken the gun even if I hadn't been stoned."

"You think so?"

"Sometimes, yeah. Maybe I wouldn't have fired it. Then again, maybe I would have. Sometimes I even wonder if I really thought I was firing at a . . ."

Her cousin's voice trailed off, and she was about to ask Charlotte to continue when the older girl abruptly resumed speaking, her voice once more rich with its characteristic flippancy.

"Anyway, I'm looking forward to seeing the shrink. Excuse me, the therapist. It'll be good for me! It'll be good for my dad's lawsuit, it'll be good for the work he does for FERAL. So, I'm serious about this, my country cousin: You don't need to get Gwen involved, you don't need to bring up the teenagers. You don't need to say anything—not a word—about the marijuana or the beer. Your dad's gun would still have been in the trunk of your car even if we hadn't smoked a little dope and had a couple of beers, and I still would have taken it. Okay?"

"I don't know," she said, aware they had hit some sort of impasse. "I should go in for dinner."

"You do that. We're about to have dinner here, too."

Before hanging up Charlotte announced that she would be busy memorizing lines and songs and doing the mountains of homework demanded of someone in the eighth grade, but they could still talk next week if the prospect of the deposition continued to frighten her.

At dinner that night Willow's parents wanted to know all about Charlotte and **The Secret Garden**—and, simply, how the child was bearing up—and she was sorry that despite the length of their phone call, there was very little she could report.

CHARLOTTE HAD TROUBLE falling asleep that Saturday night, because she was aware that she had made an important connection: Initially she hadn't wanted Willow to tell anyone about the marijuana and the beer for the simple reasons that she was afraid she would get in even more trouble and because she didn't want to imperil what she considered her friendship with the older teenager. Now, however, she understood that secrecy mattered for another reason: She feared if it came out that she had been a little bit high, a little bit drunk, it would jeopardize both her father's lawsuit against the gun company and the way FERAL was using the accident to tell people that hunting was disgusting and guns were unsafe. And after what had happened (oh, hell, **after what she had done**) she owed it to her father not to imperil either the lawsuit or his organization's antihunting media campaign.

It was the strangest thing: Her father had spent forty-five minutes with her that afternoon helping her start learning her lines. He'd spent another half hour on the Web finding her photos of the original Broadway production of the musical, so she could see what Mary and Martha and Colin and Dickon had looked like on the stage at the St. James Theater. He would never have taken the time to do either before the accident.

He'd even marked the date—the dates, all five performances of the show—on the calendar in the kitchen, and painstakingly typed e-mails with his left hand to his assistants at FERAL and to Dominique informing them that he absolutely could not be booked anywhere on those days.

Outside her open bedroom window she heard the sirens and the garbage trucks and the occasional car alarm that filled the night, and she wondered why this evening they seemed so very loud and intrusive.

Twenty-three

"Meat is a social food—a shared food," Howard Mansfield told John over lunch, dabbing at his mouth with a paper napkin between bites of his patty-melt sandwich on rye. "The family or the tribe gathers together after the hunt. They celebrate, they reaffirm their bonds, they rejoice in their kinship. It's been that way forever. And though most of us these days are pretty damn far removed from the meat when it was living and breathing, we still approach it as a ritual food."

"Thanksgiving," John murmured. "Or the great Easter ham."

"Or even the backyard barbecue. Nothing like the smell of a little seared flesh to awaken in all of us that great tribal need for connection." Mansfield was a month shy of fifty. When John had first moved to Vermont, the older man had been a partner in the Burlington firm where John practiced. Then Mansfield left to be a judge and John left to be a public defender: a job John thought would be more interesting than handling the city's municipal and real estate business—his specialty at the firm—and allow him to feel better about himself when he came home at night. And feeling good about what he did was important: He knew how entitled his childhood had been, and he understood exactly what had driven his mother to volunteer her time in the dingiest class-rooms she could find in the city. Now Mansfield was on the Vermont Supreme Court, and John was run-ning the county public defenders' office. They saw each other infrequently, no more than once a season, but it was Mansfield who had taken him hunting last fall, and it was Mansfield who had suggested ten months ago that he simply use a ramrod to extricate the jammed cartridge from his gun's chamber. The two of them were having lunch now at a Burlington diner with the improbable name of the Oasis, a classic aluminum-sided train car with a green rendering of a palm tree on the restaurant's neon sign.

"My brother-in-law would argue that meat is about power," he told Mansfield. "The only reason it became a social food was because peasants got to eat it so rarely. When they did, it was a big deal. A feast."

"Vegetarians—people who choose not to eat meat even when it's available—have always been comfort-able with their nonconformism. They're not social misfits, but they are social renegades. I'd wager there has always been a little distance between them and the bonfire."

"You know, I don't believe Spencer has a lot of friends other than his FERAL cronies. He moved a lot as a kid, so he has no buddies from childhood. And he and Catherine have been their own little world since they fell in love as freshmen, so he doesn't have many pals from college, either."

"Your sister's a vegetarian, too, right?"

"Yes, but not a vegan. And, for the record, she does have friends."

"Women friends?"

"And men."

"Really?"

"She's a magnificent flirt."

"Brothers always think their sisters are flirts."

"Are you speaking as a Freudian?"

He smiled. "Nope. As an older brother."

Outside a dairy delivery truck began to back into an alley across the street, the vehicle's horn automatically emitting the loud whooping cries it made whenever it moved in reverse, and the two men grew silent. When it was parked Mansfield continued, "So: You want my opinion on who your lawyer should be."

"That's right."

"I hate to be predictable, but I believe your best bet is our old firm. I'd ask Chris Tuttle or perhaps even your friend Paul Maroney."

The two attorneys were indeed among the candidates John was considering. And though he was pleased that Mansfield was validating his choices, he wanted to know why the older man had said **perhaps even** Paul: It suggested there was a chink in Paul's armor that he hadn't considered. And so he asked Mansfield whether he had a preference.

Mansfield raised his gray, beetling eyebrows, and put down his sandwich. "You and Paul are a little closer than you and Chris. True?"

"I don't think I've spoken to Chris in a year. Maybe

longer. I see Paul every so often for lunch or a beer and sometimes at events at Willow's school. Paul has a son a year younger than Willow."

"Well, they're both equally capable. But Chris is more likely to approach your situation with complete objectivity. And that's what you need." Mansfield was known among Vermont attorneys for both his fairness and his preternatural patience—attributes that made him an excellent hunter as well as a justice. With the exception of his three years at law school in Pennsylvania, he had never lived anywhere but Vermont.

"And you believe I need objectivity because I can't see my situation well enough on my own—because this is my brother-in-law and my niece?"

"Yes. Also, Chris hunts. Paul doesn't. It might be nice to have another hunter in the room with you when the lawyers from Adirondack are deposing you. They are, of course, your real adversaries."

"I must confess, these days I feel pretty damn antagonistic toward Spencer, too. He won't even talk to me. Refuses to take my calls, doesn't answer my e-mails."

"You have indeed widened that hunters versus gatherers canyon that seems the salient feature of your family's topography."

"Spencer and I used to be friends! Really. We used to be friends."

"Are you and your sister speaking?"

"Yes. And the girls are talking: Willow and Charlotte. I presume they all think I'm a moron—all the women, that is. My sister. My wife. My daughter. My mother. My niece . . ."

Mansfield nodded, and John watched as he put the last three shoestring potatoes on his plate in his mouth at once. John had barely touched his own lunch, a turkey sandwich. His appetite had been decreasing ever since the accident, and these days, it seemed, he never was hungry. He'd lost ten or eleven pounds from a frame that even before the last day in July had tended toward lanky.

"You're not a moron," Mansfield said when he had swallowed the French fries. "You just didn't know."

"Actually, I just didn't cope. There's a difference."

"Tell me: What kind of ammunition were you using?"

He shrugged. "Menzer Premium. Why?"

"I had a thought this morning. The lab with the gun will check this out, but I wouldn't be surprised if the trouble stemmed from the shell's casing—not the gun's extractor. Maybe it was the casing that made it so difficult for you to remove the round."

"I doubt that. I never loaded anything in that gun but Menzer Premiums, and they always worked fine when I was learning to use it."

"Adirondack machine-tools their rifles with extreme precision. Same with their ammunition. In my experience, nothing works as well in an Adirondack rifle as an Adirondack cartridge. The company is a bit like Remington in that regard: Remington rifles, in my opinion, work best with Remington ammunition."

"What are you saying, the cartridge was faulty?"

"Just conjecture. Maybe the rim on that one round was a tiny fraction of an inch too shallow for the extractor—or too wide. All it would take is one minuscule imperfection that might not make a difference with a Menzer rifle or a Winchester or perhaps even a Remington—but it did on your Adirondack. That's all."

Abruptly he felt a little sick, a little faint. He bowed his head against the sensation, and the sounds of all the conversations around him faded into one indistinguishable drone. A single thought dominated his mind: What if the problem were indeed with the casing, and the casing was gone? He knew the New Hampshire State Police had returned the gun to him on the . . . the eleventh of August. He knew the date because it was the day after Spencer had returned to his mother's house, and the very day he and his family had returned to Vermont. If, in fact, that trooper had arrived with his rifle an hour later, they already would have been on the road home.

He knew there was no reason why anyone in New Hampshire would have removed the spent casing from the chamber, but he had no recollection of seeing it in the gun when it was returned. Absolutely no visual picture whatsoever. Granted, he had barely looked at the rifle. He'd actually been repulsed by it.

But he had checked the magazine and the chamber before handing it to the paralegal who had driven up from Paige's firm in New York to retrieve it. The last thing he wanted to do was accidentally turn a loaded rifle over to someone who'd probably never handled a gun in his life.

And though he wasn't absolutely sure, he simply could not recall seeing the spent casing in the chamber. He could, however, see in his head exactly what the chamber looked like . . . empty.

"John?"

He opened his eyes and gazed up at Mansfield. "Yes?"

"You okay?"

"I . . ."

"Yes?"

"I actually thought I was going to faint for a moment."

"I'd say it was something you ate, but you've eaten so little I'd say it was the opposite: It's because you haven't eaten."

He reached for the sandwich and took a small bite, then washed it down by finishing most of the water in his glass. "I don't recall seeing the casing in the gun when I got it back from the state police in New Hampshire," he said.

"You checked?"

"I wanted to be sure the gun was unloaded before I turned it over to Paige's firm."

Mansfield was staring at him. The justice looked as if he had instantly digested this information and drawn a conclusion. He didn't look anxious—Mansfield never looked anxious—but he did seem concerned. John sensed that the older man had thus come to the same conclusion he had: If the problem had been with the cartridge's casing and the casing was gone, then there would be no apparent reason for his inability to extricate the cartridge other than mind-numbing incompetence. Yes, FERAL would still proceed with the lawsuit against the gun company, insisting that Adirondack was producing an inherently defective product because a live round remained in the chamber when you unloaded the magazine . . . but he himself would be crucified. It was bad enough to be perceived as a person who failed to take a broken rifle to a gunsmith; it was even worse to be viewed as a person incapable of extracting a cartridge from a functioning one.

He told himself this didn't increase the likelihood that his own brother-in-law would sue him to see how far his insurance policy would stretch, if only because his sister wouldn't let Spencer try such a thing . . . but anyone else in Spencer's situation would.

"Well," Mansfield was saying now, "maybe your memory is a little fuzzy and the casing was in the chamber after all. And maybe it won't matter in any event, because the extractor will turn out to be the culprit."

"Maybe," he agreed. "I think I'll call the state police anyway and see what the police report says. Who knows? Perhaps the casing is bagged up in some evidence drawer, and some minion can track it down."

Mansfield smiled at him and nodded, but John recognized it as the sort of smile he gave Willow when he was trying to make her feel better but didn't believe a word he was saying.

YOU DON'T KNOW **what I saw, you don't know what I'm feeling!** Her daughter's impassioned roar at her from the backseat of the car last week when she was driving the child to ballet. Sara didn't believe a morning or an afternoon or a 2 a.m. feeding had gone by since then when she hadn't thought of it. Yet, so far, she had made absolutely no headway learning what was behind it—what may have occurred that awful night in New Hampshire that her daughter was keeping to herself. The girl remained uncharacteristically histrionic when the subject came up, adamant that no one could understand what **she** saw or what **she** was feeling, yet absolutely unwavering in her insistence that she was hiding nothing.

Sara was resolved to change all that now. Monday was one of the two days a week when she only saw patients in the morning so she could be home when Willow climbed off the school bus. With Patrick upstairs napping, she was determined to accomplish more in their time together this afternoon than merely help her daughter with her homework and dive into a new box of cereal with her. Cereal had become the girl's after-school snack of choice these days, since the school nurse had used the first day of health class to remind the sixth grade to read the nutrition labels on packaged foods. Once Willow understood that she was getting 710 calories and 40 percent of her fat for the day from the Cobble Hill jumbo iced honey

bun, she avoided her once favorite snack like it was in-
fused with the Ebola virus.

"Can I ask you a question?" she asked her daughter,
her voice as casual and nontherapist-like as she could
make it, as she poured the milk into their twin bowls.
They were sitting at the kitchen counter.

"Uh-huh," Willow said distractedly. She was reading the back of the cereal box. On the front there was
a vibrantly colored cartoon creature—part lion, part
human, part space alien—while the back featured the
beast on its way through a labyrinth in search of all the
food groups in the nutritional period. Sara tried not to
analyze the Jungian sensibility behind the image.

"It will be about a subject I know you don't like to
talk about."

"Math?"

"No."

Willow looked up at her now, instantly understanding that—once again—her mother was going to
try to discuss the accident. "I don't want to talk about
Charlotte and Uncle Spencer," she said. "You know
that."

"I know, sweetheart. But I do." She almost added,
And my feelings count, too, but was able to stop her
therapist-speak in its tracks. Instead she continued
firmly, "And I'm your mother, and so we will."

"You're adding tension and stress to my life, you
know."

"I'm doing no such thing, and you know it."

The girl dropped her spoon in her bowl and gazed
out the window. The maples in their yard hadn't yet

started to turn, but Sara knew they would any day now. Certainly most other trees had.

"Something is bothering you, sweetheart," she continued. "That's painfully clear. And I mean that: painfully clear. Your father and I both know that you're keeping something inside you, and—"

"You can't know that. You can't know what I saw, you can't know—"

"What I'm feeling," Sara said, finishing her daughter's sentence for her. "That's right, I can't know what you're feeling. We've been around that block, Willow. The truth is, you're using that line the way your cousin would—as a very dramatic bit of subterfuge."

"I don't even know what that word means."

"It means you're hiding behind it, sweetheart. It's your defense not to talk to me. Of course, I don't **know** everything. Okay? But your father and I both **believe** that something is troubling you, and it has to do with the accident."

Willow sighed, an almost impossibly long exhalation for a person so small. "Everyone is already in so much trouble, aren't they? I feel awful for Dad. Don't you?"

"Yes, I do."

"And . . ."

"Yes?" She was sure now that her daughter was going to add that she felt bad for Charlotte, too.

"And I just wish people didn't make such a big deal about what other people eat." Willow turned from the window and stared at her with eyes that were fretful and intense. "We talk about food all the time: What's good for you, what's bad for you. White meat, red meat. Uncle Spencer's tofu. Did you get your five fruits and vegetables? You better have. Don't eat that honey bun: You'll get a heart attack someday if you do."

It took Sara a moment to register both that her daughter hadn't continued with what she presumed was the natural connection—that she was worried about her cousin as well as her dad—and that the sixth-grader was mixing in her mind two very separate issues about food. "It's one thing to try to eat right," she answered carefully. "You know, to eat healthy foods—a little bit each day from all the food groups on that pyramid. It's a different thing entirely to choose to become a vegetarian. There are people in this world who eat meat and still eat nothing but healthy foods. Likewise, there are vegetarians who eat terribly. They live on mayonnaise and cheese. Uncle Spencer isn't a vegetarian because he believes it's healthier. It's because he loves animals. I'm pretty sure—"

"I know the difference, Mom. Really. All I meant is that sometimes it seems like all we care about is eating. It's like all we think about is food."

If Willow were a little older, Sara thought she would have said to the child, **And sex. And, maybe, what our parents thought of us. Those are, alas, the big three.** But she restrained herself.

"I mean," Willow added, "this summer Grandmother was figuring out the dinner menu at nine in the morning. Can you believe it? Charlotte and I were still in our nightgowns, and she was asking us what we wanted to eat at the end of the day."

"And that's yet another issue: That's your grand-mother trying to be in complete control. What I want to discuss now is—"

"The accident."

"Yes. Why don't you want to talk about it?"

"Would you want to talk about it if you were me? I don't even want to think about it. I just want it to go away."

"I think it would help you to talk about it. I think you'll forget it sooner if you don't keep whatever's troubling you to yourself."

For a long moment the girl was quiet, staring down into the rainbow-colored pellets of wheat in her bowl. Then: "Even the accident was about food: Uncle Spencer's vegetable garden and Dad's deer hunting. Uncle Spencer just had to have a big plot of vegetables and Dad just had to start hunting. You know what I wish?"

"What?"

"I wish we could all just take one big, chewable pill in the morning—and all the pills in the world had exactly the same flavor—and that was our food for the day. Everything we needed. Not just all the vitamins and stuff: everything. All the . . . the . . ."

"The calories."

"Yes, all the calories and all the bulk—or whatever—we need to feel full."

She smiled. "Oh, you don't mean that. Imagine a world without hot fudge sundaes. Or pizza. Or even crunchy, vaguely fruit-flavored cereal. I think you'd miss them."

"Maybe. Maybe not."

Outside a gust of wind shook the trees, and the branches of the hydrangea—its conical bouquets of flowers salmon colored now—scratched against the bay window in the next room. When Willow had been a little girl, that tree had frightened her: When the flowers and leaves were gone the branches looked like talons.

Once the breeze had fallen away and the house had grown quiet again, Willow sat back in her chair and murmured, "You know what else?"

"What?"

"I never thought he was going to die."

Sara nodded. "Uncle Spencer."

"Uh-huh," her daughter said. "Even when I found him. That night it never crossed my mind he might die. When I got there, there really wasn't all that much blood. Maybe it would have looked worse if it hadn't been so dark, but the only light was the spotlight outside the garage. I remember running past Charlotte— I just ran the way she was facing—and there he was on the ground. Charlotte was screaming. His eyes were open, but I don't think he knew I was there. His skin was wet. Sweat, maybe. But maybe it was also dew from the garden leaves and the lupine. He was right at the edge of the garden. Remember? His legs were twisted, sort of. One was under the other—I don't remember which—and his feet were in the snow peas. I wondered if they were broken—his legs, I mean—and I even thought for a second that maybe he'd been shot in a leg. But then I realized all the blood was up around his shirt. And his shirt collar. There was a big, growing spot by his shoulder. And then Dad was there. I heard people running, and then I felt Dad's hands on me—I knew it was Dad even before I turned around—and he was pulling me aside. At first I thought it was just because he didn't want me to see Uncle Spencer. But then I understood it was also because he wanted to see how badly Uncle Spencer was shot. Where he was shot, I guess."

Sara reached across the edge of the table and wiped away a rebellious lock of Willow's hair that had come loose from a small butterfly clip and was falling across the girl's eyes. It wasn't that the hair was offending Sara: She simply wanted an excuse to touch her daughter.

"And then you were there," Willow continued.

"I ran outside with your father."

"Where was Patrick?"

"Patrick?"

"You know," she said, her voice brightening slightly at the chance to tease her mother. "Your son? My baby brother?"

"I knew who you meant, silly girl. I was just wondering why you were thinking of him."

"Where was he?"

"I put him in the crib. He was in your father's and my room."

"Was he crying?"

"Probably."

"And you left him?"

"Of course I did. My first reaction was that something terrible had happened. And while I guess I understood on some level that you were safe because you'd dropped off the diapers only a second or two earlier, I couldn't be sure. And so I was scared to death. Petrified. Does that really surprise you?"

"Well . . ."

"Sweetheart—"

"I just didn't realize you would leave Patrick, I guess."

She slid her fingers down from Willow's forehead to the girl's hands, which looked impossibly soft and small to her now. Beautiful hands. A young ballerina's hands. She lifted them both to her lips and kissed them, pressing the slender digits against her face. She had the vague sense that there was something more that she wanted to ask Willow. Likewise, she had the feeling that this wasn't necessarily the direction even her daughter had anticipated the conversation would take: It was similar to the unexpected connection the child had made about food a few minutes ago. But she couldn't bring herself to try to steer their discussion back to its original course, in part because it was possible that Willow had just revealed precisely what she was feeling that was causing her such angst—the altogether understandable belief that she was second fiddle to the new baby, an impression that must have grown more pronounced in New Hampshire in the days after the accident when it was all she and John could do to keep from having nervous breakdowns themselves—and in part because she was afraid if she tried to speak more than a dozen words she'd start to cry.

And so she simply sniffed deeply for control and then said into the little hands enmeshed with hers, "I love you, Willow Seton. I love you so, so much."

THE WEATHER TURNED COLD overnight in northern New Hampshire, the temperature a mere thirty-five degrees when Nan Seton came downstairs in the morning, and she knew it was time to return to New York. She called up the local handyman whom she paid some seasons to drive her between Sugar Hill and Manhattan and scheduled her return for that Thursday. She would close up the house for the winter tomorrow, depending upon the same gentleman who would be driving her south to replace the screens with the storm windows and to carry the porch furniture into the garage.

She had already pulled up what was left of the garden—mostly vines and weeds that had grown back since her son had had that paroxysm in the rain in early August and uprooted whole rows of decimated tomato and bean plants, as well as the maturing potatoes and carrots and beets the deer hadn't yet nuzzled up from the earth—but she went out there now and stood with her hands on her hips. She guessed people who took their vegetable gardens seriously would spread compost into the dirt and clay, but her family hadn't bothered with a compost pile this summer. There had been some discussion that they would have one next year, but it had been work enough simply to

get the vegetable and cutting gardens into the ground
and those rows of berries planted.

She wandered to the edge of the lupine and
thought of her family in New York City. She believed
she was standing just about where Spencer had been
when Charlotte had shot him, and she wrapped her
cardigan more tightly around her chest. According to
Catherine, he was doing about as well as could be expected, though Nan had been careful not to press for
details: The last thing she wanted to know were the
grisly particulars of either his injury or his treatment.

She gazed at the clay soil and wondered if ever
again it would grow more than lupine and weeds. She
rather doubted they would have a vegetable garden
here next summer. She presumed that Catherine and
Spencer and Charlotte would return for their summer
vacation, if only because this house was a part of
Catherine's cultural legacy, her childhood. And—at
least until he was shot—certainly Spencer had loved
the place, too. But she guessed there would be no energetic descent on this house over Memorial Day
Weekend, with the McCulloughs and the Setons arriving en masse with their trowels and their spades and
their big green boxes of Miracle-Gro.

The foreboding she had experienced the other day
on her hike in the woods had since grown more pronounced. She was becoming more certain all the time
that the next time everyone in that younger generation
would be together here in the country would be at her
funeral: a little ceremony amid the astilbe, the daisies,
and the phlox, the mourners expressly forbidden from

sharing their memories or singing any hymns. She understood that Spencer was still refusing to speak with John, and she wished she had the matriarchal clout of either her late mother or late mother-in-law. Forty years ago, young adults still listened to their mothers and mothers-in-law. Lord knows, she sure did. Neither of those strong-willed women from a more simple era would have tolerated this sort of nonsense: A raised eyebrow or spoken dagger from either of them, and Spencer and John would have been back at the Thanksgiving table together, their egos curbed and their tails between their legs. They might not have liked each other, but they would have tolerated each other. They would have been civil.

And that was what counted. Civility.

She sighed and stared at the mountains, their peaks hidden today by a heavy layer of leaden white clouds. She imagined it might be sleeting right now atop Lafayette, and perhaps the first snow was falling on Washington. She tried not to be morbid and was only rarely, but she couldn't push from her mind the vision of snow falling on a tombstone in the Sugar Hill cemetery. There was her name carved into the marble beside Richard's. She reminded herself that she still felt no pain, was enduring just a constant shortness of breath. Was weary. Constantly weary. Her heart? Perhaps. She guessed she would schedule an appointment with her doctor when she was back in Manhattan, but she had the fatalistic confidence that she was at the beginning of the end.

Suddenly, at the edge of the woods at the base of

the hill, the far perimeter of the sweeping tangles of old lupine, she sensed something move. At first she wasn't sure what she had seen because she'd barely glimpsed it from the corner of her eye. She lowered her gaze from the clouds shielding Lafayette and remained perfectly still. She squinted, wishing she had her eyeglasses looped around her neck as she usually did, and grew annoyed with herself for leaving them by the sink after washing her face before coming outside. Nevertheless, she could see that the animals were deer, even if she couldn't make out the details of their markings. There were three of them, none with antlers impressive enough that she could distinguish the branches this far away. One of the creatures, it was clear, was watching her, standing guard while the other two ate.

"Go away!" she screamed unexpectedly, surprising herself. When she was alone she barely made a sound. She never spoke aloud—she certainly wasn't the sort who would talk to herself—but here she was . . . screaming.

"Go away! Shoo!" She stamped her foot, though she knew it caused no tremor they could feel at this distance.

Still, her voice was enough: Almost as one the animals bolted into the wall of pines, their white tails as prominent for one brief second as the flags on the greens at the Contour Club golf course. Then they were gone.

She turned toward the house and started in, steaming. Hadn't they done enough? Really, hadn't they brought enough ruin on her family? She was fearful that she would never again see her two granddaughters together in the pool at the Contour Club or in the gloriously crisp waters of Echo Lake. She was afraid that she would never again witness John mixing gin and tonics at the end of the day for Sara and Catherine and Spencer or see the four grown-ups battling together on the tennis court. And while her son and her granddaughter certainly had their parts to play in this travesty—and, perhaps, even Spencer himself, with his dogged opinions about everything—the deer were far from blameless. They had the whole world in which they might browse, the miles and miles of forest that sloped slowly up into the White Mountains. Why in the name of heaven did they have to have her family's Swiss chard and kohlrabi, too?

Oh, how she missed the summer, and those long and wondrous days in July when she had no greater challenges before her than getting Charlotte into a decent swimsuit or figuring out what she could serve her difficult eaters for dinner.

Twenty-four

"I want to do something special for Charlotte," Spencer said. "We completely ignored her birthday two and a half weeks ago." He was sitting in one of the ladder-back chairs in the kitchen that surrounded a round cherry table about the size of a manhole cover. Catherine was cubing a great block of tofu and putting the squares into a bowl with scallions, zucchini, and okra. Their daughter was rehearsing at Brearley.

"We did not completely ignore it," Catherine said, hoping she didn't sound too defensive. They had only been back in the city a couple of days when Charlotte's birthday rolled around, and with Spencer's painful convalescence, the familial strife, and the chaos that greets any family when they return after an unexpectedly long time away—the towering mountains of mail, the canceled appointments that have to be rescheduled—the day itself had been downplayed. Besides, there was that small issue that the girl had nearly killed her father. Granted, it had been an accident. But it still seemed inappropriate to Catherine to make a major production of her birthday this year.

Nevertheless, she had rounded up a few books and DVDs and found her a jazzy sweater and scarf. Last year the child had been elevated (emancipated, Catherine knew, in Charlotte's opinion) from the Brearley elementary school jumper to the middle school skirt—which allowed for some fashion autonomy and accessorization—and so she also had purchased a couple of blouses that matched the uniform garment. The family hadn't had a party. They hadn't even had a cake. But she had managed to wrap the presents and offer them to Charlotte over éclairs she'd picked up at their favorite bakery on Columbus. And so while they hadn't done anything particularly special, neither had they (as Spencer put it) ignored their daughter's birthday.

"You know what I mean," Spencer said. "We didn't do as much as we usually do."

"Fair enough. What did you have in mind?"

"Well, I guess that's the problem. I can't decide what we should do. I called Ticketmaster, and there's nothing available for any of the shows she wants to see until the end of November. So I think the theater is out—at least if we want to do something soon. What else do you think she might like?"

"Were you thinking with just the two of us or with her friends, too?" she murmured. She was so focused on making dinner that she answered a question with a question to stall for time: This way she could redirect her thoughts for the moment on what their daughter might enjoy. She wasn't sure she had ever come across a vegetable as slimy as okra. It was leaving an oily residue on her fingertips that reminded her a bit of beef jerky.

"Either, I guess," he said. "Tell me: If she could

have one thing in the world right now, what do you think it would be?"

"Breasts."

"I'm serious."

"I am, too. She wants to be older than she is. Actually—" She put the knife down and turned toward him, the scraggly start of his beard once more nonplussing her. "Actually, that's not quite true. She wants to be small and young-looking until the school play is behind her so she's a convincing Mary Lennox. Then, between the final performance and the cast party, she wants to mature completely into a well-endowed Brearley senior. That is what our no-longer-little girl wants." She was reminded of the arguments she and Charlotte had had when the child had been in the third grade and had started to demand that she be allowed to have her ears pierced. Somehow she and Spencer had managed to hold firm against her increasingly desperate entreaties until the day before she started fifth grade. They might have caved in even sooner that summer, but Charlotte had been in New Hampshire with her grandmother and Willow for two weeks, which had given them a much needed respite from her pleas and her howls.

"Do you think she wants a party?" he continued.

"You mean something here in the apartment?"

"Uh-huh."

"She hasn't wanted something like that since . . . since Connecticut."

"She had that sleepover here three years ago. That was a real hit."

She barely remembered that night, because she always associated those weeks with her daughter's newly pierced ears. When she recalled it now she realized that it had been a pretty terrific evening: Charlotte had had three of her best friends spend the night, and they had watched movies until two or two thirty in the morning, and then all four girls had brought their sleeping bags into her and Spencer's bedroom because . . . because Spencer had actually been out of town the night of the party. Yes, he'd been around the night of Charlotte's actual birthday, but the evening when she had her sleepover he'd been at a conference in San Diego. Catherine knew she had been furious with him before he had left and then self-righteous when he'd returned, because the party had been a ripping success. Two of Charlotte's friends had piled onto her and Spencer's bed with her, and Charlotte and another girl had curled up in their sleeping bags on the plush carpet between the bed and the walk-in closet. They'd had waffles for breakfast, and she had made them with real milk and butter she'd bought the moment Spencer had left for the airport, for no other reason than the fact he was leaving again and she was mad.

She kept her voice even now, almost light, but she felt she had to remind Spencer of the small detail that he had been on the other side of the continent the night of that sleepover party. "You're right, it was a hit. I'm glad you heard such good things about it when you got home."

"Oh, we're not going to kick that old dog, are we?"

"No," she said, and she was indeed resolved to let the issue disappear. She'd made her point. But the memory alone had made her testy. Or maybe it was the contents of the bowl before her that suddenly she found annoying: the zucchini and tofu and okra. She would douse the blocks of tofu with enough soy sauce and sesame oil to make them tolerable, but it would take more than Chinese seasonings to make zucchini edible. She loathed zucchini and was only putting it in the stir-fry because Spencer liked it.

"So, what do you think? A sleepover, but maybe this time we go to someplace like Planet Hollywood first?"

"Spencer, they have nothing vegan on the menu, remember? Or almost nothing: I think you had a salad the time we went there, and you left seething."

"I did, didn't I? I'd forgotten."

"Yes, you did. It just wouldn't be much fun for either you or Charlotte, because there isn't enough on the menu. Besides, I think she's outgrowing places like that."

"You think so? She's only thirteen, you know. Barely."

Only thirteen. She shuddered. She knew what thirteen-year-old girls were capable of. "My sense is you either have to be eight so you can appreciate the pop rock and the video screens or twenty-one so you can get hammered in the bar," she said. "In between, the place is hell."

She turned back to the wok on the stove and tossed in a capful of oil. She had no intention of lighting the burner until her daughter had returned, but she was about to set the table and she wanted everything ready in the kitchen. She took a breath, and suddenly something in the zucchini—its seeds, its translucence, its profound and impertinent greenness—caused her whole body to tense.

"Do you think anyone else in this whole apartment building is eating tofu and okra and zucchini tonight?" she asked, pouring brown rice into a measuring cup. She was careful to focus on the lines on the glass so she didn't have to look either at him or the small torpedo-shaped grains. The truth was she preferred white rice to brown. She didn't know anyone other than Spencer and his FERAL friends who actually liked brown rice.

"Excuse me?"

"All this vegetable nonsense. Do you really think anyone in this whole big building is eating what we are tonight?"

She heard him rustling uncomfortably in his chair. "I guess. I believe the Youngs are vegetarians. And the Rosners. I mean the Rosners have never served meat when we've been to their apartment for dinner parties. And I can't believe they'd deny their other guests salmon or steak just because I'm present."

"I can."

"Really?"

She grabbed a handful of silver from the drawer by the sink and then three place mats from the cabinet above it. "Absolutely. Sometimes it's just easier to go along with your . . . your beliefs . . . than to listen to your lectures." She inhaled deeply through her nose, unsure why she was taking a perfectly innocuous conversation about what they should do for their daughter's belated birthday and twisting it into something angry—especially since Spencer seemed to have no stomach at the moment for a fight. She didn't cry often, but she felt the desire to howl now.

"I don't think they're secret meat eaters," he said softly. "I guess it's possible, but the idea of someone hiding meat—"

"I hide meat!"

"What?"

Her eyes were starting to tingle and so she dropped the place mats and the silver on the counter and dabbed at them with her middle fingers. Then she repeated herself: "I hide meat. I have a couple of Slim Jims in my purse right now and a couple more in a shoe box in my closet—the box with my dress heels. Why do you think I scarf down Altoids the way you scarf down Percocet? So you can't smell the meat on my breath!"

"I didn't know," he said, and he didn't sound angry and he didn't sound hurt. He didn't even sound betrayed. He seemed merely surprised, and this was too much for her since she'd expected something like rage.

"No, of course you didn't know, because it was just easier to eat my cheeseburgers where no one could see me, or my bologna, or my Slim Jims. It was just easier! But you know what? I'm tired of sneaking around, I'm tired of trying to accommodate you and your vegan pals. I'm tired of this whole vegan nonsense, and that includes eating tofu and zucchini, or sneaking Slim Jims like I'm some closet binge drinker. I'm tired of watching you humiliate my brother and embarrass our daughter by making a public exhibition of your lawsuit! I'm tired of . . . I'm just tired of everything!"

She stared at him, at the small, scruffy tufts of beard, and at the defenseless alarm on his face. At his wounded arm in its sling. At his limp, forever useless fingers. For a long moment neither of them said a word, and the only sound was the traffic outside the window.

"How long have you felt this way?" he asked finally.

"For years," she said.

"Always, huh?"

She nodded. "You know what I wish?"

"No."

"I wish years ago someone had told you to see a shrink so you could just get over your lobster fixation. Just talked out your . . . your guilt or your whatever, so you could have gotten on with your life instead of becoming this fanatic."

He seemed to consider this for a moment. Then: "In the hospital—in New Hampshire—I had a similar thought."

"Really?"

"Uh-huh. When I was having those dreams about lobsters. Those nightmares. And I wondered if I was starting to lose it."

"What did you decide?"

"Well, I will see someone. A therapist. Paige needs me to see someone for the lawsuit. But my sense is that it wouldn't have changed anything if I went to one ten or fifteen years ago. If it hadn't been the lobsters, you know, it probably would have been something else. I still would have given up meat."

"But maybe you wouldn't have been so extreme."

He surprised her. "Maybe," he agreed.

She heard their front door opening, the hinges groaning with the precise whine she knew well from their years in the apartment, and then the jingle of keys on a FERAL fob—that hand grenade–shaped logo with all the animals on it—and she realized that Charlotte was home. She wasn't sure whether she was relieved or disappointed by her daughter's return: Had she been a few minutes later, who knew where her series of confessions might have progressed. She doubted she would have revealed that as recently as hours before the accident she believed their marriage was in such desperately sad shape that she was wondering seriously if it was winding down. But she hadn't planned to tell him about the Slim Jims, either, so who could say what she might really have said? Perhaps, she thought, she might have dropped a bombshell that big.

"We should probably just ask Charlotte what she'd like to do for her birthday," she said simply. "If anything. For all we know, she'll tell us it's more than two weeks past and she feels no need to celebrate it now. Okay?"

"Okay," Spencer agreed, his voice barely above a whisper.

She called out into the living room that she and

Spencer were in the kitchen, and in a moment their daughter pushed her way through the swinging door, bringing with her a shimmering array of stories about rehearsal and the voice coach and the handsome older boy from Buckley who was going to play Archibald Craven.

Twenty-five

The obsessions will get you every time when they're not human—and sometimes, Sara thought, when they are.

She flipped off the small tape recorder with the remarks she had made to herself that morning immediately after Eleanor Holmes had left her office. Eleanor was a thirty-two-year-old woman with an eating disorder who was only now beginning to struggle with the fact that when she was eight she'd spent a full day alone at a New York State Thruway rest area because neither of her divorced parents was willing to cave in to the other and go pick her up. Her father had left her there a day early and just presumed that her mother would drop everything and come get her: Mom hadn't. Mom had refused to be bullied by her ex-husband and wouldn't change her plans. It was a game of chicken, and one result was that little Eleanor had lived on whopping plates of nachos in cheese sauce that day, because she was afraid she would be abducted if she left the rest area's snack shop and cafeteria. The woman believed now—and Sara thought there was some truth to this—that this was why she had become a compulsive eater and tried to use food to reduce anxiety and stress.

Sara closed her eyes. Upstairs she presumed that Willow was sleeping as deeply as Patrick, while John was . . .

John was probably staring at the pages in his book in bed. She'd noticed lately that it took him long minutes to turn the pages in whatever novel or history he was reading. When she'd first noticed the trend in their bed two or three weeks ago, she had presumed he had fallen asleep and that was why he had been on, say, page 216 for fifteen minutes. But then she'd realized that his eyes were open, staring aimlessly at the wallpaper or the window—a blank screen, inevitably, because the shades would be drawn—or simply the foot of their bed.

She hadn't spoken to Spencer since they'd left New Hampshire five weeks ago, and she knew John hadn't, either. This was yet another source of torment for her poor husband. It was a wonder he hadn't become a compulsive eater himself. (Instead, alas, he'd simply lost almost all of his appetite.) She tried to imagine how the brothers-in-law's feud—though it was actually a pretty one-sided squabble since John wanted desperately to be on speaking terms with Spencer—would play itself out. She had to believe that the next time they saw each other would not be in five or ten or fifteen years. This lawsuit would have to bring them together at some point, wouldn't it? And what about Christmas in three months or the Seton New England Boot Camp next summer? The McCulloughs actually didn't visit them all that often in Vermont, largely because when they came north everyone gathered at

Nan's place in New Hampshire, but Sara and Willow and John had a long history of seeing the McCulloughs in Manhattan. Willow loved New York City, and the three of them went there at least twice a year and stayed at Nan's. They'd see lots of Catherine and Charlotte and—when he was in town—Spencer.

Still, Sara guessed that it was possible with a man as stubborn as Spencer that he'd find a way never to speak to her husband again. It was, of course, ridiculous. Childish and ridiculous. And it was only making things worse.

She was about to head upstairs herself and get ready for bed, when she heard a knock so soft on the living room door that she knew instantly it was Willow. The girl was awake, after all.

"Come in," she said, just loud enough to be heard through the door.

Willow's bangs were falling across her eyes, and she was squinting against the light in the living room. Though it was only the middle of September, it had been chilly the last couple of days and the girl had started to wear her winter nightgown, a red and white Lanz which last year had dragged on the floor but now, Sara noticed, didn't even reach her daughter's small ankles.

"Are you having trouble sleeping?" she asked, as Willow moved with the awkward gait of a sleepwalker over to the plush armchair in which she was sitting, and perched herself on the wide armrest.

"A little. But that's not why I came down."

"Go ahead."

"I think I know what I want to do for my birthday."

"Oh, good. Tell me."

"Today in art class Ms. Seeley was telling us about the Cloisters—in New York City. Have you ever been there?"

She shook her head. "Believe it or not, I haven't. I should have by now, I know. Certainly your father has. Probably any number of times."

"She was showing us slides of the statues and paintings they have there, and the way the light moves in the stone hallways, and all these gold goblets and candlesticks that are works of art themselves. Everything's from the Middle Ages, you know. I'd like to go there for my birthday."

She was pleased that Willow wanted to see a museum on her birthday, but she was also realistic enough to understand that her daughter knew well that any trip to Manhattan would include far more than a visit to a museum. There would be dinner at a restaurant sufficiently fancy to allow Willow to wear one of her dresses she loved that were far too elegant for Vermont, perhaps lunch at a more rowdy venue such as the Hard Rock Cafe, shopping at the great palaces of consumption—Macy's and Bloomingdale's—and a detour to a downtown boutique (almost certainly Alice Underground) that would have exactly the sorts of hip, inappropriate children's clothes you couldn't find in Vermont but every girl wanted on her eleventh birthday.

"We can do that," she said, and instantly she began

to outline the logistics of the trip in her mind. Today was Tuesday, the fourteenth. Willow's birthday was the twenty-seventh—a Monday. "Your grandmother will be back in the city by your birthday. I think, as a matter of fact, she's being driven home in a couple of days. This Thursday, maybe. So we could go either the weekend before your birthday—drive down on Friday, the twenty-fourth—or the weekend after. That first weekend in October. We can check with Daddy and see if one of those weekends is better for him than the other."

"The thing is . . ."

"Yes?"

"We'd need to go this weekend—if we decide to do this for my birthday."

"This weekend? Why?"

"Ms. Seeley—she grew up in New York City, you know . . ."

"Yes, I know," she said, smiling when her daughter paused in midsentence. Grace Seeley, the school's art teacher, was a statuesque blond no older than twenty-five or twenty-six with a small blue stone in the side of her nose. She regaled her students in the weekly art class with her tales of art school in Manhattan and the strange and wondrous things people did there that they considered . . . art. This was Seeley's second year in Willow's school, and the girls, especially Willow, adored her.

"She said this is the Saturday that the Cloisters and the park right next to it—Fort something—is having a medieval harvest festival. They do it every year, and it's only this one Saturday. That's it. But she said it's really cool: It feels like you're living in the Middle Ages, except there are always a few people who forget to turn off their cell phones."

"So you want to go this weekend?"

"If we can . . ."

"This is awfully spontaneous. And your father and I are many things, but we're not exactly spontaneous people."

"I know."

She looked at the girl, saw—despite her drowsy eyes—her consuming interest in the idea.

"But you really want to go to this harvest festival, don't you?"

"I do. I've been imagining it all day."

She, too, had been thinking about Manhattan just before Willow had come downstairs. She didn't believe this was a sign precisely, but she had the amused suspicion it was something more than a coincidence: an indication, perhaps, of her and her daughter's connectedness.

Moreover, she recalled that no one had done a whole lot for Charlotte's birthday at the end of August—she had ordered online a CD of some musical and had the company tape one of those ten- or eleven-word greetings to the wrapped disc—and if they went to Manhattan this weekend, the two girls could do something special together. A sort of joint birthday celebration. Certainly they could invite Charlotte to join them for the day at the Cloisters. She liked that idea. Even if their fathers weren't speaking—

perhaps **because** their fathers weren't speaking—it was important to do all that they could to give the girls opportunities to see each other. And while she knew that Spencer didn't want to see John, it was always possible that with her husband in the city he'd have to. They could all descend on the McCulloughs' apartment when they picked up Charlotte—assuming she wanted to go with them to the Cloisters—and she couldn't imagine Spencer hiding in the bedroom. Maybe they'd even get there a little early, so he couldn't sneak out before they arrived to see his physical therapist or run errands or torment the keepers of some nearby fur vault.

She saw in her mind the awkwardness that would infuse any encounter between the two men, and she sighed. It would be pathetic. Absolutely pathetic. The male stripped of any semblance of social grace. It would be embarrassing for anyone who had the misfortune of witnessing the small spectacle.

Then again, she guessed she was kidding herself if she honestly believed there was any chance at all that Spencer would tolerate her husband's presence long enough for embarrassment to become a dominant sensation. Her family might visit Manhattan this weekend, but the only McCulloughs they would see would be Catherine and Charlotte.

"Do you think we can go?" Willow was pressing her now.

"Okay, sure, if that's what you really would like. Maybe we can celebrate your and Charlotte's birthdays together. I know your aunt Catherine didn't have a chance this year to do a whole lot for your cousin. We'll see what your father has on his schedule, just to make sure it's okay. What do you have at school on Friday afternoons this year? Just gym and library, right?"

Willow nodded.

"Well, then. If it's okay with your father, we could pick you up at school at lunchtime and then go straight to the city. We could be at your grandmother's in time for dinner. How does that sound?"

"That sounds great, thank you! Thank you so much!"

"You're welcome. It'll be fun." She slipped her small tape recorder and her notes into the attaché on the floor beside her, and rose from her chair. She shook out her leg which had fallen asleep and said, "Now let's get you back into bed. Do your sheets need to be tucked in again?"

The child nodded, hopped off the armrest with the grace of a gymnast, and then ran up the stairs to her bedroom.

AS WILLOW FELL ASLEEP that night she thought of the slide of what she believed Ms. Seeley had called a reliquary shrine: a gold box with blue enamel, angels in the corners, and a little statue of the Virgin Mary as the knob to open the lid. The box sat on what looked like a dollhouse-sized stage, with a tiny wall of stained glass behind it. She wondered what people stored in such a beautiful box. She'd have to ask someone at the Cloisters on Saturday.

She was looking forward to visiting the place, but the truth was that it wasn't something she would normally have wanted to do on her birthday. It was simply an excuse to get her parents to take her to New York City sooner rather than later so she could see Charlotte. The idea had first started to form in her mind when Ms. Seeley had mentioned that the harvest festival only lasted a single day, and that day was this coming Saturday. She still didn't know quite what she would accomplish with her cousin, but she wanted to see her before they faced their depositions. She wasn't making much headway getting resolution on what she would say—on what they would say—over the phone, and she thought she might make more progress if they spoke face to face. Sometimes she could get her way with Charlotte when they were together. She thought it was possible that her cousin appeased her because she was younger and the older girl wanted to be magnanimous, but Willow didn't care: She didn't want to lie at the deposition if there was any way she could avoid it.

She wondered what Charlotte would say when she told her she was coming to New York this weekend. She liked her mom's idea that she and her cousin might celebrate their birthdays together. It might be a little strange with her father and Uncle Spencer not talking to each other, but they'd work it out. They were grown-ups. Besides, that was their problem. Not hers. With that deposition looming, she had enough to figure out on her own.

Twenty-six

The next morning, Wednesday, Spencer was returning to work, and so he gave in completely. He allowed Catherine to put the jam on his bread—even
opening the jar for him so he didn't have to hold the
glass between his legs and hope to God that he didn't
stain his khaki pants as he struggled to unscrew the
lid—and the toothpaste on his toothbrush. She held
his cardigan sweater for him as he slid his left arm
through the sleeve and then discreetly safety-pinned
both the right side and the right sleeve to his shirt—a
considerably better plan than his big idea, which was
simply to try to wad the dangling sleeve into a front
pants pocket. Now they were standing together on the
sidewalk while the building doorman was hailing a
cab. When one arrived, Catherine offered him a restrained kiss on his cheek and then stood aside while
the doorman held open the door. He slid gingerly into
the backseat, and he was off.

Alone, he gazed out the window at the theater ads
on the buses beside him in traffic. After dinner last
night neither he nor Catherine had brought up her admission that she still ate meat. In their bedroom she
had helped him undress and get into his pajamas and
then gotten ready for bed herself, but it was clear that

neither of them had any desire to discuss her revelations further. She ate meat; now he knew it. Apparently she wasn't going to stop and he was, by then, too tired and beaten up to fight . . . or, perhaps, even care all that much. At least about the meat. After all, the issue wasn't that his wife desired dead things. The issue, clearly, was that she was furious with him, and those Slim Jims she was wolfing in secret were more filled with animosity and bitterness than they were beef and mechanically separated chicken. The truce had continued this morning through breakfast.

With the fingers on his left hand he gingerly adjusted his sling under his sweater. He wondered exactly what he had done to anger his wife so—was it years of being a pill or was all this hostility triggered recently?—and what it would take to make her happy again.

DOMINIQUE THOUGHT some men looked distinguished with beards, especially such elegant European actors as Sean Connery and Ian Holm. When Americans and her fellow Canadians grew them, however, it often struck her as a mistake—especially these days. The hip beard this season was a patchy heroin-addict fuzz, whiskers that seemed to struggle atop raw cheeks and chins the way bearberry or sandwort strained toward the sun on wind-blasted tundra. Spencer's beard, when he was through growing it out, was never going to strike anyone as distinguished. It looked like it would become the sort of close-cropped beard that might, if nothing else, be neat—she re-called her favorite image of Marvin Gaye from an al-bum she'd owned in junior high school—but it might just as easily become the kind that would hang lacon-ically down his chest like a bib should Spencer ever stop trimming it. It was spotted with white and black and traces of red. It made his high forehead look even higher.

She watched him run the fingers of his left hand over the brand-new, left-handed keyboard they had purchased for his computer and then punch the but-tons that turned on the monitor, the tower, and the printer. He looked like he had missed using them. He rolled the special left-handed mouse back and forth across the rectangular rubber pad with the FERAL logo.

"We have voice input software on order," she told him. "You'll be able to dictate your memos and news releases right into the computer."

"What fun. Thank you."

"A new sound card, too. And extra RAM. Apparently, you'll need it."

"Uh-huh."

"Did you bring your Palm with you?" she asked him.

He shook his head ever so slightly and motioned with his eyes down at his sling. "I can't use it with my left hand. Can't draw the characters, can't use the stylus."

"In time you'll be able to."

"Maybe."

"How was your cab ride this morning?"

"Fine."

"I presume you didn't get sick?"

"Not this time."

"That must have been a relief."

She heard one of Spencer's publicity minions laughing in the corridor at something Keenan had said, and wanted desperately now to be with them instead of alone in this office with Spencer. She knew she was supposed to say something about how good he looked or how wonderful it was to have him back—how happy she was just to see him alive. But she certainly wasn't about to lie and tell him he looked terrific, because he didn't. He looked horrid: That beard was a disaster, he had bags under his eyes that resembled marsupial pouches, and his skin was the color of whey. The idea that this was a man her organization actually used to trot out to news programs and talk shows and speeches before crowded auditoriums astonished her. Had Spencer McCullough ever once been even remotely telegenic? It seemed inconceivable.

But she knew that he had been. Recently, in fact. Seven or eight weeks ago.

Now he was a shabbily dressed, sloppily bearded, debilitated wretch in a safety-pinned cardigan. This was her director of communications? This guy was supposed to sit in one of those boxy armchairs opposite Katie Couric and Jane Pauley?

He picked up a sealed cardboard carton about half the size of a shoe box with a long serial number stenciled in black ink across the side. "What's this?" he asked her.

"I believe that's your headset. For your telephone. So you don't need to hold the receiver in your hand."

"Oh, goodie. I can be just like a telemarketer."

"Hands-free communication."

He put the box back down on his desk and gently rapped the lid with his knuckles. "Well. Thank you for this, too."

"You're welcome. We want to do everything we can to make your return to work as seamless as possible. We want—"

"Everything's fine," he said to her, his voice as calm and sonorous as an incoming tide. He touched her elbow when he cut her off and she was able to suppress the need to flinch. Barely. "I know what you want, and I thank you for . . . for everything. Okay?"

She glanced down at the spot where his fingers were separated from the flesh on her arm by a wisp of linen fabric. She nodded. She wished she enjoyed the touch of humans half as much as she did the warm fur of her dogs or the scratchy tongues of her cats.

JOHN THOUGHT the offices of Tuttle, DiSpiro, and Maroney, P.C., looked surprisingly unchanged from the period in his life when he'd toiled here. The only visible difference was the removal of Howard Mansfield's name from the signage and letterhead since the older lawyer had become a justice on the

Vermont Supreme Court. The offices sat in a reno-
vated brick building on the Burlington waterfront that
had once been an icehouse. When Burlington began
to gentrify the area, the icehouse was one of the first
structures to be transformed into office space. Howard
Mansfield and Chris Tuttle were among the business
visionaries who understood that its views of the lake
and the mountains were sufficiently panoramic to jus-
tify moving an upscale law firm to what was then a still
up-and-coming neighborhood.

As John strolled down the corridor, his feet positively sinking into the plush cobalt carpet, he realized
just how squalid was the workplace four blocks to the
east that housed the Chittenden County Public
Defenders' Office. The threadbare carpet there was no
thicker than cardboard, the walls—an ivory so coated
with fingerprints and grime that it now resembled the
color of a T-shirt left too long on a subway grate—
were peeling, and most of his lawyers' offices were
about the size of this firm's coat closet in the waiting
room. The difference in the two waiting rooms, in
fact, said it all: The one here had a pair of leather
couches so soft he could have slept on them, a post-
card view of the mountains in New York, and tables
with the latest issues of **Forbes, Fortune,** and that
morning's **Wall Street Journal**. There was coffee or ice
water or tea if you simply raised your gaze at the receptionist, a polite young woman who could have
passed for a Neiman Marcus model. The waiting room
back in his world of PDs was a cramped cubicle with
two badly cushioned wooden chairs and a box of half-

broken toys for the children of the drunk drivers and mentally ill street people and insolvent check bouncers who hoped that, somehow, he and his associates could finagle for them yet one more chance.

Though John didn't believe he had made a mistake leaving this splendor for the public defenders' office, he couldn't help but wish he could find within the organization's state-funded budget the money to repaint the walls and perhaps buy a decent couch for the waiting room. It wasn't simply that he believed his lawyers deserved freshly painted walls: Those forlorn denizens who depended upon the PDs deserved them, too. After all, was it too much to expect that your lawyers' offices would be clean?

Chris Tuttle rose from behind a desk the size of a small putting green as soon as he saw John in the doorway of his office and came around it to greet him. Tuttle was a few years older than Mansfield—John guessed he was in his midfifties now—but his hair was a shade of black darker than creosote, and his eyes were a vivid chestnut brown. His face was deeply wrinkled, however, and John suspected that Tuttle was dying his hair.

Unlike some of the other senior lawyers in the firm, Tuttle didn't keep a conference table of his own in his office, and so when they sat back down Tuttle was on one side of the massive desk and John was on the other. He was reminded of those images of estranged couples in their baronial dining rooms in movies from the 1930s and 1940s, the length of table between them a signal for the viewer that this marriage had ab-

solutely no hope of being saved. He and Tuttle had already spoken twice on the phone about his deposition,
and John had told him all that he could about the rifle—including his fear that when the New Hampshire
State Police had returned the gun to him in August the
casing had somehow been lost.

"So, how are the girls? Sara and young Willow?"
Tuttle asked.

He answered briefly that the girls were as fine as
could be expected, given the reality that his family was
dealing with a waking nightmare of guilt and self-re-
crimination. John knew that Tuttle didn't actually
want the details of their personal lives right now; nor
did he himself have any great desire to volunteer the
information while on this other lawyer's billable clock.

"So, the folks in New Hampshire tell me they're
still looking for your missing casing," Tuttle said to
him. "But I really have no more confidence than you
that it will turn up. They don't think there was a casing in the chamber when it was checked into the
firearms locker."

"Oh, that's bullshit, of course there was. They just
lost it is all."

"I'm just telling you what they're telling me. You
still have the box the cartridge came in?"

"Yes, absolutely. Why?"

"A gun guy thought it might be worth seeing if
other rounds from the box jam in the chamber. Maybe
it wasn't just that one."

"Interesting."

"A longshot. Obviously you loaded and unloaded

the rifle a couple of times last November, and no other cartridges got stuck. Still, it's something to consider when we get a chance to look at the gun. So, bring me that box of ammunition, okay? Now, let's talk about the deposition," Tuttle continued. On the lake outside the window John could see a ferry leaving the dock at the boathouse and starting its way west toward New York.

"Yes, let's."

"Obviously there is no justification for your . . ." Tuttle paused, searching for the right word. John considered assisting him with **stupidity, irresponsibility,** or **carelessness,** but he restrained himself. "Improvidence," Tuttle said finally. "There is no rational reason for what you did."

"Thank you."

"So what I've told Paige I want us to focus on, first of all, is the mystery of the round in the chamber. How it simply wouldn't pop out when you cycled the weapon, and then—and this will be very important—how you struggled and struggled to extract it."

"I didn't struggle. I didn't want to shoot my hand off with a ramrod or risk blowing my head off by firing it. I didn't know what would happen if I fired it, and I envisioned the damn thing exploding against my cheek."

"I understand—and we'll need to make that point. But you did try to pop out the cartridge; you did try to remove it. Multiple times. Correct?"

"Correct."

"And it just wouldn't come out."

"Yes."

"Good. It must be clear that you did what you could. Second, it must also be clear that events then conspired to prevent you from dealing with it further, i.e., bringing it to a gunsmith. All that busyness you told me about at work, the birth of young Patrick. I want the numbers, please, of exactly how many cases your office handled over the last twelve months, and the number for the previous year, too. You were down, what, two lawyers this year?"

"One. But we were also down an investigator."

"Fine. I also want to know how many cases you managed personally, in addition to all your responsibilities running the public defenders' office."

"I can get you that."

"And, lastly, I want a list of all the ways and all the hours you volunteer in the community and all the ways you help out your family—including that garden."

"You mean the garden Spencer had us plant?"

"Yup. That one. You must have helped him weed it or something."

"I spent all of Memorial Day Weekend over there putting the damn thing into the ground."

"Excellent. That's three days right there you were helping him when you could have been taking the gun to a gunsmith. That is, after all, half the problem here. You never brought the gun to a professional."

"The other half, I presume, is leaving a live round in there in the first place?"

"Okay, the problem should be divided into thirds, not halves. Forgive me. You left a live round in the

chamber. You failed to bring the weapon to a gunsmith. And then you left the rifle where a child could
get it."

"It was only where a child could get it because I was
actually going to see a gunsmith roughly thirty-six
hours after Spencer was shot. That was the whole reason the rifle was in the trunk of my car."

"You sound angry. You needn't be. It goes without
saying that you shouldn't be angry at your deposition."

He heard a small laugh escape his lips, unexpected
and trilling. **I'm not angry,** he wanted to say. **I'm depressed.** His depression might have made him sound
cranky, but one was only a visible manifestation of the
other. Some mornings it took every bit of will he
could muster to simply climb out from under the
sheets on his and Sara's bed, to emerge from the warm
cocoon he had created with a little cotton and a nighttime's worth of body heat. He might not have made it
out of bed today—the depression this morning was
almost a quilt, shielding him from all the nastiness the
world had to offer with the cozy affection of a down
comforter—if he hadn't heard Willow calming Patrick
in the kitchen (so distant, so very distant) while Sara
was trying to get one child ready for school and the
other for the Mother's Love Nurture World. He had to
help. He **had** to. If he didn't, he understood, he would
have ratcheted up the self-loathing yet one more
notch, and that might have sent him so deep into his
nest of percale and gloom that he would never have
emerged.

"I won't be angry," he said to reassure Tuttle, and he

tried to sit up a little higher in his chair. He realized he'd been slouching, just the way his own clients did when they were meeting with him.

He hadn't really thought about it until just that moment, but he guessed they were depressed, too.

PAIGE LEANED FORWARD in the ergonomic stool with a back that purported to be a chair. She used to have a chair that was a deep burgundy leather. Once she was the youngest lawyer in the firm who got to sit on the slick, supple skin of a dead animal. It was a big chair with plush cushions and wheels—an unmistakable sign of achievement and success. Then she started working with FERAL and she understood that the chair had to go. Now an associate who would soon be a partner (but wasn't yet) had it, a woman from Harvard who spent lots of time suing automobile manufacturers over headrests, fuel tanks, and air bags. Nothing she did ever wound up in trial, and she made the firm mountains of money. She was likable. She was pretty. She was a rising star. Paige knew she would have detested her if she herself weren't already a partner.

Now her eyes moved back and forth between the papers on her desk that had been faxed to her moments before and the telephone. She had known essentially what the fax was going to say for fifteen minutes before it arrived because the engineer at the ballistics lab in Maryland had called her and left a message on her voice mail. Then he'd followed up with this fax. The results? They could find nothing wrong with the extractor on the Adirondack rifle she had sent them. Not a thing. And they'd put the weapon through batteries of tests, using different brands of ammunition and test-firing the gun multiple times. Always, however, they had been able to extract both live rounds and spent casings from the chamber with ease. Never once did any round stick.

She'd called Spencer at FERAL a few minutes ago, but he was already in a meeting. She considered telling Keenan the news, but that wasn't quite fair. Spencer was her client. Not FERAL. Spencer should get the results first.

She guessed she should not have been surprised by the findings, given how little faith she had in John Seton. Fortunately, this disappointment did not derail the lawsuit. In some ways it actually meant the stakes were even higher, because now it wasn't simply one defective rifle, it was the whole Adirondack thirty-ought-six she was taking on: the model. They were going to sue a brand because there was a fundamental defect with the gun: A round remained in the chamber when a person emptied the magazine, and that—they would argue—was inherently dangerous. The company was putting an irresponsibly lethal weapon into the stream of commerce.

Well, it's a gun, that little voice of reason kept muttering inside her head. **Of course it's lethal. Hello?** She thought of the Shakespeare quote one of the malpractice attorneys in the firm had engraved in bronze on a plaque on his wall:

**When sorrows come, they come not single
    spies,
But in battalions.**

Still, this was the information she needed to finalize her theory of liability and compose the complaint.
Now, at least, she knew precisely what they were going
to argue.

THAT AFTERNOON, Keenan pulled back the bolt
on the rifle an intern in Paige's firm had purchased the
day before at a sporting goods store on Long Island. It
was the exact same model John Seton owned. Keenan
was familiarizing himself with the weapon in his office
while Paige watched, and a surprisingly articulate
mountain man from some small, smoggy city in northern Pennsylvania patiently explained to them why the
chamber and the magazine on a bolt action rifle could
not be unloaded simultaneously. Dan Grampbell must
have been six and a half feet tall, and Keenan would
have been shocked if he tipped the scale at an ounce
below three hundred pounds. His eyes were green, his
mouth—what Keenan could see of it behind the massive beaver beard that swallowed up cheek and neck—
was pink, and his hair, all of it, was the sort of orangish
red he'd once seen on poppies at the botanical gardens.
He was wearing an ill-fitting blue blazer over a worn
flannel shirt.

Yet Grampbell also had a degree in criminal science
from Penn State, and he spoke with the soft voice of a

poet. Moreover, Dan Grampbell knew about guns. He knew a lot about guns. That was why he was here and why he was being paid an hourly rate commensurate with that received by the associates in Paige's own firm.

"It's a two-step process for a reason," Grampbell was saying quietly. "If Adirondack chooses to settle, it will be because in their opinion settling is less expensive than the cost of a trial or enduring the negative publicity that would surround the case."

"Let me try unloading it for myself one more time," Keenan said. He was afraid that his clumsiness with the weapon in front of Paige was unmanly, and he was surprised at himself for giving a damn.

"Fine. It's now fully loaded," Grampbell observed. "There is a full magazine and a round in the chamber."

Paige was grinning mischievously, and she looked to him a bit like a schoolgirl. Twice when he'd been trying to load the weapon he'd fumbled the dummy ammunition, one of the cartridges dinging off the dark oak of his precious mission desk.

"You're on safety. Correct?" Grampbell asked.

He looked to make sure. "Yes."

"Now, pull back the bolt—that's right—and, voilà. The round will pop—"

Sure enough, it popped right into his nose, ejecting like a pilot from a doomed fighter jet. He yelped, and Paige's pixielike chuckles were turned into a single burst of full-throated laughter. He wasn't smiling, however, and so she put a cap on her mirth and extended her hands to him, open-armed, as if to say, **What did you expect? Really, now, what did you expect?**

"The bullet certainly popped," he murmured to Grampbell. He hoped he sounded like a good sport.

"Next, you are going to push the magazine release by the trigger guard."

He pressed the small knob and instantly four cartridges cascaded onto the floor, a pair rolling under the chair in which Paige was sitting, two others disappearing near the credenza. He'd forgotten to place his cupped hand beneath the magazine to catch them, even though Grampbell had warned him earlier that he should.

"You've now cleared the magazine. See?"

"I see."

"A good thing to do at this point might be to close the magazine door."

He looked at the dangling piece of thin metal. "Ah, yes. Remind me . . . please."

"Press it upward straight into the gun. That's all. It'll click shut."

He pushed. Sure enough, it closed.

"That wasn't difficult, was it?" Grampbell asked, a completely rhetorical question. Keenan could tell that in Grampbell's worldview, loading and unloading a weapon was child's play. Any fool could do it—except, apparently, fools who were lawyers.

"What remains unclear to me," Keenan said, "is why the chamber and the magazine cannot be linked. Why must unloading the rifle be this two-step process?"

Grampbell nodded. "The chamber is, essentially, a combustion chamber. It's designed to withstand the pressures that come with firing the round. Typically, that pressure is in the neighborhood of fifty thousand pounds per square inch. In order to handle that, the chamber can't have any slots or breaks in the metal surrounding the bullet. The rifle's bolt—along with the cartridge casing on the bullet—actually completes the seal in the rear of the chamber."

"And you need a seal . . . because . . ." Paige asked.

"Because without one the hot gases needed to propel the bullet down the barrel would escape to the rear, creating what you would have to consider an extremely hazardous situation for the shooter. The gun might even explode. Now, what this means is that the magazine can be nothing more than a reservoir of extra rounds. That's all. And that's why you need a two-step process to unload the weapon." He shook his head, then continued, "In my opinion, that rifle you have there is still a mighty impressive engineering feat. You may not be able to unload the chamber when you unload the magazine, but I think it's nevertheless pretty remarkable that when you cycle the used cartridge you simultaneously pull a bullet into the chamber from the reservoir. That's a nifty little accomplishment, don't you think?"

"And this two-step process is all the result of an . . . an immutable law of ballistics?" Paige asked. "There's no way to design around it?"

"Oh, there's an exception."

"And that is?" she asked.

"A rifle with a fixed box magazine. Remington, Springfield, Savage—they all have a model like that.

Those rifles have no floor plate like the firearm we have here, meaning the bolt must be opened to empty the rounds in the magazine. You literally cycle the cartridges one by one from the reservoir to the chamber. When you're done, there can't possibly be any rounds left in the firearm. The downside to this system, of course, is all that cycling. If not properly done, there is always the risk of an accidental discharge."

Keenan placed the rifle down gently on his credenza. Even though they'd been using dummy ammunition, the long weapon frightened him.

"Well, I think this is all just messy enough to give FERAL some ink," Paige said. "Especially since there is most definitely no indicator on the weapon telling you when there is or is not a bullet in the chamber."

"And there's that girl," Grampbell added. "I'm no lawyer, but I've seen enough of these cases to know it helps the plaintiff when there's a child involved."

Keenan thought about this, and then he thought of all those hunted deer. All those Bambis with their big dark eyes. Those animals hadn't a chance against an exploding projectile rocketed after them with—what was that number?—fifty thousand pounds of pressure per square inch. No animal did. Just look at what a bullet did to the shoulder of their communications director. He made a pyramid with the fingers on both hands, and as he spoke he hoped his words didn't sound as oddly chilly to Grampbell and Paige as they did to him: "But since the lawsuit will go to the heart of one of Adirondack's best-selling rifles, I believe we can take comfort in the reality that, in this case, they will not settle right away. Which is, of course, precisely what we want."

The mountain man looked puzzled for a moment. He was even making a small silent **oh** with his mouth beneath that great ruddy beard. But then Grampbell turned toward Paige Sutherland—and she looked downright petite beside him—and he stretched the seams of his blazer with one massive shrug.

O N LY   W H E N   C H A R LOT T E had mastered the ability to drop the final **g**'s in her words—**eatin'** and **drinkin'** and **goin'**—did she start trying to spit out the **t**'s that marked the end of some words or soften the vowels that resided in the midst of still others. Sometimes she feared that she sounded more like a Cockney aunt from a **Monty Python** sketch than a spoiled but unhappy little girl from the colonial aristocracy, but the drama teacher told her—in a stab at a British accent herself—that the accent was comin' along just fine.

She was running lines now with her father on the couch in the living room. He was holding a copy of the script open with his left hand, pressing it flat against his knees at an angle that allowed them both to see the dialogue on the page. Occasionally he would lean forward to hold the pages open with the weight of his sling-enclosed forearm and use his functional left hand to reach for a toothpick pretzel in the small bowl on the end table beside them.

"Are you goin' to be my father now?" she asked,

closing her eyes after glancing quickly at Mary's line. This was how she found it easiest to learn her part: She would read the dialogue once, repeat the words in her mind, and then say them aloud with just a hint of an accent.

"I'm your guardian. But I'm a poor one for any child," her dad answered, replicating impressively in her opinion the stoic voice of the orphan girl's tortured uncle. "I offer you my deepest sympathies on your arrival."

This time she didn't have to lean over to glance at the script because the next line—the very last in the scene—was one of Mary's best. "Did my mother have any other family?" she asked, emphasizing **other** exactly the way the young actor did on the CD she had from the original Broadway production.

Her father removed his fingers and let the script fall shut. "Very nicely done," he said. "You're good."

She was flattered, but reflexively she rolled her eyes. "I'm okay," she said.

"Your grandmother—my mom—used to have an excellent ear for accents. It was mostly a party trick, but sometimes when I was a little kid she'd leave me howling with laughter."

"But she never acted, right?"

"Just school plays."

"She never tried anything more?"

"I doubt it."

"Why?"

He nodded, apparently pondering his response.

Finally, he said, "I've always been sorry you were so young when my mother died. You would have liked her."

"I have a couple memories of her. Once we went looking for seashells together, right? I was three, maybe. It was a windy day and the waves seemed humongous—but I'm sure they weren't."

"No. They weren't."

"And didn't she finger-paint with me one time? On newspapers on a glass table?"

"She did."

"But maybe I just remember that because you or Mom told me about it."

"Maybe."

"So, why do you think she never tried to become an actress?"

"Oh, I don't know if she had the talent. Or the discipline. Or the desire. I'm not sure she ever figured out precisely what she wanted."

"That's so sad."

"She had her moments. She adored you," he murmured softly. Then, almost abruptly, as if waking up from a trance, he said, "Now, your mother and I have been thinking about your birthday. I know it was a couple of weeks ago, but we didn't do a whole lot and that was wrong. A birthday is still a birthday."

"It was fine, really. I didn't mind that we didn't have a party," she said, once more trying to sound like Mary Lennox. She decided she was unhappy with the way she had just rolled the **r** in **really** (too Scottish, she thought) but immensely satisfied with the crisp way she had enunciated **party**. "Besides, I already have what I want." There: A girl such as Mary Lennox would most assuredly have said **have** instead of **got**.

"This part?"

"Yes, Father," she replied. **Father**. Now that was a nice British touch. She had never called her dad **Father** before, and she liked how it sounded.

"Would you like a party now? I know it's late, but we could still have one."

Next Tuesday was that press conference. That meant, she presumed, that her father would be crazed this coming weekend. Almost certainly he would not be around. "Well, anything we do should wait until after the press conference. So if we have a party or go someplace special—and I'm not saying we should—I'd understand if we did it the following weekend. Or even next month. Okay?"

"Sweetheart, the press conference is a completely separate event from your birthday. And I think it's under control. At this point, it doesn't look like I'll have to do a whole lot more than show up. And so I think I can manage both—a party and my responsibilities at the office," he said, and as he spoke he accidentally knocked the ceramic bowl of pretzels onto the floor with his good arm.

The floor was carpeted and so the dish survived its plummet intact, but the pretzels scattered everywhere like small toasted Pick-up Sticks. She watched her father reflexively lean over to start gathering them up, and she glimpsed the wince he was able neither to conceal nor control. And so instantly she knelt down and started sweeping them up with her hands, telling her dad to stay put, that she could do this.

Much to her surprise, he did. "Fair enough," he said with a sigh, and he fell back gingerly against the cushions.

When she had recovered the pretzels she returned to her spot on the couch, wondering if he would say something about his clumsiness or his helplessness or his simple inability to pick pretzels up off the floor. She wondered if he would be angry. Quickly she put the cap back on the yellow highlighter they'd been using to mark the script, because she knew how difficult it would be for him with one hand.

"So: Your birthday," he continued instead, as if nothing had happened. "What would make you happy?"

The short answer was easy: Her father to have a functioning right arm once again. To go back in time to July. To no longer live with the constant, only barely suppressed awareness of what she had done.

This wasn't an option, however, it wasn't anything her father could give her. It wasn't anything her father was even contemplating with the question. And so she thought for a moment, wondering exactly what she did want. And she had the sense as she sat in the living room and learned her lines with her . . . **father** . . . a father who was at once strangely placid and uncharacteristically present . . . that right now she was indeed (and she heard Mary Lennox using precisely these words) **about as content as a girl could be, given her current circumstances.**

"I'm happy," she said, and she pulled from deep within herself a smile for her father's benefit. "I really don't want anything more for my birthday. But . . ."

"Yes?"

"Thank you, Father. Thank you for the thought."

Twenty-seven

"So Catherine really doesn't know about this?"

"Nope," Spencer said. "She doesn't. I considered telling her, but then I thought I might as well surprise her, too."

"Well, I think it's sweet. Maybe a little crazy—the not telling your wife part. Actually, that's a lot crazy. But it's certainly a lovely gift for Charlotte. You're a good dad."

He smiled at Randy Mitchell, the former Granola Girl who had become his most senior assistant, as they walked down Fifty-ninth Street to the Humane Society of New York's animal adoption center. The shelter was a no-kill facility, which meant they only euthanized animals that were terminally ill. He had asked Randy to join him because she had a dog, a mutt she insisted was part springer spaniel and—based on the way its tail stood up like a dust mitt and folds of skin hung like drapes between its fore and hind legs—part flying squirrel. Spencer had met the dog, and the creature was among the most unattractive animals he'd ever seen outside the Discovery Channel. But she was playful and happy, and Randy adored her.

Spencer was particularly appreciative that he had

Randy's help this afternoon because it was Thursday evening, a mere five days before the press conference, and Randy had better things to do than help her boss pick out a shelter dog. He imagined he would have come here alone before the accident.

Then he guessed he wouldn't have come here at all. He would have been unwilling to get a dog before the accident. He'd always told his daughter that he believed it was cruel to keep one in a New York City apartment, but the truth was that until now he simply hadn't been willing to have his life complicated by the attention a dog needed—especially one that lived in an apartment.

The animal was going to be a belated birthday present for Charlotte: three weeks belated, in fact, and if for that reason alone quite a surprise. The humane society didn't allow same-day adoptions, and so Spencer's plan today was to fill out the forms and choose the dog. Then on Monday he and Randy would return after work for the animal. At that point he'd really need his assistant, because he was quite sure that he was incapable of bringing a dog—and all of its accoutrements—back across town to his family's apartment with one hand.

"I'm not a good dad," he said. "But I'm trying."

"Oh, don't be so hard on yourself. It's a beautiful day, I bet you've got a pocketful of Percocet, and you're about to bring another companion animal into your family's life. Give yourself a break."

Randy's FERAL-speak caused him to cringe slightly—even he viewed dogs and cats as **pets** rather than as **companion animals**—but it was a lovely day, he agreed. And his shoulder actually felt a little better this morning. He was not for one moment oblivious to the pain, but today, at least, it was tolerable: a steady ache that was considerably more pronounced than the feeling of a pebble lodged inside one's shoe but no more debilitating. According to Nick, his physical therapist, the pain probably would never, ever disappear completely, but eventually it would diminish to the point it was at now—and that would be without the gloriously buffering power of the small candy jar of painkillers he was consuming daily. Moreover, he'd gone to a barber this morning and had the whiskers on his face trimmed and shaped into something that resembled a beard. He looked less like an over-the-hill grunge rocker and more like a tweedy English professor. The beard still had a distance to go, but already he liked the air it gave him, and the way the facial hair seemed to shrink his ears to something like a normal size. Granted, his forehead seemed to stretch now into Quebec. But the ears? Almost average. For the first time since the accident, the world didn't seem quite so exhausting.

THE DOG THAT HE CHOSE was a two-year-old combination of collie and something more petite, with dark eyes and fur that felt like satin against the fingers on his left hand. She weighed just over forty pounds. Her name was Tanya, and she'd wound up at the shelter when her owner had lost his job and a pet—especially a not insubstantial one with an appetite that could only be called impressive—suddenly seemed an unacceptable luxury. Moreover, she'd had emergency surgery the day after she arrived at the humane society, because she'd swallowed a small rubber ball and it had lodged in her intestines. Tanya was a quiet animal who, according to the young woman from the shelter who was assisting them, had always done well in an apartment.

The decision had only been difficult for Spencer for the simple reason that there had been so many needy dogs present, and every single one of them seemed to be barking desperately for his attention. The animals in their pens were so loud that he and Randy and Heather Conn, their guide at the shelter, had to shout to be heard over the din. And while Spencer considered any number of the smaller dogs there—the mutts who seemed to be largely terrier, spaniel, or beagle— simply because they would be easier for him to manage with only one arm, he was drawn to this serene miniversion of Lassie. He decided that Tanya would have been perfect if she were ten or fifteen pounds lighter, both because of his disability and because of the finite space in their apartment. Still, his mother-in-law's dog lived in an apartment, and that animal seemed quite content.

He had a vision now in his mind of Tanya running through the lupine in Sugar Hill with Nan's golden retriever, but then he remembered that dog hadn't run anywhere since the last presidential administration. Still, he saw Tanya racing off the porch and onto the badminton court, jumping into the air after one of the badminton birdies. He saw the dog lounging with her nose on Charlotte's lap as the girl sat on the carpet before the fireplace in the New Hampshire living room. He saw her walking at his side as he strolled out toward those apple trees, the ones that bordered the . . . vegetable garden.

Oh, there would be no vegetable garden. Never again. He knew that.

But the dog might walk between his daughter and him as they strolled down his mother-in-law's driveway late in the afternoon, the sun still high because it was only the last week in July.

As he walked the dog up First Avenue, he felt shivers of pain in his right shoulder every time Tanya pulled against her leash and yanked his left arm. The sensation rippled across his upper back and became transformed from a simple awareness of a tug to the feeling of a knife slicing through skin. It was sharp and it stung. Still, he had endured far worse over the last month and a half. Far worse. The dog sniffed everything in sight on the street, from the garbage cans to the sewer grates to the stations on which hung the antiquated pay phones.

Heather and Randy were walking a few paces behind him, chatting. He wondered if perhaps he should bring the animal home tomorrow—Friday—instead of on Monday. The advantage was that Charlotte didn't have school on Saturday and Sunday, and so she would have more time to bond with the pet. They all would. Moreover, Monday might be chaos for him because of the press conference on Tuesday, and it was certainly possible that his day would get away from him and he wouldn't even be able to make it to the humane society to pick the animal up.

On the other hand, Willow was arriving this weekend and surely Charlotte would want to see her. And Sara and Willow and ol' Francis Macomber wanted to take Charlotte and Catherine to the Cloisters on Saturday.

"You have cats, right?" It was Heather talking to him, the woman standing suddenly right beside him. Her eyes were blue and she was staring at him intensely.

"Yes. Two."

"I believe Tanya's pretty good with cats. But when we get back, let's bring her to the playroom on the third floor of the shelter. We can see how she does there with some of the cats we have right now."

"Okay."

She pushed her bangs off her face and gazed at his sling. "How are you doing?" she asked. "It looks like she's giving you a pretty good workout."

"I'm right-handed."

"When do you get your arm back?"

"Never."

"Are you serious?"

"Completely. Nerve damage."

She nodded thoughtfully and then said, "Your daughter's thirteen, right?"

"Just turned thirteen, yes."

"So, tell me: What are you going to do in four or

five years when she leaves home? When she goes to college or gets a job?"

"You mean in regard to Tanya?"

"Yup. You said this dog would be a present for her."

"I guess I'll be walking her more often, then."

"I presume you're married."

"I am," he said. Glib responses passed through his head: **For the moment. At present. Trying like hell.** But he squashed them because the last thing he wanted was to give Heather the idea that Tanya might be brought back to the shelter at some point in the next four or five years because his daughter was leaving for college and his marriage had gone belly up. And though he knew it wasn't necessary, he felt a prickle of defensiveness—that old anger—at the sensitive spot this woman inadvertently had touched, and he continued in a voice that was needlessly sharp, "Really, you don't need to worry about my commitment to this dog. I've devoted my life to trying to stop animal cruelty: The last thing I would ever do is act irresponsibly in regard to this creature or behave in a manner that would in any way make her life difficult."

"You don't need to sell me on your devotion to animals," Heather said. "I was only asking because I like Tanya, and I will do what I can to make sure she has a happy new life."

Quickly Randy took the leash from him and gently reeled Tanya in. She knelt on the sidewalk before the animal and nuzzled her. "I think you are going to love every minute of your life with the McCullough family.

Yes, I do," she said, murmuring into the dog's snout as if it were a microphone. And though she was talking to Tanya, Spencer knew she was speaking largely for Heather's benefit. He sighed, forced himself to relax. He was very glad she had joined him.

LATER THAT DAY, farther uptown in Central Park, Nan Seton walked her own dog. Though the sun had set it was still light out, and they were on the path just north of the museum that bordered the reservoir. They were passed by joggers and young people on in-line skates, and sometimes the dog would crane his nose into the air as the exercisers slid by, savoring the aromas that their exertions left in their wake.

She liked walking the dog, despite the fact that she no longer felt well, because it created routine. And Nan cherished routine. Granted, in the country it was nice also just to allow the animal to wander aimlessly into the fields of lupine that surrounded her house. But here in Manhattan? It was reassuring to have a regimen. It would not expunge the despondency that had begun to envelope her in New Hampshire, but it would take her mind off it for long moments at a time. She could focus once more on the small repetitive acts and social rituals that filled out her days in the city, instead of on her fears for her family once she was gone. No one—no thing—was irreplaceable. But some people were more useful than others. And now she had to contend with the reality that whatever was ailing her (and Nan knew it was real, because she was many things but a hypochondriac was not among them) was not merely going to take her: When she was gone, her family would still be estranged.

She had just turned around and started back toward the park's exit, the dog's leash in one hand, when she saw that woman whom she believed was her son-in-law's boss jogging in her direction. Dominique Germaine. She was wearing the sort of tight Lycra bike shorts which in Nan's opinion bordered on the indecent and a halter top that left little of the woman's stomach to the imagination. She was wearing a headset as she ran.

Nan didn't believe the woman would recognize her as Spencer McCullough's mother-in-law, though they had been introduced two or three times, including one afternoon when Spencer had lectured about George Bernard Shaw and nineteenth-century vegetarianism to a luncheon crowd at the Colony Club. (Nan had felt a twinge of guilt that the club had served salmon that day, but certainly her son-in-law hadn't expected them to serve something with beans or tofu to a group of already gaseous elderly women.) She hadn't really thought about what she was going to do—or why— but she called out to the woman as she approached, "Excuse me."

Dominique stopped and for a moment jogged in place, and Nan could tell that she was trying to decide whether this stranger who was accosting her was a FERAL friend or foe. Clearly she was accustomed to being stopped by unfamiliar people. Then she allowed her legs to stop churning and bent down to pet the dog on the leash.

"This is a beautiful animal," she murmured, and she nuzzled her face against his. "I am so sorry that I don't have any Kibble-Soys for you," she said ruefully to the dog.

"Kibble-Soys?"

"Meat-free dog biscuits."

Nan resisted the urge to roll her eyes. "My name is Nan Seton. You are Dominique Germaine, aren't you?"

"Guilty as charged. Are you a member of FERAL? I do hope so."

"Well, I give money to your group each year in December. But I don't know if I am, technically, a member."

"Certainly you are. Thank you. We—the animals—appreciate whatever you give. Truly."

"I'm Spencer McCullough's mother-in-law."

The woman rose to her feet, and Nan felt an odd and unexpected twinge of pride at her reaction.

"Well. I am so sorry about what happened," she said. "It is such a tragedy."

"John Seton is my son."

"Of course he is," she said, and instantly returned their conversation to her son-in-law. "It's so good to have Spencer back. You can't imagine. We missed him dreadfully this summer. Dreadfully."

"I haven't seen him since he was in New Hampshire. I only returned to the city a few hours ago. I may see him this Saturday or Sunday. I hope so."

"He's doing so much better this week. Really. So much better. He will, of course, never—"

"I know all the things he will never do again," she said, surprising herself by cutting the woman off. She knew she could be blunt—on occasion even curt—but rarely would she interrupt someone while that other person was speaking.

"I feel so bad for him."

"And for my daughter."

Dominique nodded. "Yes. And for your daughter."

"I'd like to talk to you."

"We are, aren't we?" She smiled.

"Spencer and my son aren't speaking. And it's making everything difficult. This weekend my son and his family are visiting the city, and I want to do something special for my granddaughters' birthdays. Unfortunately, whatever I do, it won't involve Spencer. He won't go because John will be present."

Dominique pasted on her face what she hoped was a thoughtful expression: one that was interested and winning and sympathetic. Inside, however, she was feeling peevish. She wanted to resume her run. Besides, it was this woman's son whose indefensible enthusiasm for hunting had left one of her most senior staff members permanently disabled. "And you're telling me this . . . why?" she said finally.

"Because Spencer is doing this for you. For FERAL."

"He's not talking to John for FERAL? Or he's suing the gun manufacturer for FERAL? Forgive me, but which?"

"Both."

She inhaled. She wanted to correct this woman, to explain to her in no uncertain terms that Spencer was suing Adirondack, first, because the long-term costs of his disability would be enormous and, second, because he saw no reason why so many animals should be hunted and killed with weapons capable of inflicting precisely as much pain as he himself had been enduring since the middle of the summer. Nevertheless, she would be patient. She had to. She hadn't a choice. She was a public figure, and, besides, Spencer was very good at what he did.

And so she said simply, "And you want me to do something."

The woman's jaw fell slack, and for the briefest of seconds she actually saw the gold fillings residing in the teeth in the lower half of her mouth. Clearly the responses Spencer's mother had anticipated had not included what she had heard as an offer to help. It wasn't, of course, in Dominique's mind. It was merely a confirmation of what Nan Seton was asking; but if this other person had heard more than she meant and it would allow her to disengage from this unwanted conversation quickly, so be it.

"Yes, I do," Nan answered. "You're his boss. I don't see how his refusal to talk to my son is benefiting anyone. I don't see how this press conference next week will help. It seems to me, all any of this is doing is tearing my family apart."

"I'm sorry. It shouldn't have to be that way. But I'm sure you've seen how much pain Spencer has been in since your granddaughter shot him. Right?"

Nan seemed to flinch on either the word **grand-daughter** or **shot;** Dominique couldn't tell which.

"Imagine, then: Spencer was shot with a gun and a bullet designed to inflict exactly that sort of agony on a deer."

"The deer die quickly," Nan said.

"Some do. But that doesn't make it right. And some run for hours before they die. Or days. The truth is, an awful lot of deer die slowly of their wounds or of starvation because they are unable to browse. And every minute of it they are enduring what your son-in-law is experiencing now."

"None of that justifies the turmoil my family is experiencing."

"Reasonable people could debate that. Look at your sweet companion animal here. Why is it acceptable to inflict such pain on a deer but not on this fine creature? Why is a dog more deserving of our protection than a deer?"

"I don't want to be theoretical. I'm speaking as a mother. As the head of a family. None of this justifies Spencer not speaking to John."

"Spencer's angry. Can you blame him?"

"John is very sorry."

"I'm sure he is."

"Look, I'm very concerned about this!"

Dominique scratched the dog once again behind his ears. Her patience, she realized, was at an end. "I'll talk to Spencer," she said simply.

"Will you?"

"Yes."

"Thank you. That's the right thing to do, you know."

She nodded, wished this old woman a pleasant evening, and slipped her headphones back over her ears. It was semantics, but she told herself as she started to jog that she had never said to Nan Seton precisely **what** she would say to Spencer. She guessed she wouldn't tell him anything that he didn't already know. His mother-in-law wanted the two boys to play nicely in the sandbox. And that, she understood, was no more likely than FERAL deciding not to hold a press conference on Spencer McCullough's behalf.

THURSDAY NIGHT CATHERINE phoned her brother. Spencer and Charlotte were in the living room listening to the CD for **The Secret Garden,** playing over and over the cuts in which young Mary Lennox had her solos. Though Catherine was happy to see the two of them spending so much time together, she feared if she had to hear that over-the-top feigned British accent much more—both the one that young actress had used on Broadway and the one her daughter was attempting—she would take the disc and flip it from their apartment window like a flying saucer. She called John while she cleaned up the dinner dishes largely so she could hold the phone against her ear with her shoulder. She hoped that the combination of the conversation, the running water, and the sound that she made when she scrubbed hard, blackened vegetable matter from the bottom of a cast-iron skillet would drown out the Victorian melodrama being reenacted in her living room.

"So, I gather we'll see you on Saturday," he was saying to her. Yesterday she and Sara had coordinated the logistics of the Seton family's visit to Manhattan this weekend, and Sara clearly had briefed her husband on the itinerary.

"Yes, indeed. God, I can't even remember the last time I went to the Cloisters," she said. "How old was I? Eleven? Ten? I was definitely younger than Charlotte."

"I don't know. I wasn't with you."

"You sound tense."

"Gee, I can't imagine why I might be tense. Can you?"

"You won't even see Spencer this weekend. He's going to take advantage of the fact we'll be at the Cloisters on Saturday to prepare for the press conference. And on Sunday Dominique is speaking at some rally against the cat show at the Garden, and Spencer's going to join her."

"But the point is, I would like to see Spencer. I want this cold war behind us."

"Not gonna happen."

"I know."

"The thing is . . ."

"Yes?"

"The thing is, he seems so happy these days. He really does. Or, at least, serene. He barely flinched when I told him I've been a closet carnivore all these years."

"Better living through drugs. I'm sure it's the painkillers."

"Well, clearly they're helping with his injury—though he's still hurting a lot. But what I meant is something different. His attitude. Do you know what he's doing right this second?"

"Tell me."

"He's rehearsing with Charlotte. Again. Suddenly he's become superdad."

"Spencer never does anything halfway."

"Marriage, maybe."

"Excuse me?"

She wasn't sure why she had said that, and she wished now that she could take it back. She couldn't, however, not with John, and so she told him—hoping to diminish the significance of her inadvertent disclosure—"I was just grousing."

"Indeed."

"It's been years since I've had more than half of Spencer's attention, because so much has always gone to pigs and monkeys and circus bears. And now that he has become superdad, I have him even less. He used to . . ."

She was going to say, **He used to worship me. When we were in college, the man had actually worshipped me.** And even though it was true, she couldn't bring herself to verbalize such an idea to her older brother, especially since college had been so very many years ago now.

"He used to what?" John asked her. "Go ahead."

The irony, of course, was that seven or eight weeks

ago she wasn't even sure she wanted to remain married to him. Why now was she begrudging him his composure? Here he was crippled and in pain, yet he was striving to be more giving, more tolerant. Why was she still angry with him? Was it all because of that press conference? "We don't need to discuss this," she said. "I'm fine. Really."

"Ah, that's what I like to see: our family's wondrous emotional repression in action. Good work, Sis. Mother would be proud."

"Mother's back now," she said. "She got home late this afternoon." She put the skillet in the drying rack and wiped her hands on the dish towel.

"So I hear. I gather she's joining us at the Cloisters, too."

"Yup."

"And we're doing something with you and Charlotte to celebrate the girls' birthdays, right? A brunch or a dinner or something?"

"Mother wants us to do brunch on Sunday. Someplace elegant that would give the girls a chance to get dressed up and consume vast numbers of Shirley Temples."

"Charlotte will want a mimosa."

"She might. But even she has seemed oddly composed the last week."

"Maybe it's that play."

She squirted gel into the dishwasher and pushed the door shut. "Maybe," she agreed.

"And Spencer's definitely not coming?"

"To the brunch? Nope—though he did apologize."

"Well, I'm glad Charlotte's feeling better."

"I didn't say she's feeling better. I said she's composed. It's pretty clear she's still shaken."

"Willow's a wreck. Well, maybe not a wreck. But she's very stressed by the idea of a deposition at some point in the coming months."

She stood up straight. "Really?"

"Uh-huh."

"Charlotte is, too. Or she was. She seems fine now. But she had one final meltdown before she became the great, unflappable thespian. It was last week when we were having breakfast with Paige Sutherland. The deposition came up, and Charlotte got all weird about lie detector tests."

"Lie detector tests?"

"That's right. She said she would refuse to take one. And then she stormed off to the ladies' room."

"Well, the idea of a deposition must be very scary for them. Lord knows I'm dreading mine. Alas, that's one more part of this nightmare for which I can take credit."

"Beat yourself up. There isn't enough pain going around at the moment."

"You know," he said, "if only Spencer would talk to me. It would make such a difference."

"What exactly would you say to him?"

"I honestly don't know. But the idea of us simply returning to speaking terms would be huge. We wouldn't have to discuss the lawsuit. We could talk about, I don't know, all the other things we have in common."

"Like hunting?"

"Like raising daughters. Like playing tennis."

"The two of us don't even talk about tennis anymore, and it used to be something we were pretty passionate about. Even during the finals at Flushing Meadows this month—remember how Spencer and I always got tickets when we were younger?—I don't think we said one single word about tennis."

"I wish I could talk to him about this press conference. That's the main thing. I understand the lawsuit. Really, I do. It's FERAL's involvement and the media frenzy he wants to create that I find so disturbing. It's the way my daughter and my niece are being dragged into this in such a public fashion."

"And you, too."

"Yes, obviously. Me, too. But if we were talking, there would still be hope. There—"

"John, you couldn't stop this train even if Spencer would hear you out. It's way beyond the station. He thinks his lawsuit against the gun company is a way of showing Charlotte this wasn't her fault."

"Maybe I should drop by the apartment when you're all at the Cloisters. What do you think? Spencer and I could talk this out—maybe even get to the point where he'd be willing to join us on Sunday for brunch."

"He won't even be here, he'll be working at FERAL. He's still learning to use his new left-handed keyboard and mouse, but at least he has such things at the office. His voice input software hasn't arrived yet—"

"He will need that now, won't he?"

"Well, it will help."

"God, this is awful."

"Please, stop it. Okay? Yes, it's awful." While she paused, she heard Charlotte drawing out the first syllable in the word **garden** as if she were holding a musical note, and softening the **r** almost to the point of nonexistence. Her mind was flashing back now to that breakfast last week with Paige Sutherland. She couldn't imagine there was some important detail about that horrible night in New Hampshire that she didn't know. What had occurred was pretty clear: Her brother had left his loaded rifle in the trunk of his Volvo, and her daughter had thought her husband was a deer and accidentally shot him. It was only complicated if you were a lawyer. Why then had Charlotte freaked out about a lie detector test? Why was Willow, in John's words, a wreck about the idea of the deposition?

Was it possible there was something she had missed? Something all the grown-ups had missed? Certainly she had asked Charlotte again when they'd had breakfast with Paige. And Charlotte had insisted there was nothing more to the story than what they already knew.

Actually, that wasn't quite accurate. Charlotte had retreated angrily to the ladies' room at the very suggestion something more had occurred that night. And so she decided that when Lee Strasberg was done with their daughter—or, perhaps, before Charlotte went to bed—she and her daughter would have a chat.

"Tell me," her brother was asking her, "how would

Spencer react if I just showed up at his office on Saturday afternoon?"

"Trust me, you don't want to go there. You probably wouldn't get past the guard in the lobby, anyway."

"Why don't I just see how I'm feeling that day— and whether I've managed to marshal some arguments that might make a difference to him? Play it by ear?"

She sighed. "Sure. Why not?"

In the living room Spencer and Charlotte continued to work, and Catherine wondered how she had wound up an outsider.

BY TEN O'CLOCK Spencer was sound asleep. The combination of an extra sleeping pill, the pain in what remained of his shoulder, and the ceaseless exertion of trying to learn to exist with one functioning arm had exhausted him. And so Catherine left their bedroom and knocked on Charlotte's door. She hoped the child was finishing her homework and was about to go to bed herself. She wasn't. She was on the computer sending instant messages to her friends. Catherine looked at the communications on the screen and realized that Charlotte wasn't chatting with her usual pals, but instead with the kids—teenagers, actually—who were in the upcoming musical with her.

"Who are you talking to?" she asked, hoping to elicit some specifics.

Without turning around Charlotte mumbled, "People in the show."

"That's what I figured." She pointed at one of the

responses and monikers on the screen. "Let me guess: Dudester 1035 is a boy?"

"Uh-huh."

"And he lives at 1035 . . ."

"Ten thirty-five Fifth. He goes to Buckley."

"Does Dudester have a name?"

"Archibald."

"Archibald?"

"Oh, sorry, that's his name in the play," she said, typing a response as she spoke. "His real name is Sawyer."

"How old is Sawyer?"

"I don't know. A little older than me."

Catherine had a pretty good idea that "a little older than me" meant fifteen at least. Maybe sixteen. She hoped that no fifteen- or sixteen-year-old Buckley boy was chasing after her waif of a daughter—a daughter who seemed especially tiny right now in a pair of bright red pajamas that were sprinkled lavishly with ivory moons and yellow stars. Regardless, ten o'clock was late for instant messages when you were in the eighth grade and so she asked Charlotte to log off and join her. She sat down on her daughter's bed and waited there, aimlessly stroking a teddy bear that three or four years ago had meant so much to her child, and which even now Charlotte couldn't quite part with.

When the girl joined her, sitting down by the footboard with her legs crossed at the knees, she said, "I still haven't done my history reading for tonight. But I think I'll only need fifteen or twenty minutes. Is that okay?"

"Bedtime is supposed to be ten. You know that. But, yes, it's fine to stay up a little late to finish your history. I think Sandy would be angry with me if I didn't give you that extension," she agreed, referring to Charlotte's history teacher, an older fellow on the faculty whose actual name was Sanford Clunt but (thank God) insisted that his students call him by his first name instead of his last.

"Thanks," she said, and then she jumped off the bed and retrieved her history textbook from the floor by her desk. When she returned to her mother she smiled and murmured, "Good night." Then Charlotte waited, clearly expecting her to leave.

"One thing," Catherine said, instead of rising.

"What, Mom?"

"Last Friday, when we had breakfast with Paige Sutherland, you got upset."

"It felt like you were accusing me of shooting Dad on purpose."

"I simply asked if there was something else you wanted to tell us. And the idea that there might be more to what happened than I knew only crossed my mind because you"—and she wanted to phrase this perfectly—"expressed some concern about a lie detector test."

The child nodded.

"So?" she asked Charlotte now. "Do your father and I know absolutely everything we need to know about that night in New Hampshire?"

"Scouts honor."

"You've never been a scout."

"Then yes."

"Yes?"

"Mom!"

"I'm just making sure." She sat up and pulled her child to her, and held her for a long moment. She savored the fruity smell of Charlotte's shampoo, and surprised herself by whispering into her ear that she loved her. She guessed she surprised the girl, too. Every bit Nan Seton's daughter, Catherine knew she was not particularly effusive. Then she kissed Charlotte, stood up, and went to the door. From the frame she reminded her not to stay up too late.

When she returned to her own bedroom, she felt better. Not completely reassured. But better. A little bit better.

CHARLOTTE STARED at the page in her history book, her eyes glazing and the words growing indistinct. She simply couldn't concentrate. She wondered if someday she might be a lawyer instead of a great actor. She hadn't lied to her mother; she had in fact answered her question with what she considered scrupulous accuracy. She had told her that she and Dad knew everything they needed to know about that night. That was all.

And her parents did know everything they needed to know. They most assuredly did not need to know about the marijuana or the beer. They did not need to know what she was feeling when she pulled the trigger. The truth was, she herself didn't even know anymore.

The one absolute and inescapable reality was that she had crippled her father for life, and the best way she could help him now was to do all that she could to assist with his lawsuit and his campaigns for FERAL. And if that meant not telling the lawyers everything at the deposition, then so be it. So be it.

So—and she drew out the first syllable as if she were a little British girl in the late nineteenth century, before snapping the last two together—be it.

Twenty-eight

When John arrived for a meeting in Chris Tuttle's imposing office with its views of the lake on Friday morning, he was surprised to discover a second man standing by the window, watching a lone, large sailboat cut its way south through the water. Instantly, he decided that given the way this stranger was dressed—a denim shirt with a string tie and black pants tucked into a pair of auburn cowboy boots inlaid with snakeskin—the guy wasn't a lawyer. He guessed the fellow was about his own age, maybe a couple of years older: His hair was starting to recede and his skin looked as worn as his boots. He had a pair of silver and turquoise bracelets on his wrist and similar silver rings on three of his fingers.

Tuttle motioned for the two men to join him around his desk, explaining to John as he introduced them that this stranger was a ballistics expert. His name was Mac Ballard, and since he'd been testifying the day before in a trial in Albany, Tuttle had been able to commandeer him this morning. He lived just outside of Santa Fe, and he wasn't flying back until Saturday.

"When I called his office yesterday and learned he was only a few hours south of us, I grabbed him,"

Tuttle said to John, as he retook his seat on the far side of his great steppe of a desk. "We may be a nonparty, but it behooves us to know all we can about your rifle."

"You replace your gun yet?" Ballard asked John, smiling. He spoke slowly, forcefully, his voice a deep combination of inappropriate interest and menace.

"No."

"Want a suggestion on a different piece of hardware?"

"No."

He nodded. "I see. You already got your mind set on one."

He started to say no once again, but he stopped himself. He knew it was completely unreasonable to dislike this man on sight. Ballard was here, after all, on his behalf. He just wished Tuttle had consulted him first. But, then, would he really have told his lawyer not to bring Ballard in? Of course not. His discomfort had nothing to do with surprise. Rather, it was because this Mac Ballard knew all about guns and he didn't, and possessed a critical knowledge he lacked. It was because around Ballard, he was the moron who couldn't pop out a round from a thirty-ought-six.

"John has no plans to resume hunting anytime soon," he heard Tuttle answering for him. "Why don't you two sit down? John, you want some coffee?"

"Oh, I'm fine. Thank you," he said, taking the seat that didn't have the well-worked leather pouch beside it. He wondered if the damn thing was a saddlebag with a strap. "We should get through this as quickly as possible—whatever it is, Chris, you want us to accomplish this morning—because I'm only working a half day today. And, believe it or not, I really do still have clients of my own."

"Everything all right?" Tuttle sounded concerned.

"You mean the half day?"

"Uh-huh."

"Oh, yeah. As fine as things can be in my life these days. Sara and I are picking up Willow at school around lunchtime and driving to New York City. Her birthday's coming up. That's all."

"Very nice, very nice," Tuttle muttered. "Okay, then. I've told Mac what happened, all we know about the gun, and—"

"It was a good gun you had there," Ballard said, jumping in. He had crossed his legs, his ankle precisely atop his knee. The boot—its toe looked pointy enough to gouge out a splinter in skin—was practically in John's lap. "There won't be a problem with the extractor. Trust me. It's solid. Well tooled."

"That's what I gather. A friend of mine—a friend of both of ours," John said, motioning at Tuttle, "suggested the same thing. A sportsman named Howard Mansfield. He's a justice here in Vermont. He said it might be the ammunition. I was using Menzer Premiums, you see, and he said that sometimes a Menzer Premium in an Adirondack rifle—"

"Myth."

"Myth?"

"Some people have this myth in their heads that you need Adirondack ammunition in an Adirondack rifle. What'd he say? The rim on the casing was too shallow for the extractor?"

"Essentially."

"Malarkey."

"Howard Mansfield is a smart man. As soon as we examine the rifle, we're going to try loading some other bullets from that same box into the weapon. See if the extractor has difficulties with any of those."

"Look, I don't want to malign your pal. Maybe you got that rare cartridge with a defective casing. And maybe . . ." He paused for a brief moment, thinking, and John restrained his desire to jump in and tell this Mac Ballard just how smart Howard Mansfield really was. "And maybe you loaded and unloaded so many times that you really did manage to ding the casing. You know, you ripped off a small piece of the rim so the extractor would have nothing to grab. That, it seems to me, is a more plausible scenario than the idea the round was defective to begin with."

"You realize the casing is gone, right?" John asked. "It seems to have been lost when it was with the New Hampshire State Police."

"Your lawyer told me."

"So we'll never know if that's what occurred."

"I don't think that's it, anyway."

"Then what, pray tell, did happen?" He'd worked hard to keep the disgust out of his voice, but he knew after the words had escaped his lips that he'd failed.

"Well, my granddaughter has a set of blocks—"

"You have a granddaughter?"

"Two, my friend. I fell in love young. Real young. You have any?"

"No, and I'm years away. My daughter still has a week and a half left at ten and my son is an infant."

"You got a lot to look forward to. Anyway, my granddaughter has some wooden blocks. You know the kind, you've seen them. Rectangles. Squares. Cylinders. She's two and a half. And the blocks have a wooden tray with cutouts in which she can place them. They fit snug. Real snug. As the expression goes, you can't put a square peg in a round hole. The square will only fit in the square opening and the cylinder will only fit in the cylindrical opening—like a cartridge in a chamber. They have been very—and I mean **very**—precisely milled. Now, imagine you slipped something as thin as a cardboard match into the cylindrical chamber for the cylindrical block. What do you think would happen?"

John suspected he knew the answer and he considered volunteering it: The block would get stuck. But he wasn't sure where Ballard was going with this example and he felt sufficiently stupid already. And so he decided he would allow Tuttle the chance to embarrass himself for a change. Tuttle, however, remained silent, too.

"Well, then," Ballard continued, "I'll tell you. The block will get jammed in the chamber. It'll be wedged in there so tight that you won't be able to extract it without a mighty good tug. And all it takes to wedge it right in there is that little cardboard match. And if you think those blocks are carefully milled, well, just think how carefully a gun company manufactures the chamber inside its firearms. Think how exactly the right caliber cartridge fits inside. Now, I'll bet you loaded and unloaded your gun beside your truck. You did, didn't you? Think back: It's last November, and you're loading and unloading, loading and unloading. True?"

"More or less. But it was beside my car or my friend Howard Mansfield's pickup. I don't . . . own a truck," he said, wondering why the hell it suddenly seemed unmanly not to own a truck.

"Okay. Now tell me: You ever drop your gun?"

He smiled self-deprecatingly. "Oh, yeah. That's why they have safeties—for guys like me."

"It ever fall over?"

"You mean . . ."

"You just leaned it up against your—let me guess— Audi or Volvo while getting your ammo box at the end of the day. Or the beginning. The bolt is open, and it tips." He leaned his arm upright at the elbow on his chair and then swung it toward the ground like a pendulum.

"That happened, sure. I know the gun toppled over once when I leaned it against a tree while I was having lunch and another time when I was getting ready to start out in the morning. And, yes, I was leaning it against my . . . Volvo."

"There you go."

"But I don't smoke and I certainly didn't slip a match into the chamber."

"No, but a little dirt got in. Three or four grains of sand. That's all it takes."

"Are you saying three or four grains of sand kept me from extracting the bullet?"

"Yup."

"Have you ever seen that happen before?"

"Yup."

John sat forward in his seat, and turned the chair so that he was angled away from the toe of Mac Ballard's boot. "I wish we had that casing," he said to Tuttle. "I really want that—especially if the lab doesn't find anything wrong with the extractor."

Tuttle steepled the fingers on his hands. "If what Mac is suggesting is a legitimate possibility, we can test it—and we will. We don't need that missing casing. Besides, I'm not sure it matters."

"Excuse me?"

"You're not a defendant."

"No, but I look like an idiot—a complete moron— if the extractor works and we can't find the casing!"

"Calm down. If the extractor does work—and bear in mind, we still don't know if it does—we're still left with three possible reasons for your inability to remove the cartridge," he said, and he listed them on his fingers. "It had a defective casing; the rim was damaged when you were loading and unloading it; some dirt got lodged in the chamber."

"It's number three," Ballard said, and for the first time since he'd sat down he uncrossed his leg.

"Anyway, John, the fact the casing is gone actually

gives you a bit of cover. We have three possible theories, if we ever need one. Okay?"

John felt his heart thrumming in his ears, and he imagined his blood pressure positively geysering. It seemed unfair that something as infinitesimal as a grain of sand might have cost his brother-in-law his arm and his family so much.

CHARLOTTE HAD EXPECTED the shrink to have a regular doctor's office—like her orthodontist's office, maybe, or the offices of the specialists her father had visited when they had first returned from New Hampshire. She'd expected a glut of magazines, most of them boring, that she would have to wade through until she found a **People** from her lifetime or a **Vogue** from the current season. Instead, there were magazines like **Highlights**—which she remembered from second and third grade—and **Sports Illustrated for Kids** and **Teen People**. There were books, too, some more dog-eared and pawed over than others. **The Wind in the Willows. Stuart Little.** A couple of Beverly Cleary paperbacks featuring Ramona. Moreover, the place was clearly an apartment—someone's home, it looked like—with mahogany paneling on the walls and the kinds of furniture that Grandmother owned: lots of dark wood, and couches and chairs so plush it was like they belonged in a funhouse. The only difference was that the coffee table and end tables had long, deep scratch marks, which really didn't surprise her since it was pretty clear that Dr. Warwick spent a lot of time with the Barbies and G.I. Joe playground crowd.

She'd never visited Aunt Sara's office in Vermont, but she knew it was part of a group practice. In her mind she had always seen it as a regular physician's workplace: chairs with bony armrests, beige walls, a receptionist behind a sliding glass window. Now she wondered if her aunt's reception area felt more like a living room than a waiting room, too.

Actually, this place didn't feel quite like a living room. Living rooms didn't have a person who looked more like an au pair than a doctor's receptionist sitting behind a delicate writing desk that seemed to belong in a museum. Charlotte guessed the young woman couldn't be more than nineteen or twenty, and she was writing something on the jazziest computer monitor she'd ever seen: It looked as thin as a plastic place mat.

Charlotte decided that she didn't mind having to wait with a **Teen People** instead of a regular **People** (though she definitely preferred the more grown-up scoop in the normal edition), and she felt quite content. She was, after all, helping her dad with his lawsuit. Moreover, she really was no longer sure why she had fired Uncle John's gun into the night. Maybe she would learn something. You never knew.

Her mom had picked her up right after second period and was sitting on the couch beside her, reading the short papers she'd had her English literature students write that week. She had a blue Sharpie pen in her hand—blue, she always said, because she feared students brought too much baggage to red—and was scribbling away madly on some poor kid's assignment.

Finally a door opened and a woman Charlotte guessed was her mother's age emerged, though Charlotte had once heard someone observe that heavy people were occasionally older than they looked. And this Dr. Warwick was heavy indeed, a series of round snowballs: midsized ones comprising her bottom and her breasts, a large one to serve as her torso and abdomen, and a smallish (at least in comparison to the rest of her body) one for her head. She was wearing black velvet pants and an ivory silk top that was a tad too clingy for someone so big. Still, this Dr. Warwick had the eyes and smile of a pixie and the most lovely blond spit curls clinging to the sides of her scalp. Charlotte liked her on sight.

She and her mother stood simultaneously to greet the therapist, and after they had made their introductions all around—including the receptionist named Anya who, it turned out, was a psych major at Columbia when she wasn't here three mornings a week—Dr. Warwick ushered her into another room. The doctor had her fingers pressed gently on her shoulder, and Charlotte decided that she liked the feel of this, too.

KEENAN BARRETT studied Paige Sutherland. He wished he had something that resembled her charisma. He wished he exuded the sort of telegenic charm that mattered so much more these days than an ability to frame an argument soundly. Alas, he was anything but magnetic. He was mannered . . . deliberate . . . old school. All qualities, alas, that didn't play well on CNN.

The problem at the moment was that he feared Paige was about to make the kind of mistake that young charismatic lawyers often made: She'd convinced herself that she was so smooth and attractive that she could bluster and bluff her way through anything. He hoped he could disabuse her of this notion and persuade her to rethink her plans.

"I just don't see why it will be relevant," Paige was saying in response to his concern. His office didn't have the sort of small round conference table that Dominique's had, though this was because he liked the way his massive mission desk made everyone with whom he met look small and inconsequential. Right now Paige and Spencer were sitting across from him in two straight-back mission chairs.

"It will be relevant because they are going to want to know why John couldn't extract the bullet," he told her, referring to the writers and reporters who they hoped would be at the press conference next week.

"And I'll tell them we delivered the gun to the lab," she answered.

He glanced at Spencer, who was looking down at the fingers on his right hand. His arm was still in that sling, and since his return Keenan hadn't seen him make any effort to take a single note with his left. Hadn't even seen him pick up a pen. Keenan wasn't completely sure he was listening now, or—if he was—

whether he was following the nuances of their conversation. It was as if he'd been shot in the head, not the shoulder. He was so placid. So yielding. So serene. Keenan wondered if this was the result of his painkillers or whether the ache in his shoulder and back simply precluded him from concentrating on anything outside his body. Either way, this was a different Spencer from the one who had left for New Hampshire at the end of July, and Keenan wasn't sure what he thought of him. The fellow was certainly more likable. But he wasn't especially helpful. While the old Spencer would have had strong opinions on what they should and should not say at the press conference, this new one hadn't offered more than a sentence or two in the last fifteen minutes.

Keenan decided that he didn't even like his associate's new beard. He understood why Spencer was growing it, but the sad fact was that it made him look a little dim: He resembled the cavemen Keenan saw going to Ranger ice-hockey games at nearby Madison Square Garden, the beefy, lumpish, ancient-looking hominoids who painted their chests red and blue and then took off their shirts for the cameras. This troubled Keenan for a great many reasons, though the foremost right now was the reality that in four days Spencer was going to be the focal point of a press conference.

"If that's all you tell them," he said, directing his response at both the other lawyer and Spencer so he could see if there was anyone home behind those whiskers, "then once the gun's fundamental soundness is revealed—as it will be as soon as Adirondack inspects it—we will lose a sizable measure of our credibility and our message will be undermined. People will not be listening to what we have to say about hunting if they believe the legs have been cut away from beneath Spencer's lawsuit. If the lawsuit appears groundless, we have no forum."

"I'm not going to say the rifle didn't function the way it was meant to. We're contending, pure and simple, that Adirondack has been manufacturing a dangerous product because a bullet remains in the chamber once you unload the magazine. If the extractor had been defective, that would have been a nice bonus—nothing more, nothing less."

"That isn't my point."

"What **is** your point, Keenan?"

"I believe it is in your client's interest to acknowledge upfront—next Tuesday—that Mr. Seton's weapon worked perfectly. We need to be the first to say it performed exactly as it was designed to, so reporters do not misconstrue what we are claiming and get it into their deadline-obsessed heads that we're implying the rifle was in any way defective. We simply cannot allow Adirondack to trump us in the media in a week or a month or whenever with the announcement that the gun was inspected and no mechanical defects were discovered."

"The gun worked?" It was Spencer, looking up finally from his useless right fingers.

"Spencer," Paige said, smiling gently at her client, "haven't you heard a word we've been saying? Haven't you been listening?"

"I guess the reality only hit me just now."

"Yes," Keenan said, "the gun worked." He couldn't imagine how the hell they were going to put this guy on the dais in a couple of days.

"But we're not going to say that it didn't work," Paige added. "Our point all along—"

"If the gun worked, then why couldn't my brother-in-law get the bullet out?"

"That's exactly the question we need to answer," Keenan said.

"He'd been getting the bullets out for two weeks. Probably more when you factor in the time he spent in his hunter safety courses," Spencer continued.

"We can ask the lab to look into that," Paige said. "But I'm sure it was just your brother-in-law's unfamiliarity with the gun."

"My brother-in-law's a pretty sharp guy. The hunting is appalling, of course. But he's not stupid."

"No, of course he's not," Paige said, though Keenan could tell that she didn't believe that for a minute. "But it may just be that he didn't know how to unload the weapon—which, given its apparent complexity and the fact you have to do two things to unload it, seems plausible enough to me."

"People who are a lot less capable than John do it successfully every day."

Keenan immediately sat forward. "That, Spencer, is a sentence you need to divest yourself of instantly. Do you understand? Expurgate that very thought from your mind this very second. Please."

"Oh, Keenan, I won't say that on Tuesday. I'm just telling you here in the privacy of this office that I agree with you: It's something we need to understand." Then he placed his left hand on the front of the wide desk and pushed himself to his feet.

"Where are you going?" Paige asked. She sounded alarmed.

"To get a dog. I was going to wait till Monday, but if I bring her home today my family will get to spend the weekend bonding with her."

"What? You can't get a dog now," she said, a slight tremor of panic in her voice. Keenan guessed she was afraid that her client—near catatonic for the vast majority of their meeting, and then suddenly sharp but oblivious to the party line for the rest—was losing his mind.

"Why?"

She looked at her watch. "Because it's Friday morning."

"That's not a reason why I can't get a dog, Paige. People all over the world get dogs on Friday mornings."

"I meant we still have work to do."

He paused in the doorway and smiled. "I think you and Keenan do. But I'm all set. I know my lines for Tuesday."

"Do you?"

He nodded.

"So you're just leaving to go get a . . . a companion animal?"

"No, I'm just leaving to go get a pet: a creature that will be completely dependent on my family for its food and its shelter."

"Fine, then: You're just leaving to go get a pet?"

"That idea really disturbs you, doesn't it?"

"It's just . . . weird."

"Would it make the Puritan inside you more content if I got the dog later today?"

"Yes!"

Keenan was surprised at the enthusiasm in Paige's voice. Apparently, she'd never seen a client excuse himself from a meeting with her to go get a dog.

"Okay, then. I'll tell Randy we're getting the dog later—her schedule permitting."

"And then you'll come back here?"

"No. I have plenty of other things to do. We have a Granola Girl on **Howard Stern** next week, and I want to make sure she knows what she's in for—and that she doesn't have to take her top off, no matter how many goldfish he threatens to kill if she doesn't. And Joan's 'Don't Gobble the Gobbler' campaign needs a little work: It sounds like we disapprove of Thanksgiving, and not just eating turkey. And Dominique's holiday fund-raising letter is pretty extreme. And you know what? Even if none of the projects on my list interests me this morning, I think I could entertain myself just fine by screwing around with my new left-handed keyboard and mouse." When he was finished speaking he gave them a small wave and started down the corridor to his office.

After a moment Paige asked, her voice barely above

a whisper, "Do you think he's stable? He just went from a near stupor to this zeal for some dog."

"It's for his daughter. The dog. It's a belated birthday present."

"Keenan?"

"Yes?"

"I'm worried about him. I'm worried about his health."

"You?"

"I know. I'm not just worried about his behavior at the press conference. I'm worried about whatever's going on inside his head. He really does seem . . ."

"Different."

"Uh-huh. Whatever happens, we have to make sure that we get a decent settlement out of Adirondack. He—his family—might really need one."

"Well, then. Let us be certain we do two things. Let us make it absolutely clear at the press conference next Tuesday that Spencer's lawsuit in no way rests on a malfunctioning firearm: We must say crisply and without reservation that the gun worked exactly as Adirondack designed it. Second, let us be certain that we have an explanation for John Seton's inability to extricate that final cartridge from the chamber. Are we in agreement?"

She inhaled deeply, and he thought he detected a slight shudder of real humanity inside the fortress she built from René Lezard pinstripes and a coiffure from Richard Stein.

"We are," she said, and he allowed himself a small smile.

SHE TALKED ABOUT BREARLEY and the musical she was going to be in, and she talked about being a single child. She sank deep into the cushions of the easy chair opposite Dr. Warwick and told her what she liked about her summers in New Hampshire and what she found burdensome and boring. She began with short answers, not because she was trying to be difficult but because there were moments when she honestly wasn't sure what the correct responses were. The truth was that it never had been a big deal to have her mom in the school building with her, and more times than not she actually enjoyed the sensation. But her aunt Sara once told her how much she had disliked being the school secretary's kid when she'd been growing up, and so Charlotte found herself wondering now what it meant that she wasn't disturbed by the fact her mom taught at Brearley.

Likewise, she certainly had tried to find excuses not to work in her dad's vegetable garden this summer (and everyone did seem to view it as Dad's Vegetable Garden), but if she revealed this to her psychiatrist, would the woman presume she was so angry with her dad on a subconscious level that she'd shot him on purpose just so she could escape a little weeding? That was ridiculous. But she'd heard enough from her New York friends who were in therapy to know that grown-ups seemed to love to blame the subconscious and were thrilled when it could take the fall for their kids' misbehavior.

And, she had to admit, she had no idea herself just how murky her subconscious might be when it came to her dad. Who could say what sort of ooze was deep in there, what kind of roiling animosity was festering in the gray matter behind her eyes? She loved the way he was there for her now—this week, this month—but this serious interest in her life was a new phenomenon.

No doubt about it: This conversation was a tightrope. She thought she had managed to keep her balance so far. Thank God, Dr. Warwick hadn't ushered her over to the corner of the room with the dolls and the blocks and the trucks and subjected her to toy therapy. If this nightmare had occurred two or three years earlier, Charlotte guessed, she and the shrink might be on the floor right now dressing Barbies.

"Do you want to talk about what happened in New Hampshire?" the doctor was asking. Her voice was silken, soft. It reminded her of a female hypnotist she had once seen interviewed on the Discovery Channel.

"Sure."

"Do you think about it often?"

"Every time I see my dad I think about it."

"Because of his sling?"

"And his beard."

"He didn't use to have a beard?"

"No. It's really hard for him to shave now, so he just stopped. His beard isn't in all the way yet. But it's getting there. It's mostly black, but it's got some white and some red in it, too. The red is really surprising, because he doesn't have any red in his hair."

"What do you think about when you see him?"

She considered this for a moment and didn't say a word. Unlike many adults, silence didn't seem to disturb Dr. Warwick. She just sat there and waited.

"Well, I think about how much he must hurt," she said finally, both because she did think about the pain he was enduring and because this response seemed appropriate. She guessed it was what she was supposed to say.

"What else?"

"I think about how his life has changed. All the stuff he can't do."

"Is there a lot?"

"Oh, yeah. Tons. He's right-handed. He can barely open a bottle of ketchup these days."

The doctor rested her chin in her hand and smiled. Charlotte suddenly detected a trace of perfume and she recognized it from . . . from New Hampshire. It wasn't a perfume that her mother or her aunt or Grandmother wore, that wasn't why it was familiar. Rather, it was an aroma that reminded her of one of the flowers in the cutting garden they'd put in. The tall purple ones, she guessed, but she wasn't positive. She wished she knew the plant's name.

"Has that changed your relationship with him?"

"The fact he can't open a bottle of ketchup?"

"That's right."

She shrugged. "Sure. I do a lot of stuff for him I never did before—stuff he would never have let me do before. At first, he thought he was going to be superindependent—despite the injury. Then he figured out he didn't have a prayer. And so I tie his sneakers for him. I make his coffee for him. I don't do the real personal stuff, like flossing his teeth and helping him get dressed and undressed. Mom does that. When he burnt the crap—excuse me—when he burnt the heck out of his hand, she was the one who kept putting the lotion on it. But I always feed the cats now—which is a real production, because of course we're not a normal family that feeds the cats normal canned cat food. That has meat in it, so we can't. It used to be that whoever happened to be in the kitchen would feed the kitties, but now it's always Mom or me. And because Mom is so busy making sure that Dad's zipper is up or something, I try to be the one to feed them. And that means getting down the vegan vegetable stew, the Foney Baloney, the seitan, and the vitamin supplements and then mixing them all together. And our cats are so finicky, we can't mix up a huge batch ahead of time and then store it in the refrigerator. It has to be room temperature, which means opening a fresh can of the stew each and every time and then mushing in the other ingredients, including the Foney Baloney which **does** have to be refrigerated and so it really has to be blended into the canned stuff. It is only completely impossible to do it all with one hand. Mom just wants to start buying them Friskies or something to make our lives a little easier, but I know that isn't what Dad wants, and so I figure I better be the cat chef for now."

"For now," Dr. Warwick repeated.

She nodded. She thought of that Saturday afternoon in the summer when everyone had been sitting on the porch in Sugar Hill talking about the party at the club that night—maybe six or seven hours before the accident would occur—and she'd decided to go wandering around the house to the cutting garden. She'd knelt amid the purple flowers that smelled so much like this woman's perfume. She wished she could go back there now. To that moment.

"It sounds like a lot of work," the doctor continued.

"Having vegetarian cats? Oh, yeah. It's hugely difficult. But what else could we do? I mean, think of who my dad is. He and his boss, Dominique, are, like, two of the most notorious vegetarians in the country. Dad's been on **The Today Show,** you know. Twice. And he's been on the CBS **Early Show** and **Nightline** and tons of other news programs."

"You sound like you're very proud of him."

"I am. But being Spencer McCullough's daughter is a lot of work. Do you know something?"

The doctor shook her head and waited.

"I have never been inside a McDonald's. I may be the only teenager in the developed world who hasn't been inside a McDonald's. My friends, even the ones who don't eat meat—and there are a few—think it's pretty extreme."

"Is that a good thing or a bad thing?"

She sighed and savored the smell of the perfume. That day had been warm, the parents had all arrived, and she thought she was going to dance at the bonfire that night with . . . Connor. At least she thought now the teen boy's name had been Connor. Had she really forgotten? Was the boy really that forgettable? In any case, she knew she had been very happy that afternoon. She remembered putting one of those purple flowers in her hair, slipping it underneath her headband and imagining that she'd wear it that night to the bonfire. Then she remembered taking it out because she feared that she looked like a hillbilly.

"Charlotte?"

"Yes?"

"You said it wasn't easy being your father's daughter—even before his injury. Would you like to tell me more about that?"

"About being Spencer McCullough of FERAL's kid?"

"Is that who you are?"

"I don't know what you mean."

"Not Charlotte McCullough?"

"Oh, I'm her, too," she agreed, but she understood now what the doctor was driving at. Still, here in New York she **was** Spencer McCullough's daughter—even, often enough, at Brearley, where if she had been anybody other than simply Charlotte she should have been Mrs. McCullough's kid. Or, if it was one of the older English classes filled with juniors and seniors who her mother insisted call her by her first name, Catherine's kid. But even at Brearley she was frequently defined in terms of who her father was and what he stood for. It was always good-natured and sometimes kids were impressed by her father's notoriety, though there was no shortage of celebrity moms and dads among the Brearley parents. Other kids' par-

ents were important politicians, or they ran big corporations and were frequently in the **New York Times**
business section or the **Wall Street Journal,** or they
were simply richer than God and everyone (somehow)
knew it. Sometimes their mom or dad—or their
grandmom or granddad—was a famous actor.
Nevertheless, what her dad did stood out, and so he
was the subject of conversation as often as any other
student's parent. FERAL did some pretty outrageous
stuff, and whether it was photos of naked models at
some antifur extravaganza or those horrible photos of
monkeys from research labs that her father's group
plastered on the bus stop kiosks, it was going to be of
interest. Heck, the fact that she herself had never eaten
a Sabrett hot dog was of interest, what other people ate
in the lunchroom when they sat beside her was of interest. **I hope you don't mind my eating the lasagna
today, Charlotte—it's got meat in it. Charlotte,
how can you not eat roast beef? I only eat chicken:
Is that okay? What's wrong with eating fish?
They're, like, cold-blooded, aren't they?**

"Is there a difference?" It was the doctor.

"Excuse me?"

"Is there a difference between Spencer McCullough's
daughter and Charlotte?"

She thought about this. Of course there was.
Especially in New Hampshire, where Grandmother's
friends and the kids at the club viewed her more as a
Seton than a McCullough. It was completely different
from New York. She guessed there were people in
Sugar Hill who weren't even aware of what her dad did

for a living. If anyone there made a big deal about vegetarianism and animal rights, it was likely to be her. Either she would be trying to torment Grandmother for force-feeding her cousin sausages or she would be turning up her nose with great drama at something that was cooking on the long barbecues at the club. Even the night of the bonfire, she'd made a point of telling one of the older girls what really went into a hot dog.

And that garden. Those **gardens.** Her father's **gardens.** The day of the accident when she'd wandered alone into the cutting garden: That hadn't been the first time. Did she go there as Spencer McCullough's daughter or as Charlotte? She'd actually spent more time amid those flowers in the weeks before all the parents had arrived than either her cousin or her grandmother. Yes, she hated weeding. But didn't everybody? Weeding, after all, was a chore. But flowers weren't all work. They weren't even mostly work. And alone in July she had meandered among the rows of loosestrife, astilbe, and phlox; she'd knelt before the daisies and lilies and savored the rich aromas that rose up to her from the flowers.

Especially those purple ones.

Now she breathed in Dr. Warwick's perfume and closed her eyes, recalling those days before she had shot her father. Shot. Her. Father. Oh, to be back in the garden on an afternoon smack in the middle of the summer, your parents on the porch on the other side of the house, everything the way it had always been and forever would be.

If only she could go back.

If only.

She was aware that she was crying now, the tears creating small, shallow runnels along the sides of her nose. When she opened her eyes, she saw that the therapist was handing her a box of tissues. She took one, and then she took the box. She thought she had finished crying back in New Hampshire. Apparently, she was wrong. Apparently, she was a complete mess.

She remembered she was supposed to answer a question that had something to do with her father, but she was no longer sure what it was. And so she just shook her head and blew her nose and let the psychiatrist sit there and watch since—as she'd noticed before—the woman really did seem happy enough when her patients didn't say a word.

WILLOW KNEW it was exactly 289 miles from the end of her family's driveway to the garage on Ninety-second Street in Manhattan where they parked the car when they visited Grandmother. She'd been picked up at school today which added another two miles since they had to double back past their house, and so when she looked over the headrest at the odometer she saw they were still a few miles short of the point at which they would be precisely two-thirds of the way there. But they'd been on the Taconic for easily forty-five minutes now, and she felt clearly as if they were in the home stretch. Even though they had stopped twice in the first half of the trip so they could have lunch and then change her baby brother's diaper, they would still be in the city by seven.

Beside her Patrick blinked in his sleep in his car seat, and he scrunched up his face as if he'd just eaten a lemon. She knew he'd probably wake up pretty soon. He'd given her almost two hours of peace in the car while he'd napped, and that was about all she could expect. And so she leaned over and reached for the bottle with the breast milk Mom had pumped before leaving her office. Willow guessed that the first thing her mother would do when they arrived at Grandmother's apartment was get Patrick latched onto her chest: She could tell by the way her mother was fidgeting in the front seat that her tanks were getting pretty full and it was time to start dumping fuel.

Her parents were listening to the news out of Manhattan now that they were in range of the New York City AM stations. Her dad loved it. News Radio 88, 1010 WINS. **You give us twenty minutes, and we'll give you the world.** It was one of those signals, her mom said, that thrilled Dad because it meant he was almost back to his childhood home.

She gazed out the window at the trees along the highway which, this far south, hadn't even begun to change color, and she kept her eyes open for deer. She almost always saw a few on the Taconic, usually in groups of three or four, one of whom would be staring at the cars as they sped by on the highway while the others browsed contentedly among the trees and shrubs at the edge of the forest for food.

She thought it was interesting that in the last two

months she'd never felt any anger toward the deer. She
knew this whole disaster was not their fault, but she
also knew from her mom that anger very often wasn't
rational. The closest she guessed she'd ever come to
feeling any animosity toward the animals had actually
occurred well before her cousin had shot Uncle
Spencer. She remembered she had felt a twinge of resentment toward them when her parents had first
learned that the baby in Mom's tummy was going to
be a boy, and her father suddenly announced his interest in hunting. She'd wondered why it hadn't
crossed his mind that hunting might be something he
could share with her. After all, there were girls in their
village who hunted with their fathers. Yes, it was
mostly boys with their dads. But last year their neighbors Carolyn Patterson and Jocelyn Adams had both
gotten animals during the state's Youth Deer Hunting
Weekend.

   The truth was that she had absolutely no interest in
the sport, and there was no way in the world she
would ever have gone with her dad into the woods in
search of a buck they could kill. Her dad probably understood this. She wasn't exactly the type to shoot an
animal and then pull out its guts. And she wasn't
known for being real happy in the cold. Still, it would
have been nice if her dad had asked.

   She was looking forward to the Cloisters tomorrow
more than she had expected. When she'd told her art
teacher they were going, Ms. Seeley had brought her
brochures and a **National Geographic** magazine article with breathtaking color photographs, and given her

all sorts of suggestions of what to look for. She'd reminded her to keep her eye out for the jugglers at the
festival at the park beside the museum, and to give the
guys doing the Gregorian chants half a chance.

Mostly, however, Willow was anticipating her conversation with Charlotte. She wasn't looking forward
to it in the same way she was excited about the
Cloisters, for the simple reason that she and her cousin
might very well end up fighting. And she hated fighting. But she had to see if she could change her cousin's
mind. See if they could come to some sort of agreement about what they should say at the depositions.
She understood her cousin's point that they didn't
want to get Gwen in trouble and that it was in Uncle
Spencer's best interests for them to lie at the deposition: Complete honesty might undermine both the
lawsuit and FERAL's antihunting campaign. But that
didn't make lying right. And while the truth might
make things more complicated for Uncle Spencer, she
sensed it would make things easier for her own dad.

At least she thought it would.

Though it would also make things worse for
Charlotte. And that, Willow had concluded, was the
big problem. If they told the lawyers they'd been
smoking pot and drinking beer that night, then
Charlotte would seem far from innocent.

This had to be at least part of the reason why her
cousin was continuing to insist that they lie at the deposition.

When she brought their **whole** story up with
Charlotte, the older girl would be defensive. Obstinate.

Even a little melodramatic. But she reminded herself that she could be stubborn, too. Besides, she had the high ground on her side. She was the one advocating that they reveal everything they had done that night.

Next to her Patrick opened his eyes completely and stared up at the ceiling of the Volvo for a moment, and then turned his attention to her. He smiled and reached up his arms. He wanted to be picked up, but she couldn't lift him from his car seat while they were speeding south on the Taconic. And so she took the tiny fingers on both his hands in hers and kissed them one by one. Then, still smiling down at him, she inserted the bottle of milk into his mouth.

SPENCER GUESSED that the Setons would all want to meet Tanya, especially Willow, but he had to believe that John would have the good sense to steer clear of his family's apartment. The depth of his anger at his brother-in-law continued to mesmerize him. So much else that used to annoy him no longer did, and he actually thought he was handling his disability with something that resembled grace. He hadn't even lashed out at his physical therapist today while doing his reps with the man during lunch.

He presumed that his refusal to speak with John was causing the man serious pain. It wasn't that he believed John put an exceptionally high value on their friendship or missed talking to him in a meaningful way. Even if his brother-in-law hadn't left a loaded gun in the trunk of his car, they probably wouldn't have spoken more than once or twice in the last two months. But Spencer understood that by refusing to talk to John he was placing a magnifying glass on the guilt that his brother-in-law was enduring, and—as if that guilt were a dry leaf—igniting it. John would never understand the pain he had lived with through August and the better part of September (and would live with forever to some degree) or the disability he would carry with him to the grave, but he would know what it was like to be shunned.

Just thinking about his brother-in-law got him worked up, and so he sat back in his chair in his office and gazed out the window at the gold deco letters that spelled Empire State on the building across the street. His shoulder was still aching from his therapy, but he knew from experience that it would only get worse if he brought his left hand anywhere near it to massage it. It was best just to leave it alone.

"Spencer?"

He turned, and there was Dominique.

"Yes?"

"I ran into your mother-in-law last night in Central Park."

He tried to read from her expression what Nan had said to his boss. He vaguely remembered introducing the two of them at one gathering or another, and he presumed that Nan must have taken the initiative to speak to Dominique: Heaven knew Dominique certainly wouldn't have been the one to strike up a conversation with some senior citizen of whom she had at best the haziest of recollections.

"Really?"

"Yes. I was jogging and she was taking a walk with a very lovely golden."

"Her dog."

"So I surmised."

"She just returned to the city from New Hampshire. She couldn't have been back more than a few hours when you saw her. What did you two talk about?" This was, of course, not merely his mother-in-law they were discussing: It was also Safari Master John Seton's mom, and so he was deeply interested in whether she had broached her son's monumental idiocy.

Dominique shrugged. "Oh, we didn't talk about much. She's a charming woman—as you know. I believe she wanted to tell me she was a member of FERAL."

"Well, she writes us a check once a year. But she also has a mink that she loves to trot out around Christmas, and she still doesn't believe the human species can survive without meat."

"I understand."

"That's all you talked about?"

She rested her index finger, its nail this morning a vibrant shade of plum, against the slightly bronzed hollow at the very top of her sternum, and seemed lost in thought. Then: "That's all I can remember. Oh, wait: She asked me to say hello to you."

"Very nice."

"What are you working on?"

"A bit of everything. Thanksgiving. Our holiday fund-raising pitch . . ."

"Well, if there is anything I can do to help, you'll let me know?"

"I always do."

She smiled and continued down the hall. He had the sense that there was something more to Dominique's conversation with Nan Seton, and either the woman honestly couldn't remember or didn't want to burden him with the specifics. Or, maybe, she just didn't want to tell him. He guessed if it was important he'd find out eventually, and so he returned to the pages with the recipe ideas for vegetarian Thanksgiving celebrations that Joan Robbins wanted to pitch to a variety of daily newspapers. Most of them focused way too much on tofu and squash for the mainstream media. But there were a few ideas with potential, especially her lists of halftime snacks for the football-watching crowd that were free of animals and animal-sourced products—and could be found in any local supermarket. It was the second element that made it so clever in Spencer's opinion. If you had any hope at all of keeping the average American away from the sour cream dips and Buffalo chicken wings, you had to make sure your alternatives were no more than an aisle or two away from the Budweiser and didn't demand a special trip to the natural foods grocery store.

He had just verbalized a few suggestions for Joan into his brand-new digital recorder, when he saw that Randy was waiting for him in his doorway. The young woman was wearing a white linen broomstick skirt that fell to her ankles and a red drawstring blouse with the ties so loose he could see the front clasp of her lilac bra. Reflexively, he averted his eyes. Sometimes the part of the woman that had aspired to be a fashion model—that exuberant exhibitionist who had been so comfortable as a nearly naked FERAL Granola Girl—still dressed like a catalog tart. It was a tendency, Spencer knew, that served her well when she was working the male contingent of the press face to face.

"Ready to become a doggie daddy?" she asked.

"Yes, indeed," he said. He rose, surprised by the sharp ache he felt in his left wrist, and he wondered if he had overworked his left hand and arm today with his physical therapist. Fortunately, it only seemed to hurt when he bent it, and so he didn't anticipate any problems bringing their new dog across town. He glanced at his watch. It was barely twenty past three. Catherine and Charlotte were still at school, and would be for another two hours because rehearsals this week were lasting till almost five thirty. Assuming there were no last-minute hitches at the shelter, he and Tanya would be waiting to surprise them in the living room when they walked in the front door.

THE PLAN WAS SIMPLE, especially since they would be taking a taxi from the humane society to the apartment. Spencer would walk the dog to and from the cab, and Randy would carry the paperwork, the ratty pillow Tanya loved, and the goody bag with plastic dog toys the shelter was giving them.

Unfortunately, Tanya wasn't real happy about the serpentine cab ride through Central Park. Twice she fell against Spencer in such a fashion that the first time he fell forward and cut the palm of his left hand against a jagged edge of the half-open ashtray that was built into the back of the front passenger seat, and the second time he bounced against his right shoulder and cried out in agony—which, in turn, caused the poor dog to dive onto the floor of the cab where she cowered for the remainder of the ride. By the time they arrived at West Eighty-fifth Street, his pants were speckled with drops of his blood, he was on the verge of vomiting in the back of a New York City cab for the second time in the month, and the dog was whimpering at his feet.

Then when Spencer pushed open the door with his left hand, the leash wrapped carefully around his wrist, Tanya made a sudden leap for daylight. Spencer had no right arm to brace his fall, and so he was pulled down onto his knees on the sidewalk, his shins cracking so hard into the curb by the cab that he feared for an instant he'd broken both his legs. Still, even that pain was nothing compared to the excruciating, lights-flickering torture he was experiencing in his shoulder as a result of falling atop his right arm.

"Fuck!" he hissed into the pavement. "Fuck, fuck, fuck!" He rarely swore, but this seemed an occasion on which it made little sense to bother stifling a profound and much needed desire to vent. The only good news was that he had managed to hang on to the leash, and so Tanya—though straining hard—was still with them. He had a vision of her racing down the sidewalk, dragging her leash, until someone or something spooked her and she ran into the street, where a delivery truck slammed into her and sent her cartwheeling through the air to her death.

Randy raced around the other side of the cab and knelt before the dog, stroking her behind her ears and murmuring that she was okay, she was going to love her new home, and she wouldn't have to ride in any big, bad cars for a long, long time. She didn't, he noticed, make any effort to see if he, too, was going to be all right, but he guessed that an animal was always going to get more sympathy than a human from Randy Mitchell. She did, after all, work for FERAL.

He slowly climbed up onto his knees, glancing briefly at the dirt and tiny pebbles that were lodged in the stinging cuts in his hand, and turned back toward the taxi. The driver had emerged from the vehicle, and for a moment Spencer was touched: The fellow apparently wanted to see if he was okay, and he felt a small, grateful smile forming on his lips.

"Eight seventy-five," the cabbie said, his voice not exactly menacing, but a far cry from compassionate. "One of you two owes me eight dollars and seventy-five cents."

Randy put down the pillow and the papers from the shelter and started to rummage inside her purse, and Spencer was about to stop her. But then he stopped himself. He couldn't imagine how he could possibly reach into his pocket for his wallet with a dog's leash wrapped around his one good wrist and his one good hand a bloody mess, while every cell in his shoulder and his shins and his left palm was screaming for mercy. And so he just turned from the cold eyes of the cabdriver to the confused and frightened ones of his dog and tried to compose himself. He could pay Randy back upstairs. She could wash out his hand for him, and— though it would incapacitate him further—cover the gashes and little cuts with gauze. He could change his pants, time-consuming as that little act might be. Or not. These khakis were goners already, so he probably wouldn't bother. Either way, soon he would be inside his home with this dog, a gift for his daughter, and he would fix himself a gin and tonic and Percocet. And then everything would be fine.

Or, at least, as fine as things got these days.

Twenty-nine

Sara watched Nan serving the plump chicken breasts and the rice, and spooning the boiled peas and carrots from a gold-rimmed china bowl that had probably been in the family since the turn of the twentieth century. She envisioned Nan's grandmother as a young bride ladling creamed onions from it when Theodore Roosevelt had been president.

Nan liked to sit at the head of the long cherry table, surrounded by the different components of the meal: the meat, two vegetables, and the starch. She would have the assembled family pass their plates to her one by one, the farthest from her first, and so she was always serving herself last. It was a small ballet.

The New York table was set tonight with the usual elegance—and it was indeed a dramatically different presentation from the chaos that often reigned in New Hampshire—despite the fact that the only guests were her son and his family from Vermont. Everyone but Patrick had two pieces of Waterford crystal before them, a claret wine goblet and a water glass, each with a series of wedge-cut sparkles that resembled a castle's turret. There was sufficient silverware (and it was indeed silver, not stainless steel) bordering the linen place mats to exasperate poor Willow (why

Grandmother wanted them each to have two sizes of each utensil was a frequent source of conversation on the drives back to Vermont), and they all had cloth napkins rolled neatly inside personally monogrammed silver rings. Even Patrick had a napkin ring now with his initials.

"Spencer is not going to join you tomorrow," Nan was saying. "I don't know what his plans are exactly, but Catherine said he's not going to the Cloisters."

"Yes, she told me he'll be at his office," John said.

"He's being quite pigheaded," Nan continued, her exasperation evident in even the set of her mouth.

"He's angry," Sara said, offering Patrick some applesauce. "And he believes he's punishing John."

"He's punishing the whole family. Think of how much fun you'd have at that festival tomorrow if you were all there together—like the old days!"

"Mother, Spencer was never the life of the party!"

"No," Nan said, "of course he wasn't. But his absence will be a damper, precisely because we will all know why he's not there. And the same goes for this Sunday. I want to take my granddaughters someplace special for their birthdays, and this . . . spat—"

"Call it a feud," John said, his voice edged with sardonic resignation. "This constitutes a feud, not a spat."

"Fine, then. This **feud** is complicating everything. What is Spencer going to do, mope the whole time you're here?"

"He'll be working, Mother. It's how he deals with adversity. He'll do whatever it is that he can right now, whether it's writing a speech or telling the French not to eat foie gras or planning that nightmarish press conference," John said.

"Dad?" It was Willow.

"Yes, sweetheart?"

"You're not going to the press conference because it's not till Tuesday. Right?"

"I'm not going to the press conference because I don't want to be there. Even if we happened to be in town for some reason, I wouldn't be going. You don't actually want to go, do you?"

"You will most assuredly not be at that press conference," Nan said to her granddaughter. "And neither will your cousin."

"No, Nan, of course they won't," Sara told her mother-in-law.

"And I don't want to go," Willow said. "I was just wondering: Will the people at the press conference have to take an oath?"

Sara studied her daughter intently. Though the child was only a week and a half shy of eleven, she looked tiny. Small, petite. A pipsqueak. She was smart and she was articulate and she was wise beyond her years . . . but she was still a pipsqueak.

"No," John said, answering slowly and carefully, "they won't. The press conference is not simply to announce that your uncle is suing a gun company. It's also about propaganda. Your uncle and whomever else FERAL has up there won't be lying, but they are going to offer an extremely selective compilation of the facts. It's very different from a deposition. I certainly don't want to romanticize the law, but the purpose of a deposition is to reconstruct history and learn as precisely as we can what actually occurred."

"Which is why they make you take an oath," Willow murmured. She picked up the bigger of her two forks, and started pushing the rice around on her plate.

"Which is why they make you take an oath," her husband repeated abstractedly. He seemed only to have half-heard the melancholy in their daughter's voice. Sara wondered what he was thinking—what both her husband and her daughter were thinking—but sensed that she shouldn't ask either right now.

CATHERINE STOOD for a long moment, the plastic bags full of groceries dangling like weights at the ends of both of her arms. She watched her daughter drop her knapsack and the grocery bag she was carrying onto the rug just inside the front door and run across the living room toward her father. He looked insane right now, a complete madman. His hair was a mess, there were bloodstains all over the legs of his trousers, and his one good hand was swaddled in white hospital tape and gauze. But he was sitting serenely in the easy chair by the fireplace as if he were hosting **Masterpiece Theatre,** his legs crossed, cradling a drink in his working fingers. And perched attentively by his feet was a dog, an animal that looked a bit like a collie but was considerably smaller. It started to shrink at Charlotte's imminent approach, but then it figured out this human meant it no harm and began to sniff the child energetically. Then it started to lick Charlotte's face, practically painting her cheeks with its tongue.

Though a small part of Catherine was holding out the feeble hope that the animal belonged to someone at FERAL and it was only going to be a weekend guest at their home—though even that would have demonstrated, in her opinion, a colossal indifference on her husband's part to the amount of work she already was doing as well as to the feelings of their two cats—she knew instinctively that this was supposed to be a keeper. And so despite the reality that she understood she was about to say exactly the wrong thing, she put down her plastic bags beside the one Charlotte had been carting and said, her voice a robust combination of pique and disgust, "Where are the cats?"

"And good evening to you, too. Welcome home." He raised his glass in a mock toast.

She saw then that the doorway that led down the hall to their bedrooms was closed. "Are they in our room?" she asked.

"They are."

"What's her name?" Charlotte was asking, the three short syllables merged into one blissful cry. "Does she have one yet? How old is she?"

"Her name is Tanya, and she's two. I got her at the humane society." He put his glass down on the side table, the tumbler balanced precariously on the coaster because he had failed to center it atop the small wicker mat. Then he labored to his feet, his bandaged palm pressing hard against the armrest of the chair. "She's very good with cats," he said, directing this last statement at his wife. "I watched her with some."

"That may be," Catherine said, "but our cats are not necessarily very good with dogs. And they were here first."

"They'll be okay."

"Are we keeping her?" Charlotte asked, though it was hard to understand precisely what she had said because her face was buried in the thick ruffles of fur that surrounded the dog's collar and neck.

"Yes, of course, we are. Happy birthday."

"She's a birthday present?" the girl asked.

"A belated one, yes. I was going to bring her home next week, but then I decided a Friday was best because this way you can spend more time with her. You won't have to desert her first thing in the morning for school, and you won't be gone until nearly dinner with rehearsals."

"Spencer?"

"Catherine?"

"This weekend will be no better than next week—at least in terms of time. My brother and his family are coming for a visit. Remember? And while you seem to have no interest in seeing them—"

"I can't wait to see Sara and my beautiful niece."

"Fine. My point is that Charlotte is up at the Cloisters and Fort Tryon tomorrow, and my mother is taking the girls to brunch on Sunday, and I'm sure we'll all want to do something tomorrow night. And so I don't know when you think we're going to have the time to bond with this—"

"This weekend. We'll bond this weekend. And next week. And throughout what's left of September and October. We'll be fine. It won't happen overnight. Never does. But, as you can see"—he motioned down at their daughter and the dog—"the two of them seem to be getting along just fine."

"Is she house-trained?"

"She is."

"And who's going to walk her? And feed her? Did you think for one moment about how much work an animal is? How much work it will be for me?"

"No," he said evenly, "I don't think much about animals and their care."

"Spencer!"

"Lighten up, will you? Look, I can walk her—"

"And scoop her poop? And—"

"I can walk her, Mom. And I already feed the cats most of the time. I can feed her, too."

"It's not a big deal, Catherine. Really. I didn't bring her home to start a fight. I brought her home because Charlotte has always wanted a dog. I don't want to make your life any harder than . . . than I've already made it. Okay?"

She wandered over to the dog and knelt beside it, so that she and her daughter were surrounding it. The dog turned her deep eyes toward her and then licked her, too. "I just wish you had talked to me first," she murmured.

"Then it wouldn't have been a surprise," he said.

She took a deep breath to calm herself. She presumed she was angry because she didn't like surprises and because she was indeed fearful about the additional work the dog would demand. Perhaps she was even jealous of the way Spencer had ingratiated his way into their daughter's heart with one dramatic, unexpected gesture. But she wasn't really that worried about the cats. They'd be fine, she guessed.

"How did you bring her home? You must have had help," she said.

"Randy Mitchell."

"And your hand? What did you do to your hand?" Charlotte looked up from Tanya and noticed the bandages and the blood on her father's pants. "Dad, what happened?"

"I cut myself in the cab. On an open ashtray. It's not a big deal."

"Is that how you ruined your pants?"

"More or less."

She looked at her husband's scruffy beard and his pot holders for ears and the way his eyebrows were raised with bemusement. "I'd get you a drink," he said to her, "but it would be warm. I still haven't mastered the ice tray." She saw that his glass had no ice cubes in it. A few days before she had watched him whacking the tray upside down against a kitchen counter, and the ice cubes had indeed slipped out . . . and then slid like lemmings off the counter and onto the floor. She climbed back to her feet and smiled down at her daughter. Then she kissed her husband and went to retrieve the groceries from the front hall. She wanted to get the perishables into the refrigerator. Once that was done, she would get herself a gin and tonic, too, and some ice for his.

WITH PATRICK SOUND ASLEEP and Willow ensconced in Nan's bedroom, channel-surfing through the seemingly endless array of television stations they didn't have in Vermont, John and Sara took a walk. It was considerably warmer than in Vermont this time of night, and they walked down Lexington as far as Seventy-ninth Street and then back north to Nan's via Park. They needed only sweaters, and John guessed they would have been comfortable in simply their long-sleeved shirts. He hadn't yet told Sara his idea, because he was still playing out the design of it in his mind: If he did **x,** what would likely be **y?** And what would happen after that? He sensed in any event that it was all just a fantasy.

His plan, still only half-formed, was that he would threaten to show up at the press conference on Tuesday, if FERAL went ahead with the event. He would say all of the things about conservation and the understory and the plight of the northern deer herd without a rifle season that would never be addressed in a media show orchestrated by FERAL. The reporters would be all too happy to talk to him since he was, after all, the idiot who had left a loaded rifle in the trunk of his car—a rifle that had shot Spencer McCullough. They didn't have to know that the very thought of holding a gun these days made him nauseous. As he'd told his daughter at dinner, this press conference was about propaganda.

His goal was to convince his brother-in-law that he would be such a disruptive influence that it would not be in the organization's best interest to forge ahead. The problem, of course, was that if he told Spencer his plan beforehand, FERAL could do any number of things. They could tell him they were postponing the press conference indefinitely and then conduct it when he was back in Vermont. Or they could go ahead and hold it as planned but be prepared to refute anything he had to say. He knew they had amassed small mountains of statistics, and with enough numbers you could convince anybody of anything.

More important, he did not want to undermine Spencer's lawsuit. The man was crippled, for God's sake: The last thing he wanted to do was decrease the likelihood of an impressive settlement package. He **owed** Spencer that. That alone should preclude him from going on the offensive.

Sara took his hand and squeezed his fingers. "What's on your mind?" she asked him.

"A lot of things, I guess. The press conference, mostly. I'm somewhat less enamored with the idea of being the sacrificial lamb in this nightmare than I was a few weeks ago."

"Meaning?"

"No one told our niece to start shooting my rifle into the night. In fact, our own daughter specifically told her not to."

She released his hand, and he turned to her. She was staring straight up the avenue as they walked, her arms folded across her chest, nodding ever so slightly. It was, he could see in profile, her therapist's nod, and he couldn't help smiling to himself. "And what are you proposing to do with these feelings?" she asked. "Anything?"

"I'm torn."

"Go ahead."

"I was wondering if I should go to the press conference. Or, to be specific, I was wondering what would happen if I told Spencer this weekend that I would show up at the press conference if he goes ahead with it."

"And the point would be?"

"Talk him out of having it. Convince him that I would cause such chaos with my presence that it wouldn't be worth it to FERAL or to his lawsuit."

"And you would do this . . . why? So you're not humiliated?"

"So Charlotte and I both are not humiliated. I've spent the last few weeks worrying about this. I've worried about how I will look to Willow. To you. To our friends. I've worried about how Charlotte will deal with the notoriety that will surround her. At dinner tonight it dawned on me that perhaps I don't have to take this lying down. I thought I had to because I owed it to Spencer. But I'm less sure of that now."

"And you believe you could scare Spencer out of having the press conference by telling him you'll show up?"

Her voice was thoughtful and soft: questioning his idea, certainly, but offering at least the courtesy that she thought his plan had a small kernel of potential. Hearing it verbalized by someone else, however, made it clear to him how completely absurd the notion was. Spencer wasn't going to cancel the press conference simply because his brother-in-law had announced he was going to be present. And Spencer's associates would actually revel in the reality that he was there. They could make the public pillory that was about to become his life even more uncomfortable, even more unpleasant.

"Unfortunately, it doesn't make sense when the idea is spoken aloud, does it?" he said, putting his arm around her shoulder and pulling her to him as they walked.

She shrugged lightly. She'd made her point.

Nevertheless, he vowed that he would talk to Spencer this weekend. Face to face. And though he didn't believe he could persuade his brother-in-law to abandon the idea of the press conference, perhaps he could convince him to be kind. Perhaps he could re-mind him that once, not all that long ago, they had been friends.

CATHERINE PHONED her mother and told her about the dog, and then John got on the phone and she told him. When John asked to speak with Spencer, she pleaded his case to her husband, but he refused to pick up the receiver.

And so an hour and a half later, having avoided her husband since hanging up the telephone, after kissing her daughter good night and petting her daughter's dog—the animal was on the carpet in Charlotte's room as the girl tapped away on her computer, sending instant messages to the Dudesters and Dreamdates and Lexicon-Domos who were her friends—she climbed into bed beside Spencer. She was still as miffed as she'd been when she'd informed her brother that her husband had no intention of removing even a single brick from the Berlin Wall he had built between them. He was thumbing through color layouts of the pages from the upcoming FERAL holiday catalog, pressing blank Post-it notes onto some of the corners with his left hand. Both of their cats were curled on the chaise lounge by the window, but Emma's eyes were open and they were wary: She was watching the door for any sign of the dog.

"You're mad at me because I won't talk to John," he said when she was settled in on her side of the bed.

She considered ignoring him, but then decided against it. She'd ignored him for the last ninety minutes and it hadn't proven particularly satisfying. "Yes," she said. "I am."

"I'm sorry, sweetheart, I can't. I simply can't."

"That's apparent."

"Would you like to discuss it?"

"What's there to discuss? We've been over this ground so many times . . ." Her voice broke, and she was surprised.

He put the pages down on his nightstand and

turned to her, contemplating her for a long moment. He knew she wanted to say something, but he didn't know what. "Where's Tanya?" he asked finally.

"With Charlotte."

"We had a nice walk tonight," he said.

"I'm happy for you."

"But you're not happy for yourself? Are you really that angry with me for getting our daughter a pet?"

"I'm angry . . ."

"Yes?"

"I'm angry at you for a lot of reasons."

"I know."

"And . . ." She paused, wondering whether to continue. Finally: "I just don't know how I can go on this way. How we can go on this way."

"I know that, too."

"Do you care?"

"Of course I care. And I'm trying, Catherine, really I am. Haven't I seemed less cranky? Less a pain in the ass? Tell me honestly."

"Oh, you have. But . . ."

"Talk to me. Please."

She thought of the different sources of her annoyance, the springs that were feeding her resentment—including, she had to admit, his sudden placidity and tolerance when it came to her eating meat, behavior that seemed more punishing and hurtful on some level than if he had chastised her, because it was as if he'd simply concluded that she (like her mother and her brother) was beyond redemption. She decided as well that she could rail at him for not talking to her brother, for getting a dog without consulting her, even for the last year of neglect. Hadn't he himself just alluded to this issue? But when she considered what really was troubling her most at the moment, she concluded it was the sheer inconsistency—the utter irrationality—of his behavior toward their daughter these days. On the one hand, he had become Jim Anderson from **Father Knows Best;** on the other, he was going ahead with that hateful press conference next week. That was the issue, and it had been driven home to her this evening by his unwillingness, once again, to speak with John. "Okay," she said, trying to remain as calm as he was, "one minute you're getting Charlotte this sweet dog and the next you're planning to embarrass her at the press conference. I just don't see how you can do that."

"Charlotte won't be embarrassed. And I hope John won't be—at least not too dramatically. Paige doesn't think much of him, but eventually she'll need him as an ally against Adirondack. She'll be careful. And even if John is a little uncomfortable, well, the fact is he was the one who left a loaded rifle sitting around in the trunk of his car."

"Charlotte **will** be embarrassed. How can she not be? I know she was crying with Dr. Warwick today."

"Really?"

"Yes!"

He brought his left fingers to his mouth in a tight fist and blew onto them. These days they sometimes grew cold. "I guess I shouldn't be surprised," he said softly. "For the rest of her life she does have to deal with this. And though I know it's not her fault, we both know she feels guilty."

"And the press conference will make her feel even worse!"

"See, that's where we disagree. I won't let that happen. I know what I'm going to say. I know what Paige and Dominique are going to say."

"Her name will be splattered all over the newspapers and on the TV news for shooting her father! How can that not make her feel horrible?"

"Her name won't ever be mentioned at the—"

"You're kidding yourself! You're being ridiculous! You should have heard Paige warning her about the media at breakfast last week."

He gazed at his fingers and then did something he hadn't done in a very long time. Slowly, as if the digits extending out from the gauze and the tape were breakable twigs of glass, he moved them toward the side of her neck, and then—as if her neck, too, were a fragile wisp of porcelain sculpture—he stroked her. He petted her. He ran his hand gently along the skin as if he were touching it for the first time, his eyes focused on her neck and then on her face. Her eyes.

"It'll be fine," he whispered, his voice so soft she barely heard him. "It'll be fine."

"How?" she asked. She felt the pulse in her neck beneath his fingers. She considered pulling away: She was almost too angry to be touched. But it had been a very long time since he had touched her like this, and she couldn't bring herself to move.

"I just know it will be. I am trying . . ."

"Yes?"

"I am trying to treat people like animals. I am trying not to be angry."

"I've noticed. Sometimes, I have, anyway."

"I'm sorry I didn't tell you about Tanya. I thought you'd like the surprise, too."

She nodded, and she felt the soft skin of his thumb on the side of her jaw.

"And I am sorry about . . . oh, there's lots I am sorry about, Catherine. Lots. There is so much I wish I could do over. And so these days I'm trying. Really, I am. I'm trying."

Now she did reach for his hand, and she pulled it before her face and stared at the dots of blood that had soaked through the bandages there. He **was** trying, she had to agree; she didn't know quite what that meant, but she guessed that trying was better than not trying . . .

"Please, then," she said, "for me and for Charlotte, will you talk to John? You don't want the next time you see him to be in court, if it comes to that, or at my mother's funeral."

She heard the thump of one of the cats bounding onto the foot of the bed, and she looked up and saw that Emma had leapt from the chaise to the mattress and was walking now across the bedspread. The animal waited by Spencer's legs, and then hopped over them and into her lap, where she started to knead at the cotton of her nightgown.

"I guess I'm not all that popular," he said.

She realized that because she had been holding

Spencer's left hand, he'd been unable to pet or massage or hold Emma—to show the animal that her presence was welcome.

"Emma just wants a little physical reassurance," she told him. "It's what we all want, I guess."

"Could you help me change into my pajamas? Is now a good time?"

"Of course. It's fine."

"Thank you."

"And will you talk to John? Will you at least consider the idea?"

He exhaled a long breath and sounded tired. "Yeah, I will," he said finally.

"Yeah, you'll consider it?"

"Yeah, I'll talk to him. I'll . . ."

She couldn't quite believe what she was hearing, and she was afraid that she might have misunderstood him. She brought his fingers to her mouth and kissed them. She kissed each one, and when she was through she heard him murmuring something about how he might join them all at the Cloisters in the morning, and maybe he and John would go for a walk. He didn't know, he'd play it by ear. But he would definitely go with them to the Cloisters.

Thirty

When the two girls had been younger, they would run into each other's arms when they were reunited in New York or New Hampshire and hug each other like lovers, their bodies colliding in a minor ecstasy. They would wrap their arms around each other's backs and there had even been a time—he guessed it had been when Charlotte was seven or eight—when his niece would actually lift his daughter into the air and spin her beloved younger cousin around as if they were in a perfume commercial. Even now, however, one girl thirteen and the other on the cusp of eleven, ages when they could be self-conscious about everything, they still scampered playfully toward each other like baby colts. Charlotte no longer lifted Willow off her feet and their embraces weren't as long as in years past, but whatever the ties were—blood, history, friendship—they still were solid. The girls held each other, and Charlotte patted her shorter cousin on the back.

A dozen yards behind Charlotte, winding their way through a small crowd surrounding a pair of musicians dressed up like Chaucerian minstrels, he saw his sister and a strange man with a beard. It took him a moment to realize it was his brother-in-law. Behind them he could see the western tower of the George Washington Bridge and the graceful, sloped curves formed by the stay ropes and suspender cables on the New York side. The families had planned to meet at the top of the stone steps at the entrance to the Cloisters itself, rather than here in the middle of Fort Tryon Park, but here they all were—even Spencer.

He'd never seen Spencer with a beard, and the combination of the whiskers and the mere fact that the man was present caused him a brief second of disbelief, then incredulity: **Is that really Spencer? Has he really come along?** The giveaway was the sling. Spencer's right arm was strapped in a sling across a blue cotton tennis shirt, the fabric a pale echo of the cobalt sky above them.

John knew that even if he and Spencer hadn't been feuding, they never would have greeted each other with anything like the exuberance of their daughters. Given, however, that they were sparring (rather, that Spencer was sparring with him), he tried to decide how much ardor and warmth he should manifest now. He felt a September breeze coming up off the Hudson, warmer than the wind in Vermont, riffling the leaves on the park's maples and oaks.

Willow was pulling Charlotte over to them, and he and Sara both took turns hugging their niece. She looked like she had grown since New Hampshire, but then John decided it was something else. She seemed more poised. He wondered if a few weeks in eighth grade could change a girl so much. She was wearing a denim skirt and a balsam-colored cotton cardigan, and now that she was done greeting her cousin she was carrying herself as if she were . . .

And then he got it. She was carrying herself as if she were that kid in the play she was in. That proper British orphan. He thought he might even have heard the suggestion of a British accent when she had said hello.

"Heavens! Spencer has a beard!" It was Nan speaking, apparently more taken aback by her son-in-law's facial hair than the reality that he had deigned to join them. Gently she pushed the stroller with her grandson back and forth, fearing, perhaps, that her small outburst had upset the child. Patrick wasn't sleeping, but at the moment he was content to bat at the small plastic boats that dangled before him from the awning of the pram.

"Yes, isn't it nice that Father chose to come along, too?" Charlotte said, allowing that small hint of a British accent to become almost overwhelming. John didn't believe he had ever heard his niece refer to Spencer as **Father,** and he was quite certain that collapsing an **er** sound into an **a** was a new affectation.

He smiled at her and then offered his sister and Spencer a small wave across the crowd. His sister waved back, but Spencer remained almost completely motionless. A juggler in harlequin tights drifted through the crowd, tossing garish cloth beanbags into the air, and John remembered that Willow had expressed an interest in the jugglers. And so he made eye contact with the jester and motioned for him to join them. When he was sure that the juggler had seen them, he murmured to his mother and to Sara that he thought he would go say hello to Spencer. He didn't know quite what he would say. But Spencer was here, and even if they resolved nothing, at least they could talk.

INSIDE THE STONEWALLS of the Cloisters, Spencer stared at Bartolo's massive **The Adoration of the Shepherds,** but he was less interested in the depiction of the humans' veneration of the baby Jesus than he was in the awe that he saw in the eyes of the donkey and the cow. Arguably, they were more prominent in the painting than the shepherds. Luke, he knew, had never said specifically in his account of Christ's birth that there were animals present, but neither did he say that the barn had been empty. Certainly it was impossible for Spencer to imagine the Nativity without them. He couldn't envision how, years ago, Charlotte could ever have built her own crèche scenes without carefully finding a place for each creature. Their metaphoric importance to the story was profound, and certainly Bartolo had understood this. Most medieval artists did.

"I like the name Tanya. Did you choose it, or did it come with the dog?" he heard John asking him. Everyone else was outside on the terrace overlooking the Hudson River. They had fled as a group as soon as they saw that he wasn't going to shun his brother-in-law from Vermont, in theory leaving the two men alone to iron out their differences. So far, they hadn't said more than a dozen words about anything other than medieval altarpieces and twelfth-century wooden sculptures. Now John was bringing up the dog.

"She's two years old. The name came with her," he said, keeping his eyes fixed on the great cow eyes in the painting before him.

"Charlotte sounds very happy to have her."

"She is."

"She seems to be in a good phase right now. Is it the play?"

"Maybe. Maybe she's just growing up."

"Does she talk about what happened in New Hampshire?"

He turned away from the Bartolo. This was the first time John had deviated from small talk. He sighed. "Well, we don't discuss it much. She's started to see a therapist, and the first session may have opened up some doors for her."

"Does she seem okay about it—about the accident?"

"Now, have you thought about why you're asking me that?"

"Spencer, please. Come on."

"I'm serious. Why do you think you're asking? Is it so you can feel less guilty about what you did—be reassured that your niece is not going to be traumatized for life—or is it because you're interested in my daughter's mental health? Personally, I think the answer's a combination of both."

Two young women, one in a Fordham sweatshirt, pressed close to the painting. They had clipboards, and they seemed to be scribbling notes about the image.

"Yes, I'm sure my guilt is a factor. Is that what you need to hear? If so, I'm happy to admit it. But the primary motivation behind my question just now was my niece and how she's doing. And I'll tell you something else: As bad as I feel for Charlotte, I feel a thousand times worse when I think of how my stupidity led to your injury."

"I'm sorry. I shouldn't have made such a big deal about your question," he said.

John looked taken aback—almost dazed—by his apology. Only after a moment did he continue, "So . . . you and Charlotte really don't talk much about what happened?"

"Nope. But it's not like it's a subject we avoid, either. It is in our faces. After all, I'm still learning to eat with my left hand. I can no longer tie my own shoes. It's impossible to hold a book open and turn the pages. A hardcover novel, I've learned, is really quite heavy."

"Does she blame me? If I were her, I might."

He resisted the urge to chastise John for bringing this all back to him. **Does she blame me?** Yes, they were in the midst of relics touched by the true pioneers of the hair shirt, but if only because John's voice sounded so pathetic his question didn't seem quite so narcissistic. "Did she seem to blame you a few minutes ago in the park?" he asked in response.

"No."

"Well, there's your answer."

"I'm glad."

Spencer wandered toward the glass looking out on the garth garden and the fountain from a twelfth-century French monastery. It felt good to be strolling through here with John. Anger, always an exhausting emotion, was particularly trying when you were already investing so much energy in simply trying to button your shirt. The main reason, he guessed, he had agreed to resume speaking to his brother-in-law was precisely because not speaking to him was becoming so much work. "Can I ask you something?" he said when he felt John standing beside him once more.

"Absolutely. Ask me anything."

"How much weight have you lost? You look like hell."

"I don't know. Ten, maybe fifteen pounds."

"That's impressive. All since mid-August?"

The man shrugged with both shoulders, a motion Spencer noticed largely because he couldn't do it. "Early August, mid-August. I don't know."

"Why are you on a diet?"

"I'm not. I'm just not hungry."

"Well, the two of us look pretty scary."

"I know. I saw in the paper today that there's a play opening downtown about the Bataan Death March. We should have auditioned."

He grinned in spite of himself. "I'm amazed I'm not losing more weight. I spill more food than I get to my mouth. At breakfast this morning I overturned a bowlful of cereal. Sent the whole thing somersaulting onto the floor. Fortunately, Tanya was right there. To be honest, that's the main reason I got the dog. It wasn't for Charlotte. It was for me. She'll eat anything."

"Even soy milk?"

"Oh, yeah. I checked her references. I made sure she was a vegan."

"Really?"

"I'm kidding. The animal shelter doesn't categorize its animals that way."

"But you will try to make her a vegetarian—like your cats. True?"

"Oh, I don't know. I may even pick up a few cans of Friskies for the cats one of these days. Just leave them on the kitchen counter for Catherine and Charlotte to discover one evening when they go to feed them. Everything is so much harder now, and not just for me. Sometimes I need to give in and accept the fact that I can't do as much as I'd like."

"You're getting mellow in your old age."

"You learn to compromise when you're down to one arm. And the truth is, Catherine eats meat—did you know that?"

"She told me a few weeks ago."

"Yup: My wife eats meat and the sun continues to rise."

They were quiet for a moment. The garden was starting to empty, and he wondered if something special was about to occur in the park. The jousting, maybe. That would explain why people were beginning to leave.

"Spencer?"

"Yes?"

"I was thinking of staying in town for the press conference."

"That would be interesting. Did you discuss this with Paige?"

"I'm not going to stick around. At least I don't think I will. And I wouldn't have been staying to help you. I was going to **threaten** to stay—**threaten** to talk about the benefits of hunting—to try to convince you not to announce your lawsuit with a press conference. It was a stupid idea. And I'm only telling you now so you understand the depth of my concern. I mean, I have no objections to the lawsuit itself. Absolutely none . . ."

Spencer circled his left index finger at John, signaling him to continue.

"But if I were at the press conference," John said, "a lot of reporters would want to talk to me. It would be chaos. And, in the end, less time and space would be devoted to the FERAL message, because the writers and producers would have the chance to quote me—the guy who owned the gun. And I would talk very reasonably about managing the size of the deer herd through hunting, and how contraception only works in very controlled little worlds. But it was all just brinkmanship. Public relations brinkmanship. I couldn't have gone through with it."

He thought about this, picturing John in the rear of that large conference room in Paige's firm where they were going to announce the lawsuit, and the vision didn't make him angry. Certainly it would have once. Mostly, he guessed, he was surprised that John—exactly like his sister—had so little faith in what he was going to do at the event, in what he was going to say.

"You sound like Catherine," he said after a moment.

"Was she threatening to go, too?"

"No. It's that both of you seem to think I am going to mismanage the press conference, and my daughter is going to be humiliated. That's not going to happen. I know what I'm doing."

"I won't ask what your plans are, but . . ."

"Good," he said, "it's too nice a day and it's too good to see you again." He reached into his left pants pocket for one of the Percocet he carried there loosely like change and popped it into his mouth without water. When he had swallowed it he continued, "Seriously, John, you can sleep easy. I know what I'm doing, and I would never embarrass my daughter. Now, shall we rejoin our families and see if the jousting is about to begin?"

A MAGICIAN dressed up like Merlin was throwing bolts of fire into the autumn air from his fingertips, while a group of costumed adults were performing a living chess match on the tournament field. Willow decided that her art teacher, Grace Seeley, had been correct: This festival was wonderful. She had to remind herself that the whole reason she was here was to talk to her cousin about their depositions, a conversation toward which she had made no overtures thus far. Mostly they had discussed the school musical in which Charlotte had a lead and her cousin's new dog. When she put the two subjects together, it almost made

Willow breathless with envy: How interesting her New York City cousin's life was compared to hers!

They were walking alone now, a dozen yards ahead of their mothers, their grandmother, and Patrick, when Charlotte surprised her by saying, "Are you still worried about those oaths we may have to take?"

"Yes." She considered adding more, but since her cousin had brought this up she had the instinctive sense that she should remain patient and see what Charlotte had to say.

"I've been thinking about them, too."

"Really?"

"Uh-huh. And I know you don't want us to lie, but I believe we have to. We have to for my father. This whole lawsuit could crash and burn—isn't that a powerful expression? I learned it from my history teacher—if people find out I was stoned when I pulled the trigger. And that would be a disaster for him both personally and professionally. This isn't about you or me, and it sure as heck isn't about Gwen. It's about my dad. Your uncle."

She worked hard not to raise her voice. "But what about **my** dad? It isn't fair to him if we don't tell the truth—"

"Your dad isn't crippled. Mine is. Your dad doesn't have a cause here that matters to him. Mine does."

"But lying is wrong. It's—"

"Willow, have you ever told someone you couldn't come over to their house because you were going to visit your grandmother? You know, told a little white lie so you didn't hurt someone's feelings? In my opinion, not telling the whole truth at the depo-what-ever—"

"Deposition," she said, unable to restrain herself from correcting her cousin.

"Right. Deposition. Not telling the truth at the deposition is like a white lie. It makes things better than telling the truth, which would only make people's lives worse. Do you see the difference?"

"We're not talking about a little white lie. We're talking about a really big one."

"No. The point is—"

"Here's what I think the point is. Your dad can't use his arm anymore and my dad is in trouble because you picked up his gun and started fooling around with it. And why were you fooling around with it? Because we were both stoned."

"First of all, your dad is **not** in trouble. Second, I would have taken the gun even if **we** hadn't been smoking pot," she said evenly, her voice lowering a register and picking up a slight trace of a British accent. "That's **my** point, and I am quite certain of it now."

"So, you know what's going to happen, then?" Willow responded, hoping to keep her tone equally as measured. She stared straight ahead at the chess players in their medieval garb, wondering suddenly where they'd gotten all those costumes. Everyone looked like they had just arrived here from Middle Earth. "You won't say anything about the pot and the beer, but I will. They'll find out anyway—everyone will—and that certainly won't make your dad's case look very good."

"You can't do that!"

"I can! I won't lie in the deposition, Charlotte. I won't. It's wrong, and it's not fair to my dad."

"You can't—"

"Girls, is everything okay?" It was her aunt Catherine's voice. She turned around, and the grown women—her aunt and her mom and her grandmother with the pram before her—all looked slightly concerned. Willow didn't believe they had overheard enough of their conversation to understand exactly what they were discussing, but clearly they'd heard their daughters fighting.

"Oh, we're fine, Mother," Charlotte called back in that new voice of hers. "Just two girls bickering."

"Are you hungry? There seem to be some vendors along that road over there," Aunt Catherine told them, and she pointed at the row of food carts on the street, closed today to automobiles, that wound its way up to the Cloisters.

"Cousin, are you hungry?" Charlotte asked her.

"No."

"That's probably good. I smell a lot of seared flesh," she murmured softly. Then she raised her voice for their parents and said, "We're both fine!"

"Okay, then. Just let us know if there's something you want," her aunt said.

Charlotte picked up her pace and Willow had to walk faster to keep up. When they had some distance once again on the grown-ups, Charlotte spoke: "This is very complicated, you know. I'm trying to do the right thing."

"Me, too."

"But here's something else," she said firmly. "How could we be friends after you revealed everything? How could we? Telling everyone everything would be so hurtful to my dad. That's what I don't get: Here I am trying to make up for what I did—yes, what **I** did, I know I'm to blame—by making this lawsuit and this press conference go perfectly, and you're trying to stop me."

"I'm not trying to stop you."

"Oh, but you would. You would undo everything if you talked," Charlotte said.

"But—"

"Look, we're not going to figure this out right this second. Would you do me a favor?"

"What?"

"Think about what I've said. Okay? Just think about it today, and we can talk more tonight. Deal?"

Willow couldn't imagine she'd change her mind, but they really were getting nowhere. And so she nodded and mumbled, "Okay." Then she halted where she was to watch a pair of tumblers who were dressed like the court jesters on her grandmother's playing cards, while Charlotte walked on ahead.

"What were you and Charlotte talking about?" She turned and saw her mother standing beside her. Her grandmother and her aunt were continuing to walk, slowly narrowing the gap between them and her cousin. At some point her mother had taken the carriage back from Grandmother, and so Willow peeked inside now and saw her brother smiling up at her. He seemed to be batting his eyelashes like a baby flirt.

"Oh, nothing."

"It didn't sound like nothing."

"I'll tell you later," she said, though she had no expectation that she would tell her mother the real subject at any point soon. How could she until she and Charlotte had come to some sort of resolution?

But then, maybe that shouldn't matter. And maybe it wouldn't matter. This had to resolve itself this weekend, because it was possible that after tomorrow she wouldn't see Charlotte again before their depositions. And so it crossed her mind that she should simply tell her mother and father tonight what had occurred that awful evening at the club in New Hampshire. Let them figure out how to deal with the information.

An idea began to form. She wasn't sure if it was a good idea or—even if it was—whether she had the courage to go through with it. But it was certainly a notion that intrigued her. With her uncle Spencer now speaking to her father, she had no doubt that later that day or that evening both families would have a meal together somewhere. Maybe a nice dinner at a Japanese or Chinese or Indian restaurant on the Upper East or West Side. Then, with everyone gathered together, she would reveal the details that both she and her cousin had withheld since that horrible night. Charlotte would be furious—there would be no dignified British orphan scene once this word got out; this would be a performance, she guessed, comprised largely of screaming and hysteria—but wouldn't it be better to expose everything here in New York, with all the grown-ups assembled in one place, than as a complete surprise in a deposition?

And, she knew, one way or another it was going to come out. No matter how hard she tried, she could no longer keep that part of the story to herself.

HOW ODD, Catherine thought. Spencer was here and she was walking with him, and he had just had a long talk with her brother. This was exactly what she had wanted, exactly what she had hoped would occur but hadn't thought possible. They were strolling along the terrace that overlooked the Hudson River, while everyone else was back in the park getting something to eat. But then Spencer had told her of his conversation with John about the press conference and she had grown angry. Their family was lurching spastically toward public humiliation, estrangement, or both, and their daughter was, according to Dr. Warwick, a volcano of guilt and despair just waiting to explode—despite whatever serenity she was projecting on the surface. And here Spencer was bringing up the press conference. Again. The gentle feel of his fingers on her neck last night—their taste when she kissed them—seemed very far away to her now, and she knew exactly what she would say.

She paused against the stonewall and gazed out at the Palisades across the water.

"I've made a decision," she said, and she could feel him stopping beside her, though she couldn't imagine he knew what she was thinking.

"Oh? About what?"

She took a breath, exhaled. Took another and began: "If you go ahead with that press conference on Tuesday, I will leave you."

"What?"

"I will pack up our daughter and we will go across town to my mother's, and I will immediately start looking for a new home for us. For Charlotte and me."

"Whoa. Where is—"

"You know where this is coming from. At least you should. Things haven't been right between us for a very long time. As a matter of fact, if the accident hadn't intervened, I was going to tell you in New Hampshire that I wanted us to start counseling. Marriage counseling. At the very least I wanted that. Certainly we **needed** it. I might even have left you then, but you got hurt and so I couldn't. I just . . . couldn't."

He was leaning against the stones beside her, and she wondered why she wasn't crying. She thought she might if she turned to look at him, and so she didn't. She focused on the shore across the water, on a plane descending toward Newark.

"Why isn't counseling an option now, then? Why this threat—"

"Maybe we could explore counseling once I've left. Maybe not. Right now I don't know. But I am quite sure that I cannot live with you if you are capable of subjecting our daughter—and, yes, my brother—to the indignities that will follow your press conference. It's just that simple."

"But it will help the lawsuit," he said, a quiver of panic marking his voice. "And it's such a great opportunity for us to point out the horrors of hunting. Good Lord, the pain I'm enduring is precisely what deer experience—"

"I don't care. For once I want you to put your family first. You know, those animals you live with, those animals who are a part of your very own little herd. Charlotte and me. My brother. Go ahead with the lawsuit, sue the hell out of Adirondack—though I would certainly hope that you and Paige would have the common sense not to let this thing ever get to a trial. But you hold that press conference to announce it on Tuesday—you so much as have Randy Mitchell pick up the phone to start calling people on Monday morning to tell them about the event—and your daughter and I are out the door. We are gone before the sweat from Randy's hands has left a palm print on her phone."

"Why didn't you tell me you felt so strongly about the press conference sooner?"

"What?"

"Why didn't—"

"I did! I told you every way I could! But it wasn't registering! That's why it has come to this."

"An ultimatum. And all because of a press conference."

"The press conference is just the tip of the iceberg. My God, Spencer, didn't you hear what I just said? I considered leaving you this summer."

A couple of seagulls swooped down onto the stone

terrace and started pecking at something between the stones. Beside her she heard him breathing, and she couldn't imagine what he would say next. She was hoping, she realized, that he was going to announce that the press conference was now a dead issue. Over, done with. He would call Paige and Dominique that afternoon to put an end to the nonsense.

Finally he spoke: "I've tried the last few weeks to behave better. I know how difficult I can be. Has it made any difference? Any difference at all?"

"Yes, absolutely. I've noticed. And I've seen how attentive you've been with Charlotte."

"But it's been too little too late . . ."

"That's how it feels," she said. "I'm sorry."

"And you're serious about this?"

"Yes." She almost said more, but she felt a shudder in her throat and now, finally, her eyes were starting to mist. She could feel it, and it took every bit of willpower she had not to wipe them. She knew if she did, that would be it: She would be sobbing and that was the last thing she wanted. Not here, not today.

"Okay, then."

She tried to read meaning in those three short syllables—resignation or anger or acquiescence—but they were indecipherable. Completely impenetrable. The birds flew up past the two of them, apparently unsatisfied with the pickings in the stones at the foot of the wall, and she watched them wheel up and out over the wide river. She wanted to ask Spencer what he was going to do, but she didn't dare open her mouth.

CHARLOTTE SIPPED her bottle of orange juice and nibbled at a very doughy, very salty pretzel and watched the contingent from Vermont eat frozen yogurt. Nearby, another family was eating "Medieval Festival Fowl"—turkey legs the size of bowling pins. They were using their hands, and their fingers glistened with fat.

But her father didn't seem upset. If anything, he seemed oblivious. She wondered if his shoulder was hurting more than usual.

Everyone was sitting on a massive beach blanket that her grandmother—who thought of everything—had brought with her. She and Willow hadn't spoken any more about her cousin's determination to tell everyone about the dope and the beer, but she, at least, hadn't stopped thinking about it for one single minute. The whole thing was making her a little queasy.

She stood up now and looked at the stone edifice of the Cloisters itself, the museum perhaps a hundred yards away from their spot on the grass in the park. She imagined it was a real monastery for a moment and tried to envision the monks inside it doing whatever it was that monks did. She wasn't exactly sure. But she guessed they prayed and baked bread and they chanted. It probably wasn't a whole lot different from being a nun, except she presumed that nuns sang instead of chanted. For some reason, in her mind's eye she could see nuns wandering among those gardens and terraces inside the Cloisters, but not small gatherings of monks. Maybe it was the name of the place itself. **Cloisters.** It sounded feminine to her. Girlish. She'd learned that morning that a cloister was just a covered walkway in a religious building, but she understood that it was also the root of the word **cloistered**. And that meant something else. Something more. Separation. Isolation. Purity, maybe.

The gardens and the terraces reminded her of the secret garden: that walled garden from the play, that secluded little world of magic and—what were the words in one of the songs in the musical?—spirit and charm. When Mary Lennox tries to get the little crippled boy to rise up out of his wheelchair in the second act of the show, she sings precisely that: Come spirit, come charm.

She saw Willow pushing up off the ground now and walking toward her. She acted as if she hadn't noticed and wandered a dozen yards closer to the Cloisters itself. Her cousin followed, exactly as Charlotte suspected she would.

"Have you ever met a nun?" she asked Willow when the younger girl was beside her.

"No. I don't think so. You?"

"No. How about a monk?"

"No. I know I've never met a monk."

"Me neither," she said. Then: "The gardens in there made me think of the secret garden. Maybe it was the little walkways and stonewalls. It's like in the play."

"And the novel."

"Yes, in the novel. I don't mean to relate everything

back to the play." She finished her pretzel and put the paper napkin in her pocket. Willow looked so little to her right now, but also so strong. So courageous. So much more like that fictional Mary Lennox than she was. "You're really going to tell them, aren't you?" she said.

"About what we did? Yes. I'm sorry, Charlotte. Really I am. But I can't lie."

She nodded. "During the deposition later this year?"

"Actually," her cousin said carefully, "I thought I might do it before the deposition."

"So it isn't a complete surprise for everyone."

"Uh-huh."

"I was beginning to suspect that," she said. "If possible . . ."

"Yes?"

"If possible, would you wait until after the press conference? Let my father have that?" She could see that her cousin was pondering the idea, and so she added, "After all, the depositions won't be for a little while. But the press conference is this Tuesday. You'll have plenty of time to tell everyone what happened afterward."

"I could do that."

"Thank you."

The girl licked at a drop of frozen yogurt on the back of her spoon. "What about you?"

"What about me?" Charlotte wondered.

"Are you going to tell your parents—or wait until they hear it from mine?"

"Oh, I'll have to think about that," she said, but her

sense immediately was that it would be better for them to hear it from her than from Uncle John. Or from Uncle John's lawyer. Or, perhaps, from Paige. "But I'll probably tell them myself," she added.

"Do you want to pick a day now?"

"No, I'd rather not," she said in her most mannered, most adult voice. "Is that okay?"

"Sure. Charlotte?"

"Yes?"

"We're still friends, right?"

"Yes, Cousin. We're still friends." She knew she should say something more reassuring to Willow, but she couldn't. Not yet. She was not happy with this turn of events, and she felt as if she had been needlessly cornered by . . .

Not exactly by her cousin. But by the events themselves. What had happened. On the one hand, she understood that her cousin was correct and they shouldn't lie; on the other hand, telling the truth seemed to be almost a betrayal of her father. First she shot him. Now it comes out that she'd been smoking dope and drinking beer, and—worse—she hadn't told anybody. She had seen enough courtroom dramas on television to hear in her head some lawyer from the gun company telling a jury that while this was all real sad, the fact was that Charlotte McCullough was stoned when she ignored her cousin and shot her father. This was a real tragedy, but it sure as heck wasn't the fault of the Adirondack Rifle Company.

She turned back to her family on the beach blanket and stared for a long moment at her father. He still looked a little dazed to her, as if he weren't listening to a word of whatever Aunt Sara and Grandmother were saying. She saw he had an unopened can of Diet Pepsi by his left leg, and she noticed that he was the only one there who wasn't drinking anything.

Afraid that her father was thirsty but was unwilling to be a bother, she loped over to the blanket and knelt beside him, and there she popped the top of his can of soda and held it to him like an offering. The goblet of wine at communion. That gold chalice she had just seen inside the Cloisters. **Drink,** she said to him in her mind. **Drink, drink.**

Thirty-one

On Monday morning, while he and Charlotte were taking Tanya for a walk before breakfast, he told her. The plan he and Catherine had agreed on the night before was that he would break the news to their daughter and then leave early for work so she and Charlotte could discuss Mom and Dad's immediate plans before heading across town to Brearley. They'd considered telling her together, but it was clear to them both that they'd end up squabbling if they tried to work as a tag team on this one. He guessed he could have been more eloquent (or, perhaps, more assertive) in his defense when he and Catherine had argued, though in hindsight it really hadn't been much of an argument. They hadn't discussed her ultimatum at all since she had presented it to him at the Cloisters. He'd thought about it, he'd thought about it all the time. But mostly it had just exhausted him. He felt simultaneously defensive, convinced that she didn't appreciate how hard he'd been trying lately, and disappointed in himself that it had taken him so long to understand that his self-absorption was gnawing away at their marriage. His life, it was clear, was now completely unraveling.

"What have you decided?" she'd asked simply when they both were in bed Sunday night.

"About?"

"Please. The press conference."

"It really has come down to that, hasn't it? Just that one . . . thing?" He was too tired to say more. He'd spent most of Saturday afternoon and all of Sunday numbed by the realization that his wife wanted to leave him. He felt sorry for himself **(I am crippled and in pain and my wife is leaving me),** but it had been so obvious in hindsight that his marriage was trending this way that he wasn't surprised. Just fatigued.

"That one thing is a gauge of where we are—and where we're going."

"It will be fine, you know. The press conference. You can trust me. I know what I'm doing."

"You're bringing needless attention and ridicule down on our daughter and on my brother. That's what you're doing."

"No, I—"

"Yes, Spencer. That's all there is to it."

Maybe if she'd said something less adamant he would have been less stubborn. Maybe if she hadn't interrupted him he would have said something else. Who knew? Certainly he didn't. "Well, I can't cancel it," he told her in response. "Not now. It's far too late for that."

"You can cancel it. Absolutely you can. But you won't."

"Catherine—"

"No. I told you how I feel," she'd said, and she had actually climbed out of bed that moment, something she rarely did once she was settled under the sheets, and pulled out her suitcase from the back of the walk-in closet.

"You're going to pack now?" he'd murmured.

"I'm going to get a few things ready, yes. Enough to tide me over for a few days across town. Tomorrow I'll need to help Charlotte gather her things, and so I might not be able to focus on my needs."

"Your needs," he had repeated, but that was as close as he'd come to saying something hostile.

Now he watched his daughter hold Tanya back as they started east down Eighty-fifth Street, the road still in shadow and quiet since it wasn't quite 7 a.m. The air was chilly, and he was wearing his windbreaker in his usual fashion: His left arm was through the sleeve, but the right side of the jacket was clipped to his shirt as if it were an opera cape. He himself, of course, hadn't done the careful work with the safety pin: Charlotte had. He'd tried and failed.

"Your mother and I made a decision about something last night," he said once they were well beyond their building's front awning. He noticed she no longer wore the scarves that had been a crucial part of her accessorization last year. Instead, this fall she seemed to be wearing the most simple and conservative headbands she owned. He guessed this was another element in her transformation into Mary Lennox. A part of him liked this new child a lot, but he also worried that she was taking it all a bit too seri-

ously. Then, precisely because he himself was taking
her accomplishment so seriously—and the opportunity it had presented him to be with her—he wondered how he would be able to run her lines with her
daily. She was doing well, but the kid seemed to be on
stage practically every minute of the musical: They
still had a ways to go.

"About what?"

"Well, we disagree about the press conference this
week, and she thinks it would be best if we spent a little time apart—"

"You're separating?" She stopped so suddenly that
the leash went tight as a clothesline and poor Tanya
was yanked to a halt.

"I don't know if I'd say that exactly. Your mother
simply thinks it would be best while we iron things
out if you two moved across town to your grandmother's. But I really don't know if I'd call it a separation, and there's no reason to think all this could ever
end in divorce," he said, not happy with his obvious
lies but convinced it was better to ease his daughter
into this—break the bad news a little at a time over
the course of weeks—than drop it all like a fireplace
andiron on her foot.

"You two . . ." she said, looking at him with eyes
that had grown thin with rage. Tanya squatted and
peed, half on and half off the sidewalk.

"Us two . . ."

"You two are so selfish! Do you ever think of anyone but yourselves?"

He restrained his initial instinct to remind her that she couldn't speak to either of her parents that way and responded instead in his most measured tone, "Your mother has recommended we do this precisely because she is thinking of you. She's worried that I am going to lose control of this press conference tomorrow, and you'll be embarrassed."

"So she thinks the solution is to move me to Grandmother's? Well, I'm not going."

She turned and allowed the dog to pull her quickly down the street. He scampered to catch up, and once he was beside her tried to decide whether he should simply allow her to vent or tell her firmly why this was the best thing for her. The problem was that he himself didn't believe this was the best thing for her. And, speaking selfishly **(Good Lord, is she right?),** he did want her with him. They were having more fun together this month than they'd ever had when he was healthy.

"It just doesn't make any sense," she continued. "First of all, you can't live in the apartment alone. Who would feed the cats? Who would feed you? You'd all starve to death. I mean, you can't even open a can of Pepsi on your own. You couldn't even put on your windbreaker without my help."

"Oh, I'd get by," he said, though he honestly wasn't sure that he would.

"No, you wouldn't. You still need people—a lot. And that's only one of the reasons why this idea is so dumb. We both know that bringing Tanya across town wouldn't be fair to Grandmother's dog. Not at his age. And it probably wouldn't be fair to Tanya, either. She's just starting to get used to our apartment."

She was looking straight ahead, but he thought he detected a slight quiver in her voice.

"And then there's me. I don't want to go there, period. It's not that I don't love Grandmother, because obviously I do. I mean, I stay with her part of every summer, don't I?"

"Your mother and I thought you liked going to New Hampshire!"

"I like it fine. But I don't want to live in her mausoleum of an apartment this fall. Especially not with the play coming up in November. Don't I have enough to deal with as it is?"

He nodded, more to himself than to her because she was watching Tanya sniff at the side of a building as they walked. "So what would you propose?" he asked.

"I'm not worried about this press conference. What are people going to find out? That I shot you by accident? Well, duh. Like every single person at Brearley and every single person in the apartment building already knows that. I screwed up," she said, and—there it was—he heard the tremor in her voice grow into a small sob and when he turned toward her he saw she was starting to cry. Instantly he knelt before her, a sudden ache coursing up and down his side because he had moved too quickly, and he used his one good hand like a football player to hold her. Grabbed her around her waist and brought her to him.

"I screwed up and I shot you," she said again, crying fully now. "Fine. Well, now I'm not going to leave you alone. I don't care what Mom says, I'm not going. She can go if she wants, but I'm not leaving—and no one can make me."

He held her as close as he could, even though the pressure against his sling-cradled arm was causing him literal spasms of pain, and the dog was resting her paws on his knees—he was poised like a baseball catcher, and the ledge of his legs was too tempting for Tanya to resist. The pain was considerable, but the real issues were that his daughter was crying, a response that he'd certainly thought possible, and that she was refusing to leave him, a notion he hadn't even considered.

Suddenly, despite the fact they were on the corner of Columbus and Eighty-fifth, his eyes were tearing, too.

NAN REMEMBERED a moment one morning in the vegetable garden in New Hampshire. It was either the day her children had arrived this past summer or the day before. She no longer knew which. She had been examining the damage caused by the deer and wondering how Spencer would react, and suddenly she had begun to worry about Catherine. She'd worried that Spencer was more interested in animals than in humans, and the thought had crossed her mind that someday her daughter would leave him and her marriage would end.

Well, here it was. It was happening. It was playing itself out exactly as she had feared. Spencer was putting FERAL before his family, and Catherine was leaving him and—this part, she had to admit was an unforeseen twist—coming here. With Charlotte. And that new dog. Returning to the apartment in which she had spent a large portion of her childhood.

"Why isn't Spencer the one who's leaving?" Nan had asked Catherine just now when her daughter had phoned with the news over breakfast. Apparently, Spencer was telling Charlotte what her parents were planning that very moment, while the two of them were taking the dog for a walk. "Normally, isn't it the husband who moves out?"

"He's crippled."

"Oh."

Nan knew there was plenty of room for everyone—even Tanya, she guessed—but she was still deeply troubled by the news that Catherine's marriage was hemorrhaging. She was also disconcerted by the unexpected reality that Catherine's arrival later today meant that she was going to have **both** of her children under her roof this evening.

"That sounded like bad news," John said after she had hung up the phone. He had wandered into the kitchen in his pajamas, finishing a buttered English muffin as she had spoken with Catherine.

"Yes," she said. "Very bad news indeed."

Sara and Willow and Patrick had driven back to Vermont yesterday afternoon as planned, but John had decided to stay until tomorrow afternoon.

Tuesday. He'd remained behind because he'd resolved at the very last moment that he would attend Spencer's press conference, after all. He'd concluded, for better or worse, that he couldn't stay away from it. He had no plans to be a bomb-throwing, deer-hunting anarchist. But if he had to be part of it, then he was going to witness the event up close and personal.

When it was over, he would take a cab to LaGuardia and catch the 5:25 flight to Burlington.

He hadn't yet told Spencer he was going to be present, and he hadn't decided whether he would call him at some point today or just show up tomorrow. Nan guessed that Catherine's presence here tonight might force him to call Spencer first. But you never knew. Catherine was so angry with her husband that she might be comfortable with the idea of her brother launching what Spencer might construe as a sneak attack.

"It sounded like Sis is coming home to Mother. True?"

"True," she murmured distractedly, her mind focused on the image that evening of John and Catherine and Charlotte and Tanya all here with her. And then she thought of Spencer alone on the West Side with his cats, and of Sara and Willow and Patrick in Vermont. How had it come to this? She'd thought when everyone had been together on Saturday that the cold war was thawing, but in reality all that had occurred was a shifting of alliances. She sat down heavily in one of the kitchen chairs, depression insinuating itself through the creases and trim of her nightgown—

it was a dowdy piece of work, she decided—and coating her skin like a lotion. What would happen when she was gone? Really? Would anything like a family remain?

"Can you give me the details?" her son was asking. She looked up at him. She didn't feel well at all, and she honestly wasn't sure she had the strength.

CATHERINE WAS AWARE that the dog was sliding her water bowl along the trim that ran underneath the kitchen cabinets in the pantry, an idiosyncrasy that had struck everyone as cute on Friday and Saturday when the animal had initially shown the inclination but had begun to grow tiresome yesterday when first Spencer and then she had forgotten the bowl was there and accidentally stepped on the dish. Catherine didn't make an effort now to suggest to Tanya that she should give this practice a rest, however, because the minor inconvenience posed by a dog's overturned water bowl was absolutely inconsequential compared to the human meltdown she was trying (and failing) to halt. Charlotte was standing beside the refrigerator and screaming at her, yelling in a manner that Catherine hadn't witnessed in a good long time, the child's affected British refinement a mere memory, while Spencer was squatting beside their daughter, his forehead in his one functioning hand, looking as if he had given up completely any hope that he might be able to reason with her.

"I am not leaving!" she was shrieking, her cheeks

and her forehead so pink they looked sunburned, the tears descending down her face like twin waterfalls. "Tanya is not leaving! And you would be horrible if you left! Horrible! How could you even think—"

"I will not be called horrible!" she snapped back. "You will not talk to me that way!" The words were out before she could stop them. She hated herself for sounding precisely like the angry mothers she saw snapping at their children in grocery stores, but she couldn't help it. She couldn't help herself.

"You are! You don't care about Dad, you don't care about me! All you care about are your precious students and precious Eric—"

"That is enough!"

"Precious Eric, precious Gary, precious Hank—"

She grabbed Charlotte by her upper arms and squeezed, trying physically to rein her in. She had a vague sense that if she didn't have something in her hands—even her daughter's shoulders, so small and frail underneath a thin cotton sweater and the blue blouse that she wore often with her Brearley skirt—she would slap the girl. Strike the child (strike anyone) for the first time in her life.

"You're hurting me!"

"Charlotte, you must settle down!"

"Just go, then! You—just go! Get out!"

She felt the girl struggling, but she wouldn't release her. It was, she realized, a test of wills, and her ability to reason was slipping away. She tried to think of what she wanted to say, but she couldn't. She understood on some level that when Spencer and Charlotte had re-

turned from walking Tanya, they both had been crying. But then they were quiet, very quiet, the two of
them. And somehow—in the space of, what, sixty seconds?—a little moment of domestic sadness had been
transmogrified into this cataclysm of accusations and
rage, and the bubbling up from deep inside their
daughter's mind of all these . . . issues . . . that had
nothing to do with her parents' problems. At least in
Catherine's opinion, they didn't. Dr. Warwick might
view it all somewhat differently.

"Get out! You want to leave, well, leave!"

"Charlotte," Spencer began, his voice muffled
slightly because his fingers were still on his forehead
and so he was speaking down into the tile floor.
"Charlotte . . ."

It was apparent he, too, wasn't sure what to say, but
still Catherine was grateful that at least now she had
an ally.

"Charlotte . . ." he murmured once more.

"What!" It was a screech, not a question.

"You need to calm down. To stop yelling. Your
mother and I—"

"Don't you dare!" she said, and abruptly she wres-
tled free of Catherine's grasp and whirled across the
kitchen, one foot flipping the water dish—which, inevitably, had wound up precisely in the girl's path—
into the air like a giant tiddly-wink, sending the water
into a spray that coated them all. "Don't change your
mind! You said outside I didn't have to go. You said I
could stay right here!"

"Yes, Charlotte, you're not going anywhere," he

said, and Catherine couldn't believe what she was hearing. The notion of Charlotte staying here was inconceivable. Unthinkable. Spencer could barely care for himself. How in the name of God could he care for their thirteen-year-old daughter, too? What was he thinking telling the girl she could remain with him at this apartment? More important, how could she—the child's mother—allow Charlotte to stay ensconced in the home of the man who was going to use her so shamelessly in a press conference tomorrow?

"Spencer, did you just tell Charlotte she didn't have to come with me across town?" The horrible shrillness in her voice disgusted her.

"Yes, I did."

"Spencer—"

"Mom, I'm staying! You can leave, if you want to—"

"I don't want to! I'm not leaving—**we're** not leaving—because I **want** to!" she said, and some small part of her actually began to focus on how wet her stockings were. Thank God it was only water, because she'd never have time to change before school. "We're leaving because your father and I have agreed that it's best—"

"Catherine, no: I don't want you to go, either."

She turned from her daughter to her husband and saw there on his face an almost unrecognizable hangdog look of despair.

"This isn't something we agreed on," he was saying. "It's something I am enduring because I don't know what else to do. But I don't want you to leave. You don't know . . ."

She wondered what she didn't know, and she was about to ask him if only to give herself time to think. To refocus on this—and as the words formed in her head and she felt the chilly dog water on her legs she almost nodded at their rightness—sloppy mess.

"What don't I know?" she murmured. "Tell me."

"Neither of you knows anything!" It was Charlotte this time, still crying, still angry, her face still that ugly pink mask of despair, but at least she hadn't shrieked this accusation. She'd actually spoken with sufficient quiet that Tanya nosed her way closer: The dog was seeming to decide whether it was worth the possible noise-induced hearing loss to venture any nearer this odd little group that constituted her new pack. "Neither of you knows anything," she said again, sniffing in a manner that was at once dramatic and necessary: All that crying had made her nose run like a softening glacier.

"Charlotte," Spencer said. "What don't we know? Tell us."

"You don't know," she said, shaking her head. "You two—and Uncle John and Aunt Sara—you don't know what I did. No one but Willow does. This is all my fault, and you two can't get a divorce because of me. You just can't"—her voice a plea now—"because I couldn't stand it if I caused that, too!"

The girl's small sobs and sniffles made it difficult for Catherine to understand every single word, but she was getting the point. She crabbed over to her daughter and held her again, this time not grasping her shoulders as if she were about to shake some sense into

her but instead enfolding her in her arms and pulling
her head to her chest. The dog came over to the two
of them and started trying to wedge her snout in between them, and Catherine didn't stop her. Any moisture left on her skirt or her blouse by a wet dog nose
was nothing compared to the impressive stream of
tears flooding against her chest.

"I was stoned when I fired the gun, and drunk,"
Charlotte was saying. "I'd been smoking marijuana
and I'd drunk a whole beer. Maybe I would have tried
to shoot a deer anyway, I don't know, but I do know I
wasn't thinking clearly. I didn't tell you because I didn't
want to get Gwen—"

"Gwen? Who's Gwen?" Spencer asked.

"She's a lifeguard at the club," Charlotte answered,
hiccupping as she cried. "I stole the joint from her bag
at the bonfire that night. At first I didn't tell you because I didn't want to get Gwen in trouble. But then,
when I saw what you and FERAL were doing, I didn't
tell you because I was afraid if I did you couldn't sue
the gun company and hold your press conference.
And that seemed so important! And after I'd ruined
your life by shooting you, I had to make sure I didn't
wreck anything else. I had to! But, please, don't get a
divorce now because of this! Please! I am so sorry for
everything, and I've tried to hold it together, but, no,
no, not this too, not this, don't make me have to live
with this, too! I couldn't handle it, really, I couldn't!
Please, no! Please—no!" and her voice rose into an almost classically tragic ululation—the widows of all
those ancient Greek sailors—before trailing off into

nothing but those wrenching, pathetic sobs. Gently Catherine rubbed her child's back, her hands making slow, tender circles. She looked across the floor and Spencer raised his eyebrows and shook his head. Then he, too, scooted over the damp tile to them, wincing once when he must have moved his shoulder too quickly, and there the three of them—and their dog— held each other as if they were the most fragile objects in the apartment.

Which, Catherine decided suddenly, they were.

Thirty-two

Paige liked this conference room. She liked it a lot, and not simply because it was massive. It sat on a corner of the twenty-ninth floor, high enough that the east-facing windows offered an ashy view of the East River and the dusky, saddle brown warehouses, industrial waste, and municipal detritus that stretched toward the sunrise—and, indeed, the sun was rising now—on the water's far bank. There were panels in the walls behind which sat a wireless Panasonic projector, a Polycom view station for teleconferencing, a prohibitively expensive Toshiba DVD player, a forty-two-inch Sanyo plasma display screen, and an Advantage Electrol matte white panel that descended from the ceiling and offered a perfectly square field for presentations that was a dauntingly impressive eight by eight feet. The firm rarely used these high-tech toys, but everyone enjoyed knowing they were there. Especially the litigation group. And tomorrow, after she announced the lawsuit—lambasting Adirondack for profiteering at the expense of safety—and turned the press conference over to Dominique, they were going to use a good many of these audiovisual baubles. There would be images of motherless fawn, eviscerated deer, and Spencer McCullough's shoulder, in-

cluding some of the photographs she'd had taken in
New Hampshire the Tuesday after the shooting.
They'd swamp the group with all manner of statistics
about deer hunting that would convey the sheer size
and brutality of the slaughter, the numbers of humans
and dogs that were killed and wounded every year, the
figures that supported their contention that buck-only
laws actually resulted in wildlife overpopulation.

The reporters and the women and men with their
cameras and bright lights would enter the room from
the two main doors near the reception area. When
they were settled, she and Spencer and Dominique
would enter from the lone door that faced west and
opened onto a corridor that led to the suites where the
partners toiled. Already in her mind she could hear the
humming in the conference room, a buzzing not unlike the burble of conversation you hear in a crowded
restaurant or a courtroom before the judge has entered. The mammoth cherry conference table—its ve-
neer always so polished that one time Paige had
actually used the reflection it offered to refresh her lipstick—would be gone, as would be the smaller side tables. The sixteen leather swivel chairs with their
comfortable armrests would be carted away, too, slid
together like shopping carts into smaller meeting
rooms at the far end of the firm. They would be replaced by forty folding chairs laid out in four neat
rows of ten, and another eighteen along the walls. She
was confident that most, if not all, of those seats
would be taken and behind them there would be tele-

vision cameras. In her head she saw three, and one of them was from a cable news network.

And in addition to the newspaper reporters and the curious magazine journalists, there would be a good number of FERAL's allies. People from organizations with all manner of interesting acronyms, including representatives from PETA and PAWS and IDA, as well as the leaders of antihunting organizations, including the Committee to Abolish Sport Hunting (CASH) and People Opposed to Deer Slaughter (PODS). It would be glorious, absolutely glorious.

She was pulled from her reverie by the trill of the receptionist's voice on the speakerphone. Keenan Barrett had arrived for their eight thirty meeting.

BY QUARTER TO NINE the two of them had finished their coffee and were settled comfortably in her office. Spencer was supposed to join them, but he hadn't arrived yet. And while they most certainly would not have started without him before the accident—he wouldn't have stood for such a thing, he would have lit into them both like an acetylene torch if they had—they figured these days they might as well go ahead. This postshooting Spencer was noticeably more serene than the old model. And so they dialed their mountain man in Pennsylvania, Dan Grampbell, and began their scheduled conference call. The subject was basic, and Paige had e-mailed Grampbell on Friday to inform him precisely what they wanted to discuss: Why, in his opinion, had John Seton been unable to extract a cartridge from the chamber of a rifle the ballistics lab insisted worked perfectly?

"Ah, yes, the Adirondack with the reluctant round," he said, once they had dispatched with the social pleasantries.

"Have you had a chance to give some thought to the question?"

"A bit," he said, "but without examining the weapon myself I can only speculate."

"That's precisely what we're interested in: your speculation," Keenan said.

"Well, it was probably the ammunition. That's what I would surmise if the lab can't find a flaw in the gun. That is, after all, your only other variable. And so either the cartridge was defective to begin with—a factory defect, maybe—or somehow Mr. Seton damaged it. Damaged the rim. Either way, the extractor couldn't grasp it to remove it from the chamber."

"How would someone have damaged the rim of a bullet?" Paige asked, sitting forward in her chair.

"That's a tough one. For obvious reasons, they don't damage easily. But I have seen cases where loading and unloading the same round over and over eventually dents the rim. The extractor is biting into the tiny lip on the casing multiple times, and—on rare occasions—ultimately breaks it down. Imagine stripping the head of a screw. It's not unlike that. What did the lab say about the cartridge?"

"They didn't say anything."

"Why?"

"I don't know. I don't know anything about guns, Dan," she said, trying to keep her voice light. "That's why we have you."

"Well, I'd give them a call. Ring them right up!"

DAN GRAMPBELL was replaced on the speakerphone in her office by Myles McAndrew, the engineer in Maryland who had examined John Seton's rifle and written the report.

"We didn't look at the casing because it was gone when we received the firearm," McAndrew said. "We presumed the owner or the state police in— where was the accident, Vermont?"

"New Hampshire."

"That's right, New Hampshire. Thank you. We just assumed that someone in New Hampshire had removed the casing before your paralegal brought the rifle to us." The man sounded a bit like a public radio newscaster: His voice was calm and even and assured. Unflappable.

"Why would someone do that?"

"Remove the casing? I would only be hypothesizing."

"Please, Mr. McAndrew," Keenan said, jumping in. "We seem to be surrounded by people whose opinions we prize enough to pay handsomely for them, yet who seem, at the moment, constitutionally unwilling to offer them. So, please: Hypothesize. Is a spent casing dangerous?"

"No. Of course not."

"But someone removed it?"

"The rifle was empty when it arrived here in Maryland."

"Could it have fallen out accidentally?" Paige asked.

"Not easily it couldn't," McAndrew said. "The bolt would have to be open—which, as you know, in theory should automatically eject a casing that remains in the chamber. This time, apparently, that didn't happen. But the bolt has to be open. That's the first thing. Then, perhaps, if the firearm were cracked solidly against something, it's conceivable the tremor might dislodge it. But that's a lot of accident to happen to one gun and one casing."

"What are you implying?" Keenan asked.

"I'm not implying anything. I am, per your request, Mr. Barrett, offering my opinion because you prize it and are paying the lab what you consider a handsome fee. Remember? My suggestion is that you call the owner. Or the state police. Maybe they can tell you where the casing went."

She watched as Keenan drew long blue lines with his fountain pen on the pad before him. He was pressing so hard that she could see the nib was slicing through the top sheet of paper.

IT TOOK TIME to find the right people at the state police, but by midmorning she had spoken with a trooper who could review the Seton paperwork at the firearms locker at the barracks, as well as Sergeant Ned Howland.

And, still, there was no Spencer McCullough. He'd actually called while they'd been on the phone with McAndrew and left a message on her voice mail—both she and Keenan thought he'd sounded a tad less somnambulant than usual—saying that he was running late and would have to pass on their meeting. He said he would probably just go straight to his office and catch up with Keenan there.

Howland finally called her back from a cell phone on the road a little before ten thirty, his clipped voice disappearing briefly at first into the black hole that seemed to suck in so many syllables of cell phone conversations in New England. Still, she could hear enough of Howland's replies to her questions to understand clearly that he was corroborating exactly what that other trooper at the barracks had told them: There had been no casing in John Seton's gun. Howland said that until he learned the rifle had had a live round jammed in the chamber, he'd simply presumed the casing had been ejected. When he first picked the rifle up off the ground near the trunk of an apple tree at the end of the old woman's driveway, he thought the bolt had been open.

But he wasn't absolutely positive about that.

He was, however, confident that the chamber was empty.

"So, no one at the state police removed the casing?" Keenan inquired.

"Mr. Barrett, you're a lawyer. I shouldn't have to lecture you about the collection of evidence. When I confiscated the weapon there was the chance this would become a criminal investigation. I therefore tried to preserve the weapon in the condition I found it."

"Thank you," Keenan said, not exactly contrite but humbled slightly.

"You're welcome. Forgive me, sir, but I wish someone in this case—you or Mr. Seton's lawyer—knew the first thing about guns. I wish Mr. Seton had known the first thing about guns. I hate to be glib when a man has been so badly injured, but the truth of this matter is that all of your questions combine to make for one great argument for serious gun control."

"Tell me," Keenan said. "You said you found the weapon by an apple tree."

"That's right."

"But in the drawing I saw of the accident scene—the reconstruction, if you will, that showed where the players were that night—when the child fired the weapon, she was closer to the driveway itself than to those apple trees."

"That's correct."

"Why weren't the locations where the rifle was discharged and where you found it the same?"

"The girl's mother wanted the firearm as far from the child as possible after the shooting. It was a gun, she'd just seen firsthand its ability to inflict monumental damage, and she didn't want the girl anywhere near the thing anymore."

"So she moved it?"

"I believe that's what she told me that night. I could check my notes. But I believe she said she tossed it."

"And then you recovered it?"

"Yes."

"Then where did the casing go?" Paige asked.

"If this were a criminal investigation, we would have begun our search on the property. Near where the child discharged the firearm and then where we found the rifle."

"But you didn't . . ."

"Ma'am?"

"You didn't search the property . . ."

"No. The state's attorney chose not to press charges. It was pretty clear it was an accident."

"A horrible one," she said simply, and breathed in deeply through her nose. In somewhere between twenty-six and twenty-seven hours, she was going to have to say something. No one in that press conference was going to ask about the missing casing: There was no reason to believe they would even be aware it was gone. But someone was bound to ask why John Seton had left his rifle loaded, and that would demand they have an explanation for his inability to extract the cartridge.

"Yes," Howland agreed. "A horrible one."

"I guess we should try to find the casing," she mumbled, though she knew also that this wasn't going to happen—at least not in the next twenty-six hours. And even if, by some unprecedented miracle, the casing did turn up that afternoon, it couldn't be analyzed in time for the press conference. She wondered briefly if they should postpone the event, but these things had a momentum of their own. They had been working toward tomorrow since well before Spencer had returned to work. The lawsuit was just about ready to be filed: Sections of it were being proofread in a room down the hall that very moment.

But the casing could still affect it. Their contention was that the rifle was inherently unsafe because a round remained in the chamber when you emptied the magazine, and there was no mechanism on the barrel to warn a person that the gun was still loaded. Perhaps if they had the casing and could show that the rim was damaged, then they could sue the ammunition manufacturer as well.

"Thank you, Sergeant Howland," Keenan was saying. "We appreciate your getting back to us."

She thanked the trooper, too, but her mind already was elsewhere. She was trying to imagine what she would say tomorrow when someone asked her why that dimwit in Vermont—though the reporter would not frame the question quite that way—had been unable to pop out the cartridge that remained in the rifle.

Thirty-three

"In college," Spencer was saying, "I never thought I would be a bald, angry man when I hit middle age."

"No one does," John answered, and he guessed it was the truth. Certainly he'd never presumed that he would hit forty with a receding hairline and eyeglasses.

On the other hand, he wasn't angry. Not like Spencer, anyway. Lately he'd been pretty damn pissed at his brother-in-law, but that irritation had been triggered by a fairly precise set of circumstances.

It was Monday morning, not quite nine thirty, and the two of them were sitting in his mother's living room with its sweeping views across Park, Madison, and Fifth, and into Olmstead's vast commons—these days a series of baseball diamonds, skating rinks, and paths for exercisers on their in-line skates and air-cushioned Nikes. His mother's dog had lumbered over to Spencer, sniffed out Tanya's scent, and—satisfied— was sitting now with his snout draped on the man's lap. Nan was somewhere on the other side of the apartment, in that long series of rooms that looked south on the spires of midtown Manhattan, and Catherine and Charlotte were at Brearley.

"I mean, why didn't someone tell me I had so much rage?" Spencer said.

He shrugged. "We did. We tried, anyway."

"And I wasn't listening?"

John considered agreeing that, yes, this was precisely the problem: Spencer didn't listen to anyone, because he was right about everything. At least he believed that he was. But his brother-in-law already was so abashed that John saw no reason to make him feel any worse. "We are who we are," he said simply. "And you have your strengths." He watched the light through the gauzy curtains accentuate a flying buttress of dust.

"But listening is not among them."

"Guess not."

The dog rolled over onto his back, imploring Spencer to stroke his tummy. His brother-in-law reached down awkwardly to pet the animal with his left arm, grimacing slightly at the effort.

"Look, Catherine says you've changed in some very positive ways since the accident," he continued. "And this weekend Charlotte told Willow that she's having a great time working with you on the musical she's in."

"Getting shot does wonders for one's priorities—that and being crippled. I wouldn't recommend it for everyone, but it seems to have worked in my case."

He sat forward in the heavy chair in which, years earlier, he would watch his father flip quickly through **Advertising Age** and the **Wall Street Journal**. "Can I ask you something? And this is none of my business, so feel free to take the Fifth. But are you and my sister going to seek counseling? Or will you two crazy kids try to figure out your next steps on your own?"

"Counseling."

"Good."

"But she's not leaving and we're not separating. I've gotten a stay of execution."

"I'm relieved."

"Me, too. I think we both are. And Charlotte. Charlotte might talk a tough game, but it's all bravado. Inside she's a cupcake."

John wasn't sure if he could ever envision his niece as a cupcake, but he also wasn't about to disabuse the girl's father of this notion.

"Anyway," Spencer went on, "that's not the only reason I'm here." He pulled himself away from the dog, wincing as he sunk back into the couch. The animal looked up at him with wide eyes that, alas, reminded John of a deer's. "Given my morning, I'm glad you stuck around."

"Honestly, Spencer, I really don't know why I'm going to the press conference. At one point I'd had some vague idea that I could defend myself. But I gave that notion up. Yesterday I just decided I had to be there to . . . to see it. It was all very spontaneous."

"Look, don't say another word: I'm canceling the press conference."

"Are you serious?" He wasn't sure whether he heard mere incredulity or giddiness in his voice. He supposed there was a little of both.

"Yup. I haven't told anyone but Catherine yet. I tried Dominique at her home before leaving, but I missed her. She'll be disappointed, of course, but—"

"Disappointed? Catwoman? She'll be furious!"

"She's not a bad person, John. She simply sees things in black and white. Once she knows that I'm doing this because of my family—when I tell her about Charlotte this morning—she'll understand." He raised his eyebrows. "I'm actually supposed to be at Paige's office right now. Paige and Keenan are talking to our gun experts about why you couldn't get the bullet out of your rifle. I need to break the news to Paige later when she's alone."

"Your ballistics lab has had the gun since mid-August! How can they not know what the problem is?"

"They couldn't find anything wrong with the rifle. You knew that, didn't you?"

"No!"

"Paige didn't tell your lawyer?"

"No, but in all fairness there's no reason she would have. I'm not her client. I'm sure she would have gotten around to it eventually," he said, working consciously to answer Spencer's question, because if he didn't—if he focused only on the reality that his worst fears about the gun were coming true—he thought he would faint. He heard a tiny ringing in his ears, and his vision was growing slightly fuzzy.

"You okay?" Spencer was asking, the voice sounding almost as if it were on the other side of a large wall of ice.

He nodded, put his head between his legs, and breathed slowly and carefully.

"I'll get you some water," Spencer said.

Still he said nothing. He heard his crippled brother-in-law rising from the couch, and then walking—the click of the dog's toenails on the tile in the hall an indication that he was being followed—to the other side of the apartment for a glass.

WHILE SPENCER was getting him water, John forced himself to concentrate on what this news about the gun meant. He saw a couple of ways Adirondack might respond. They might argue the lawsuit was so completely frivolous—so monumentally groundless—that it should be dismissed. At the same time, they might point out that Spencer should be suing his brother-in-law in Vermont. The guy who left a loaded rifle in the trunk of his car.

Or they might see this as a trifling nuisance to be disposed of quickly. They would convince Paige Sutherland that it would be impossible to wrest a sizable chunk of change from them in court because she would be unable to contend the gun was defective. It was thus in her client's best interest to accept a token payment and go away.

It was not, of course, in Paige Sutherland's best interest to acquiesce to a token payment. Not by a long shot. She might care as deeply about the rights of animals as Spencer or Keenan or Dominique, but there was also a big pile of money on Adirondack's side of the table, and her goal was to convince them to slide it over to her.

Besides, Spencer didn't want a token payment. Actually, John wasn't sure that he wanted any payment. Oh, he understood the damages could be enormous, but for Spencer this nightmare had never been about the money. It had been about animals and hunting and violence.

He looked up when he saw Spencer returning with his water. He took a sip and wished he felt better than he did. Spencer sat down and watched him.

If only they had the casing, he thought, and it had a definitive ding or dent. A rim that was defective.

"I wish we had the casing," he murmured simply. He half-emptied the water in his glass and placed it down on one of the coasters he remembered from his childhood. It had an artist's rendering of the **Mayflower** on it. "I might look a little less foolish. And your lawsuit might be more viable."

"John, it's fine. Let it go."

"No, it's not fine. With the gun working perfectly, this lawsuit—"

"There isn't going to be a lawsuit."

"What?"

Spencer pushed himself to the edge of the couch, and John saw a glimpse of the intensity that once ran through his brother-in-law like river water in March.

"There's something you need to know. Something Catherine and I just found out this morning."

His mind was still centered on Adirondack; he couldn't imagine what Spencer was about to tell him.

"Go on."

"Charlotte was stoned when she shot me."

"Stoned? What are you talking about?"

"Charlotte had been smoking dope that night and she'd had a beer. A whole beer. She'd stolen a joint from some older kid's bag at the bonfire the teenagers were having, and she and Willow—yes, little Willow—were wasted. Maybe not falling-down-drunk wasted, but somewhere between careless and unthinking. You've been there, John. Me, too. God, we've been there together."

"Not at ten years old," he said. "Not at twelve, even!"

"If it makes you feel any better, your daughter has been trying to get mine to come clean for almost two months," Spencer said, shaking his head slightly, before continuing with details John understood he was only half-hearing. Something about two beers, a bottle for each girl, and a joint that, according to Charlotte, was as thick and round as a crayon.

The image of his daughter, her tiny legs in her shorts, passing a joint to her cousin on a summer night in New Hampshire disgusted him. He wasn't angry with her—the child was ten, for God's sake, still a week shy of eleven—but he was furious with himself. How had it come to this? he thought, and then he decided he knew. He knew.

Here was one more thing for which he could feel guilt and remorse, one more reason to kick himself in the ass. Unlike the weapon he'd left loaded for eight long months, however, this was a gaffe he could fix. He and Sara both. He didn't know whether it was before Patrick was born or after, he didn't know whether shipping their girl off to her grandmother's in the summer was a mere symptom or a part of the cause, but he was confident now that at some point he and his wife had managed to lose sight of their daughter.

"Who knows what she was thinking when she shot me," Spencer concluded. "All I can say is that it's evident she wasn't thinking real clearly."

"Oh, you can say more," John said. "Me, too."

Spencer began to use his left fingers to toy with the ones on his right, and John had the sense that this wasn't an unconscious mannerism. He wondered if his brother-in-law was supposed to do this to keep the blood circulating. Spencer then offered the smallest of smiles: Resignation. Capitulation. Fatigue. "Anyway," he said, "this little bit of information sealed the deal in my mind. There can't be a lawsuit. Not now. I doubt we could win if this information were known, and we certainly can't try to bury it and proceed. I'm going to tell Paige this morning."

"Are you going to mention the marijuana?"

"Yes. And I'll explain that I don't want my daughter and my brother-in-law to become public spectacles—Catherine's concern all along. I'll tell her how Catherine almost left me this morning."

A few minutes ago, John thought, he had been speculating on how little interest Paige would have in a token payment. But dropping the lawsuit completely? He hadn't even contemplated that. He started to estimate how many billable hours she might have amassed but quickly turned off the calculator in his head. He didn't want to know. Besides, she was bound by a fiduciary duty to follow her clients' instructions. If Spencer McCullough wanted the suit dropped, then dropped it would be.

"She won't be happy," he told Spencer simply.

"No, but she has a good heart. Really, she does. She'll understand that I'm doing this for my family."

He was surprised: He hadn't realized that Paige Sutherland had a heart, much less one a person might argue was good.

"Anyway," Spencer continued. "I thought you should know."

"Thank you," he said. "Thank you for telling me about . . . everything."

The dog was returning now, and—as he did always when Spencer was present—the animal went directly to him.

"You're welcome. And John?"

"Yes?"

"I forgive you. Really and truly: I forgive you."

John thanked him for this, too: for pardoning him, for letting him off a hook that by all rights could have left him dangling for life. Then he climbed from his chair and went to the dog at his brother-in-law's feet and stroked the animal, trying to see nothing more than the gray that dappled the old animal's snout and feel nothing other than the luxuriant softness of his mane.

Thirty-four

This was bad news. Unutterably bad news.

Nevertheless, Dominique had learned that sometimes with bad news it was best to do nothing. Now was one of those moments. Spencer had left to tell Paige his decision, and she was alone in her office with her erotically charged paintings of tropical birds, and for a moment she pushed her chair away from her desk and simply tried to sit quietly. So: Spencer was calling off the press conference. And dropping the lawsuit.

She sipped her tea, the mug grasped tightly in both her hands, and allowed the warm porcelain rim to rest a long moment against her lower lip. She guessed the main reason she was doing nothing was because there was absolutely nothing she could do. It was over. There would be no surprise broadside on the hunting industry, at least not this week. Or this month. Or, barring some unforeseen accident or tragedy in the hunting season, this year.

One of the things she had learned from Spencer's injury was that it helped to have a human casualty to point out the horrors that hunting inflicted on animals. Spencer had put a human face on a bullet wound. On what it felt like to be mistaken for a deer and then shot.

In theory, it didn't require so very much imagination to understand that sort of pain, now did it? As Jeremy Bentham had asked about animals well over two hundred years ago, the question was not whether they could reason or talk, but could they suffer? And yet, somehow, it seemed to take more imagination for humans to identify with animal suffering than it did to conceive of space flight or cloning or nuclear fusion. Yes, she was a fanatic in the eyes of most of the country, an uncompromising extremist without any patience. Mostly, however, she just lacked patience for people who wouldn't accept her belief that humans inflicted needless agony on the animals around them, and they did so in numbers that were absolutely staggering.

The press conference would have been a real eye-opener.

Still, the story would get out. Maybe not with the orgiastic fanfare she once had contemplated. But already the word was traveling among their friends in the animal rights community that Spencer McCullough had been shot. The story had been on the street ever since Spencer had returned to work in the middle of the month and begun to return people's calls. **We are a litigious society,** she thought with bemusement, **and there is little we like more than a good courtroom drama.**

And Charlotte, apparently, was a wondrous little drama queen. She would have been sensational.

Nevertheless, Dominique had to admit that she was relieved for the girl. She was disappointed for her group and the animals they represented, but she was sincerely happy for the girl.

She stood up, stretched, and went to try to cheer up Spencer's young minions—an admittedly uncharacteristic gesture, but one that she told herself she had to consider more frequently—reassuring them that although this press conference was off, there would be others.

There would always, alas, be others.

THAT AFTERNOON Adirondack's lawyer had sounded predictably mulish when he'd first taken Paige's call, presuming—with cause, Paige readily admitted to herself—that she was phoning to torment him with still more conjecture about how a jury would respond to the presence of a traumatized thirteen-year-old girl on a witness stand.

But once he understood why she was actually calling, she could hear in his voice the way his eyes must have widened and how he couldn't wait to finish their conversation—as if this good news might evaporate if he stayed on the line a second longer than necessary, or feared he might say the wrong thing and somehow cause this great gift to be taken back. He wanted to tell his boss. And his boss's boss. And anyone in the manufacturing headquarters of the Adirondack Rifle Company who would listen.

Perhaps he would take credit for this change of

heart on the part of Spencer McCullough and his counsel. Perhaps he would concoct a reason why Spencer McCullough and his animal rights nutballs had decided suddenly to slink silently into the night.

She really didn't care.

She felt sunken, deflated, a little sick with sadness. It wasn't just about the money, though lately whenever she had pondered the money that might have been theirs, she had had to breathe in slowly and deeply through her nose to calm herself, as if she were a . . . a hunter. A hunter about to squeeze a trigger. Now, the money that seemed once to demand nothing but patience and journeyman competence had vanished. Vanished completely.

And, yes, she felt bad for Keenan and Randy and Dominique.

But mostly the sorrow that tugged at her now was the result of those claws and paws and hooves, all abused, that surrounded her. That surrounded them all.

So tomorrow it wouldn't be deer. It might be dolphins or whales, elephants—the ones who were shot in the wild or the ones who were beaten in the circus—or mink. It might be the hogs who were driven up the chutes to be clubbed to their death. It might be cattle. It might be the monkeys with their wondrous brains—gray matter perhaps fully conscious of the fact that the virus these humans had injected into their blood was slowly killing them—or the rabbits blinded by cosmetic companies. It might be the whole arks of creatures we were either endangering with our gluttony for trophies or breeding for no other reason than our insatiable desire for meat.

The litany was endless.

So what if it wasn't the deer's turn? It was inevitable their day would come. Somewhere out there was another John Seton. Good God, the woods were full of them.

Suddenly, her eyes were watering and she was unable to blink back her tears.

CHARLOTTE GUESSED instantly that the person leaning against the lockers twenty or twenty-five yards down the corridor was a reporter. She was her mother's age but Charlotte knew that she wasn't a teacher and nothing about her signaled parent. She was wearing khaki pants and a windbreaker, and she had an attaché strapped over her shoulder. Her hair was the color of honey and it fell to her shoulders.

Given the kind of day that she'd had—a day that had begun ten hours ago with her parents trying to separate and then (much to her own astonishment) her fessing up to the marijuana—Charlotte briefly considered turning tail and running back into the auditorium, where a couple of kids from rehearsal and her drama teacher were still hanging out. She was supposed to meet her mom in her mom's classroom, but this woman was a roadblock between the two of them.

Before she could do anything, however, before she could either retreat or plow ahead, the woman saw her. The reporter, assuming that was indeed what she was, offered a small wave and then started to march down the hall toward her.

She stood up a little taller, not that she believed that her height—such as it was—was going to help her much now, and waited.

"I'll bet you're Charlotte McCullough. My name is Lorelea. Lorelea Roberts." She stuck out her hand, and Charlotte took it. "I'm with the **Times.** I'm a writer."

"I had a feeling."

The woman smiled. "Can we talk?"

Reflexively, before she could stop herself, she glanced back toward the auditorium, hoping someone was emerging who could rescue her. But there was no sign of any help in that direction.

"I heard there was going to be a press conference tomorrow," the woman continued, "but then it was canceled."

"Really?" She hoped she sounded surprised, though after she spoke she honestly wasn't sure what was supposed to have surprised her: the fact there had once been a press conference scheduled or that it had been canceled.

"It was going to be tomorrow afternoon. At some law firm. Your father's law firm, I presume. True?"

She nodded, and as she moved her head she feared that already she had revealed too much.

"Ah, but then it was canceled."

"I should go meet my mom," she said quickly. "I'm supposed to catch up with her in, like, five minutes."

"You're meeting her in her classroom, I bet."

"Yes."

"Then can I have just a few of those minutes? Please? When we're done, I could walk you to your mom and ask her a couple of questions, too. The truth is, I already have my story, and I just want to confirm the facts. That's all. I won't ask you anything I don't already know, I promise. I just want to do what I can to get it right."

"You already know what happened?"

"Uh-huh. Absolutely. I've talked to a lot of your father's friends in the animal rights community—folks he's spoken with since he got back to work. And I've connected with a number of people in New Hampshire."

"Have you spoken to my father?"

"No, but I'm trying."

Charlotte swallowed hard and tried to think. She made a production of switching her backpack from her left shoulder to her right to give herself time, because the disparate strands of an idea were starting to coalesce in her mind. Her dad had wanted a press conference because he was pissed off at the way hunters blasted a bazillion deer a year. Well, the press conference may have been off, but this Lorelea Roberts seemed nice enough. And very professional. Perhaps, she reasoned, she could use this interview to say some of the things her father would have wanted said if the event had gone forward as planned. Given her unfortunate history with firearms, she guessed she was in about as good a position as anyone to talk about the evils of guns. And she'd certainly grown up around her share of animal rights propaganda, so some of it had to have registered.

At the very least, she could make the point that, clearly, it hurt like heck to be shot.

Besides, she wouldn't be telling this lady anything she didn't know. Hadn't the woman said that she already had the full story and was just checking her facts?

"So, what do you think?" Lorelea was asking, her voice a low, seductive, almost conspiratorial whisper. "Can you give me four minutes?"

"Okay," she agreed slowly. She had the sense this could be a huge mistake if she weren't smart. She'd have to play this one carefully.

"Good. Thank you," the reporter said, instantly pulling a pocket-sized digital recorder from her windbreaker pocket as she spoke and clicking a button on its side. "This happened on July 31?"

"I guess so."

"A Saturday?"

"Yes."

"And you thought you were shooting at a deer?"

She started to nod and then caught herself. She saw the trap: If she said she was shooting at a deer, the newspaper would have the daughter of a senior FERAL executive taking a potshot at a wild animal. That would do no one any good. And so instead she changed direction and answered (and she could almost see how proud of her Father would be), "I didn't know the gun was loaded. It was one of those horrible mistakes that, like, just happens."

"Why were you even holding the gun?"

"Curiosity, I guess. I mean, the thing is, you saw the damage it caused. My dad practically lost his arm. He was nearly killed! That's what a gun can do. That's what a gun does to all those deer—to any animal. Hunting is just the most gross thing. And it's not a sport. Please. What chance does a deer have against something like that? Like none, that's how much. Zip, zero, nada. And my dad is in constant pain," she said, and behind the reporter she saw her mother and the headmaster stomping down the hall, but she was on a roll and she didn't care. This was a stage, she was discovering, she could handle.

Moreover—and this was a point that mattered to her—she was doing this for her dad.

"How does that make you feel?"

"I feel terrible, of course. And that's the lesson here," she said, as her mother and Mr. Holland surrounded Lorelea Roberts. "We are inflicting a lot of pain on a lot of animals. And what for? Do we need deerskins for clothing anymore? I don't think so. Do we need to eat deer meat? No way. I mean, my parents' freezer at home has got all kinds of imitation meat that tastes just fine. They even make imitation chicken fingers now, and—as we all know—chickens don't even have fingers. Am I making sense?"

"You'll have to leave," Mr. Holland snapped, unwilling to hide his annoyance with the reporter.

Normally, he was a pretty good-natured guy, especially since her mom was one of his teachers. "You didn't check in at the front office and—"

"I'm an alumna," the reporter said, smiling. "My mother is an alumna. My grandmother was an alumna. Lorelea Roberts." Now she offered her hand to Mr. Holland. "You arrived five or six years after I graduated, but I've read in the alumnae magazine about the terrific work you're doing here. I'm sorry we haven't met."

"You still should have checked in at the office, Ms. Roberts."

She spread her hands palms up in a gesture that was a little like an apology and a lot like a dismissal. Charlotte saw the eyes of the other two adults land squarely on the small recorder.

"And you have to turn that thing off," her mother said. "Right this second."

"No, it's okay," she told her mom, surprising herself.

"Charlotte?"

"Really, I know what I'm doing and I know what I want to say," she went on. Then she reached for Lorelea's hand with the recorder and actually steered it toward her face. "There's one more thing I want to add. Actually, it's two. Can I?"

She could tell that her mother and the headmaster wanted to stop her, but either they didn't want to make a scene in front of this reporter—who happened to be what Grandmother Seton liked to call a Brearley girl herself—or they trusted her just enough that they

were going to let her plow ahead. When they remained silent, Lorelea said to her, "Looks to me like
you're good to go."

"Okay, here we are. I think the company that made
the gun should make it really obvious when the darn
thing is loaded. It would have been nice to know,
thank you very much, that there was a bullet in the rifle when I picked it up. Second, I made a huge mistake
that night, the biggest one I will ever make in my life.
At least I hope it was the worst mistake: I hate to think
what worse shi—" She caught herself before she had
finished the word, then resumed as if nothing had
happened, "Anyway, I love my dad. I love him a ton. I
would give anything in the world to be able to go back
in time and give him back his right arm. Okay?"

Lorelca looked at her and seemed to be considering
this. Then she nodded and clicked off the recorder.

"Good. Let's go home, Mom," she said, taking her
mother's long fingers in hers. With her free hand she
gave the headmaster a small salute and then walked
with her mother down the hall. Three words formed
in her head in the almost old-fashioned courier font
from her **Secret Garden** script, and the image in her
mind made her smile:

Exit, stage right.

THAT EVENING Nan Seton had dinner alone with
her dog in her dining room. Across the wide expanse
of park the three McCulloughs ate with their new dog,
the cats watching warily from different perches on a

living room couch. Far to the north the Setons ate at an Italian restaurant near the airport in South Burlington: Sara and Willow and baby Patrick had met John there, and they all had agreed they were far too hungry to wait till they were home to dine. Patrick ate Cheerios one by one from a restaurant high chair and sucked on a bottle of milk.

None of the Setons or the McCulloughs was feeling particularly celebratory, but they all felt relieved.

Three hundred miles apart the grown men both brought up the missing casing, and each time their wives told them—gently—to drop it. Just shut up (please) and drop it.

The two girls thought of the vegetable garden in New Hampshire, and—again, similarly—hoped their parents would not get the notion into their midlife-addled brains that it could possibly be worth the effort to try once again next year. Charlotte liked the gardens the students were building for her stage play, especially the hedges. They were constructed entirely from green paper cocktail napkins and walls of mesh screen. They looked real enough, and they demanded no serious care.

But the girls also knew instinctively that they would never be alone in New Hampshire with their grandmother again. It wasn't that Grandmother couldn't manage them: Good Lord, she probably managed them better than their own parents. Rather, it was their sense that their parents, pure and simple, were going to want them with them. Not because of their dalliance with underage drinking and dope, but because they loved them and did the best that they could.

This attention might grow tiring. Still, it was reassuring.

Some of the people ate meat that evening and some did not, but those who did were aware of the flesh on their plates. They told themselves, however, that there was enough in their small worlds about which they could feel guilty—myriad, endless failings and whole catalogs of disappointments they heaped on others— and so they chewed and smiled and swallowed.

And Spencer, at least for the moment, looked the other way. He looked only at his wife and his daughter, grateful, grasping his Good Grips easy-to-hold fork, and hoisted chickpeas and artichoke hearts across the great divide that separated his dinner plate from his mouth.

THE GIRLS WERE CORRECT when they surmised they would never again be alone in New Hampshire with their grandmother: That night the old woman died. Even so vigorous a heart was not immune to the unsubtle havoc wrought by time. Besides, some hearts are better than others, and though Nan's was generous, it was weak. Had she not been so vigorous, she might have died a decade sooner. And though it would have been simpler for everyone if she had lived another five years—even five months—she lasted just long enough. She made it by hours. The boys had reconciled in the morning, and she passed away in her sleep a mere half spin of the Earth later. And so while John and Catherine and Spencer were devastated, they were devastated together. Sara helped them all, the therapist in her surprised by the depth of her own sadness, as did Nan's granddaughters. The girls' presence was comforting, because they seemed so very grown up.

Nan died dreaming of a woodpecker in one of the trees that ringed her house, the drumming in actuality the last beats of her heart before it spasmed, then stopped. The sudden spike of pain woke her body, but Nan was never conscious of what the pain was or that she was dying. Her eyes opened reflexively, then shut, and she was gone. It was all very similar to the way her friend Walter Durnip had died in the country that summer, except she had her dog with her at the end instead of her spouse.

The animal, much to everyone's surprise, actually outlived her. He spent his last days with the Setons of Vermont.

Nan was buried in the cemetery in New Hampshire, with a service beforehand at the homestead. The afternoon was raw but bearable, and the family stood together with Nan's friends near the dead stalks of the cutting garden, the rented trellis exactly the one Sara had seen in her mind when the days had been long in July. Then they all sang a hymn and went out—but they sang only one, and it was short.

Thirty-five

The clouds were moving like whitewater, streaming in lines to the south. Occasionally the sun would appear, adding bright, fibrous stripes to the oyster-colored mass.

Each time the sun would emerge the crow would look up, his dark eyes attracted by the sparkle.

Still, it was chilly and there was less sunlight every day. Winters here were just cold enough and the hills just high enough that soon the crow would fly south, as would the female pecking now at something in the ground far below, and their offspring. Three smaller birds, each about half his size. Altogether, this extended family—this small series of nests atop the white pine—numbered fifteen, and together they would leave for a slightly warmer climate.

This particular crow was the biggest. He was just about a foot and a half long and he had a wingspan of thirty-five inches. He weighed almost exactly a pound.

At the edges of the distant woods the deer were starting their walk up the hill toward the garden. They used to come only at night, but lately they had grown considerably bolder and would venture here during the day. One of them, a male, had even begun to scrape at a thick maple tree beside the garden as the rutting season began to draw near. The animals were growing their winter coats, a grayish brown shell of hollow, kinky fur that insulated them against the cold.

The crow turned his head from the deer when he saw something moving on the ground near his mate. A raccoon, perhaps, was stalking her. He screeched and the other bird rose instantly into the air and landed on one of the lower branches of an apple tree. His eyes darted back now to the source of the motion, and he saw it was merely a twig from a rosebush scratching against the side of the gray house.

The place had been empty for a week. No longer was it a source of almost ceaseless activity, with humans constantly coming and going, their cars rumbling up and down the long driveway. The deer, of course, had noticed their absence, too, which was why they had extended the small world of their browse to the remains of the garden during the day as well as the night.

Humans didn't seem dangerous to the crow, at least not this bunch. But they were noisy.

Especially that one night in the middle of the summer.

The bird no longer remembered the details of what he had seen from the top of the pine, and—entranced by the lights that flashed everywhere, the lights atop the cars and the lights waved by the people—he hadn't even witnessed the precise moment after that nearly deafening blast when a woman had picked the rifle up off the ground and heaved it hysterically against an apple tree. He hadn't seen the brass casing fly free of the chamber when it slammed into the trunk.

It was actually the next morning, while one of the little girls was curled up in the strawberries, that he first noticed the twinkle, the flash in the grass. It was irresistible. Whatever it was, it was glimmering in the high early August sun. And with the child absorbed in her strawberries, he had been able to swoop down and gather it up.

He gazed now at the cylinder in his nest. It was bigger than the other items: the thin, crinkled piece of aluminum foil that he could actually bite through with his beak if he wasn't careful and the perfectly round bead that had come off the wrist of one of the girls. The casing was a bit heavier than his galvanized carpenter's nail, but the tube was hollow and so it hadn't been particularly difficult for him to lift it off the ground and deposit it here in the nest. It was lovely to look at, and he treasured it. So did his mate. It wasn't as flawlessly shaped as, for example, that bead: There was a dimple near the opening where he had lifted it off the ground, and a section of the rim—that lip at one end—had an ugly flat patch. But, still, the crow thought it was beautiful. The bird wouldn't take it south with him—he took nothing with him when he flew south—but this summer and autumn it had given him a pleasurable sensation that, in his small mind, was rather like being full.

Now his mate lifted off the apple tree and flew up to their nest in the pine. Below them the deer started to dig at the weedy dirt. A squirrel scampered abruptly across the gravel driveway. A rabbit crouched behind the lowest branches of the hydrangea, his ears high, his nostrils twitching as he sniffed the crisp, autumnal air.

And behind them all, the house sat perfectly still.

EPILOGUE

The Race to the Face

My cousin was eighteen the autumn her father finally had his arm amputated. She was a freshman at Yale, and even in southern Connecticut the leaves had mostly turned. It was a Wednesday, a detail I recall because I was a junior in high school and I had a double block of organic chemistry that day. Uncle Spencer checked himself into a hospital in Manhattan shortly before breakfast, and the dangling appendage was gone before lunch. It was, by then, as thin and frail-looking as a very old man's. I don't believe he ever missed it.

The following summer, my cousin's and my family convened in Sugar Hill the very last week in July. We knew we would be there for the anniversary of the accident, but we were no longer fixated on the date and certainly those of us from Vermont didn't discuss it. We had returned there any number of times since that long and awful night when my cousin had shot my uncle, and the principal strangeness we experienced inevitably was due to my grandmother's absence—not to any awkwardness that we were vacationing at the scene of the crime. The big old house just never seemed quite the same without her.

The summer after my uncle had his arm amputated, however, my father, my cousin, and my now one-armed uncle did have a commemoration of sorts. A short triathlon is held in Franconia every summer, usually on the first Saturday in August. It's called the Race to the Face, because the route winds its way to a spot at the peak of a mountain not far from the ledge where the Old Man of the Mountain once had resided. And though a fair number of serious triathletes compete, a lot of athletic dilettantes participate as well. After all, the biking portion is only about seven miles long (though, in all fairness, it is uphill and almost half of it follows a deer path in the woods), the swim is a mere three-quarter-mile sprint across Echo Lake, and the final segment is a two-mile run up the ski slopes on Cannon Mountain. These are not intimidating lengths. Moreover, many people participate in teams of three—which is where my father, my cousin, and my uncle fit in.

Years earlier my father had sold his hunting gear, bought a mountain bike with the proceeds, and become a pretty avid cyclist. He was going to handle the first third of the triathlon, the ride from Franconia to Echo Lake. There my cousin would take over, wearing (for a change) a completely suitable Speedo. My uncle would be waiting for her at the other side, where, as soon as she had emerged from the water, he would start his one-armed run up the mountain.

The rest of us—my mother, Aunt Catherine, Patrick, and I—waited for the athletes at the finish line high atop Cannon.

I don't recall precisely where they placed among the sixty or seventy teams that had signed up that summer, but I know they managed to sneak into the top half. This wasn't bad for two middle-aged men who had only three arms between them and a young woman who rarely swam in the university pool more than twice a week. They attributed their success either to being directly related to the impressively energetic Nan Seton or, in my uncle's case, to coming of age on her watch.

Nevertheless, what I remember best about that day isn't an image of my father leaving in a heat of almost two hundred bicyclists, or my beautiful cousin racing down the beach at Echo Lake and diving gracefully into the water, or my uncle starting his trek up a ski slope with grass so green that the sun made it look almost neon. When I think about that morning I envision instead the moment when my uncle finally reached the summit. He was greeted there by my father and my cousin, who, upon finishing their portions of the race, had taken the tram to the top. The three of them threw themselves together into the sort of ecstatically loopy embrace that had never marked the conclusion of any previous tennis match, golf game, or badminton contest in Seton or McCullough family history, jumping up and down and laughing with an exuberance rarely manifested by any of us. And when they posed for a photograph—the two men surrounding my cousin—you wouldn't have known that my uncle had lost his arm or that once, a long time ago, he had almost lost his family.

ACKNOWLEDGMENTS

I am enormously grateful to a long list of doctors, lawyers, hunters, animal rights activists, physical therapists, EMTs, and firearms experts. I am particularly indebted to Paul Bonzani; Lauren Bowerman; Armand Compagna; Richard Gaun; Dr. Mark Healy; Reverend Gary Kowalski; Carter Lord; Jonathan Lowy; Kevin McFarland; John Monahan; Dr. Turner Osler; Bob Patterson; and Whitney Taylor. You are exceedingly patient and I thank you all.

Among the small library of books that I read while researching this novel, two were especially helpful: Richard Nelson's **Heart and Blood** and Matthew Scully's **Dominion**. Both Nelson and Scully are thoughtful, candid, and wise.

Finally, once again I am deeply appreciative of a great many people at Random House, including Marty Asher, Jenny Frost, and Shaye Areheart. Shaye is a great editor—and an even greater friend.

ABOUT THE AUTHOR

CHRIS BOHJALIAN is the author of nine novels, including **Midwives** (a **Publishers Weekly** Best Book and an Oprah's Book Club selection), **The Buffalo Soldier,** and **Trans-Sister Radio,** as well as a collection of magazine essays and newspaper columns, **Idyll Banter: Weekly Excursions to a Very Small Town.** In 2002 he won the New England Book Award. His work has been translated into seventeen languages and published in twenty countries. He lives in Vermont with his wife and daughter.

Visit him at www.chrisbohjalian.com.

ABOUT THE AUTHOR

Before You Know Kindness

CHRIS BOHJALIAN

Reading Group Guide

Questions for Discussion

1. **Before You Know Kindness** opens with a blunt, clinical description of Spencer's injuries. Is the preface a purely objective report or does it begin to develop some of the general themes of the novel? What does it convey about the Setons and their way of life?

2. Spencer's speech [pp. 21–26] and Nan's descriptions of his behavior [pp. 40–45] offer varying insights into his personality. Does the tone of the writing influence your impression of him? What specific details bring out the differences between Spencer's self-perceptions and the way others might view him?

3. How does Bohjalian portray FERAL and the people who work there? Do you think this is an accurate portrait of the animal-rights movement? What reasons might Bohjalian have for modifying their attitudes and activities?

4. Sara thinks, "The problem with Nan—and with John and Catherine, and yes, Spencer when they were all together—was that they could never just . . .

be."[p. 57] In what ways is this attributable to Nan and Richard Seton's marriage and the atmosphere in which John and Catherine grew up? Why does Spencer, whose background is so different, demonstrate the same quality?

5. How persuasive are John's explanations of why he took up hunting? What does the argument that hunting "is the most merciful way humans had to manage the herd" [p. 110] imply about the relationship between humans and the natural world? Does John's anguish after the accident alter his view of hunting in general? Do you think that it should?

6. In talking to Willow about Catherine and Spencer, Charlotte says, "Sometimes I get pissed at both of them. I don't think Mom would be the way she is if Dad wasn't this public wacko." [p. 174] Are Charlotte's complaints typical of a teenager or does Spencer's profession put an unusual burden on her? Is her criticism of her mother's flirting well-founded?

7. Bohjalian suggests several times that Charlotte may have subconsciously wanted to injure her father. She herself says, "There were lots of reasons for pointing Uncle John's weapon at what was moving at the edge of the garden. . . ." [p. 197] and acknowledges that others might think, **"She was just doing it to get your attention."**[p. 200] Is this speculation supported by the way Bohjalian describes the accident? By Charlotte's subsequent behavior and her conversations with Willow?

8. The accident and Spencer's permanent disability provide FERAL with an irresistible opportunity to make their case against hunting. Is their decision to bring a lawsuit totally reprehensible? Do the depictions of Dominique, Paige, and Keenan undermine the validity of their case?

9. Self-interest plays a part not only in FERAL's reaction to the tragedy. Are you sympathetic to John's concerns that the lawsuit will affect his professional reputation, as well as his fear that "for as long as he lived he would be an imbecile in the eyes of his daughter" [p. 210]? How did you feel as Catherine vacillates in the second half of the novel between wanting to help her husband and wanting to leave him?

10. "Nan was a particular mystery to [Sara]. Exactly what was it that she didn't want to think about?" [pp. 262–63] Were you puzzled by Nan as well? By the end of the novel, did you feel you had a better understanding of her?

11. What would have happened if Charlotte and Willow had not confessed to drinking and smoking pot on the night of the shooting? Were you relieved that Spencer decided not to pursue the lawsuit?

12. Although the plot revolves around Spencer, at various points in the novel each character moves to center stage to comment on the events and their repercussions. Which members of the family most appealed

to you and why? How successful is Bohjalian at capturing their individual points of view and personalities? Did your opinions of them change as the novel progressed?

13. Does Bohjalian present both sides of the controversy in an evenhanded way? Which characters appear to embody his own point of view? What is the ultimate message of **Before You Know Kindness**?

14. Do you think that the issues Bohjalian examines in **Before You Know Kindness** are more important (or more relevant) than the topics he explored in (for example) **Midwives** or **The Law of Similars,** or **Trans-Sister Radio**?

15. Why did Bohjalian use a passage from **The Secret Garden** as one of the epigraphs? In what ways is the children's classic relevant to **Before You Know Kindness**?

16. Why did Bohjalian take his title from the poem "Kindness," by Naomi Shihab Nye, a portion of which serves as the other epigraph?

If your reading group would like to schedule a half hour with Chris Bohjalian via speakerphone or e-mail, please visit his website (www.chrisbohjalian.com) and click on the Reading Groups tab.